The Long Way Back

The Long Way Back

Fuad al-Takarli

Translated by
Catherine Cobham

The American University in Cairo Press
Cairo • New York

English translation copyright © 2001 by
The American University in Cairo Press
113 Sharia Kasr el Aini, Cairo, Egypt
420 Fifth Avenue, New York, NY 10018
www.aucpress.com

Copyright © 1980 by Fuad al-Takarli
First published in Arabic in 1980 as *al-Raj' al-ba'id*
Protected under the Berne Convention

Dar el Kutub No. 17888/00
ISBN 977 424 646 2

Designed by the AUC Press Design Center/Moody M. Youssef
Printed in Egypt

Translator's Note

The action of *The Long Way Back* is focused mainly on an old house in the Bab al-Shaykh area of Baghdad where the author himself was born in 1927. Four generations of the same family live in this house which is built around a courtyard open to the sky. Overhanging the yard on the first floor is a gallery, and the rooms of the various members of the family open on to it, as does the large alcove where they gather to eat and drink tea. Bab al-Shaykh is an important part of old Baghdad situated around the famous mosque of Abd al-Qadir al-Kilani (al-Jilani), with its big dome, minarets, and chiming clock. The quarter is bounded by two gates, one opening into Kilani Street and the other into the opposite end of Bab al-Shaykh, near the Kurdish quarter, where some of the events in the novel take place.

These events, although they concern the individual dramas and preoccupations of the characters, are set in a very precise historical context in Iraq between 1962 and 1963. The modern state of Iraq was founded in 1920 in the aftermath of the 1914-18 war as a constitutional monarchy under indirect British control. A group of military officers seized power in 1958 and overthrew the monarchy, bringing an end to the old political order. This revolution was led by Abd al-Karim Qasim who governed Iraq for the next five years, until he was overthrown on 8 February, 1963, which fell in the month of Ramadan that year, by a Baathist-Nasserite-Arab nationalist junta. Qasim took refuge in the Ministry of Defense for twenty-four hours, but was executed the next day. The Baathists fell out with the Nasserites and other Arab nationalists nine months later but finally returned to power in 1968. The character Adnan in the novel belongs to the Baath party, as is clear from numerous indications in the text.

The Kurdish quarter was a poor area in the northwest of Baghdad, inhabited mainly by Kurds and Shia Muslims. In 1963 its inhabitants were known to be leftists and communists who supported Abd al-Karim Qasim, and following the overthrow of Qasim it was blockaded and shelled by the nationalists and Baathists, and all those inside were killed or arrested.

The novel has a somewhat unusual publishing history. The Iraqi censor asked the author to cut out the character of Adnan. The author naturally refused and sent the manuscript to Dar Ibn Rushd in Beirut, who agreed to publish it in 1980, incidentally at the beginning of the Iran–Iraq war. Subsequently the novel was distributed in Iraq without the censor appearing to notice.

In 1989 Dar al-Adab in Beirut offered to republish the novel on better quality paper with a clearer typeface if the author would simplify the Iraqi dialogue in it to make it accessible to a broader readership. He agreed to this and the novel was republished in 1993 when it aroused the interest of a new generation of readers and critics. Despite the simplification of the dialogue in the more recent version of the novel, the nuances and variations of usage and register remain as strong indications of the generational, educational, and regional background of the characters, giving it an imaginative dimension that is inevitably reduced in English translation.

Although it is not the purpose of this note to analyze the novel's technique or subject matter, a passing reference should be made to its polyphonic structure, of which much has been written elsewhere. In the author's view this multiplicity of voices and perspectives was inevitable, given the nature of the content. He started writing the novel in 1966, when he was in Paris studying law, and continued writing it for the next eleven years while he was working full-time as a judge in Iraq. In his words, he conceived of its structure with the specific aim of "implicating the reader, trying to construct a world which moves within each reader," although his postscript to the novel is a poignant or ironic counter to such aspirations. Nevertheless, the exquisitely skillful building-up of the overlapping but conflicting worlds of the characters within a brief and clearly determined period of recent history is a bold, intelligent, and profound portrayal of the ambiguous strengths and weaknesses of Iraqi and wider Arab culture and tradition, which has yet to be surpassed. Its language is sometimes vividly pungent, sometimes elegant, and sometimes delicate and lyrical. In addition, the dramatization of the relationships between generations, social groups, and men and women is achieved with a mixture of humor, bitter irony, and compassion which identifies it as a great work of art, regardless of its provenance.

Fuad al-Takarli was born in Baghdad and graduated in law from Baghdad University in 1949. He worked in the Ministry of Justice and was made a judge in 1956 and rose to be head of the Court of Appeal in Baghdad. In 1983, he resigned from this post to devote himself to writing. He studied law in Paris from 1964 to 1966 and lived briefly in Paris again during the 1980s. Since 1990 he has lived in Tunis. In 2000, he was awarded the prestigious Owais Prize for the Arabic Novel.

He published his first short story in Beirut in 1951 and his first collection in Baghdad in 1960. Since then he has published a number of short stories and one-act plays and, as well as three novels, most recently *al-Masarrat wa al-awjaa* (1998). A new collection of short stories is forthcoming.

The Long Way Back (*al-Raj' al-ba'id*) was first published in Beirut in 1980 and a revised version was published there in 1993. A French translation of the novel was published in 1985 (*Les voix de l'aube*, J-C Lattes). Al-Takarli's short stories have been translated into a number of languages, including French, Spanish, Croatian, and English, but this is his first novel to be translated into English.

I would like to thank Fuad al-Takarli for all his help and encouragement over the years since I first read *al-Raj' al-ba'id* and wanted to translate it; Ronak Husni of the University of Durham, UK, for many useful discussions on linguistic and cultural matters relating to the translation; and the Honeyman Foundation for a grant enabling me to visit Tunis for detailed consultations with the author in the final stages of the translation.

The Long Way Back

Chapter
One

The two of them walked slowly, crossing Kilani Street through the long shadows, and began climbing the unpaved alley. Nuriya spoke to her granddaughter. "Don't walk so fast, Sana dear."

"All right, Bibi."

It was shortly before sunset and the street was busy behind them, but a light breeze carried the noise away. They managed to see where they were walking, although the streetlights hadn't come on yet and the faces of the passers-by were indistinct.

"This bread's very hot," said the little girl.

"May God always bless us with bread."

"God willing, Bibi."

"Good girl. That's the way to talk. Never let God's name be far from your lips."

"No, Bibi."

The bag of fruit and eggs and vegetables was heavy, and Nuriya found it harder to breathe with every step, as the road continued to rise steeply. She slowed down and changed the bag over to her other hand and noticed the little girl staggering under the weight of the bottle of milk and rounds of hot bread.

"Shall we rest for a bit, Bibi?" the little girl asked. "You're tired."

"No, dear. It's no distance to the house."

It was then that she saw him coming round the corner of the next alley, tall, broad-chested, walking unsteadily. She was surprised she could recognize anybody in this forest of shadows, especially someone she had thought was far away.

"Stop, Sana, dear. I want to have a rest."

"All right, Bibi. I said you were tired."

He stumbled violently and almost collided with the wall, but recovered his balance at the last minute. She heard him cough and saw his whole body shake. It was for the best if the little girl didn't see him. What freak wind had brought him back from Kuwait? He stopped to light a cigarette. The smoke rose in the air behind him as he walked on, his head up but his gait strangely uneven, as if he'd had a blow to the temple.

"Bibi, this bread's really hot."

"Yes, dear, I know. Let's go now."

She watched him walking away and thought he could have been anybody. Who could tell, this monstrosity might outlive them all! It was possible the little girl hadn't noticed him, but he was as stubborn as a mule, moving forward a few steps, only to come to a halt again. She busied herself with her bag of shopping and, trying to catch her breath, began to speak to distract Sana. "Yes, dear. Never let God's name be far from your lips. You can give me the bread if you like. I'll carry it for you."

"No, Bibi. I'll manage."

"Good girl. Come on, let's go."

And off they went again.

"Last night I had a dream, Granny, but I've forgotten it now. I told Suha about it in the morning and she said I shouldn't have dreams. Why shouldn't I, Bibi? Because I'm younger than her? Why does that mean

4

I shouldn't have dreams? Anyway, whenever I go to sleep I ask God to let me have a nice dream. Better than Suha's."

Then she pushed open the door of the house with her foot and hurried in. Nuriya cast a last glance at the figure weaving its way along close to the wall, then followed her granddaughter inside. She hoped Sana would carry on chattering as they walked along the dark, narrow passage, but the little girl was silent, paying close attention to where she was putting her feet.

"Look out for the creepy-crawlies, dear."

"Yes, Bibi. I'm scared of the dark."

"No you're not. Why would a sensible girl like you be afraid of the dark?"

The big inner door squeaked loudly as they pushed it open, and the noise of the house surged up to meet them.

Nuriya heaved a sigh of relief as her feet struck the familiar bricks of the courtyard and she watched the little girl hurry towards the kitchen. She heard her daughter Madiha calling her from the first floor.

"Who's there? Mother? Sana?"

"Yes, Mum. It's us," answered the little girl.

Nuriya sank down on to a low chair in a corner of the kitchen and put her shopping bag on the floor. She was tired from the long walk and felt vaguely uneasy. What had he come here for, and why now? She watched Sana opening a large pot and stacking the discs of bread inside it, then going towards the fridge with the bottle of milk. Perhaps they'd thrown him out of the company when they'd discovered what he was really like, but was he going to go through the same farce with the family all over again? Madiha called her once more from the upstairs gallery.

"Mum, Mum. Where are you? Are you in the kitchen?"

"Yes. Why don't you come down?"

"I'm coming."

All the noise was from the room where the old women sat—Nuriya's mother and sister-in-law. They were constantly squabbling

5

about nothing. Madiha's tall, full figure appeared dimly at the foot of the stairs.

"Switch on the light, Madiha," Nuriya called out to her.

Her daughter paused for a moment, then the kitchen doorway was flooded with light.

Nuriya got up to put the eggs in the fridge and noticed her grand-daughter was no longer there.

"Where's Sana?" she asked.

"Upstairs," answered Madiha, then went on hurriedly, "Come on, Mum, please. Let's make dinner quickly. They've been pestering me for two hours now."

"Who? Your aunt?"

"My aunt and my grandmother. For the past hour Aunt Safiya's been saying, 'I can smell kebab, dear,' and my grandmother's got fantasies about mutton broth."

Nuriya lit the small gas cooker.

"They're only getting fried eggs and spinach," she said. "Is your father home?"

Madiha sat down on the vacant chair. Her mother thought she seemed tired. "Is your father back?" she asked again.

"Mum, is it true you saw Husayn when you were out?" asked Madiha, pushing some strands of black hair off her forehead with a gesture which confirmed her weariness to her mother.

So the child had noticed after all. "Did Sana tell you?" she asked. "I thought I'd stopped her seeing him. He seemed drunk. He's nothing to do with us any more."

"I know." Madiha let out a long sigh.

Her mother was silent, sensing that although Madiha was her daughter she couldn't speak her mind about Husayn.

"I knew he wasn't going to stay in Kuwait long," Madiha went on Madiha. "Since Abd al-Karim Qasim said Kuwait belongs to us, things have got worse for Iraqis over there. And that just suits Husayn. It's hot in Kuwait, and there's nothing to drink. What would he stay for?"

Nuriya was busy taking food out of the fridge to make the dinner. She turned to her daughter. "He's nothing to do with us. It's two years since that man left you and the children. He hasn't sent you any money, he's never dropped you a line. You've had no news at all. You don't know where you stand. Do you think such behavior's acceptable to the Lord?"

Madiha sighed heavily. "Yes, Mum, I know. That's what I'm saying."

The two women heard a quavering voice from above: "Nuriya. Nuriya, my dear. Are you going to make the food? Your Aunt Safiya's faint with hunger. She says she wants some hot bread, two shish kebabs, vegetables, and pickles."

"She's at it again. Give me strength," said Madiha. "That's Granny. Auntie's sent her to see what's happening. What is it, Bibi?" she called.

This time the voice was gentle and imploring. "My dear little Madiha, your Auntie wants kebab and I'll be happy with mutton broth for my dinner. You can put it all on a tray, and I'll send Sana to fetch it. Hurry up, Madiha, and may God send your little girls' father home to you!"

Nuriya went out of the kitchen and called up to her mother. "Why do you keep going on, Mother? There's only eggs and spinach, and we're all going to sit down and eat when Abu Midhat comes home." Then she turned back to Madiha. "Where *is* your father, for God's sake? And Midhat and Karumi? Where are they all?"

"Father's still out, and Midhat's on the terrace."

From above the same voice grumbled, "This is so unfair! Oh well, I suppose those who've eaten their fill don't know what it's like to be hungry. Did you hear what they're saying? There's nothing to eat! There's no dinner! All those lovely smells that keep wafting up to us, and they say there's nothing to eat! No kebabs, no mutton broth!"

"Be patient," said a sharp voice from inside the upstairs room.

"Mum, they're going to make such a scene if we don't shut them up," said Madiha. "Why don't you go away? I'll get the food ready."

"Where would I go to? Your father will be back soon and then we'll make the dinner. Where's Karumi gone?"

Her daughter let her hands drop between her knees and stared at the floor dejectedly. "I really don't know, but he seems very busy these days. He goes out every afternoon and doesn't come back till after midnight. I've no idea what he can be doing."

Nuriya's heart gave a faint lurch. Was there something going on in the house that she didn't know about, even though it concerned her younger son? "What do you mean, Madiha? What's wrong with him? I haven't noticed anything. Perhaps he just likes to go and study with Fuad. Has he said anything to you?"

"No. Why should he? If they're studying for the exams already, then that's fine."

They heard the sound of heavy footsteps as someone came along the passage.

"There's your father. Give me the frying pan, Madiha dear. I'll fry the eggs."

As she got to her feet, her daughter whispered to her, "Mum, don't say anything to Dad about Husayn. Perhaps it'll all blow over."

She said nothing for a moment, then answered, "God willing. God willing."

The main door squeaked, and her husband was standing in the kitchen doorway. "Good evening, everybody."

"You're late, Abu Midhat. It must have been some funeral!"

He took off his black *sidara* cap and sat down on the chair. "It was the last day of the wake. They wanted to keep me there for dinner but I declined. I didn't like the way those boys were behaving. There was a steady stream of people paying their respects but they couldn't take their eyes off the door, hoping someone from the government would come to offer their condolences. Weren't we good enough for them, for God's sake? Since when have they had connections in the government?"

"It's not their fault," she replied, taking the eggs and the pan from her daughter.

He mopped his brow and turned to talk to Madiha. "Where are the children? How is it I can't hear a sound out of them?"

"I left them upstairs doing their homework. They've got a test tomorrow."

He got to his feet. "I'll go up and see them. Where's Midhat?" Without waiting for an answer, he trudged off towards the stairs.

The lighted rings on the cooker gave off an uncomfortable heat, and the cooking pots and the smoking fat in the big frying pan grumbled and whispered to one another. Nuriya was aware of her daughter standing in a corner of the kitchen in the shadows, near where the white plates were kept neatly stacked. She turned to look at her. Slowly, with a distracted air, Madiha was wiping some glass object. She didn't want to say anything, but she couldn't help it. "What's wrong, dear?"

Madiha's hand went up quickly to brush her cheek. The round shape of her face showed up indistinctly and her mother couldn't tell if she was really crying. She was about to repeat her question when Madiha whispered, "Why do I have such a hard time? And the girls, too? We're so unlucky!"

Nuriya moved the frying pan off the ring. "Listen to me! Why are you complaining? You're living in your father's house with your family, aren't you? You should be grateful. Your father's alive and in good health, thank God. And there are your brothers, too, God bless them. As for that man Husayn, he'll get what's coming to him. Just leave him to get on with it. You're sensible, Madiha, and you know how much I love you. You're my only daughter." She embraced her gently and kissed her damp cheek. She thought her daughter was acting like a five-year-old who had seen nothing of life and its hardships, and this worried her.

"I know all that," whispered Madiha again. "But I'm living in limbo, and I'm not getting any younger."

"Patience is a virtue," quoted her mother briskly. "It's not the first time he's come back. This is just the way things have turned out for you, dear, and you never know when your luck will change."

She turned to put the frying pan back on the ring, while Madiha went on in a firm voice, "No, Mum. I want to see him this time. He came back to see the girls, I know, but I've made up my mind to settle things with him face to face. We don't need him. I've got a job and a regular salary, and my daughters and I have a roof over our heads, thanks to Father. He has to know I'm not just sitting waiting for him in case he feels like coming back to me. That time's passed."

Madiha was interrupted by the voice of her daughter Suha. "Mum. Mum. I'm hungry. Bibi Umm Hasan says are we getting something to eat this evening or not?"

"Yes, of course we are, Suha. It's just about ready. Have you finished your homework?"

"I have. Sana hasn't though. Grandpa says she's lazy and good for nothing."

Sana could be heard shouting from their room: "That's a lie, Mum. I have finished. Grandpa never said anything about me. Suha's a liar."

"I'm not a liar. Grandpa did say you're lazy."

"When?" asked Sana.

This bickering didn't make Nuriya feel any happier. She wanted to get dinner over so she could talk to her daughter in peace and try and find out what exactly she was planning to do.

"Have you put the food out, Madiha?"

"Yes."

"Then send Suha to fetch her Uncle Midhat. What's he doing up on the terrace in this cold weather? I wonder if Karumi's eating somewhere else?"

She looked at Madiha setting the white crockery out on the table. The kitchen had got hot and she could feel the sweat collecting on her forehead and running down between her breasts. All her misgivings returned with a vengeance as she watched her daughter moving about mechanically like a puppet with no mind or spirit of its own, then step-ping out of the murky kitchen, wiping her face with the palm of her hand and calling, "Suha. Suha."

The child answered from a distance, and her mother told her to go up on to the terrace and tell her uncle dinner was ready. Her voice trem-bled as she spoke, and it occurred to Nuriya that her daughter had sud-denly aged.

———

Nuriya came out of the bedroom, leaving her husband to smoke his last cigarette.

A dim light shone on the gallery and lit up part of the big alcove where the family often sat. The dark sky was studded with stars and smudged here and there with white clouds. She stood leaning on the worn wooden balustrade. The courtyard of the house was as dark as the mouth of a well. It was true her son Abd al-Karim was back late so reg-ularly that it was beginning to look suspicious. She saw a light in his brother Midhat's room and went towards it. She was tired. It was an effort to lift her feet, and she wished she could go to sleep like her hus-band in the warm bed next to him. He hadn't understood why she want-ed to go to the girls' room, but assumed that she felt like watching the late film on the television.

She put her head round the door of Midhat's brightly-lit room but there was nobody there. She heard a voice from the other side of the courtyard. "I'm here. Do you want something?"

She turned quickly, but could not make out the shadowy figure at first. He was looking in her direction. She could just see him with difficulty in the faint light. "Midhat, my dear. What are you doing outside?"

"Having a walk," he answered testily.

"That's fine, dear. Take your time. Aren't you cold?"

"No, not at all."

"Fine. Don't get annoyed, dear."

She was afraid to ask him why his brother stayed out late every night. He grew impatient if he talked to her for long, although she was sure he loved her. She watched the short figure moving slowly away as she walked laboriously along the gallery. He had some of her father in him, especially his edginess. God preserve him from ending up like her father!

She could hear the noise of several different voices raised in conversation in her daughter's room before she opened the door. There was only a miserable light in the large, high-ceilinged room and the walls were in dark shadow. She saw her mother, Umm Hasan, and her sister-in-law, Safiya, sitting on the iron bedstead watching television. Madiha was lying on one of the big beds near her two sleeping daughters. She was in time to hear her sister-in-law finishing her story: "Our orchard used to be where the Unknown Soldier is buried. It went from the Soldier down to the river, and you could walk along beside the river right up to the neighbor's house. It was a huge orchard, my dear, a wilderness! A donkey could get lost there for four days!"

"What donkey?"

She stopped short and appeared to be considering Umm Hasan's question, then went on, "What do you mean, what donkey? A donkey that was around at the time."

Nuriya sat down on the bed next to her daughter. "Are the children asleep?" she asked.

Madiha nodded. She was undeniably pale, and in among the waves of her black hair threads of white gleamed. Although Nuriya saw that she was looking attentively at her aunt, she questioned her again, in an undertone: "Are you tired, Madiha?"

She sighed deeply and nodded her head again, so Nuriya was none the wiser. Madiha was leaning on her elbow, resting her cheek on her hand.

"Why are you staring at your aunt? Are you fed up with her stories?"

Madiha smiled faintly. "I'm looking at her red hair. Every week she puts henna on it. Why does she bother?"

Nuriya turned to look at her husband's sister. She was a little bundle of bones crowned by a thick mass of white hair stained with henna. She didn't hate her any more after all these years, and anyway Safiya was afraid of her and avoided crossing swords with her. She seemed to have given up her claims on her brother at last, although she still clung firmly to the image of her noble ancestors, and never tired of talking about them.

"My father was very tall, God rest him," she was saying now. "We children didn't take after him. We took after our mother. She was short, God rest her soul. He was extremely tall. He had to duck when he went through doorways. And his legs! I can see them now, sticking out over the end of the bed when he slept on the terrace. What a figure! He was so handsome! Like the moon on the fourteenth day. A face, they used to say, like a circle of bread, so round and fair. And when he walked, he positively undulated! Sayyid Ismail bin Hajji Abd al-Razzaq. A man to be reckoned with! With his navy blue suit and the gold watch gleaming on his chest, you couldn't miss him. And his fez always slightly at an angle."

"Aren't you hungry, Safiya?" interrupted Umm Hasan.

"Why, what's the time?" asked Safiya, after a moment's pause.

"They haven't had the call to prayer yet."

"Which one?"

"The evening prayer."

"You're showing your age, Umm Hasan. They gave the call to prayer a couple of hours ago when that windbag was singing the praises of her crazy leader on television."

"Do you think I watch television?"

Nuriya noticed the slight smile returning to Madiha's lips as she listened to her aunt and grandmother talking. It must be past ten o'clock, otherwise her mother wouldn't be mentioning food again.

"If you're hungry, Mother," she said to her, "there's a bit of bread and cheese in the kitchen. Shall I go down and get it?"

"Don't bother, Nuriya. I'll go and see if there are any sesame pastries left. Karumi brought me some a couple of days ago, God bless him. Lovely ones!"

"I'm starving, too," said Safiya. "Come on, my dear. Let's go and see what we can find."

The two of them went off slowly and unsteadily, holding on to each other, leaving the door open behind them. The fresh night air of springtime blew gently in on Nuriya. Silence closed around the big house, and she felt her body drooping with tiredness. She saw her daughter's eyes were closed and spoke gently to her: "Madiha. Go to bed if you're falling asleep."

Madiha sat up on the bed and rubbed her eyes, then tucked the covers firmly round the two sleeping children.

"Were you dozing? Go to bed, dear. I'm going now. I thought there might be something on television."

"There's nothing on but trashy films, or songs and speeches."

Madiha slid down under the covers and pulled them up to her chin. Her mother didn't know whether to cross-examine her about her husband Husayn or leave it for another time. She told her that she hadn't mentioned seeing Husayn to Madiha's father, but Madiha's only response was a faint grunt. Arranging the covers around her and the two children, Nuriya whispered, "Madiha. Listen. You're not to do anything without telling me first. Do you understand? I don't want to be kept in the dark next time. Madiha . . . She's fast asleep. I'm wasting my time."

She got up and switched off the lights, then left, closing the door behind her. She couldn't see Midhat on the gallery. There was a slight chill in the air and the sky was clear. He must have gone back to his room. Her mother and Aunt Safiya were talking in abnormally loud voices in their room nearby. She hesitated. She didn't want to intrude on them, but wasn't ready to sleep, despite her tiredness. They were sitting cross-legged, each on her own bed, nibbling at sesame pastries, which they first softened in a glass of water on the floor between them. In the red glow of the light they were talking, both at the same time and with unaccustomed fervor. Her mother turned to address her as soon as she walked through the door: "It's Nuriya. Please come in. See what you think." Safiya had gone quiet and was concentrating on eating, while Nuriya's mother kept talking: "Nuriya, you know Maliha, who's married to that shaykh in Baquba?"

Safiya interrupted her: "What shaykh, Umm Hasan? You're mad. He's got a fruit and vegetable stall."

"What does it matter? Shaykh or greengrocer, he's got pots of money and good luck to him."

"Yes, good luck to him. But he's not a real Arab shaykh."

The mother directed her conversation to Nuriya: "We're talking about Maliha, Adnan's mother. How many sons has she got, and how many daughters?"

"Three sons and three daughters," Safiya cut in.

"That's right," agreed Nuriya. "Count with me. There's Adnan, the oldest. Then Sakban and Salman. And the girls, Salima, Fahima, and Badaa. Salima and Fahima are twins."

"And Munira, the pretty one who's a teacher," said Umm Hasan doubtfully. "Isn't she Maliha's daughter, too?"

Nuriya laughed and was about to reply, but Safiya got in first: "My dear Umm Hasan, you're out of your mind. Don't you know your own granddaughters?"

"It's true, mother. Why are you getting so mixed up? Munira and Maliha are sisters, the daughters of my sister Najiya—my nieces in other words. How can you have forgotten?"

"Who says I've forgotten, Nuriya? Does anyone ever forget their own children? But they live a long way off, God save them, and it's months since I last saw any of them. I want to go to Baquba as soon as it gets a bit warmer."

"You'd do better to stay where you are," said Safiya. "You'd have to come back the minute you got there! They're coming here in the holidays."

"Who is?"

"What do you mean, who is? Munira and her mother, who else? Do you want to have Maliha and her family here too?"

"No, my dear. Who wants her? Nobody's seen her for years. She spends all her time getting pregnant and having children."

Nuriya went slowly and sat down on the edge of her mother's bed and stretched her feet out in front of her on the rug. She wasn't comfortable like this, and every bone in her body ached. The old women's conversation about her sister and two nieces stirred some vague memory. They were busy eating their pastries dipped in water while she tried to recollect it more clearly, when she heard her mother say, "There's someone at the door, Nuriya."

Safiya's jaws immediately stopped moving and she listened attentively for a few moments. Then she said, "No. It's nothing. Who'd knock on the door at this time of night?"

But Umm Hasan whispered hesitantly, "Really, I can hear someone knocking all the time. Or at least sometimes I think there's someone there, and then I think maybe I'm just . . ."

". . . just imagining things," finished Safiya.

"All right, then. I'm wrong."

They heard footsteps approaching and Midhat put his head round the door and said to his mother, "Someone's been banging on the door for five minutes. Hasn't Karumi got a key?"

She jumped to her feet, and heard her mother saying, "You see? You can't say anything round here without somebody jumping down your throat!"

"How could he not have a key?" Nuriya said to her son. "We never hear him when he comes in at night. Why would he knock tonight? And how do you know it's him?"

"I don't," he said, walking away. "I just thought it might be. I'll go down and see."

She hurried after him as he moved lightly along the gallery, heading for the stairs. She suddenly felt anxious as she struggled to catch up with him. People didn't usually knock on the door at this time of the night. As she went cautiously down the stairs, she wished she could tell her husband about it. The knocking gathered strength as they crossed the courtyard in the semi-darkness. Her heart was beating violently, and she couldn't help thinking that Husayn might have something to do with it. Perhaps he'd come to reach an understanding with them in his own particular fashion, after knocking back a bottle of arak!

Midhat switched on the light over the main door, and she saw that his thin face was hard and tense. The narrow passageway continued to reverberate to the heavy thuds even when they were only a few steps from the door.

"Who is it?" called Midhat.

Abd al-Karim's voice came back at once: "It's me. Me—Karim."

She relaxed at the sound of her younger son's voice and managed to speak: "Do you think this is funny, Karumi? Scaring us all stiff in the middle of the night like this!"

Midhat was unlocking the door without a word. His shoulders looked narrow in the dim light and she felt a surge of tenderness towards him.

She noticed nothing particularly odd about Abd al-Karim as he apologized for having lost his key, then walked ahead of them into the house. Perhaps his voice was hoarser than usual, his speech slightly jerky, and he seemed to be in a hurry for no apparent reason.

She followed him, leaving Midhat to lock the door, and begged him to slow down a little, but he showed no signs of having heard. She stopped and waited in the dimly lit courtyard by the trees in the little garden, listening to him going upstairs. He stumbled several times, but she didn't tell Midhat this when he caught up with her and walked slowly along beside her. The two of them crossed the yard and went up the dark staircase with her leading the way, battling to keep ahead. Realizing what was in her mind, Midhat said to her as he went off to his room, "Go and see what he wants, Mother. He might be more comfortable with you."

She nodded and hurried into Abd al-Karim's room, next door to Midhat's. The light was dazzling, its effect heightened by the white walls. Abd al-Karim was sitting on his bed, his jacket off, staring bewilderedly at his trousers, then at his hands. He looked up at her, and she could see the anguish and confusion in his eyes. He seemed to be imploring her to help him. A large dark stain on his trousers and the edge of his white shirt caught her eye. The emotion on his face scared her, and she hurried over to him and knelt down beside him. "What's wrong, Karumi? What is it, my dear?"

His hands were shaking. "That's blood. Fuad's blood, Mother," he shouted in a frenzy.

She embraced his trembling legs impulsively, then began calling out to Midhat.

Chapter Two

They were in the alcove talking, drinking tea, talking some more. From my sick bed I listened to them and guessed they would come to see me here. I would have preferred to go on listening without encountering them face to face, although I knew the sight of her would make me happy, and so I lay there waiting for them to finish their conversation.

The last red rays of the sun were falling high up on the neighbors' wall and the sky was still blue. By now we would usually be sleeping up on the terrace. Most years we would start towards the end of May, but it was early June and we were still in our rooms, making do with opening the windows wide at night. I hadn't seen her for several months, five or six probably. Since she'd got a job as a schoolteacher outside Baghdad she hadn't been around much. I wished I wasn't ill like this, feeling lightheaded after any conversation that lasted more than a few minutes, or after reading just a page or so. That was why I hadn't been able to sit the first round of exams. She would definitely have heard all about it. Nothing was a secret for long around here. Anyway, it was impossible to avoid being ill altogether, especially since I hadn't received proper care.

Love can't solve everything. That's why my mother couldn't cure me with her love alone, and I was still cooped up in bed for no obvious reason. They were coming towards my room. If illness is taken to be a natural, physiological occurrence, then it's open to being understood and treated. They came in, greeting me. She and her mother, Midhat, my mother and Madiha. But if it's psychological, or a response to some obsession, then it's very doubtful if it can be treated at all. She was dressed in black, which accentuated the effect of the kohl round her gold-brown eyes. They sat round my bed and asked me trivial questions. Her black *abaya* was still draped over her shoulders, and her beautiful face reflected the sadness that came from being intelligent like her. Why had I been separated from her for so long? Then I noticed the pain in her eyes. Her blonde hair fell carelessly over her forehead, and she fiddled with her lower lip whenever she wasn't talking. Where had I seen that look of anguish before?

I stared at her, drawn in by the aura of pain surrounding her. She was trapped in it, like me and Fuad on that awful day, and I could feel Fuad, almost see him all around us, binding us together.

That evening back in the autumn, Fuad's eyes had been glowing like dying embers. He had been trembling in spite of the warm weather and infecting me with the anxiety that he transmitted even just by moving his fingertips or lips slightly, or glancing sideways. He never used to reveal his inner thoughts or feelings to me when we met those evenings last autumn; I often watched him silhouetted against the sunset and the anemic sky, on the terrace of the Café Belkis down by the river, and there was the same unfathomable look in his eyes as there was in hers now.

She was talking to me uneasily, asking me about my illness, my exam, what I'd been reading, what was really wrong with me, and I wasn't listening properly. I could feel my forehead damp with fever. I smiled at her, and she responded with the ghost of a smile, excusing my lack of good humor. I was not the person she thought I was: she was ignorant of much that had happened to me during these past few months, although the fact that I had been ill was no secret. I lived my illness conscientiously because I couldn't think of any alternative, and it was what brought us close to each other. Illness united us. Mine and hers. They suddenly got up to go, cutting short the brief moments when she had lit up my room with her presence, all because of my mother who had apparently noticed that I was exhausted.

Munira hung behind briefly. She stood at the door, her face turned towards me. Her brown skin was pale, and all I could make out of her features was her gold-flecked eyes. She said in a serious voice that she hoped everything would work out. Her *abaya* revealed the swell of her left breast, and from the waves of despair in her voice I realized she was talking about herself as well.

The room was strangely empty after they'd gone. I lay on my bed wondering not for the first time why I was ill like this. I longed to follow them out of the gray shadows where they had abandoned me and become one of them. The sight of her made me want to be a healthy outdoor type, and yet I was incapable even of getting up to switch on the light!

From my tall window I could see a piece of the sky, white and soft against the light blue, and below it the neighbors' dark, depressing walls. I got up slowly and walked and stood in the doorway. I wasn't as weak as I had imagined, so I ought to accept the illness as it really was: no exaggerating it and no adolescent pretending it didn't exist. The sky opened out above me, and the sight of it made me feel calm. They weren't in the alcove, and I heard their voices coming from my Aunt Safiya's room. They were talking with a liveliness that they hadn't shown when they were with me. They were more aware of my illness than I was myself. They experienced it at a profound level sometimes, my mother especially, but their fellow feeling didn't move me, although it should have done.

Suha came running out of my aunt's room and noticed me standing there. She looked slightly taken aback, then her face lit up and she began telling me enthusiastically how they'd all decided to go up on the terrace to sleep from tonight on. She was like a little bird, twittering with excitement. Since Munira and her mother had arrived I'd expected the family to move up there, as it wasn't easy to find suitable accommodation for two extra people. I felt as pleased at the idea of the move to the roof as if I'd been going to join them myself, but then I had a dizzy spell which forced me back into bed where I became immersed in my own thoughts again.

The police officer took two or three steps forward and came to a halt a short distance from the chair where I was sitting, bound hand and foot. He stood like a peacock, his eyes blazing. Sometimes he was a Gestapo officer, sometimes an interrogator from the Spanish Inquisition. He began to address me, fixing me in the eye: "I have to inform you that it is my duty to arrest you on charges of murder, desertion, and treason."

Then he gave a Nazi salute that frightened me more than what he had just said. My limbs were numb and stiff, and the sweat was pouring off me. I wasn't really tied to the chair, but I might as well have been.

"You'd do well to understand," he began again, "that my duty as an honest official and a citizen obliges me to arrest all those accused of murder, desertion, and treason. What do you think we're in this world for?"

Another strange salute. Then for the third time: "Don't allow yourself to think about anything but your arrest for murder, desertion, and treason."

He wore a little round badge on his chest, which he insisted on pointing out to me when he finished speaking. This time there was no salute. The image on the badge zoomed towards me, and I saw it in close-up. It was only then I began shouting. The picture was a jumble of lines, like ant-tracks in the dust, but from it a clear image emerged: Fuad's face in the last few moments of his life.

I felt like shouting and weeping to exorcise my anguish in the first light of dawn. I sat up in bed staring into space. I was bathed in cold, sticky sweat, and my breathing was rapid and uneven, constricting my chest. I wiped my sweat with the cloth my mother had left by the bed, then stood up and went towards the door, my limbs trembling. The cold air of daybreak revived me slightly, and I made slowly for the fridge in the alcove. I drank some icy water and splashed the remains of the glass over my face. The world was as quiet as an open grave. There was nobody about but me. I held on to the wooden balustrade and rested my weight on it. Why did these dreadful things happen to me? I wanted to be ill and get better like normal people did. But it wasn't the illness that was eating at me: it was an idea, an obsession, a devil on my back. I returned to my room feeling drained and empty and lay down on the bed. Through the open door I could see the sky glistening like the waters of a stream. The sun wouldn't be up for an hour or more. I'd been on my own like this for a while now. I couldn't remember how long, and if time had no meaning in such situations, then surely I was destined to end up like this, neither guilty nor innocent. No one but me would ever know what had happened to me, and perhaps I was the only one who could look for a solution. If I continued to be afraid of pain, sorrow, guilt, remorse—the specters which haunted my nights and often my days too—then I would be actively inviting a harsh judgment on my behavior.

The surface of the sky grew brighter. If only the hidden corners of the soul could be lit up in the same way! I decided Munira wasn't like Fuad. There was no physical resemblance. But spiritually, in the aura that surrounded them both . . . Fuad was walking parallel to the curb, thin and upright, apart from the slightly hunched shoulders and an unsureness in his steps. The yellow light defined him from all angles. That particular night we had left earlier than usual. The big house had been empty. I'd believed for a short while, after I saw the object of his affections coming out of the room and gesturing to me in a way which

I took to mean that things had gone normally at last, that he would now find something approaching peace of mind. I saw his face as soon as he came through the door. It was blotchy and very pale, and his blazing eyes had gone empty and dead. He propelled me along in a rush, not wanting to see her, and his fingers felt cold and clammy and limp. He went out ahead of me and took a few steps along the street, then leaned against the fence of the next door house. I went up to him anxiously, thinking he was about to throw up, but he wouldn't have had the strength. His entire body was trembling. Without a word I put my arm round him and he was still, like a dying sparrow, and my heart was sore for him as I held him. I said nothing, although I didn't understand what was going on. The moments passed like long years of torment, and we were two old men approaching death. I saw him close his eyes, then he let out a sigh that was more of a sob and moved away from me along the edge of the curb. This was the picture of him I would preserve for the rest of my life. He wasn't dead then. He was like a flower in full bloom covered with the early morning dew. No one would benefit from him ceasing to exist. He was a bright star in the surrounding darkness, and I could only be true to myself if I saved him from extinction. From now on this would be my reason for living.

I was almost calm as I lay there on my bed listening to the first chirpings of the birds in the barren olive tree. I realized that the lame way I was solving my problem—if indeed I was—by forcibly holding myself apart from everything, trying to remain immobilized inside time on a sick-bed, couldn't be sustained for much longer. So much mental activity in one day, before the sun had even risen!

These reflections were interrupted by the sounds of someone coming down from the roof. The lightness of the tread made me think it must be my mother. She always walked softly like that, as if she was scared of hurting the feelings of the ground beneath her feet. Was she an infinite source of love? Perhaps it was anxiety about me that had woken her up so early in the morning. Since the door leading to the stairs was opposite my room, I was expecting to see her at any moment, as soon as she'd crossed the gallery separating us. It was only a few minutes to sunrise, and the crystal sky bathed the courtyard and gallery and old wall in a soft flood of light.

The moment the figure emerged through the door at the bottom of the stairs leading to the roof, I saw it was her, treading slowly, light as a bird, then stopping to lean against the balustrade. She looked thin in her long blue dress. Her shoulder blades stuck out, and part of her neck and chest showed pure white. Both hands were resting on the railing, and she was looking down. The moments that followed were magical for me, immeasurably beautiful. I was surprised and enthralled to see her in such a way and at such a time. She wasn't Munira, my cousin, but an explosion of light in my confused life. She was my sorrow, my painful past, my love, my longing, my sickness and misery. She stood there without moving and looked unearthly, ethereal. She raised her hand to push a strand of her long hair back off her forehead. Then as she turned her gaze slowly to look round the house, her eyes brushed past my room, and I was seized with horror at the idea of her seeing me. My presence, or even the sight of me, might sully her, bring her down to the level of ordinary mortals. She was at worship, contemplating her soul and something heavenly to which I had no access. I felt insignificant as I watched her finish this dawn prayer of hers, then glide like a phantom towards my aunt's room.

After she'd gone I felt tired, and it didn't occur to me to go out and speak to her. A cool breeze caressed my hot face and I closed my eyes. Maybe I was feverish, about to have a relapse, but unfamiliar emotions were raging inside me, making me uneasy. I was reliving the whole painful episode. I hadn't lost Fuad; he was still part of my world. Nor had I betrayed him, not for a single instant. He was alive in some way in this creature of uncertain dimensions whom I hardly knew. From my dark night he was drawing me towards him.

That autumn evening his eyes had been ablaze as he sat facing me at the dirty, dusty table up on the terrace of the Belkis, where we'd gone to avoid the dull company inside. I'd watched him trembling with emotion, which wasn't like him, and it had alarmed me. He wasn't given to impetuosity. I was used to his deliberation and careful reasoning, but from what he told me he had been swept off his feet without realizing what was happening. She was the daughter of some neighbors who'd lived in a shabby building near their large family house for a couple of months, then moved away. They were the sort of people whose past mistakes hound them all their lives. Her mother was on her own, and people said her father was a British officer who'd fallen in love with her mother, a beautiful Bedouin woman, married her, had a boy and a girl with her, then gone off with his regiment. She'd received a few letters, then nothing more was ever heard of him. As the son wasn't able to give the family security, the mother had to do what she could to support them all.

Fuad had been seventeen at that time, and the girl no more than fifteen. A boy's love, but it had lasted. He only talked to me about her after a lot of hesitation. It was hard for him, even embarrassing in a way. He'd never said a word to her, had no desire to, but had kept track of them for the whole four years after they'd left the neighborhood. She was everything to him, a symbol of life and the world as he dreamed they could be. She knew nothing of him, and that, too, was as he wanted it to be. Involuntarily, she had purified him by her presence inside him and kindled a flame in him that would never die. He would have liked to reject the categories bequeathed to him by his forefathers, which delineated the beginnings and endings in life. Then he would have come to a halt at the peak of his burning love for her and not done anything with her, so preserving his feelings intact, undiminished, for the rest of his life. He suffered continuously because what he was going through didn't seem normal or right. He wanted to write to her, talk to her, marry her! Then he thought it would be more logical and in keeping with his views of life if he forgot all about her. It was pointless to follow her about like this, keeping watch on each successive house the family moved to, and observing her as she came and went. Their paths were clearly never going to coincide.

On this particular evening he was silent and buried his face in his hands. I watched the red sky fill up with dark clouds scudding southwards and didn't dare break the silence. I was helpless, unable to comprehend. He had told me before that he'd lost all trace of her for more than a year and felt anxious about her without knowing why. It was as if she was heading for disaster, and it was just a case of finding out when and how it would happen. Suddenly, without removing his hands from in front of his face, he said he'd seen her by chance in a brothel.

I took hold of his hands and pulled them away from his face. I needed to see his eyes to know if he was telling the truth. They were red and wet with tears. He looked away from me and squeezed my fingers. With him sitting beside me and the sky overcast and the smell of the river on the cool autumn breeze, I sensed a whiff of tragedy in the air. There was no emotion, no hint of tears in his voice, as he recounted how he'd seen her and sat watching her for an hour without the strength to move. She hadn't paid him any particular attention. He reminded himself that he'd chosen in one way or another not to get involved in her life and realized he had to get out. Sitting watching her was sheer hell. He didn't have the courage to go back and see her on his own, and the nights of anguish and heartbreak were becoming more than he could stand. I realized from the way he looked at me, from the dark circles under his eyes, which were tired despite the passion in them, from his silence and his hands lying resignedly on the table between us, that he was appealing to me to share these difficult times with him. I never thought for a moment that a thing called death was awaiting us, and so with a light heart I patted his hot hand and asked when would be a good time for us to go.

We entered the hall of the big house and, as we sat waiting for her, I became convinced he must have resolved his feelings and abandoned his past illusions about love and all the rest of it. She was terribly thin and moved heavily. There was nothing attractive about her face except for her eyes, which had very black lashes. She sat down beside us. I was examining her, trying to fathom the mystery of the strange sort of purity that enveloped her and pervaded her features and gestures, when I noticed the sound of Fuad's rapid breathing. His pale face, turned towards her, wore a deeply tormented expression, and he clasped and unclasped his hands. She arranged her short black hair and didn't look at anyone. The arteries in his neck throbbed violently as he breathed. The two of them were obviously going nowhere together, and I began to think that perhaps I'd been influenced by what he had said and by my genuine feelings of friendship toward him when I had momentarily sensed a certain purity in her. I only existed on the fringes of their tragedy, and it would have been easy for me to say that she was an insipid girl without much to her. It wouldn't have done me any harm, and I could then have searched dispassionately for a way of sorting things out for Fuad. But that night was too short; we were prevented from taking stock because some idiotic punter beckoned her and we had to leave.

That was the start of the vicious circle: days of talking, when Fuad gave vent to his apprehensions and anxieties, then night time visits cut short by unnecessarily hasty exits. I can't say I was ever bored, but I began to share in his helplessness and embarrassment, and sometimes his fear. In the end a deadly feeling of futility and shame began to creep over me. That particular night I had wanted to speak out but hadn't had the courage. She was wearing a light green dress, and all her gestures and glances had a lightness about them. For a moment I thought she was treating us lightly, with contempt, and I had it in mind to say something to her. Perhaps it would have been a reproach or an invitation, but in the event I said nothing. I watched him gently take her hand and go off with her, and I'll never forget the quick look he gave me as he disappeared into the room with her. Was it possible that he had had an inkling of what could so easily have happened between me and her?

Afterwards, when he was walking ahead of me, I wanted to ask him what he had been going to say. As I watched him moving away from me, I felt a knot of guilt tightening round my heart. He stumbled and I called to him. He was walking parallel to the curb, his thin, upright form silhouetted against the yellow light and his steps unsure. I called to him again and saw him raise his right arm to show me he'd heard. Then he brought it down to his face. Was he crying? I hurried to catch him up but never made it. The car passed me first and in the next few moments the world exploded around us. He fell under the car wheels without warning. He didn't slip, but he hadn't wanted to die either. How was it possible to justify or explain the event? I dragged him to the side of the road and cradled his head in my lap, then took his hand in a farewell gesture, the two of us alone together, isolated from the rest of the world. He was in great pain and it took him a few minutes to recognize me. A tear ran down his cheek, and he couldn't speak. There are moments in a person's life which loom so large and figure so profoundly that after them nothing is ever the same again. The world erupting with noise all around us was as far away as the stars in the sky. I watched his breathing become more and more difficult, and my heart was pounding. Our life together was not yet completed, and I didn't want to lose him in the midst of my own personal crisis, so when he gave a faint gasp and his head lolled, this marked the beginning of my troubles. They extricated him from my arms and took him away somewhere. After that, sitting on the pavement with my arms empty, I didn't know if I was crying for the face I would never see again, or in terror at the thought of the dreadful uncertainty that lay ahead.

———

Husayn was surprised to see me sitting in a corner of the bus. He wanted to pay my fare but I beat him to it. I'd heard he was back from Kuwait but hadn't seen him. He was unshaven, and his beard was black and greasy. His hair was unkempt, and his breath smelt of arak. I was on my way back from the university and it was nearly noon. I'd stopped to buy sesame pastries for my grandmother before I bumped into him on the bus. He asked me how I was, how my studies were going, how the family was, and was obviously skirting round the subject which most concerned him. It was an uncomfortable situation for us both, and I didn't want us to move on to sensitive topics where I wouldn't be able to give him my views. He told me he visited Midhat regularly in the office and on several occasions had been about to visit me when I was ill in bed. Even though it wasn't that hot, he smelt terrible. I hoped I wouldn't have to talk seriously about anything. I was still convalescing; going back to university had made me tired, and I was irritated by the way they had treated me there. As we talked I noticed his eyes wandering, and he looked out of the window and scoured the street names as they went slowly by. He seemed conscious of all the complications involved in our interaction and our attitudes to one another. His pale face was visibly anxious. When I stood up to get off the bus he looked slightly taken aback, but then returned my goodbye with a great show of politeness.

I bought some more cakes for my grandmother and aunt, then began to go back home along Kilani Street. I felt in a somber mood since seeing Husayn and wondered if the fact that he hadn't asked me specifically about his daughters or Madiha meant he thought I wasn't the right person to discuss such matters with.

The sun was hot and the street long and empty of any welcome distraction. I didn't see why the university wanted a doctor's certificate confirming that I'd been ill and explaining my absence from courses. Although they'd been kind, they had made me feel stupid and isolated from the other students. I was sweating profusely and forgot to pass by my father's office as my mother had made me promise to do. Going to the university hadn't done anything to make me feel better. I was still cut off from other people, and because of my feeling of being rusted up inside and distant from everything round me, I had deliberately avoided two of my friends. My behavior perplexed me. A feeling, or perhaps it was an idea, or a mixture of both, would come to me when I was confronted by certain people or situations, making me want to explain aspects of them which were not immediately obvious. Did I have some characteristic that marked me out from my peers? An ability to read between the lines with some people—Munira, for example?

Some evenings when Munira was sitting in the alcove near my bedroom, she would be holding her glass in her delicate fingertips and raise it slowly to her lips. Sometimes when she thought she had abstracted herself from us, the glass would stop just short of her mouth, and I'd watch her hazel eyes mist over, drifting on strange waters. Then she'd tilt her head to one side and fiddle with strands of her hair, which was tied back from her face, and down would go the glass without having touched her lips. Was she having private conversations with herself, or with creatures that did not exist?

The courtyard was empty as I crossed it and went slowly towards the stairs. I could hear them all talking in my aunt's room. I sat down on my bed, and it didn't occur to me to take off my outdoor clothes. She was on my mind; I had often thought wearing pajamas round the house wasn't decent and was particularly aware of it in her presence. I took the pastries to my aunt's room, expecting to hear all the morning's news. Munira was lying on her bed, with one arm flung across her forehead, and her mother was sitting on the floor beside her. Munira sat up and straightened her dress although I made my excuses and said I would leave. She gave me such a beaming smile that I had no choice but to go on standing there. My aunt and grandmother greeted the pastries with delight and fell on them greedily. Munira's mother said nothing and looked unusually blank. I sat on the edge of Munira's bed. She was dressed simply in dark colors, as she had been since they arrived. She asked me how I was, what it had been like at the university, whether it was very hot outside. I was aware of my aunt talking at the same time, demanding to know why I was late back. I told them about meeting Husayn, hoping that they would leave me in peace, but it didn't have any effect. Munira looked pale and appeared to be lacking in energy. Her mother took hold of her hand a couple of times, but she drew it away slightly sharply. I asked about my sister Madiha and was told she'd gone to the school to do some extra work and taken the two little girls with her. My aunt continued to fire questions at me, asking me why I'd been held up, what had happened at the university, whether I'd had an exam or been to any classes. Munira was silent throughout, like her mother, and for no obvious reason I had the feeling that my aunt's talking was upsetting her. I tried to make pleasant conversation, asking her how her morning had been, and was aware of her mother sighing. My grandmother, Umm Hasan, rushed to reply for her and began telling me all about Adnan coming to our house that morning while I'd been away. As she spoke I looked warily at my aunt, and sure enough she interrupted her before long and told her to go and see when lunch would be ready, because she was famished. The situation annoyed me, and I didn't understand the significance of my grandmother's story, or know who Adnan was. I asked where my mother was, and when they said she was in the kitchen I stood up to leave, glad to escape the oppressive atmosphere. I smiled at Munira and noticed that she lay down again as I left the room.

My mother was sitting in a dark corner of the kitchen, smoking a cigarette with an air of resignation. She didn't brighten up much at the sight of me and repeated the same boring questions about how I was feeling, why I was back late and what had happened at the university. Her fair-skinned face was heavily lined. I stood without talking for a few moments, then asked who had come while I was out. She gave me a surprisingly fierce look, then took a drag on her cigarette and blew it out through her mouth and nose, and said coldly that Maliha, Munira's sister, had sent her son Adnan to tell his Aunt Munira that they wanted her back at the school and she should return to Baquba.

I stood looking at her without understanding what she was trying to say. Adnan. Baquba. The school. What was I supposed to make of it? Although I waited, she didn't give me any more hints, and I felt I wouldn't be able to stand up for much longer. My limbs were shaky, and the heat in that stuffy place was making my head throb. I didn't care what she was talking about any more. The world and all its mysteries made me sick and I didn't have the strength to carry on fighting it in this tortuous way. When my mother saw me keep wiping my forehead, she took my arm and sat me down on a chair. My stomach was churning, and a cold sweat broke out on my forehead. I buried my head in my hands and closed my eyes, a hollow reed shaken by nausea.

I heard my mother walking rapidly away and felt a faint breeze. I took a few deep breaths, felt slightly calmer, and lifted my head from my hands. I was alone in the hot kitchen. I went over to the tap, washed my face, dried it on my handkerchief, and sat down again. I heard my mother calling, then the squeak of the heavy inner door and the little girl Sana shouting my name. I called her, and she came hesitantly into the kitchen, rosy-cheeked, her hair disheveled, telling me that an old man was looking for me. They'd met him at the end of the road and he'd asked where our house was, so they'd brought him along with them, she and her mother and sister. Madiha came in while her daughter was telling me her strange story in her childish voice, and said she thought it was Fuad's father who had come to see me. I stared dumbly at her, my weary brain unwilling to take in what she was saying. She muttered that she could tell him I wasn't at home. I heard my mother backing her up from a distance, begging her to say I wasn't in. With a sudden feeling of alarm, I got up abruptly from the chair and hurried out of the kitchen down the long passage in a sort of dream. Wasn't I the one who should have sought out such a meeting, looked for a final word from Fuad coming to me from beyond the grave like a burst of sunshine?

I was caught up in a whirlpool of thoughts and emotions as I approached the big front door. He was standing some distance away, leaning against the wall, a slightly bowed figure nearing his seventies. I hadn't remembered him looking like this at all. His face was lined and jowly, and his cheeks were covered in white stubble. His small eyes gazed into space, and he didn't notice me standing in front of him for a few moments. I greeted him and woke him out of his trance. He advanced with short steps and held out his hand. It was big and blue-veined, and the skin was soft. I couldn't take my eyes off his face. He could be the key to rebuilding my life. He asked me in a quavering voice if it was true that I was Abd al-Karim, his son Fuad's friend. I nodded my head, flinching at the name, which he pronounced in a strange way, and pictured that this broken-down old man had been sent by his son. I went on nodding my head until he began to speak again. He said he didn't remember seeing me with Fuad.

"Weren't you with him when he died?" he asked me suddenly.

I leaned back against the wall and said nothing. My mouth was dry. I didn't know what he wanted me to say. I felt he was waiting for me to conjure up some more positive image for him by speaking about his son. He said he didn't want to be a burden, but in the hospital they'd told him unbelievable things about how much Fuad had suffered. His eyes shone with tears as he looked into my face, waiting for an answer. He was clearly in agony himself but I remained silent, motionless, removed from him. I was sitting on the dusty pavement, cradling Fuad's dear head in my lap. Then they took him from my arms in the middle of the night, under the stars, and everything went still and a black cloud enveloped me. I went back home, and life continued to run in my veins even though I screamed and shouted for days afterwards. I had embraced death and gone on living. He hadn't died in agony. Such things weren't allowed to happen to him. He had died in my arms, and it was like the light dying when the sun sets.

The tears were streaming from the father's pale eyes as he looked at my arms stretched out in front of me. I didn't realize what I was doing or saying until he took hold of them. I shuddered as if I sensed death around me. His mouth contracted, and the tears ran down his wrinkled cheeks. He couldn't speak, and he shut his eyes and shook his head a number of times as if he wanted to convey something. My limbs were like jelly. I had let my arms fall to my sides and stood watching him in silence. There was nothing I could do to comfort him.

He loosened his hold on me, stepped back, and stood looking at me for a moment, then turned and walked away slowly, his back bent, staying close to the wall. I couldn't stop trembling. I didn't call out to him, but it crossed my mind that he didn't know I'd been ill since the day Fuad died. I turned back into the house and walked unsteadily down the narrow passage. They told me afterwards that I'd reached the heavy door at the end and then collapsed. I didn't remember feeling faint, but I knew for sure I didn't want to carry on living as I was.

Chapter Three

A unt Safiya was sitting up in her bed, which was a mattress on the floor. She watched Sana intently through the open windows as she came towards their room treading carefully, carrying a tray of breakfast. The birds were singing on the gaunt branches of the fig tree and the pigeons called intermittently. It was a little after sunrise and the air was still cool. She wondered what Nuriya had sent her to eat. She had been plagued by hunger for an hour or more. It would be nice if there was cream cheese, apricot jam, warm bread. Sana stood in the doorway, looking inquiringly at her.

"Come in, Sana," she whispered. "Gently, now."

The little girl nodded and descended the high step. Aunt Safiya saw her looking over at the big bed where Munira lay. She had come down from the roof at dawn and was asleep under a light cover.

"Don't make a noise, Sana," the girl's great-aunt whispered again.

Sana came towards her slowly and put the tray carefully down on the floor by the bed. On it were two glasses of tea, a flat disc of bread covering the plate and a little dish of black olives. She lifted the bread up quickly and saw slices of white cheese underneath it and some cucumber and tomatoes. Sana sat down on the edge of the bed. "Why are there two glasses?" asked Aunt Safiya.

"One for you and one for Bibi Umm Hasan. Is she still asleep? Shall I wake her?"

"No, dear. What for? It's not as if there's a great spread here. No meat, no *patcha* or *harisa*. Let me eat in peace."

She began stirring the glass of black tea. You had to eat what you were given here, otherwise you could easily die of hunger. She wrapped a slice of cheese and some salad in a piece of bread and bit off a chunk before addressing the little girl with her mouth full: "Have you eaten?"

Sana nodded, and her great-aunt went on, "Has your mother gone out?"

"No. We're going out now. Mum and me and Suha."

"Where are you going, dear?"

"To school."

"Why? Munira's a teacher, and she's come to Baghdad on holiday."

"Maybe Mum has to work."

"What work? It's the holidays now."

"I don't know."

"What are you talking about, Sana dear?"

As she prepared another mouthful for herself she looked across at Munira. Her hair was strewn over the pillow, and the curves of her body were visible under the cover. She and her mother had come to live with them several weeks before, quite out of the blue. They had only been in Baquba a few months, living with Munira's older sister Maliha, who was married to a greengrocer who had grown rich mysteriously overnight.

Safiya shifted the bread from one side of her mouth to the other. Munira had been appointed to a school in Baquba and she and her mother had moved there. They were supposed to have been there some time, according to her contract, but they'd cut short their stay and been with them in Baghdad for the last few weeks. They had no family in the capital except Nuriya, Munira's aunt, because Munira's brother Mustafa was in the North, and his wife and children were with the wife's family.

"Auntie, shall I wake Bibi Umm Hasan? You're going to eat it all."

Safiya gestured dismissively and took a long drink of hot tea, then said, "Why do you keep on about her? Let her rest. Where's your Uncle Karumi? I heard he's going out today."

"Yes, Auntie. He's going to the university. He's shaving at the minute."

This was good news. She would ask him to buy her some sesame pastries from Sayyid's patisserie. She'd give him the money to buy her nice fresh ones. She scrabbled around in a little purse she'd taken from under her pillow until she found two dirhams and put the purse back in its place.

"Here's a hundred fils, Sana. Give it to your Uncle Karim to buy some pastries from Sayyid's. Hurry so you catch him before he goes out."

The little girl took the coins and slipped out of the room, and Safiya turned back to her breakfast. When all that remained were two puny bits of cheese and a burnt end of bread, she decided it would be wise to stop there. Umm Hasan was breathing noisily through her mouth as she lay fast asleep in an untidy heap on her bed. When she woke up she'd be certain to ask for more cheese, and her daughter, Nuriya, wouldn't stint her, while Safiya's own requests always went unheeded. She drank the rest of her tea and returned the glass to the tray, then, wiping her mouth, she shouted, "Umm Hasan! Umm Hasan! How is it you're still asleep? You're like one of the seven sleepers of Ephesus!"

She noticed Sana hurrying back. As she came into the room she tripped and knocked against the door. Munira raised her head from the pillow, and Sana stopped dead in her tracks, shamefaced.

"Sana. What's wrong?" asked Munira.

"Sorry, Auntie Munira. I tripped. Good morning."

Munira smiled at her. "Good morning."

She lay back down. Safiya indicated to Sana to come and sit on her bed. "Look where you're going, Sana. Has your Uncle Karumi gone out yet or not?"

"Not yet. He said he's at your service."

She patted the child's arm contentedly, then addressed Munira: "Munira dear." Munira lifted her head again and half sat up, frowning inquiringly. "Where's your mother gone?" continued Safiya.

"She's gone downstairs with Aunt Nuriya."

Her eyes were dark with kohl and her hair fell abundantly round her shoulders. Safiya turned to Sana: "Wake Umm Hasan, Sana. The tea's getting cold."

The little girl went over towards her great-grandmother's bed. Munira sat up and swung her legs over the edge of her own bed. Her thin nightdress revealed her neck and part of her chest and shoulders. There was no question that she was beautiful, thought Safiya, but what had she come to Baghdad for? She and her mother had turned up at the door like refugees. Two more mouths to be fed and poor Abu Midhat, her own brother, slaved all day long as it was. Still, she was a pretty young woman. Everything about her was an invitation to a man. Marriage wouldn't be far from her mind, Safiya could guarantee. It was what girls of her age mostly thought about. Munira was sitting in silence looking at the floor, her hands folded in her lap. Was there something on her mind besides marriage? Or perhaps she was considering Midhat. Who could say? His age, his job, his family background all qualified him as a suitable husband. She wouldn't find anyone better. But somehow she didn't look as if such things would interest her. She seemed to be in another world. Who could say, perhaps this was a new way of catching men. Everything was permitted these days. She noticed Umm Hasan waking up and talking quietly with Sana, but kept on watching Munira. Munira yawned and covered her mouth with her hand, then stretched so that her breasts stuck out slightly. She was thin, her complexion on the dark side, and her large eyes lit up her face like lamps. It would be good for this disturbed creature to get married. She was aware of Sana gently taking hold of her arm and heard Umm Hasan mumbling: "There's no pity or compassion in this house. If you died of hunger, they'd dance for joy. What's going on?"

"Bibi says there's not enough cheese for her breakfast," whispered Sana to Aunt Safiya.

Safiya remained silent. Umm Hasan leaned over and felt under her mattress, then took out a tattered brown paper bag. She sat clutching it in her fist, looking at Safiya out of the corner of her eye.

"You must know what kind of food they give us by now, Umm Hasan," Safiya said to her. "They collect up the leftovers and instead of throwing them in the bin they send them up to us. How can you be so naive?"

Umm Hasan pulled the glass of tea towards her. Stirring it, she muttered, "May God punish all sinners."

Then she began rummaging in the paper bag and a moment later Safiya saw her holding two pieces of sesame pastry in her fingers. She was completely taken aback. They'd run out over a month ago and been unable to replenish their stock because of Abd al-Karim's illness. And now it seemed Umm Hasan only had to wave her hand and they descended on her like manna from heaven.

"The Lord looks after His own," said Umm Hasan. She dunked a piece of pastry in her glass of tea, still looking furtively at Safiya. Sana got up from the edge of the bed and went out smiling.

"Where did you get that from?" Safiya asked, with some annoyance.

Umm Hasan didn't reply. Safiya watched her put the pastry in her mouth and begin chewing it in a disgusting manner.

With mounting anger she asked, "Why make such a fuss when you've got things worked out so well?"

Umm Hasan chewed less vigorously, then swallowed what was left in her mouth and washed it down with a swig of tea. "I knew the breakfast would be inedible this morning," she said, and went back to dunking the pastry in her tea in silence.

41

Safiya was about to reply, when she noticed Abd al-Karim through the open window. He was coming out of his room and walking slowly along the big gallery. His shoulders were bent, and he was taking small steps. She hoped Umm Hasan wouldn't see him, so that at least she could have the pastries he was going to buy to herself. She turned to Munira, who was still sitting on the edge of her bed and was also watching her cousin. He was several years younger than her. He hadn't graduated yet, and his illness had stopped him taking the exams. He would be quite unsuitable as a husband for her. Safiya was sure she couldn't be wrong about this. However strong the bond between them seemed to have grown, it couldn't last. Munira was watching him gravely, as if she was still asleep, her hands interlaced in her lap. Safiya was convinced she was never wrong in such matters.

"Is your mother going out today, Munira dear?" she asked her.

Munira emerged from her stupor with a violent jerk of her head, and Safiya fancied she flushed slightly.

"What? What, Auntie?"

What was the stupid girl thinking about? Did she honestly believe he'd make her a good husband?

"Isn't your mother going out today?" she asked again.

"No. Why?"

Her voice was lifeless and her reply sounded hostile, as if the question made her uncomfortable.

"I was just asking," Safiya answered. "I wanted to see her. Maybe she'll be coming upstairs in a while."

Munira suddenly rose to her feet and went towards the door. "I'll go down and tell her."

Her shoulder blades were plainly visible, giving her youthful body a womanly frailty. She walked with a quick, light tread. Safiya didn't feel animosity towards her. She wanted to be certain her suspicions about her were correct and decided to watch her more closely. She turned to Umm Hasan and found her leaning back on her pillow, biting on something and looking towards the window with a far-away expression.

"Aren't you tired of eating?" she asked her. "That's enough now."

Umm Hasan switched her gaze towards her and halted the movement of her jaws. "Are you going to start telling me how to behave?" she demanded. Then she looked away again, feigning indifference, and her jaws resumed their regular motion.

Safiya retorted angrily, "And they say she's senile! You think you run the place, don't you?"

The jaws stopped momentarily then went back to work.

The sun had only just hit the windows of their room, and lunch was still a long way off. There'd be no harm in a short nap. She lay down, resting her cheek on her left hand and facing into the room. Umm Hasan was motionless nearby. Perhaps she'd finally finished eating. Safiya closed her eyes and tried not to think of anything in particular. But they wouldn't leave her to doze in peace. She opened her eyes when she thought she heard someone coming into their room and was dazzled by the sun. Munira had come back. She wore a dark-colored dress and stood doing her hair and face in the little mirror hanging on the wall. Mechanically she brushed her long shiny hair. Her preparations were interminable. Munira's mother, Najiya, came in after a while and sat down on the floor next to her own mother, Umm Hasan. The two of them lit up cigarettes, and Safiya heard Umm Hasan singing in a low voice:

Forsaken, forsaken, we've been forsaken
No point sighing, no point crying, we've been forsaken.

Silly old fool! Munira and her mother were smiling. It was as if none of them realized she was trying to sleep. Munira went out and Umm Hasan clapped in time to the song she sang in her fading voice. The light was glaring white, unbearably strong, and silence hung over the house. Safiya closed her eyes. Umm Hasan's song and the clapping of

43

her bony hands no longer bothered her, and she sensed that sleep would not elude her this time.

———

They were talking together but she couldn't make out the words. They tossed short sentences back and forth and gestures concealing fearful memories. Munira was leaning against the wall by the bed, resting her hand on the rusty black metal headboard. She was pale, and her eyes grew unnaturally large and bright, and her lips moved rapidly as she talked. Her mother stood some way inside the door.

Safiya moved her hand away from her ear and raised her head slightly from the pillow. Munira sounded breathless: "Why? There's nothing going on between us. Do you understand? Nothing at all."

"He's your nephew, and he came from Baquba to see you. What else are people going to say?"

Her mother spoke slowly, the words barely making it out of her mouth. Munira's eyes blazed, and even the finger she raised in her mother's face seemed to emit sparks. "Don't talk like that. He's nothing to do with me, and I don't care what people say. Do you understand? Tell me, do you understand what I mean or not?"

Neither of them spoke for a few moments. Safiya thought she could hear her own stifled heartbeats. If the conversation had gone on just a bit longer, she would have known everything. Munira sat down heavily on the bed and gradually withdrew into herself. She bent her head and put her hands in her lap, and her hair hung down, hiding her face. Her mother stood with her hands clasped and for the first time there was a look of distress on her face. Mother and daughter were clearly not happy.

Nuriya's voice rang out from the ground floor: "Najiya. Najiya."

Munira looked up, dry-eyed and very pale. "That's Aunt Nuriya calling you. Go down. Tell her I'm not here."

Her mother turned to the door, and Nuriya's voice called again: "Munira, my dear. Munira."

"All right, I'm coming," called back Munira's mother as she went out of the door.

Nuriya continued to shout: "Najiya. This fellow Adnan won't take no for an answer. I don't know what's wrong with him. Come and see what he wants. Please. He won't come in and he won't . . ."

Then her words were lost in Najiya's mutterings as she made for the stairs. Munira withdrew into herself again, sitting huddled and dejected. Safiya did not contemplate addressing her, but she would like to have heard the two of them talking for longer. So the unknown person at the door was Adnan. Maliha's son. Maliha, Munira's sister. Perhaps he'd brought bad news to Munira and her mother. They had lived in Baquba for some time and might go back there if Munira couldn't get a transfer to Baghdad. All the two of them had to live on was Munira's pitiful salary. She'd only been qualified as a schoolteacher for three years. Maliha and Munira's older brother Mustafa was an army officer, but he was married and was in the North now anyhow. A poor family with no history as far as anybody knew. To this day Safiya didn't understand how her brother had come to marry one of them. People said it was fate, whom you married. And granted, Nuriya hadn't been a bad girl luckily. She wouldn't have dared behave improperly, anyway, especially towards her, Safiya. Noble origins made an impression on people like these, and they'd be as well to remember their place.

The room was lit by the sun's rays reflecting off the high white wall. She was fed up with pretending to be asleep. She hadn't found out what was going on down below, and that was torture to her. She moved around in the bed, then sat up and immediately noticed that Umm Hasan's bed was empty. In the anxiety which this provoked she forgot herself and shouted, "Where's Umm Hasan gone? Can't that silly old fool stay in her bed?"

Munira raised her head and looked at Aunt Safiya in astonishment.

"What, Auntie? What?" She was leaning forward slightly, her hands clasped in front of her.

Safiya stared at her. "Where's your grandmother?" she said.

"I don't know, Auntie. Maybe she went downstairs. Or to the bathroom."

"Why the bathroom, dear? Is she washing her hair now?"

"No, sorry. I mean the toilet."

"Where's your mother? Have we got visitors?"

Munira looked upset. "My mother's with Aunt Nuriya. There's no one else there."

Her eyes were clear and unclouded despite her discomfiture, and her hair fell in gentle waves on her shoulders. She wasn't the same fierce girl who'd scolded her mother not long before. Safiya heard footsteps, then Umm Hasan put her head round the door: "Munira dear, please come and help me up this step. It'll be the death of me."

Munira hurried to take hold of her grandmother's arms and hoisted her over the high lintel, then walked her to the bed.

"Where were you?" Safiya asked her.

Umm Hasan was walking slowly, her back bent, and she was panting hard.

"Allah! Muhammad! May God answer your prayers, Munira. Allah! Allah!" she groaned.

She sat down on her bed, shaking her head, breathing heavily and blowing air out through her mouth. Munira went back to the other bed, and Safiya asked again, "I said where were you, Umm Hasan?"

Trying to catch her breath she said, "Give me a chance. I was in the toilet. What's the matter with you?"

Safiya was silent as she watched Munira leave the room, then she said, "Can't anyone talk to you these days? What's wrong?"

When Umm Hasan did not reply, she went on, "I thought you'd gone downstairs. That boy Adnan came from Baquba. I don't know what he wants, but they were all in a state."

Umm Hasan looked up. "Adnan? Which Adnan? The shaykh's son?"

"Maliha's son. His father sells vegetables, he's not a shaykh. I wonder what Adnan wants."

"I've no idea. Leave me in peace. Hasn't Karumi come back yet?"

"Why do you ask? No, he's not back."

"I hope he'll think of bringing some pastries with him."

Safiya stiffened and asked loudly, "What? Why would he bring you pastries now?"

Umm Hasan turned towards her, not appearing to have understood. "I meant perhaps he'll be feeling generous. God! You don't have a kind bone in your body!" She turned away irritably, muttering, "Anyone would think the world was coming to an end. She's yelling at me as if I've spent her inheritance. What have I done wrong?"

Safiya was about to explain what she had overheard, as she didn't feel like embarking on a battle of words before midday, but Munira and her mother came back in. They looked worn out. Munira lay down on her bed straight away, and her mother sat on a cushion on the floor. They remained silent. Everything happened in silence with the two of them. Safiya watched them for a while, then heard Umm Hasan talking to her daughter: "Who's downstairs, Najiya?"

"Nobody."

Umm Hasan looked worried and she went on, looking at Safiya, "What do you mean, nobody? Who's going to make lunch then? I've been famished for an hour."

Munira's mother looked stonily at her, without replying, then Safiya spoke. "Why are you going on at them?" she asked Umm Hasan. "Can't you see Munira's not well?"

"There's nothing wrong with Munira. She feels a bit lightheaded, that's all," interrupted Najiya hurriedly.

"No. Look at her. Her face is as yellow as turmeric. Why did Adnan come to see you? We're wondering why he didn't even look in to say hello to his grandmother."

47

Munira sat up in bed. She was pale and had circles under her eyes. She addressed Safiya angrily, without raising her voice: "I'm not ill. There's nothing wrong with me, but I'd be better still if you weren't so nosy, Auntie."

Her eyes flashed with suppressed anger, and she began to talk slightly louder: "We're not hiding anything from you, but you shouldn't interfere all the time. Go and ask the lady of the house who came, and why. Don't talk to me about it, and don't interfere in my business. Leave me alone. Do you understand?"

This astonishing stream of abuse shocked and saddened Safiya. Munira continued to glare at her and Umm Hasan for a few moments, and they averted their gaze from her. Her features were hard, and she showed no signs of dissolving into tears. After a bit she lay down on the bed again. Najiya was silent, smoking her cigarette as if she hadn't heard a thing. Safiya noticed Umm Hasan looking at her and said in a low, slightly shaky voice, "Did I do something wrong, Umm Hasan? Tell me."

Umm Hasan shook her head emphatically and whispered, "I can't be bothered with it all. Aren't you hungry yet?"

"Don't remind me. How could I not be hungry? I'm dying of hunger! Call Nuriya to see if the soup's ready. We can at least eat some warm bread and soup. What choice do we have, my dear? God can't be happy at His creatures being treated this way."

"I haven't got the strength to call her. I'm absolutely famished." Umm Hasan looked at Munira and her mother out of the corner of her eye and made another despairing gesture.

The room was silent, and a spiral of smoke rose up from Najiya's cigarette. Safiya didn't know what to do. Had she been right to let Munira talk to her like that without responding? An unknown page in the two women's lives had been revealed to her that day, and she was inhibited from defending herself by a vague feeling that something broken, something abnormal in the girl's life had provoked her harsh words. Munira gave a long sigh, then inhaled deeply. Her high breasts rose and fell slowly. Safiya could see her smooth pale legs and the edge of her dress covering her knees.

"What time is it?" she asked Umm Hasan.

"Arab time or government time?"

"Government time."

"I don't know."

"Arab then."

"I still don't know."

She examined her face, unable to decide whether she was joking at this critical point, or if she just talked nonsense every now and then, depending on her mood. The sun had moved round away from them, and the house was wrapped in silence. It was past midday, and there was no sign of anyone making lunch. Were they going to have to repeat the same bitter experience of waiting for Midhat and his father to come back from the office?

The sound of footsteps in the yard, followed by the door slamming, interrupted her gloomy thoughts. She listened intently, holding her breath. Was it Abd al-Karim at last? She fastened her gaze on the top of the staircase. She would find out in a few moments whether he had managed to get the pastries or not. Her companions appeared not to have heard anything. He was walking slowly, his shoulders hunched and didn't look as happy as he should to be carrying a large bag of pastries. He went along the big gallery and into his room. None of them had noticed him. Were they blind? Umm Hasan was fiddling with her toes, and Munira's mother was vigorously stubbing out her cigarette. Then Safiya saw him coming out of his room still carrying the bag and heading for their room. She didn't want to tell Umm Hasan, but couldn't contain herself: "Good news, Umm Hasan! Karumi's brought us pastries. I gave him some money, as God's my witness. Now you can get to work on them!"

He was standing in the doorway, smiling. He greeted Munira and her mother. Munira sat up, withdrew to a corner of the bed, and returned his greeting, arranging her hair.

"You're a ray of sunshine, Karumi," shouted Umm Hasan. "Welcome, welcome."

He was pale, exhaustion written all over his face. He handed Safiya the bag of pastries and her two coins.

"Aunt, here are the pastries. They're on me this time. Here's your money. See, I haven't broken into it. Just tell me when they're finished, and I'll be happy to get you more."

"God bless you dear! Why were you late?"

He turned back and hesitated slightly before sitting down, and she noticed a barely perceptible change come over Munira. Her expression softened, and in some vague way she seemed to relax. Safiya didn't hear what the two of them said to one another, as she was distractedly opening the paper bag and taking out the pastries.

She gave Umm Hasan her share, then as she was returning the coins to her purse she suddenly heard Umm Hasan talking about Adnan's visit and raised her head to listen. Abd al-Karim was smiling foolishly, uncomprehending, and Munira was staring at the floor looking a little flushed, or so it seemed to Safiya. Munira's mother sighed several times. Awkward moments of benefit to nobody. Safiya broke the silence by asking Umm Hasan when lunch was, and Abd al-Karim inquired about his mother and sister, and his nieces. When he was told his mother was downstairs, he stood up hesitantly and went out. Munira smiled at him as he left, then lay down again, and her mother lit another cigarette. Umm Hasan looked from one to the other without a word. They were silent, each busy with her own thoughts.

Safiya couldn't properly make out the low voices coming up from the courtyard. More than an hour to wait before Midhat and his father came back from the office. This was the hardest time of day: you couldn't eat or sleep or talk. This waiting made prisoners of them, and they didn't know what to do with themselves. She rested her left arm against the pillow with her cheek in her palm. She couldn't even snatch a nap because no one would wake her and that might mean she missed lunch, and then all would be lost.

She heard the noise of the two little girls coming up from the ground floor, and they rushed in together shouting. Safiya straightened up attentively. So Madiha was back at last. Now she would pick up some snippets of news from the outside world, although Madiha wouldn't come upstairs until she'd helped her mother prepare lunch. That was just as well. She couldn't let Nuriya work on her own all day, and perhaps they'd be able to organize the cooking more quickly together. This waiting was unbearable, especially for people of her age. On top of that, she and Umm Hasan did not even know for sure what they were going to be given to eat. This was unacceptable. They should at least be asked their opinions on the subject.

She suddenly heard the big door downstairs slamming with unusual force, rattling the windows, then there was the thud of a heavy body followed by screams from Nuriya and Madiha. She looked up and saw both Munira and her mother getting to their feet. Her heart was pounding, but she said nothing.

"God protect us," whispered Umm Hasan.

They heard Nuriya call hoarsely, "Madiha, Karumi's fallen. Run and get some cold water. Hurry, dear." Then, unsteadily, "What's wrong, son?"

Munira, pale-faced, was on her way over to the door. She stopped and leaned against the wall for a moment.

"Go down and see what's happened to the boy," Safiya shouted at her. "Lord, what's gone wrong now?"

The noises coming from down below—Nuriya wailing, the children screaming and crying—appeared confused and troubled like echoes from a shattered world. Munira pulled herself together and ran out. For a second Safiya glimpsed the anguish in her eyes. Her mother followed her without any apparent haste.

Umm Hasan started to get up too.

"Where are you off to?" asked Safiya. "Go back to bed."

Umm Hasan arranged the pillow and sat back in her bed muttering, "I'm worried about Karumi. God protect us." Then she began playing with her toes again. "I don't think we're going to eat till the late afternoon today. What do you think, Safiya?"

Safiya didn't answer. She was listening dispiritedly to the sounds from below. Abd al-Karim hadn't been right since his friend's death several months ago, but he was still a young man with a healthy body, and his family ought to find out why he had collapsed like that in the courtyard in the middle of the day, when only a few minutes before he'd been talking and laughing, the object of admiring looks from his pretty cousin.

———•———

Safiya was sitting with the family in the alcove in the late afternoon, a little apart from the rest on one of the comfortable sofas, observing what was happening and wondering about what was not happening. The sun had not yet set, as it was towards the end of June, and they had only just finished their post-lunch tea. Her glass was still on the table next to her brother's and her nephew Midhat's. Lunch had been late that day, and for this reason she had not eaten a pastry with her tea so as not to spoil her appetite for dinner. The doctor had come more quickly than they had expected and given Abd al-Karim a cursory examination. Watching from a distance she had had no confidence in him, although she could not have said why. She was told he had prescribed a tonic and a tranquilizer to be taken one after the other. When he'd gone they had put a bed for Abd al-Karim out on the gallery where it was cooler, close to the alcove where they often sat, and his mother squatted down near him, her eyes never leaving his pale face with its prominent cheekbones.

She heard her brother Abu Midhat saying her name and turned towards him.

"Tell me," he said. "Did Mr. Khalil's children marry before the family moved away from Bab al-Shaykh?"

"The boys, Hashim and Qasim, weren't married because of their older sister Rahmat. The family wanted her to marry before them."

"That's it," said Abu Midhat. "Of course. Rahmatallah, their older sister!"

She was gratified by his faith in her.

"Their cousin Salim came to see me," he went on, passing his yellow prayer beads through his fingers. "He had some business with us at the Land Registry. He said Qasim married a few years ago and had his own house, Rahmatallah died after her brother's marriage, and Hashim still lives with his mother."

"Midhat, my dear," said Nuriya to her son, "won't you go and see what Munira and Madiha are doing in the kitchen? They've been heating up that tinned soup for an hour!"

Midhat stood up without a word and went out.

"Why did Rahmat die?" Safiya asked her brother. "She was a strong woman. She had a temper, even if her name did mean mercy. But she worked in the house from dawn till dusk and went out visiting in the evenings. Every evening the same. She never failed the other women. She'd sit herself down with them and sometimes talk about Hashim, sometimes Qasim, wanting to marry them off and yet not wanting to. She died at the right time!"

"Does anyone not die at the right time?"

"I suppose not. That's what I meant."

There was the sound of steps along the gallery and Munira appeared, followed by Midhat. She was carrying a tray with a steaming bowl of soup on it which she put gently down on the table by Abd al-Karim's bed. Nuriya got up to help her while Midhat went back to his place. Munira was in the same dark dress she had put on that morning, and her hair was tied back. Her face was radiant, and her movements graceful. She sat down opposite Midhat and said in a low voice, still smiling, "Madiha made this soup, you know. I just carried it up."

Abd al-Karim sat up in bed with his mother's help, and Safiya heard him saying, "Thank you, Munira. I don't know when I'll be able to serve you like this. Perhaps it'll never happen." His voice cracked. Munira looked upset, and the smile disappeared from her face.

"What are you talking about, Karumi?" said his father. "You're only human. Everybody gets ill sometimes. It would be strange if they didn't!"

Safiya noticed Midhat looking at Munira.

"Whenever he talks like that, I can't see for the tears in my eyes," said Nuriya.

Midhat was examining Munira with an obvious gleam in his eye. Safiya hadn't even seen him talking to her before, but the way he was looking at her intimated that he liked doing it and dreamt of it.

The sun cast its fading red rays high up on the walls, and calm reigned inside the house, interrupted only by the clatter of dishes in the kitchen as Madiha and her daughters washed up the lunch. They were late today because of Abd al-Karim, whose unexpected relapse had saddened them all: they felt indebted to him for the many little services he performed and the happiness he gave them. They would never enjoy seeing him lying there like that, not exactly ill, but not well either.

"Where were you today, Karim?" Midhat asked his brother.

Abd al-Karim stopped drinking his soup and was silent for a few moments before answering, "I went to the university. They said I had to provide a medical certificate so I could resit the exams. I didn't feel too good. It was very hot."

"Who came to visit you at midday?"

Abd al-Karim looked vacantly at Midhat as if he didn't understand the question.

Their mother intervened: "Drink your soup, Karumi dear. It'll get cold."

Then she turned to Midhat: "Let him rest, Midhat. He hasn't got the strength to talk much."

"I know, Mother. But I wanted to find out whether Adnan came to see him."

"Adnan! What do you mean, Adnan?" said Abd al-Karim in a jerky, lifeless voice. "Adnan didn't come to see me. It was Fuad's father."

"Why did Adnan come then?" Midhat asked his mother.

Munira was staring at her hands, which lay in her lap.

"Fuad's father wanted to talk to me," went on Abd al-Karim. "I was with Fuad—that night."

"That's enough, Karumi," interrupted his mother. "Don't wear yourself out."

Abd al-Karim looked at her for a long time without saying anything, then handed the bowl of soup back to her. He turned away from them and lay facing the wall. Safiya noticed Midhat watching with a preoccupied air. Nuriya picked up the tray and turned unhappily to her husband: "You see how they torment me?"

"Why don't you drink your soup, Karumi?" exclaimed his father. "It's very good for you. It'll build you up."

Abd al-Karim did not answer his father, and silence descended briefly on the gathering. Nuriya went off downstairs. Midhat turned suddenly to Munira. "Sorry for asking, Munira," he said, "but did Adnan come to see you?"

There was an unaccustomed gentleness in his voice. Munira raised her eyes to look at him. "What did you say?"

Large, brilliant, golden brown eyes. She continued to look at him without saying anything, almost defiantly.

"Did Adnan have some business to discuss with you?" persisted Midhat.

They exchanged chilly glances. Safiya noticed Munira's obstinate expression.

"Why hasn't he been to see you and your mother before?"

Midhat's father broke in unexpectedly: "Tell me, has Adnan left school yet? Is he working with his father in the greengrocery business now?"

Midhat turned to him impatiently. "I don't know for sure, Dad," he said, "but I don't think he's passed his third year exams."

"That's odd! How old is he? Safiya?"

She was following their conversation intently, so she answered at once, "Eighteen. He's Maliha's oldest child." Cautiously, she addressed Munira: "That's right, isn't it, Munira?"

Her irritation was plain to see. She looked coldly at her. "Yes," she said.

"Then why's he driving about in a car and disturbing the peace if he hasn't even got a school certificate?" demanded Midhat's father. "What kind of a world are we living in?"

Safiya answered him: "God made them rich, Abu Midhat. Why shouldn't he drive a car and make as much noise as he pleases? Not so long ago his father was a peasant and worked for Hajji Muhammad, running hither and thither with holes in his sandals. So what? Look at him now. He's a businessman, and his stomach's so big you'd think he was an Arab shaykh!"

Midhat laughed, and even Munira smiled. "Have it your own way, Auntie," said Midhat. "But you know there aren't any shaykhs left. Haven't you heard what our president says?"

"Every time I say anything you quote that madman at me."

"Mad or not, he's governed us for four years now, and maybe there's nobody better around."

"What do you mean, son?" said Abu Midhat. "That's not the calculation you should be making. You should count how many years he's got left, how many months, maybe even days, then you'll be able to tell what kind of a hell he must be living in."

"No, Dad. If we did that, we'd all be in hell."

"Yes, you're right. If you could work out how much time you had left, life would be unbearable. Our lives are in God's hands."

"What am I alive for then? Let me live my own life as well as I can. I mean," he turned to Munira as he spoke, "even if our lives are in God's hands, my life belongs to me. It's in my hands. Nobody's got the right to ask me to explain what I'm going to do with it."

Munira was watching him in astonishment as he talked. "If you don't want anyone to ask you," she said, "then you mustn't ask anyone else either." She was more in earnest than he was.

"No, you're wrong," interrupted Midhat's father. "That's not how the world works. You're not hermits. There have to be questions and answers. Our lives are in God's hands."

Munira didn't reply.

"So? What do you mean?" Midhat asked her. "Are you talking about people and their freedom?"

"I don't know. Perhaps it's a philosophy I don't know much about, but what you're saying wouldn't work here. Everyone questions you and interferes in your life, whether you want them to or not."

"I refuse to let them. I can refuse any interference in my life."

Safiya noticed how worked up he was. She didn't understand everything they were saying. The alcove was growing steadily darker and obscuring their faces from one another. She wanted to recount one of her memories to them. She heard Abu Midhat's voice: "What do you mean, you refuse? Do you mean people can do what they want? God forbid! For example, I'm your father. Am I not allowed to ask you what you're doing with yourself, for God's sake?"

They heard light, rapid footsteps and Nuriya appeared with Sana. "Why are you sitting in the dark?" she cried. "Put the light on, please. For Karumi's sake."

She pressed the switch and the alcove was flooded with light. Abd al-Karim had his head turned towards them and appeared to be listening to their conversation with interest.

"How are you, Karumi?" asked his mother going over to his bed. "Shall I heat up the soup for you?"

"No, Mother. Thanks. Not just now."

Sana went and sat down beside Munira. "Where's my mother?" Safiya heard her ask the little girl.

"In the kitchen with Mum. They're making the dinner."

Munira stood up and Sana did the same.

"Munira," said Safiya. "Will you see whether your grandmother Umm Hasan has eaten or not?"

"Of course she hasn't," interrupted Nuriya. "What is there for her to eat? We haven't made dinner yet, Safiya. If you give me a chance, I'll go down and help Madiha in the kitchen."

Munira went off with Sana, and Safiya saw Midhat watching her as she disappeared into the darkness on the gallery. He wiped his forehead assiduously and turned to his father. "Husayn wants to see his daughters," he said. "He's been to see me in the office several times."

"I'm surprised he knows he's got any daughters," snapped his mother. She was sitting on the edge of Abd al-Karim's bed facing him, with her back to the others. "A father who abandons his family for two years," she went on, "doesn't have the right to see them."

"Why doesn't he come and see them here?" said Midhat's father calmly. "He can visit us like anyone else, see them, and then leave." He was addressing his son as if he hadn't heard what his wife said. "We're not denying him his rights," he continued. "He doesn't recognize the claims his wife and daughters have on him, but that doesn't mean we're going to act the same as him. We're not denying anyone their rights." He turned to his sister. "Safiya," he said, "do you remember what our father, God rest his soul, told Hajji Shakir? He came to ask our father's advice about his aunt, an elderly woman living on her own who worked as a maidservant and washerwoman. She was poor, and none of her family helped support her. Hajji Shakir had heard that she was working in a house of ill repute and was planning to kill her. A woman of over sixty! Our father said to him, 'You've never recognized your obligations to her, so why are you now asking about your rights over her?' But the Hajji didn't take any notice of what he said. He went and killed her, the miserable wretch. An old woman like that!"

"What happened to him?" asked Midhat with interest.

"Nothing. His friends had a collection for him in the cafés where he was a regular, they found a lawyer to defend him, he was sentenced to three years in prison, came out in less than two and walked the streets a free man. A poor old woman of over sixty!"

"He was a hajji too," commented Safiya. "He'd visited the holy places. But God doesn't accept a pilgrimage made by someone like that."

"Husayn has no rights over his daughters," repeated Nuriya. "He hasn't given them a penny for two years now."

"Why don't you let him see them, Mum?" Abd al-Karim asked suddenly in a hoarse voice.

"What's it got to do with me, Karumi?" Her voice trembled and she sounded upset. She turned to the others: "God can't approve of him behaving like that to his family."

"He must know they're safe, living in their grandfather's house with their mother and not wanting for anything," said Abd al-Karim.

"What do you mean, not wanting for anything? Please!" She looked at her husband. "Let's stop talking about it. I'll bring you some soup. Unless you'd like to eat it with us."

Midhat backed her up. "Yes, Karim, you must eat something. Just a few mouthfuls to keep us company." Then he added to his mother, "Mum, what did Adnan want coming here this morning? Did you see him?"

"He didn't want anything. I was in the kitchen when he came. There was nobody around. I opened the door to him. At first I didn't recognize him. His face was red, his shirt open, and he didn't look me in the eye. He asked for his Aunt Munira. No greeting. Just 'Is my Aunt Munira there?' What's happened to young men these days? Not our sons though, dear. They're different. But that one hasn't been brought up properly."

She was talking unconcernedly. When she stopped, Midhat asked again, "Yes, but what did he want? Didn't you find out what he wanted?"

"I told you he didn't want anything. Not from us at least. He wanted to talk to Munira and her mother. I heard him say to them, 'Why don't you come back to Baquba? They need Munira at the school.'"

"What's it got to do with him? Coming knocking on people's doors like that! Why doesn't he go and sort himself out first?"

Safiya watched him talking with such unaccustomed heat, then his father said, "Don't worry about it, Midhat. He's just an impulsive young man who thought he was doing his relatives a kindness. Nuriya, are we going to have dinner soon? It's getting hotter these days, and I want to go up to the roof in good time."

"I'll go down now," said Nuriya, getting to her feet. "Shall we eat here?"

"Yes, dear," Safiya butted in. "Where else would we eat? This is the best place. Call them to help you carry the food upstairs."

Nuriya didn't look at her. It was as if she hadn't heard her. When no one else said anything she went off down the stairs. The sky appeared black through the darkness in the house. Safiya could hear the muffled voices of the girls and Umm Hasan coming from the girls' room as they watched television. They forgot everything when they were sitting in front of that little screen. Since the beginning of summer she had wanted to go up on the roof to sleep, but the stairs frightened her. She would expire halfway up. Midhat got to his feet and went off unhurriedly to his room. He was of average height and slim. He had strange preoccupations these days. He never usually asked who had called or what had happened at the house during his absence.

"Don't you have any plans to get Midhat married off?" she whispered to her brother.

"Why do you ask? Have you heard something?"

"Should I have?"

"What then?"

"I was just saying . . ."

Voices calling from below interrupted her, then the light went on in the small gallery and Munira appeared, accompanied by the two little girls. As they ran laughing past the alcove, Munira glanced briefly at Abd al-Karim. Her eyes were bright, and her hair flowed over her shoulders. Abu Midhat cleared his throat a couple of times, then rose to his feet. "God bless you. You start to say something, then stop in the middle! I'm going to wash my hands."

She was glad he talked to her like this. She wanted to wash her hands too, but was afraid she'd miss seeing the food arrive. There was noise rising continuously from the yard, and the lights were on all over the house. Umm Hasan came into view at the far end of the small gallery and began her slow progress towards the alcove, holding on to the wooden balustrade. Safiya watched her as she made her way unsteadily along, then realized that Umm Hasan's appearance on the scene meant dinner would be there any minute.

Chapter Four

Usayn opened his eyes, and they were assaulted by the bright light flooding through the window. He shut them firmly again, raised his left hand, and pressed it against them, then let his fingers relax and felt a throbbing under his fingertips. He was afraid to open his eyes again and abandoned himself to the darkness inside him. His heart, stomach, eyes, and head were all pounding and churning violently. He'd never felt such a trembling in his body before, although he hadn't registered when it began. He wasn't going to open his eyes. He would remain shut up inside himself. Yesterday he had got up after ten, and today he wasn't even going to leave his bed. What had they been doing in Uwanis's miserable bar last night? He groaned. That lunatic Adnan. He was an egomaniac. But he hadn't registered that at the time either. Adnan had stood in the midst of them talking, and it had seemed as if he was dancing. The mischievous lock of hair on his forehead gave him a feminine beauty. He hadn't been saying anything in particular, and Husayn had felt drawn to him and exasperated by him at the same time. Shit. His head was throbbing. He sat up in bed. He hadn't eaten anything yesterday and couldn't remember who'd paid for the drinks. Perhaps the quarter dinar was still in his pocket. He would try and remember things more clearly after he had washed. He moved his hand down his face to wipe his mouth and nose, then opened his eyes. He was only wearing underpants and a thin vest. The hair on his thighs was thick and black and curly, and the flesh underneath looked dirty. He felt his sprouting beard. When had he last shaved? His mind was a seething mass of unstable memories. He didn't like this time of day: the waking up, the sense of defeat, the slide downwards. If only he could wash properly all over today. In a Turkish bath, despite the hot weather. In cold weather, in the past, he'd spent an hour or more enveloped in steam, his feet on the warm floor and the smell of Abu al-Hil soap in his nostrils. The smell of the soap as he sang Umm Kulthum's song, "*Ya habibi, ya habibi*, O my love, O my love," his eyes watering! They were the happiest times of his adolescence, without a doubt. Then he discovered masturbation and everything was hell. The delicious, deceptive hell of sex.

Life's biggest illusion. "O my love, O my love" didn't work any more. Afterwards he used to draw in his limbs like a fetus and remain still, listening to the heavy silence of himself in a world with a wholly unfamiliar resonance. Then he poured the hot water over his legs and shoulders, and the dense steam rose and hid him from sight.

He scratched the skin on his left thigh determinedly and examined the pieces of encrusted dirt that his fingernails dislodged. Protect the skin, avoid blocked pores with regular baths and massages and by softening the body, with steam naturally. Steam was especially beneficial. He put one foot to the floor then stood up and leaned against the bed. The walls spun round and he closed his eyes. He waited a few moments, abandoning himself to the sudden vertigo. Every time his emotions reached crisis point, he closed the windows on the world and withdrew into the darkness inside himself. A temporary escape, or a short breathing space. He was caught off guard by a violent pain in his stomach. He clutched hold of it. His guts were writhing and contracting. He could feel his heart beat faster. He pressed his stomach, rubbed it, afraid he'd throw up. Shit. The storm was beginning somewhere in his intestines. Terrible hands were gripping them, pushing whatever remained there up to the surface. It was coming. There was no resisting it. Since childhood he'd been afraid of vomiting. He remembered once he'd flung his arms around his mother, begging her not to let him vomit, and then spewed the contents of his stomach over her black dress and rough *abaya*, and she had wept with him. His legs suddenly began to give way. He knelt down beside the bed. The first wave of nausea rose into his throat and he began swallowing and breathing heavily. A cold sweat was gathering on his forehead and chest. It was agony. How terrible it was to die! He felt a cool breeze from the window on his face. The arm pushed relentlessly towards his heart. He was curled up in a ball on the floor, gripping the bed. The fateful moment would come in a few seconds, a few years of torment. Then he let out a choking noise, a convulsive rattling from his mouth, nose, eyes and ears, and a bitter stream of liquid poured from his throat. He swallowed. The bitter liquid oozed out of the corners of his slack mouth and down his nostrils. He was panting, his eyes closed and the sweat running slowly down off his temples. Then his innards dropped back into place. A savage force had played havoc with him for a few moments and reduced him to a heap of flesh dripping with cold sweat. A gentle breeze blew over him, and he took a deep breath of fresh air. He felt a drop—a tear or something similar—descending hesitantly from his closed right eye. Then an unexpected shudder gripped him. He might be no more than a mound of cold flesh, but at least he was no longer suffering or about to die.

This beautiful, strange-looking girl had gazed into his eyes. He had taken hold of her gentle fingers. People said she was a prostitute. Her hand was soft and innocent. They hadn't had a lot to say to one another. There were thick clouds of steam around him in the baths as he sang, "O my love, O my love," and poured warm water over his legs and shoulders. The delights of childhood and sex. The childhood of sex. Sex the child. The shuddering returned and he opened his eyes. The light in the room was appallingly bright. He rubbed his eyes and head, then pulled himself up on the edge of the bed and sat down on it, wiping his face again. It had been a sudden attack—that was where its power lay—and it had left him with trembling limbs and a thumping heart. His watch said half past ten. Nobody in the house had noticed him throwing up, and there was still time to shave and visit Midhat in his office. He looked out of the window at the wall opposite. The sun's rays seemed brighter than usual. Perhaps it was the weakness of his body making the sun stronger!

He got down off the bed and took a few steps and was seized by another wave of nausea. For a minute he couldn't focus. He stopped and leaned against the wall. It would pass when he washed in cold water. This wasn't the first time, but he had to confess it was one of the worst. He opened the door of his room. There wasn't a sound from the floor below. Where had his miserable relatives gone—the Hajji and his old wife? He could hear the rumble of the street in the distance. He belched a couple of times and went off towards the bathroom.

To wake up vomiting or vomit up your awakening. Take your pick. The point is that your mouth is full of the acids of your corroding insides. Lebanese lemons. And that you have to begin your bright shiny day like this.

The alleyway is as muddy and twisted as the lives of its inhabitants. And you bob up and down as you walk along, you bastard. Al-salam alaykum, Hajji Wahib. Upon you be peace and God's mercy. Shall I borrow some money from him? He's looking at you as if you're the devil or a naked woman. You go up and down and down and down, then up again. You must walk straight. Like that. Stick your chest out. That's it. Up and down you go again, son of a bitch. And the quarter dinar? No trace of it. Pockets full of holes. You paid for the drinks. That must be it. The last few hours of the evening will always remain a blur. You're walking as straight as the canon of Abu Khizama, without a penny in your pocket. But here's the missing coin, bastard. What about the woman who pretended to forget my name for some reason? And she turns to look at him, the beautiful Kurd with smiling eyes, before she closes the door. You rush in after her, pull off all her clothes and hold her against you, smelling her and kissing her.

He goes up and down, up and down. What can she say? You see her. She sees you. What does it mean? I understand. The fact that we're here in front of you, gentlemen, is irrefutable proof of the prostitution of this woman. So she's killed and revives and is killed again, and again. You cowardly farts. Tea is important only to those who have no importance. You sit down on the wooden seat, the bench actually, to give it its real name. So he comes towards you, undulating, preening, dipping to the right and the left in response to orders, Arzuqi the One-Eyed, waiter at the café. He's all pride and vanity, never mind how filthy he is and how dreadful he smells. Make for the real depths, gentlemen. There you'll find the genuine corpse. His tea is like him and like these respectable people sitting to the right and left of you, judging your actions with their prayer beads. Click click click. He stops, she stops. He walks on, she walks on. He follows her, she follows him. He does it with her, she does it with him. And what about us, the honorable people? Where should we stick our noses? Or rather that other part of us. Where should we stick it? Tell us. Tell the men of honor wrapped in their *abayas*, oozing foul sweat. Click click click. Isn't it odd that Arzuqi the One-Eyed can despise you, look down on you? Throw a cup of tea down on the table so it slops into the saucer? He finds this normal, in keeping with his station, which he's not allowed to forget. If you ask him why, he evades the question and weeps with his blind eye and accuses anyone, whether he knows them or not, of things he knows or doesn't know. Why don't you put the tea down properly? Don't you want to? Why should I, he would say, his eyes full of bits and his chest covered in disgusting black hair exposed proudly to you. There's the man of the future, in his faded damp trousers. There he is, the old aristocracy. The aristocracy of ideas and taste. His tea is worthy of him. And you, you old crow, what's your involvement with these aristocratic café waiters?

It's enough to incline your head to this damp-trousered, half-blind man. Don't waste your time on anything else. You've got a long journey ahead of you. It's pointless to cut through the mosque. The schools are closed and it's not possible to see the girls. Suha and Sana. Sana and Suha. The stupidity of families. Of everything, if you think about it. Bastards. Your children are like your own liver, so they say. Mine's as hard as wax these days. So put them in a waxwork museum if they're made of your ruined liver! Don't argue. It's purely a question of logic. A broad logic, and people bow to logic, just as they bow to Arzuqi. Therefore, without complicating things, logic is Arzuqi the One-Eyed. That's it. Let's go. To Muazzam. To my brother-in-law's office.

He'd tell him without preamble that he had to see his daughters. Wasn't this the father's right? Any father on the face of the globe, even in Iraq! All the laws in the world would confirm his visiting rights. But the problem—was there a problem? Go and see them whenever you want, says Midhat, damn him. Who's trying to make you take responsibility? You've never paid a penny so far, my friend. Damn him. Let's look at things on another level. The human level, where all values can be blurred or redefined. Everything: duties, obligations, rights, etc. That was the reasonable way to look at things, appropriate to someone of his age, culture, status. Let's avoid the material twists and turns and the hot sun, and cross over to the objective side where there's more shade. Then we can lay out our current situation on the dissecting table so we can take it apart and examine all its aspects. The father's rights first, gentlemen.

His assured and guaranteed rights. He'd done it all ways in order to produce his children. No, come on, no pornographic literature, please. Once these rights have been established, we can discuss the existence or non-existence of duties. Tell me your rights, and I'll tell you who you

68

are. Animal. Human being. Dinosaur. Insect. First-class horse. Third-class. Yearling. The important thing is to establish your rights and exercise them. As for duties, who's bothered about them round here? After me, duty! Après moi, le devoir!

Good morning, Mr. Husayn. Good morning, my brother. I hope you're well, God willing. Whose was this face from the past? How are you? Fine, thanks. How about you? He was wearing a jacket and a red tie in this blazing heat. What are you up to these days, Husayn? If you were asked a question like this, it meant people were interested in you. His eyelids flickered, as if he was embarrassed. But who was this? I was in Kuwait, brother, working. His jacket was carefully ironed; he satisfied his wife in bed. What are you doing now, brother? Company director. Shit. Wasn't he mad, this company director, to stick his nose into what didn't concern him? Excuse me, I have to go. Goodbye. Then the company director fled. Fled in every sense of the word, literal and metaphorical. Husayn still didn't know who he was. Mean bastard. He comes up to you without being invited, betrays you like Judas Iscariot as soon as he senses you're thinking of asking him for a loan. Were his intentions written so clearly in his eyes? The only solution, my friends, is dark glasses. Then they won't guess the secret before it's revealed, anticipate the disaster before it occurs. You'll be able to surprise them, both with your dark glasses and your demands for a loan, coming at them like bullets out of a gun. Quick, guaranteed loans. A quarter dinar. A half dinar. A quarter. A dinar. Half. Half. Half. You'll amass more and more money. A new economic theory: infinite borrowing. A loan covered by a loan covered by a loan covered by a loan and so on and so on. Why had you forgotten who this company director was? Wasn't he the branch manager at the bank in 1959? An opportunist communist. Numan Sallum. A name which didn't tell you for certain whether he was a Christian or a Muslim! An evident disguise or evidence of a disguise! Backstage types, who stick a hand or a foot out under the lights every now and then, and when they've warmed up a little draw them quickly back in so as not to attract attention. Company director, yes, branch manager, and if you want a more precise description of him: thick-skinned, indestructible, and a real shit. A person protected by the times. But strip him of his clothes, both the external material ones and the invisible trappings. First take away his jacket and his name, then his trousers and his job. Rip off his elegant shirt and confiscate his car. At this point, let's stop for a break to laugh at the tragic results. But do you ever really hear of this kind of thing happening? Those would be pure, genuine acts. So what if you drink every day and you're bankrupt and have no income whatsoever? The jacket, the trousers, the smart shirt: they're the outer layers; the underpants and shoes are a different story. Supposing Numan Sallum was a drunk who'd lost his home and his job, what would he do? But it was inconceivable he could ever sink to such depths. A complete coward.

This sun's unbearable, and you're hurrying as if you're going to meet a lover, you silly bastard. You and Numan Sallum are on different sides of the fence, but you're walking the same road. You're both scared. It's terrifying, this life. You sat up in bed at daybreak once, ages ago, trembling with fear. You had no need to wake up at such a time. You'd only gone to sleep around two in the morning after pointless fighting, bitter words, rebuffs and abuse from Madiha, and you were tired and dejected. That was the third time you'd spent your entire salary days after getting it, without giving her a penny. Permanent drunkenness, unquenchable thirst, gambling, sordid sex. You woke up before dawn, still tired. The first light didn't penetrate the small room where you sat huddled on your single bed, alone and isolated, your heart beating. The room was almost bare. She'd driven you out of her room, and you were on your own like a counterfeit monk, when fear crept up on you. The fear of death, the fear that you were finished, that nothing was any use any more. Everything you did, anybody did, was futile. You shook, your sweat ran cold as you sat in bed alone, a traitor to yourself and your world. A sense of desolation welled up from all four corners of the room and encircled you, and from that day onwards you began to go gradually downhill.

———

He went into Midhat's office at the Ministry having been told by the janitor that he'd be back shortly. He sat in his usual chair by the window overlooking the river and avoided looking outside. His eyes hadn't yet recovered from the bright light in the street assaulting them. He shut them, letting them rest in the soft light that filled the room. The damned long walk in the blazing sun from Bab al-Shaykh to Serail had worn him out. His body was more weary than usual; the poundings inside him continued their work, and the griping pains hadn't altogether subsided. The phone rang two or three times before the janitor hurried in to pick it up. He noticed a packet of cigarettes and matches on the desk, but waited for the janitor to go out before he got heavily to his feet, lit a cigarette, and took a long, slow drag on it. The smoke tickled his lungs and relaxed him a little. He felt he could consider himself empty of everything, without worries or ties. A boat floating between heaven and earth, rocking gently, touching neither sky nor land. This was true equilibrium, the best sort. The pleasure of remaining effortlessly in a zone of equally balanced forces. Let them do what they liked. Was there any point in beginning again, in beginning at all? He sucked greedily on his cigarette and coughed several times.

The door was opened hurriedly and Midhat came in, smiling and cheerful, carrying a parcel of books. They shook hands. He wasn't surprised to see him and, if anything, seemed to be pleased.

When he had sat down and pressed the bell, he asked, "Have you been here long?"

"No," answered Husayn.

The janitor came in: "Yes, sir?"

71

"Something to drink, Abu Suha?" Then he carried on talking to the janitor: "Qadir, I saw the kebab seller at the entrance of the souk. Go and fetch some meatballs and bread for Abu Suha." He gave the janitor some cash. "And bring us a couple of teas on your way back."

"Who are the meatballs for, Midhat?" exclaimed Husayn.

"You, of course."

"What am I meant to do with them?"

"Go on, Qadir," said Midhat, ignoring him. "Hot meatballs and bread. Be quick."

As the janitor hurried out, Midhat turned back to Husayn: "If you looked at yourself in the mirror you'd know you hadn't had breakfast. Did you walk here?"

Husayn nodded and took a last drag on the cigarette.

Midhat was sorting through papers on the desk, dividing them into two lots and scribbling notes on them from time to time. He looked smart in his pale gray suit and green tie, was more friendly and open than usual, and sprucer. Perhaps he imagined all this cleanliness and friendliness and openness in people because he had lost these characteristics himself.

"What were you doing in the souk, Midhat?" he asked, stubbing out his cigarette.

Midhat looked up. His eyes were small and dark and deep set. "I bought—you know—a few light novels for Munira. She likes to read sometimes."

"How are they? Are they happy with you?"

"They're fine, I think. Munira ought to transfer to Baghdad. They weren't comfortable in Baquba. We might be able to arrange a transfer for her by the end of the summer."

Husayn felt there was something important he had forgotten to ask Midhat, but the way he talked about Munira and said her name distracted him.

"Is she a primary school teacher?"

"Who? Munira? No. Secondary school. There's a big difference. Mind you don't forget!"

"Okay, I'll remember next time!"

The janitor startled him, bursting in carrying bread stuffed with meatballs, followed by the teaboy. He had no desire to eat and sat holding the bulging sandwich and looking at the black tea which had been put down carefully in front of him. The janitor went out, and Midhat returned to his papers. The smell was overpowering, and as Husayn breathed in warily the saliva accumulated in his mouth. He looked over at Midhat and saw he was stirring his tea absent-mindedly, completely absorbed in his work, so he took a bite of the hot bread and meatballs. He felt the fat and meat and cracked wheat and spices mingling pleasantly in his mouth. He wouldn't need anything else to eat till the evening. This was a good solution to the food problem. He should make sure he remembered it at the relevant times.

"Excellent meatballs, aren't they?" he heard Midhat saying.

He was drinking his tea, calmly, looking over towards him. Shit. He swallowed his large mouthful with difficulty, then took a swig of tea himself.

"Not bad. Not bad," he replied. "It was a very good idea of yours that I should eat."

Midhat reached for the cigarettes and lit one and took another swallow of tea. "About the girls," he said.

Husayn listened carefully. That was the thing that had slipped his damned memory.

"The family doesn't have a particular idea. Madiha's against you, of course, against everything to do with you." He made a circular gesture. "What happened between you, I don't know. That's your business. I don't suppose either of you is completely innocent. The important thing is . . ."

"What do you mean, against me?" Husayn interrupted sharply.

The absurdity of people, their regrets, their hopes!

"Look, Husayn. You know how I feel about you. Don't make me take sides in a cause I think's lost anyway. Let's first of all try and procure . . ." he made the same circular gesture, ". . . the things you consider essential to your peace of mind."

Silence descended on them. This time Husayn wasn't going to interrupt it with futile questions. He stopped moving his jaws and began staring attentively at Midhat. Midhat's dark eyes were untroubled. There was an arrogant look in them, not easy to fathom.

"My father supports you in general," he heard him saying. "That's important. It might influence Madiha eventually." Then his face brightened suddenly. God, how that face brightened! "Munira always stands up for you."

"Is that true? How strange."

He felt a kind of happiness sweep over him as he chewed his last mouthful of bread and watched Midhat announcing that there was someone who gave him unsolicited support.

"You're still staying with your aunt, are you?" asked Midhat.

He nodded and drank the remains of the tea with relish, his stomach comfortably full.

"Where's that? The Kurdish quarter?"

"Yes. The other side of Bab al-Shaykh, behind Café Yas. Why?"

"I thought I could bring the girls to visit you one afternoon. What do you think?"

"No, no. Why come into those dark little alleyways? We could meet in Bab al-Sharqi or even in a park near you. I mean—seeing them for a few minutes would do me. I used to see them going to school. I watched them from a distance. Once I talked to Sana. I mean—I don't want to cause a problem. You know how things are better than I do, Midhat."

Midhat nodded, stubbing out his cigarette. "Fine, fine," he said after a pause.

"You know, Midhat," said Husayn, "I don't want them to see those places, and the house I'm living in, even though it's only temporary. I mean—maybe a walk in the park would be good for them."

"Fine. Fine."

Husayn was not satisfied with his short, disjointed sentences, but was scared that if he continued to talk so clumsily he would show himself up even more. He had never claimed to be an exemplary father. They all knew that. But something had risen to the surface during this conversation, something vaguely related to his cowardice, his mediocrity, his lack of serious interest in his daughters, and it diminished his status as a human being. He had wanted so much to leave all that behind, and instead it was mushrooming by the minute as he spoke, putting a brick wall between himself and Midhat. He noticed Midhat was talking on the phone. He felt he was in the way, and this pained him. Midhat and he had always been affectionate and honest to one another. They had been friends before Husayn married Midhat's sister and had continued to be close despite the marriage breakdown, the separation, and his job in Kuwait. Husayn did not hide much from him and if he did sometimes, it was purely from shame. He always felt he should be at his best with him, intellectually and as a human being.

"What do you do with yourself these days?" Midhat asked him.

The question somehow made him feel more at ease. "Honestly, Midhat, it's difficult to know how to pass your time, or where. There's nothing worth doing. No one has any ideas these days. There are no cafés worth going to, or cinemas. And I haven't read anything for ages." Midhat was looking at him with a mixture of sarcasm, curiosity, and incredulity on his face. This approach obviously wasn't working! "There's a cheap bar," Husayn went on. "It's really a bottle shop with a little space behind it where you can sit. Uwanis's place. It's not bad. I go there sometimes. It's quite cheap. Come for a drink one day if you want to. Really, Midhat, do. You sometimes find good company there. That guy Adnan came yesterday."

"Which Adnan?"

"Adnan, the son of your cousin Maliha. I've forgotten his father's name, dammit. He's a relative of my mother's as well."

"I know who you mean. Is he your idea of good company? How's he related to your mother?"

'You know my mother's originally from Houider in the Diyala region, north of here. His father's from the same village. He was poor, really poor, I'm telling you. And illiterate, couldn't read or write and still can't. How he got rich and acquired a brain, I don't know. Good for your aunt! How did she find him for her daughter?"

"My aunt? Munira's mother, you mean? It's past history." Then he began to look more interested. "Tell me, Husayn. This boy Adnan. What's he like? What sort of person is he?"

"An adolescent. A bit wild, impulsive. Doesn't have a job. Has a car, though, and drives back and forth between Baghdad and Baquba. I really don't know what he does with himself. Something irregular, for sure."

"He came to the house a few days ago. Or yesterday, it could have been. I don't know what he wanted from Munira and her mother."

"Don't let him in. He's a spoiled, irresponsible kid."

Midhat stared at him. "You're very prejudiced against him. Why?"

Husayn didn't reply immediately. He had no time for lucky fools like Adnan. To him they seemed as coarse, crude, and stupid as animals, and yet they lived well, and had no crises or serious problems in their lives. "Prejudiced against him? Why do you think that?" he replied. "I don't know. Maybe I am. I just don't like him."

The night before Adnan had not paid for the drinks and had refused to give him a lift. So he had suffered the added humiliation of being at the mercy of such a person.

"I'd really like to come and see you one day, Husayn," Midhat was saying.

"Where?"

"In that café. Uwanis's place. Tell me where it is."

"In Bab al-Sharqi near the Dar al-Salam cinema," said Husayn enthusiastically. "It's not a nice area, but that can't be helped. That son of a bitch Abu Kamal—Uwanis—sells cheap drink, and there's nowhere else around there. Do come, Midhat. Come tonight. Have you got anything on?"

"I'll try. What time will you be there?"

"Whenever you want. Seven-thirty. Eight. What suits you?"

"Yes. Eight, eight-thirty's fine."

"Okay."

Husayn stood up and took the packet of cigarettes off the desk and lit one, then went back to his seat. "I saw someone who used to work at the bank with me today. Numan Sallum. I didn't recognize him at all. He says he's a company director now. He offered me a job. I told him I was waiting for my money to come from Kuwait before I decided what to do next."

"What company?"

"I've forgotten. He told me but I've forgotten. I'm always forgetting things. I don't know why. I said to him, 'They have to send me my money.' Would they think of trying to do me out of it?"

He was silent. The question remained unanswered. Midhat went back to his work without showing any interest in what Husayn was saying. This topic of conversation had become unsavory. It wouldn't do him any good to pursue it. Pity! The cigarette was pleasant after the meatballs and tea. He wouldn't try again. With the change from the fifty which he still had in his pocket he could take the bus back. Then have a long nap until the late afternoon or early evening. Too bad that he hadn't managed to borrow any money. It didn't matter. The light in the room was mild and gentle, like the temperature. He had no desire to leave. Everything here soothed him. Slowly he exhaled cigarette smoke.

The janitor came in with some papers, put them discreetly on the desk, and went out again. He heard a clock strike in the distance. It could have been twelve midday, the hottest time. Shortly he'd have to get up and plunge into the ocean of light and heat and sweat and stinking bodies. There was no way of avoiding it or fighting against it. It's our heritage, so let's get on with it. With empty pockets and an empty head. He stubbed out his cigarette when he felt the smoke burning his tongue. Then he stood up.

"Right, Midhat. See you later, I hope." His tone was sad and gloomy.

Midhat looked up in surprise. "Where are you going?"

"Home."

"What are you going to do there?"

"Nothing much. Have a rest. Read a bit," said Husayn, somewhat taken aback.

"Have a seat for now. It's hot outside. Wait till I finish work and we can go together."

He didn't accept the invitation. This exchange made him even gloomier, and he was determined to go and sleep.

"No, Midhat, I'd rather go back now. I think I'll have a bit of a sleep after my lunch."

"As you wish. We've got a date tonight anyhow."

Husayn raised a hand in farewell and went out, shutting the door gently behind him. His spirits did not revive when he was confronted by the burning sun and the deserted square, then the street filled with cars and people. He felt in his pocket and came across a few coins, enough to take the bus back. He was neither hungry nor tired, but he felt his body failing to respond as he walked. This might be due to some kind of spiritual fatigue, he thought, for which he would soon have to find an explanation.

———

He saw Abu Shakir putting his glass of arak down carefully on the floor beside him, then wiping his mouth and looking at him. Abu Shakir was sitting hunched in the shadows near the doorway, his dark glasses and tall black *sidara* cap making him look as if he was in mourning.

"Brother Husayn . . ." He was slurring his words, his mouth slack.

You look like a bat, you evil bastard.

"I can see . . ."

He can hardly speak.

"If you don't mind me saying . . ." His beard took up most of his thin face, and he was dressed in somber colors.

He must have been drinking for hours, the lazy bum.

"I can see you now, brother Husayn."

You can't see a thing.

"Why aren't you drinking? I mean, if you don't mind me asking."

"Go ahead, Abu Shakir. Why should I mind?"

If that was my only problem!

"No, I mean . . . Is my watch wrong?" He shuffled around uneasily and looked at his watch. "See. It says a quarter past eight."

As if he'd discovered oil in the middle of Baghdad! His spectacles gleamed, and Husayn thought he saw his mouth twist to one side in the dim light.

The arak has made him lose control.

"Don't worry, Abu Shakir," he answered. "I'm waiting for someone."

Abu Shakir looked amazed. "That can't be your first beer!"

Worse things have happened.

"It's fine, Abu Shakir. We'll make up for it later."

And who's going to pay for it, you moron?

Abu Shakir laughed and sat back on the wooden bench, drawing in his limbs like a large beetle. "I like the sound of that, brother Husayn! In the morning they'll be weeping."

What kind of meaningless crap was this?

The curtain dividing them off from the shop was pulled aside and Abu Nazim appeared. "Al-salam alaykum! I've walked all the way from Bab al-Muazzam!"

"God is great!" shouted Abu Shakir.

Bloody bastard. You really made me jump.

"Alaykum al-salam. Why, Abu Nazim? Weren't there any buses?" he asked.

Abu Nazim sat down on the wooden bench next to Abu Shakir, took out a dirty kaffiyeh and began to mop his face with it.

"The cars aren't moving in Rashid Street. The buses are crawling along, stuffed with people. What's going on, my friends?"

He was dripping with sweat, cross-eyed and plump, his hair thick and wiry.

"Why? What's happening?" shouted Abu Shakir. "Tell me."

"Nothing, Abu Shakir. I just said to myself rather than paying to suffocate, I'd walk and save the money. Is that all right with you?"

"Well done, Abu Nazim. Well done," said Abu Shakir, still talking at the top of his voice.

What kind of a night is it going to be with this idiot for company?

"Abu Kamal, Abu Kamal," called Abu Nazim.

Uwanis put his head round the curtain.

"Yes."

"Quarter of arak, please, Abu Kamal."

"Right."

Would Midhat show up in the end? Surely he couldn't lose his way.

"How are you, Abu Suha?" Abu Nazim asked Husayn.

"Well thanks. And you?"

"Very well. Tiptop."

Abu Shakir whispered something to Abu Nazim, who leaned towards him. They were like two crows in their dark corner. It was uncomfortably hot. Uwanis came in briskly and put a quarter bottle of arak and a glass next to Abu Nazim, then went out with a glance at Husayn's empty glass. Was Midhat not going to turn up? He lifted his glass and drank the dregs of warm beer in the bottom. His hand was shaking slightly, and he felt almost feverish. He hadn't eaten since the morning, since the unforgettable meatballs! They had enabled him to have several hours of untroubled sleep in the afternoon. The sleep of the dead, without dreaming or feeling the heat. But then he had woken up sober, and the anxiety and trembling hands had returned. He knew very well he couldn't last long like this. He would begin on the arak shortly. He didn't need to be very cunning to negotiate the price of a quarter of arak, even if it meant being forced to borrow from Abu Nazim. The two men were still whispering together in a dubious fashion.

"If you two want me to go," he began, "feel free to say so."

"What are you talking about, brother Husayn?" shouted Abu Shakir.

"We've got nothing to hide," said Abu Nazim. "You know Abu Shakir! He tells thousands of stories with no point to them whatsoever. Let's drink."

He bent to pour himself an arak in a glass full of ice cubes. Can't the fool see that I don't have anything to drink? How am I going to manage it with these assholes? Abu Nazim added water and the liquid turned milky in the glass. He put it on the floor then took a small paper bag out of his pocket, which he opened and offered to Husayn.

"Roast peanuts. Help yourself, Abu Suha. They're still warm."

I've made it!

"Thanks, Abu Nazim."

He heard someone talking to Uwanis in the front of the shop and jumped to his feet, recognizing the voice. He felt cheerful as he brought Midhat back, introduced him to the others, and gave him his seat. Pulling up an empty barrel, he sat down next to him. He realized how isolated and alone a person was without money or drink. He wasn't used to interacting with drinkers when he was sober. He ordered a quarter of arak and a bottle of cold beer. Abu Shakir and Abu Nazim were engaged in another mysterious conversation: two crows without importance now. Midhat looked young and elegant to him and smelt good. Husayn told him this after two large swigs of the magic liquid. Midhat smiled without replying. It was almost nine.

"Did they like the books?" he asked.

Midhat took a quick look at their two companions. "Munira, you mean?" he said in a low voice.

Husayn nodded. Such a beautiful name, Munira!

"Yes, she liked them," said Midhat.

Midhat took a large gulp of beer, and Husayn did the same. He needed to move on to a different plane. The fact that there were no snacks with the arak didn't bother him much.

"I saw Karumi a few days ago," he said to Midhat. "He looked very weak and pale. How is he now?"

"Not bad. Well, and not well. You know he was ill. I told you. He was ill for a long time. It was a strange illness. You couldn't tell what was wrong with him. It was as if he didn't want to go on living."

"Why? He's better now, I hope."

"I don't exactly know. It's complicated. He had a friend he really loved. He was knocked down by a car and killed in front of him. It had a big effect on Karumi. He never mixed that much with the rest of us, even when he was a child. A day or two ago he collapsed in the courtyard. It really worried the family. I don't know what's going on with him . . ."

He was talking slowly, forlornly. He didn't complete his sentence and took another big gulp of beer. Husayn, too, raised his glass in silence.

Midhat seems to have decided to let himself go tonight.

Midhat lit a cigarette and offered one to Husayn. Abu Shakir and his friend were enthusiastically discussing something incomprehensible. Husayn was afraid of them interrupting his conversation with Midhat, and so he kept his head turned away from them to show that he wasn't interested.

"How are things at home, Midhat?"

"What do you mean?"

"How are you getting on, and the family? Are you happy?"

Midhat nodded and gestured vaguely: "Sort of." Then suddenly he demanded, "How are you, Husayn? I mean, how's your life really? What are your plans?"

Husayn rubbed his head. Not a very good start. He blew smoke out through his nose. "I don't think I've got any. Why should I?" He laughed and saw a depressed look on Midhat's face. Not a good beginning, old son. "Look, Midhat," he went on. "I know you like me like I like you, and you're not asking me just because you're my daughters' uncle but . . ." he felt himself smiling. ". . . the time's past."

"What are you talking about? The time's past for what?"

"Don't deceive yourself. There's nothing you feel passing as much as your own life. Don't tell me life begins at forty, or sixty. Look at me now, the state I'm in, and make me any age you want, then what? Do you think I should go back to my job, to Madiha and the girls? You know neither of those things is going to happen. And there isn't a job for me since . . ." He raised his glass in the air. "Cheers!"

He took a good long drink. A nice piece of acting! He was almost moved by his own speech. He had never managed to talk to himself so honestly and had not intended to talk to Midhat like this.

"Listen, Husayn, can't we leave these domestic and social problems aside for now?"

"What else is there, Midhat?"

"You. Who you are, really."

He wants to start philosophizing. God help us.

"Me? This is me. I'm not hiding anything. I'm the dregs of society and the black sheep of the family!"

"We're all like that. Everybody in the world. That's not what I meant. The important thing is . . ."

"There's nothing important, my dear Midhat," Husayn interrupted, warming to the topic. "Everything's the same. Freud, God rest his soul, Freud's the same in the end as any Iraqi street sweeper from Houider, and *The Origin of the Species* is the same as . . ." Midhat raised his hand to stop him, but Husayn carried on: "Just a second. I'm not a nihilist by nature, or an atheist. It's just that my life's a failure. I've done nothing. But I'm not desperate. Not at all." He couldn't find the words to express the thoughts whirling round in his head. "What have I got to be desperate about? I don't actually want anything from the world, so why should I be desperate? Take it from me, the world will be the same in a hundred years, two hundred, a thousand. So what does that mean? Anything? If it doesn't, that's the end of the discussion, and if it does, then please tell me."

He picked up his glass sadly. His evening had just begun. This was the time when he was most himself. He noticed Midhat smoking stiffly, not looking at him. He could face any horrors now, any conspiracies against him. Nobody would be able to get the better of him. At this time of day his intellectual, physical, and emotional powers were at their height. It was annoyingly hot, and their two companions' noisy debate was disturbing their conversation.

Midhat turned towards him, looking irritated: "Look, Husayn, I can't discuss these ideas with you now. I'm thinking about a particular version of the future, and you're closing all the doors."

"What future?" Then he continued, not knowing why, "You want to get married. That's it, isn't it, Midhat?"

Midhat stubbed out his cigarette and drained his glass, then sat in silence staring in front of him as if he was alone. Finally he said in a hoarse voice, "The truth is you don't want a future. You don't want to have to think about it. That's easier, more comfortable. Especially if you're able to do it, if you're quite happy with yourself."

He stopped and Husayn saw on his face in the semi-darkness and through the fog of cigarette smoke something close to anguish. He half turned to Husayn and looked him fiercely in the eye: "You can't deceive me with this kind of talk, Husayn. What kind of relationship do you have with yourself? That's twice I've asked you the same question." He suddenly lowered his voice: "How do you react to the voice inside you, Husayn? Tell me, do you have a voice hounding you wherever you go, asking you about everything, commenting on everything? What's this? Why did you do that? That's right. That's wrong. That's hypocritical. That's unjust. That's a mess. That's a failure. A voice that never sleeps, talks to you whether you're talking or not, whether you're alone or with other people. Do you have one of those, Husayn? Do you?"

Husayn's heart was beating unreasonably as he tried to avert his eyes from Midhat's tortured face. What could he answer? Should he tell him about the disappointments and setbacks and the moments of embarrassment and shame? Could he tell him honestly that it was the other person inside him who had done these things?

"What do you mean, a voice, Midhat?" he said hesitantly.

"I've got nothing to add. Either you understood what I was saying from the start or you didn't."

Had he chosen his life? It was certain crucial moments over a long period of time that had made it what it was. A word too many or too few. A moment of boredom that he hadn't been able to overcome. The temptation in a glass. The curve of a buttock. A sexual failure.

"If you mean . . . I really don't know." He stopped. "Why am I talking to myself? I must be stupid. Please, Midhat."

Midhat's eyes clouded over. He turned away to light a cigarette, and Husayn heard him saying quietly, "Have it your own way, Husayn. If you don't want to talk, that's fine. But do you understand why things have got so desperate?"

Midhat's dejected tone saddened him. "I told you, Midhat, I'm not desperate. I've messed up my life, that's all. You thought I was being funny or exaggerating. But it's the truth. What can I do?"

He raised his glass. I'll finish this in one go if it's the last thing I do.

"I tried to put myself on the dissecting table once. Peel the layers away. See who I was." His enthusiasm increased as the familiar heat was kindled inside him. "Who am I? What makes me what I am? How have I got like this?"

The words felt heavy as his slack lips pronounced them. For a moment his head went round, then the spinning subsided. The glass in front of him was empty. He picked up the bottle and poured more arak into his glass, and added ice and water. He felt like saying something original, to surprise Midhat, impress him, but the damn words wouldn't come. His memory grew dim at times, and he was left in a heap of fragmented sentences, lost and humiliated. He had no desire to repeat such experiences, but here was Midhat sitting beside him, something he'd wanted for years.

"Do you know, Midhat—how can I explain? In Kuwait, do you know how much I used to think about you?"

"Are you going to Kuwait, brother Husayn?" exclaimed Abu Shakir. "Bring me some cigarettes, brother. Rothmans. Please!"

"There is no Kuwait any more, Abu Shakir. Who goes there these days? It's a changed world."

Midhat was turned expectantly towards him, not listening to Abu Shakir at all.

He takes the thing so seriously.

"My life in Kuwait was miserable," he continued. "I wasn't settled at all. You could drink, of course. But you couldn't relax in the hotel. Anyway . . ."

"Is it true you tried to find out who you were, as you said?" asked Midhat insistently.

Husayn began searching through his pockets for cigarettes and did not find any. "What a mess I'm in today. I'm hopeless!"

Midhat offered him a cigarette. He accepted, lit it, and took a long drag. He felt he was about to reach his accustomed peak, when the world was full of joy, life was amazing, truth and fantasy were indistinguishable, and the walls came tumbling down. He didn't want to lie to Midhat: "I don't know. Maybe. One day I went out and didn't go home. I was working at the Rafidayn Bank at the time, and I'd been married three or four years. I don't remember exactly. We were all right financially, and I was on the fringes of some progressive political and literary groups. So, I went out, but I don't know where I was planning on going. There was one thing on my mind—I didn't want to go on living the life I was living."

His friend Faruq had persuaded him to join the famous poker game held in a whorehouse which some of them frequented. Drink, gambling, and most likely women too. They'd left work together with their salaries in their pockets and gone to the place in Karrada. He hadn't even phoned Madiha to tell her he wouldn't be coming home. They had been given a warm welcome and were soon playing cards in a group that grew over the course of the evening as more people arrived and joined in.

"I didn't have specific plans to take a room in a hotel. I just wanted to be by myself, to feel I didn't have any ties or responsibilities. I was obsessed by the idea of finding out what I'd be without my job, my family, children, home, friends."

It had been a wonderful night. Amazing cards. Money piling up in front of him. Whisky flowing. And Marie. She had squeezed in next to him, her breast pressing against his shoulder, her buttock resting on his chair, whispering flirtatiously to him every now and then, and the hours had passed like minutes.

"What would I be, I used to ask myself, if I was dropped naked as the day I was born on an island or out in the wilds somewhere? What would I be without my language and my past? And to tell you the truth, it was as if I was imprisoned by these thoughts the whole time, as if thinking had become a disease with me. I went without food or drink the whole night."

The cards had been extraordinary all night long, and sweet Marie had stayed at his side pouring him drinks and flirting with him. The hours had gone by, and when dawn broke they had only paused briefly for a light meal, and he had caressed Marie's breasts and kissed her in a dark corner. When they went back to the table his head had been empty, beating like a drum.

"I fell asleep and didn't wake till the afternoon. I stayed in bed without eating or shaving. I saw no one that day. I wanted this solitude."

It had got to past one in the afternoon. He had no longer been able to see the cards properly and asked if he could have a rest. He had simply wanted to sleep. It hadn't occurred to him to go home to his family, or even to make contact with them. He had been winning a large sum of money—how much he couldn't remember any more—and wanted to screw Marie. She'd asked him for however many dinars, which he'd given her without hesitation, and taken him off to a room at the back of the house.

"I paced up and down the room. I can remember it so clearly. It was as if I was chasing a shadow—something I couldn't quite grasp. And I came to one conclusion: I couldn't, being the person I was, in that situation and mental state, come to any conclusion, because I couldn't be certain of anything, and I didn't know where to start."

What a fiasco! For him and coquettish Marie. The soft bed had been like a drug. His body had been unable to keep fighting the exhaustion. As soon as he'd put his head on the pillow, intending to relax for a moment, he'd plunged into a profound sleep, which had taken him away from Marie and her warm body.

"But these hours of reflection made me feel a kind of peace of mind I hadn't felt before. It was night time. I left the hotel and went to the nearest bar. I drank and drank, as if I was drinking the spirit of life itself. I was terribly drunk, but I went on drinking till midnight and I still hadn't had enough, so I bought a bottle of whisky to take back to the room, and went on drinking till dawn."

They had woken him up in the late afternoon, and Marie hadn't been there. She had gone without leaving anything behind, not even her smell. He had sat at the table feeling, for no obvious reason, that a part of him was missing. He could still remember those few moments before the other players arrived. Through the window the sky had looked clear and blue, full of light and joy, a pure distant world that had suddenly terrified him. When he started playing again, all his luck had deserted him. He had fought back vehemently and hung on to his last bit of cash, but it was pointless: he felt that some stern judgment had been passed on him when he was looking at the sky. The game broke up at dawn, and he left the house empty and drained.

"I left my room at dawn, feeling empty, and walked alone through the deserted streets. I was beaten, finished. Completely shattered. I knew who I was then."

Midhat was still listening intently to him. Smoke filled the room, and the heat was unbearable. Husayn picked up his glass and took a large mouthful of the cold, burning liquid. His body sagged, and something was vaguely irritating him and making him on edge. He wanted to talk to the other two and hear them tell a joke or a dirty story.

"What's this rubbish you're talking?" murmured Midhat.

Husayn remained composed and kept listening. Perhaps his ears were deceiving him. He looked more closely at Midhat's face. He had heard right. It was obvious from the way Midhat was pursing his lips and narrowing his eyes, that he was about to speak again.

"I thought you were honest with yourself. I thought you'd say something that made sense," said Midhat in a quiet, angry voice. He picked up his glass abruptly and knocked back what remained in it. Husayn felt a shudder pass from his throat into his chest and back. He waited, silent and apprehensive. There was no way he could take back anything he'd said. No way at all. He wasn't ready for a fight with Midhat about life and reality.

"What's wrong, Midhat?" he asked. "Did I say something wrong? Have I upset you?"

His voice was dry and uncertain. Midhat didn't answer. He asked for another bottle of beer and Husayn shouted to Uwanis, who came hurrying over. It relieved the tension to hear himself calling out, and that was good.

"I respect your position, Husayn," Midhat continued. "It's not for me to say where you went wrong. Maybe I understand your weakness and some of your behavior. But lying to me, you know, that's what I can't take. Why do you pretend you've had these intellectual and spiritual adventures, when you know very well you're making them all up? I want to know what you've suffered from this sordid life, how people treat you, what abuse you've had. The ignominies of life. I want to know if you understand, if you're in control, if you know what's happening to you."

Husayn's mouth was dry, his jaw mysteriously slack. Abu Shakir and Abu Nazim interrupted their conversation to stare at the two of them. Husayn didn't know what to answer, how to react. Midhat smoked indifferently, as if he was alone.

"Why are you insulting me, Midhat?" he asked finally. "I love you like a brother."

Midhat took a deep breath: "I couldn't insult you, Husayn. You know that very well. On the contrary, I want to respect you, I want to feel you've got some hope. But, as I said before, don't try and deceive yourself or me. I haven't got time for that kind of thing, Husayn. I've got problems too, which I wanted to discuss with you."

These words cheered Husayn up. They seemed sincere somehow. He stood up and kissed Midhat on the head.

"You're my brother, Midhat. And you know what I'm like better than I do."

"Everything all right, people?" called Abu Shakir. "Nothing wrong, I hope."

"That's right," Abu Nazim chimed in.

"Nothing wrong," said Husayn. "Why should there be? We're brothers. We're from the same family. Your good health, my friends."

Husayn was not ashamed, but he wished he was in bed in his lonely room or squatting in the steam-filled public baths, pouring hot water over his shoulders. Perhaps then he'd forget what had been said to him, stop thinking about his past and what ought to be done. Midhat had genuinely wanted to help him in his trouble, and he didn't know how to tell him that there was no point.

He and Midhat drank slowly, without talking. He sensed that Midhat wasn't going to stay much longer and chose to keep quiet so as not to annoy him again.

"Brother Husayn," said Abu Shakir. "Who's your good-looking friend?"

Abu Nazim choked with laughter and Abu Shakir joined in. Husayn smiled and looked warily at Midhat. He saw he was busy with his thoughts, not entirely with them. He wanted to unwind a bit by sharing a joke with the other two, but a new arrival spoilt his plan. He was tall, tieless, and his shiny black hair fell carelessly on his forehead.

"Good evening," he said and remained standing in the middle of the room, when he saw there was no place for him to sit.

"Evening," shouted Husayn. "Hello, Adnan. Hello!"

"Hello. We were just wondering where you were," said Abu Shakir.

Adnan stepped back and called loudly, "Abu Kamal. A chair please."

"Come and sit here if you want," said Husayn, pulling an empty barrel out from behind his own.

Adnan shook his head, then noticed Midhat and stepped away from the table again. "How are you, Mr. Midhat?"

Husayn thought he detected a slight catch in his voice.

"Fine, thank you, Adnan. And you?"

"Very well."

Uwanis arrived carrying a wicker chair which Adnan took and placed in the doorway.

"A cold beer. A Diana. Quick, Abu Kamal."

"Coming up."

They exchanged greetings again, and Husayn finally took out his precious packet of cigarettes and offered them round. Midhat refused and sat watching Adnan curiously.

"Why were you in such a hurry yesterday, Adnan?" Husayn asked him. "You could at least have given me a lift."

Adnan crossed one leg over the other. "I had things to do, Abu Suha."

Husayn felt his irritation mounting. Idiot! He thought a few dinars in his pocket gave him the right to look down on whomever he pleased.

"You came to our house yesterday, Adnan," said Midhat suddenly. "What did you want?"

Adnan's facade crumbled. He took the cigarette out of his mouth, uncrossed his legs, and put them together in front of him. "Yes, I did," he answered hurriedly. "I came to ask Mun . . my aunt . . . They want my aunt back at the school in Baquba."

"What for? And what's it to do with you?"

He swallowed. Husayn saw him swallow. He hadn't seen him like this before. Son of a bitch. He was as fidgety as a ewe.

"My mother," he stuttered. "My mother went to the school. It was nothing to do with me."

Uwanis came in carrying a bottle of beer, misty with condensation. Adnan snatched it from him and hurriedly poured its contents into his glass. The white foam rose to the top and ran down the sides.

"No, no," scolded the assembled company, "Do it slowly. It's a shame to waste all that lovely beer!"

Adnan plunged his lips into the glass and took a long draught, wetting the sides of his mouth and his moustache. Then he raised the glass: "Your health, everybody. Sorry. Your health."

"And yours. Cheerio!"

They all drank. Midhat observed Adnan in silence, paying no attention to what was going on around him. Their racket did not distract him from his careful scrutiny. Husayn hoped he wouldn't repeat his questions to Adnan. It created an uncomfortable atmosphere, and he didn't understand their implications on the personal level.

"What are you reading these days, Midhat?" he asked, trying to divert his attention.

Midhat turned to him, but said nothing.

"And the girls," Husayn asked him again, "how are they doing at school, Suha and Sana?"

"Well, both of them. Sana gets higher grades than Suha. She seems cleverer."

"Ah! Suha's very clever too, though."

"Husayn. What's wrong with you?" shouted Abu Shakir. "They're your daughters. Don't you know how they're doing?"

As Husayn picked up his glass and brought it to his lips, he had the crazy notion of hurling it and its contents at that lined, sunburned monkey face. He poured the cold arak down his throat and felt its heat exploding inside him and spreading through his body. He wouldn't answer. He turned to his right and looked at the wall, wiping his nose and mouth. He wouldn't answer. He'd pretend he didn't feel the pricks of conscience.

"Don't blame someone who doesn't know you, doesn't know about your life," whispered Midhat.

Husayn turned to Abu Shakir. His head spun more violently with each passing moment. He was afraid the time was approaching when he'd no longer be able to control himself. His own voice rang in his ears when he talked, and he slurred his words slightly: "Abu Shakir. We're all from the same village. Each of us . . ." he coughed violently and made an expansive gesture with his arm which was meant to be obscene, "knowth—knows—his brothers."

He was controlling his tongue with some effort in order to be comprehensible.

"That boy in Kuwait who you made a marriage contract with." He raised his voice. "Where's he gone? What's become of him?"

Adnan laughed uncontrollably. Red in the face, his hair falling over his forehead, his glass in his hand, he shouted, "Alas! Your health, everybody!"

"Brother Husayn," said Abu Shakir, "Why are you asking me, as if you didn't know? Everybody's free to do what they want. You and me included." It looked as if a light had gone out in his sagging, wrinkled face. "Excuse me, everybody," he continued, "I'm a human being. I don't have any secrets, and it's no business of mine what other people do. Everyone's searching for happiness. Am I right or wrong? Is it any of my business if brother Husayn drinks day and night and can't see straight any more? If he chases women and falls over every ten seconds, what's that to do with me? He's enjoying himself and that's his business. So what does it matter to him if I make a marriage contract with a girl, or even a boy? I'm minding my own business. Looking for something to pass the time, to make me happy. True or false, my brothers?"

Adnan's laughter rang out again. Husayn noticed Midhat listening intently to this long-winded chatter. Rather than feeling angry, he thought the whole situation was ridiculous. Abu Shakir was always like this when he'd had too much arak, not able to give a serious answer.

"What do you mean by something to make you happy?" asked Midhat.

Abu Shakir picked up his glass and drank from it slowly. "It's like I said just now, brother. Something to make me happy. What I need. What I want deep down inside. What's on my mind. You see, sir?"

"A beautiful boy, of course! A handsome youth!" shouted Husayn. They all laughed. "But for your information, Abu Shakir," Husayn went on, "I've never fallen over in the street. Why do you make up these stories about me?"

"Brother Husayn, I've seen you with my own eyes." He pointed to his dark glasses.

"Ah! With those eagle eyes?" shouted Husayn. "That settles it then."

In the brief silence that followed, he was invaded by the image of that strange girl who had appeared in the street in front of him out of nowhere. Brown-skinned with black hair and dark eyes, she had been no more than twenty years old. He had followed her into a shop. She had been dressed in white brocade and had a couple of women with her. When he saw her he'd been tired after a long day's work and a boring get-together with colleagues, and felt hungry and uncertain what to do next. And he had found in her young face with its strange allure an indescribable peace. He would have liked to contemplate it forever, drown in the sea of those bewitching eyes for all eternity. He had got close to her several times, but she had moved away again. He'd been able to tell from her accent that she wasn't Kuwaiti. Her full lips were accentuated with dark lipstick and her black hair fell heavily on her shoulders and hung down her back. He had wanted to touch her. Those delicate brown fingers, kohl-rimmed eyes, the movements of her head. This longing had seemed out of the ordinary to him, despite his craving for sex. His attraction to her had stemmed from something more profound than a desire for a few minutes of pleasure. She had seemed like an embodiment of his highest feelings towards women, an encounter with his sweetest dreams about love. Then when he was almost touching her, he had caught sight of his reflection in a big mirror: pale, unshaven, sallow and lost-looking, and had been shocked at the sudden appearance of this specter in front of him.

Abu Nazim started talking again: "I said to them, where am I going to get food for you, you bastards? They said to me, if you want us to die of hunger, fine. If not, get hold of some food for us. What a mess! There were five ordinary policemen and me, the newly commissioned officer in charge. It's an old story, mind you. Could have been twenty years ago. No, fifteen or sixteen maybe. I told them to come with me. We were in the desert, and it was a week since any food had reached us from Samarra. We were marching in the desert, fully armed. I sat and thought for a long time. How could I get hold of some food for them? They were capable of anything if they were starving. In the distance I saw a cloud of dust, a big cloud of sand coming towards us. I ordered them to halt and said, 'You wait there, I'm going on ahead.' I knew what the cloud of dust was: a flock of sheep. When it was in my sights, I fired and hit the first sheep. It fell at once. The herdsman—some bedouin— came towards me, signaling with his cloak and yelling, 'Friend! Friend!' Bastard. I told them to fire a few shots in the air. And sure enough, that made him wrap his cloak around him and run. What else could we have done. We took one or two sheep and left the rest. The point is . . ."

When Husayn had recovered from the shock of seeing himself in the mirror, she had gone. He had run after her in a state of agitation and tripped and fallen flat in the shop's narrow doorway. He'd never seen her again.

"Why are you so quiet, Husayn?" Midhat asked.

He roused himself from his reverie. In the small, smoke-filled room people were hardly talking.

"Would you like another quarter of arak?"

"No thanks, Midhat. I've had my fair share today. But you have a drink. Do you want a beer?"

He called Uwanis without waiting for an answer. Adnan was drinking slowly with two empty beer bottles in front of him. He noticed Abu Shakir watching him and didn't pay any attention. He knew Abu Shakir couldn't hurt a fly, but all the same he had not relished his reference to his daughters.

"I met a bear cracking nuts, I killed the bear and ate the nuts," bellowed Abu Shakir suddenly, breaking the silence.

Abu Nazim turned to him: "What's that, Abu Shakir?"

"A tongue-twister, Abu Nazim. Can you say it quickly?"

He repeated, dragging out the words, "I met—a bear—cracking nuts. See? I killed the bear—and ate the nuts. Do you see how it goes, my brothers?"

Adnan roared with laughter: "I'd like to see you killing a bear!"

"It's a tongue-twister, I told you. I didn't kill a bear. I didn't even see a bear. The point is, can you recite it fast? I met a bear . . ."

Adnan interrupted him, planting himself in front of him, tall, his shirt open to reveal his chest. "I . . ." He stopped for a moment. He looked as if he enjoyed saying that word. He pushed his hair out of his eyes. "I, sir, can lead you to the bear's den. Would you like to know where it is?"

Abu Shakir and Abu Nazim were watching him with a mixture of bewilderment and curiosity, while Midhat looked at him out of the corner of his eye.

"Do you know where the bear is, sir?" demanded Adnan. He made a vague expansive gesture with his arm. "Over there. In Bab al-Muazzam."

"Don't let's talk about politics," said Abu Nazim. "We don't want anything to do with that kind of bear."

"Is he talking about the president?" asked Abu Shakir anxiously.

"I don't know," replied Abu Nazim. "Didn't you understand? Has your brain stopped working?"

Adnan continued to stand there stiffly, waving his arms, his face covered in sweat and an odd smile on his face. "That bear, sir. That's the one we have to kill."

"When the lion gets old, the jackals mock him," murmured Abu Shakir.

"What?" roared Adnan. "We're not jackals, sir. Don't you know who you're talking to?"

"Sorry, sorry. I was talking about myself. Nothing to do with you."

"What's wrong with you? We're defending honorable citizens like you. And you ought to stand up for your rights. Yours and mine. They're the same. What's wrong with you?"

"Nothing's wrong with me. But you can't expect miracles from an old donkey. That's all."

"Don't talk like that, my friend. You don't represent the people. We . . ."

"We? Who are you, anyway?" interrupted Abu Nazim all of a sudden.

Adnan brought his arm slowly down to his side. "Who are we?" His eyes narrowed, and he looked as if he was about to launch into a speech. Then he made a disparaging face and turned away. "You'll be hearing about us soon."

With a sharp, sidelong glance at Midhat, he vanished behind the curtain into the front shop.

They sat in silence after he had gone. They heard him settling up with Uwanis and going out into the street. He'd never spoken to them like this before: sarcastically, but stupidly too, acting as if he knew a secret which no one else knew. Midhat lit a cigarette and took a long swig of beer.

"Do you know this lad, Husayn?" asked Abu Nazim.

Husayn nodded. The heat was getting on his nerves and affecting him more than Adnan had.

Abu Nazim turned to Abu Shakir. "See, they know him. He's nothing to do with us."

"Yes, right. D'you know what the time is, Abu Nazim?"

"Ten thirty-five. Let's go."

"Yes, right."

In unison they emptied their glasses, stood up, muttered their farewells and left, all of this done quickly and quietly.

Husayn wiped the sweat from his face and neck. Midhat was smoking in silence, apparently unaffected by the amount he had drunk. Husayn himself was not pleased at the way things had turned out and the words that had been spoken. He had initially felt stimulated, but then the usual euphoria hadn't followed. He'd drunk his accustomed amount but it hadn't made his head spin or taken his cares away. His damned bad luck! He picked up his glass and found it was empty and quickly put it down again. He wanted to say something sincere and meaningful to Midhat, something central to his life and his past. There was a heavy silence between them.

"I'm sorry, Midhat," he said. "I thought we'd be able to sit quietly for a while and have a talk."

"It doesn't matter. Another time."

"Let's hope so."

"This guy Adnan," Midhat exhaled smoke from his nose and mouth simultaneously, "what type of person is he? Does he have contacts—or is it something else?"

"No. I don't think so. Why?"

"He says odd things."

"It's all rubbish. Kids' talk. Things he's heard."

"Maybe. But they must have had some basis this time."

"Meaning what?"

Midhat extinguished his cigarette. "I don't know exactly. There's definitely something in the air. It seems our friend Karim Qasim won't survive until this time next year."

"What do you mean? Is there really some connection between the things Adnan says and the future of the president? That would be too much."

Midhat waved his hand vaguely and didn't answer. He took a drink. It crossed Husayn's mind to order another arak. There was an oppressive silence again.

"Look, Midhat," he said. "I want to tell you something. I don't know how I got into this situation. Don't say I'm drunk. I'm not. But nothing's clear in my mind. I'm like a stone thrown from a mountaintop. Perhaps I always will be. How did it happen? I mean, does there have to be a hidden reason for all this?"

Midhat was looking at him with interest. "Are you content, Husayn?"

"What does that mean? I don't have any plans, or a future. But I'm content in a way, maybe, because I don't want to do anything else with my life. I don't have the patience, my dear Midhat. The people in my life or, I should say, the people who've got out of it, must be thanking God. What's a person doing in this world if he doesn't have any character or powers of perseverance?" He noticed Midhat smiling and went on. "I've tried different things, that's true. I've had experiences, as you say. I've wreaked havoc, gone hungry, slept rough. Lots of people have humiliated me. I've felt degraded and—lots of things. But do you know, Midhat, I don't remember a thing when I get up in the morning. What should I make of that?"

"What's the matter? Why are you talking like this, Husayn?" Midhat was making fun of him.

"You're right," agreed Husayn. "It's not the time for such a conversation. You talk. Tell me how you get on with them all."

"Who?"

"How do you get on with Munira? She's an excellent girl."

"Meaning?"

"Really. Pretty and intelligent. Perfect."

"Drop it, Husayn, please. I don't want to think about it."

"Why? Do you have any choice? If only life was always like that. We'd all be in Paradise."

"Anyway," Midhat looked at his watch. "Time to go. It's late, and I've got to go to work tomorrow."

Husayn nodded and called Uwanis. Midhat paid for their drinks, and they stood up and went out. The street was empty and the breeze was almost cool. They walked a few paces towards Bab al-Sharqi. Husayn suddenly felt dizzy. His head hurt and his guts heaved. He stopped and leaned against the wall.

"What's wrong, Husayn? Don't you feel well?" asked Midhat anxiously. He put an arm round his shoulders.

"No, no, it's nothing," answered Husayn quickly. "It's just the effect of the cold air." He pressed a hand to his stomach, then raised it to wipe the cold sweat from his face. He felt a slight tremor in his body. These were the signs of imminent collapse, like the powdery dust that falls shortly before a roof caves in. He walked on slowly. Midhat was close beside him. "You know, Midhat, maybe on a night like this, I'll fall down on the pavement for the last time. I don't know when it'll be. Tomorrow or in two years' time. But I don't think I'll die any other way."

Midhat took his arm and squeezed it hard. "Do you think that's a heroic way to die?" he said roughly. "Like a dog. A mangy dog." A sudden harshness came into his voice. "Why do you want to live in this unnatural way, Husayn? Why do you think about death, instead of life? Or instead of going into a clinic and getting yourself cured? Why do you have to be a drunk and die on the pavement?" He let go of his arm and pushed it away with some violence. "I want you to tell me one thing. I don't care about you just because you're my sister's husband. Maybe it's because you're my friend. Maybe. I want to know why you're so feeble, why you give in so easily. I'm not talking about strength of will or love of life. I've no interest in such chat. But perseverance, Husayn. Determination. You don't need to pretend your life has meaning. Life no longer has any meaning for us these days. But how can you bow to circumstances in this humiliating way? Why do you do it, Husayn?"

Husayn didn't answer, didn't look in his direction. He continued walking disconsolately along beside him. He understood what he was saying perfectly. He always did. He was hungry, nauseous, weak. Out of the corner of his eye he saw Midhat light a cigarette and blow smoke into the air.

"Goodbye," he heard him saying. The sound of his footsteps resounded in Husayn's ears as he walked off, taking another road back home. Husayn turned to look and could make out the shape of him and the glowing tip of his cigarette. He was hurrying, swinging his arms jerkily. Husayn didn't hate him; he just hadn't known how to answer him, that was all. The evening had been a failure, anyhow. So that Midhat wouldn't think he harbored any malice towards him, he decided to visit him the next day or the day after.

Chapter Five

The janitor came to turn out the lights in Midhat's office shortly before he left, then locked the door firmly after him. Midhat went along the dark, empty corridor. There was nobody around. He went out into the wide, bright square. The sun was gentle and the weather warm. He couldn't see his father. He must have gone home before him. He hadn't phoned. Or maybe he had, when Midhat was out of the office. He wouldn't buy newspapers today or books. Mutanabbi Street. A long street when you were hungry. He wasn't going to buy newspapers and books at all this week. A temporary period of abstinence. The town bus. A queue of faceless people waiting. He wouldn't be home before four today. He walked on and turned into Amin Street. The sun was pleasantly warm on his back and neck. He crossed the square where Amin Street met Jumhuriya Street, and kept going. Ghazi Street. Kifah Street. Crowds everywhere. Featureless faces. People running and shoving, using their shoulders and hands. Like kids. He squashed himself into the front seat of an old taxi. The heat of the engine and the stink of the driver's feet. God, what a stink! He blocked his nose with the tip of his forefinger. When he still couldn't stand the smell, he held his breath several times. A few minutes and he'd be there. Nothing comes to an end if we focus on it too much. What a terrible smell! Then suddenly he saw it. First it was just the shining eyes. It was lying in the middle of the sunny street on the black crumbling tarmac: a decrepit old dog of no identifiable color. Its black eyes pulsated with a strange light, like nothing he'd ever seen before. Two liquid lumps of black crying out for help. The body was shattered, the blood still not dry on it, and it showed no signs of life. But the eyes kept shining, fighting for the animal's last breath, pitying it in its suffering. The driver had noticed it at the same time and swerved towards the pavement to avoid running it over; then, cursing and swearing, he had swung the vehicle violently back on course. When they reached the crossroads of Kifah Street and Kilani Street, Midhat got out beside the café, inhaling the fresh air. He walked slowly. The dog's eyes appeared in front of him once or twice, the final gutterings of a candle. He found the door of the house ajar, went in, and walked down the long passage. It was almost four o'clock. His mother spoke to him from the kitchen the moment she heard his footsteps in the courtyard. He went up to his room and lay down on the bed. An old dog crossing the street gets knocked down by a car. A dog is walking slowly and a speeding car hits it. The dog crosses the street, then suddenly its back is broken and it's left to suffer, to watch itself die without a word, a cry, a shout for help, only the moist, lively eyes to express itself with in the middle of the street in front of everyone. He heard his mother calling. The twilight of life is unlikely to pass without suffering. A dog is squashed crossing the street, its limbs scattered here and there, then along comes the dustcart to pick up the pieces with the rest of the rubbish. Another dog goes by and into the slaughterhouse, and another and another. A chorus of black eyes singing of suffering, saying farewell to life. His mother was calling insistently. He went down to her. She asked where his father was, raising her white face to look at him. He gestured to indicate that he had no idea. Had he telephoned him? He hadn't.

104

Did Midhat want to eat alone? Why not? He washed his hands and face to remove the dirt and dust of the street. And what of the dust of the images and memories implanted in his heart? The suffering in the streets. The suffering of dogs. But he mustn't mix unconnected subjects. His personal life was based on non-negotiable principles: honest self-esteem, controlled egoism. And therefore no agitation before a meal or during it, and, preferably, not after it either. Give me raisins soaked in water, my heart is worn out with love. The lover should not forget to fortify his heart. What about us, we who want to live a full life, without restrictions? We pilfer avidly and consume what doesn't belong to us. What's the point of all the fuss about private property? We come from dust, and to dust we return. So everything belongs to us. We belong to it and it to us. Anyone who objects to this philosophy lacks judgment and intelligence, and should be told so. But what's the point of statements? Action. Action. We loot and steal out of conviction. This is the age of honorable thieves, and we represent them because we understand their thinking. We're their successors from necessity, so let's cheat one another faithfully. Give up anarchy and concentrate on controlled egoism. Let it be your point of departure, your base. Keep going straight round all the bends. Be an infidel, but a pious, devout one. What's the point of cheating, swindling, and fraud, if it's not to keep to the law?

His mother was sitting to one side, slightly behind him. In front of him was a meal of spinach and fried eggs, rice, salad, and bread. She was on his left hand side, slightly behind him. He could see the dark mass of her if he twisted his face round as he chewed his food, or if he sat back slightly in his chair.

"Who came to see you? What did they want? Why didn't your father phone you?"

That was how the authorities and the law operated. They didn't sit directly behind you, but to one side. Behind you, but to the side. He turned to her. Her white face, framed by the black scarf, formed a complete circle, and he noticed the wrinkles under her eyes, on her cheeks, and around her mouth as she asked about everything in an anxious manner. Spinach, rice, fried eggs, and salad. The salad, then the rice and spinach and a bit of bread. What about the eyes of dogs and sweethearts? To hell with them. We eat therefore we are. Food for all. Let's stuff ourselves. Let's die of overeating, my brothers. Forget about everything else. Food for all. Beware of other things. Books and the like. Close the bookshops, gentlemen, and let's open more restaurants! Kebab restaurants especially, if you want to know what I think. He heard his father's footsteps, then he came in smiling in spite of his hunger and exhaustion. What a hero! He stands up, sits down, comes, and goes. Explanations and elucidations. Explanations of the elucidations, and elucidations of the explanations. Phone calls which didn't happen, and others which happened in the mind. Then, as he turned to go into the kitchen, he whispered to Midhat, "I was in the café with Hajji Muhammad. I got a nice set of prayer beads out of him. Don't tell your mother."

She was coming with the food. Another batch of explanations as to why he'd come home late, along with what amounted to an orderly retreat and a more profound gloss, backed up by quotes from the Quran and the Prophetic tradition.

What people normally did—Midhat left his parents and went off across the courtyard—was to adopt a certain attitude to the world, maneuvering, retreating, negotiating, retreating again, then advancing a little. Towards a goal, naturally. Midhat climbed the stairs slowly. He should adopt an attitude to his world. Now. However you interpreted that, being honest it meant dealing with the present. That was all you had to play with, to make something of. He was walking along the big gallery. The past was over. Let that be understood. Over. What was known as the future was only the present in the process of being constructed. As soon as that was understood, life could begin. Then the possibilities for change emerged, with all their constraints, constraints which science and philosophy helped you to recognize and overcome if possible. It was worth considering.

He went into his room and began undressing, then stood in front of the mirror in his vest and pants. Thick hair, narrow chest, shining eyes. This was the world. Its beginning and end. He should take advantage of all that humanity had thought down the ages to help him live the best life possible. He was the center of the world. Nothing was demanded of him, no gift or talent extracted from him. Nobody approached the fortified castle. He was happy to be left to himself, with no commitments, no worries, empty of mind and spirit, jumping joyfully over the rocks on his desert island.

He put on his pajamas and lay down on the bed. The dying dog was still on the tarred surface of the street, and he was lying in the dust beside it. Together they watched the cars rushing towards them to crush the dog's bloody remains. Knowing that you're dying. That it's really you. Then someone says to you, "Forget the joke and let's begin again, since death's only a dream. Let's begin again."

Each person is in a certain position regarding the world. Now, at this moment. I realize that. And this includes me. I have four hundred dinars in the bank, a checkbook, a civil service job. I'm twenty-seven years old and have a sex drive which shows no sign of abating. I don't ask too many questions or demonstrate unjustified doubt or concern over what should and shouldn't be.

The family? It was based on weak foundations, but luckily it was close-knit and determined to stay that way: the best conditions for escaping its oppressive hold, without fuss or emotional confrontations. You had to free yourself by disappearing from their world, slipping out unscathed. Paid leave to study? Study with paid leave? It didn't make any difference. The main thing was to put them, the family, where you wanted them, and they could help you stay where you were.

He looked around at the small bookcase with its carelessly arranged books, the sparse furniture, the rug on the floor, the white unpainted walls, and faded, unironed curtains, and felt a pang of remorse, which astonished him. He heard nothing in the moments before he fell soundly asleep, and felt sad.

At the beginning of a long road that looked familiar to him, he met someone and the two of them agreed that it was a European road outside a city. He wanted to demonstrate to this person that he knew its name in different languages—autoroute, autostrada, motorway—but his shabbily-dressed companion kept repeating that there were a lot of dogs in the area. He was waiting for him to finish speaking so that he could ask him in English, "Why did we come here if the dogs die in the road here too?" Then he saw that the man understood what he wanted to say. The man made a helpless gesture and went to sit down on a park bench, so he sat next to him. He was heavy-hearted, and an overwhelming desire to cry took hold of him. He turned to his companion and found he was looking at him. The eyes of the dying dog shedding silent tears.

The room was dark, except for the faint light coming in through the window. Traces of tears in his heart and water rolling down from one eye. He breathed rapidly. What a joke human beings were! The noise of the family below sounded as if it came from another world. He sat up in bed, wiping his eyes and nose. Here he was crying in his sleep about things he knew nothing of, obscure symbols, yet there were plenty who would not even shed a tear over their own mother and father!

He got up and turned on the light. His figure in the mirror, pajamas unbuttoned to reveal his white underclothes. Human form distorted in a mirror. The title of a picture. He went out of the room, and the cool breeze caressed his face gently. He made for the sink nearby, washed and dried his face, and took several deep breaths. Abd al-Karim's room was empty. He was always out. Broadening his horizons, as they say. Drink, political gossip, and whores. They were busy preparing dinner, and there were still streaks of light in the sky. A clatter in the kitchen, and people calling from upstairs to downstairs and vice versa. The celebrations of the table. He heard light footsteps. Sana came up and squeezed herself in close to him.

"Uncle, we've just seen Dad. He was walking along smoking a cigarette and coughing. Me and Bibi. He didn't see us."

Husayn, that stupid chancer. What insane reason had brought him back to Iraq? Sana rushed off. His father came out of his room and went towards the stairs. The cries grew louder and more insistent, demanding dinner instantly. A forced commotion, an artificial celebration, a failed marriage, children, drunkenness, confusion, a non-future. Negation of the future, of time. Those courageous, happy-go-lucky people, drunks and beggars, who chose these goals! Could they achieve them without a struggle, without suffering? Husayn would be sure to visit him.

He was walking in the long narrow part of the gallery away from their rooms, in the darkness. He usually came to this part of the house after the evening meal to be alone for a while. They hurried off to watch television, Madiha and her two daughters, his Aunt Safiya and his grandmother, once they'd finished washing the dishes, and they closed the door of Madiha's room behind them. His mother was the last to come out of the kitchen and go upstairs. Her shoulders were slightly bowed, and she walked slowly. She passed the room she shared with his father and put her head round the door of his room, where the light blazed. He called out to her from his distant spot on the other side of the house, and she turned towards him. "Is that you?" she asked anxiously.

"When will your troubles be over, you poor woman?" he wondered.

She opened the door of Madiha's room, and their voices could be heard, mingling with the sounds of the television. It was not unpleasantly cold. The floor of the gallery was uneven, and the sky and the walls around him were silent and black. The light was pouring out of the half-open door of his room, splitting the darkness before burying itself in the leaves of the olive tree. He caught sight of his father through the dark glass of his bedroom window, sitting in bed reading and telling his prayer beads. A tranquil life sentence. His father, and before him his mother, were the ones he had to break all emotional ties with. An interest in others and their world, God, destiny, was counterproductive. Such topics were surrounded by gratuitous questions, including thinking a great deal about the origins of existence and the past and future of mankind. Although there were situations when this sort of idle speculation could bring you fame and wealth, in which case it wasn't such a waste of time. Then you could con whomever you chose, since you would be within your rights to do so.

The cold caught him on the back of the neck, and he rubbed the spot a few times. If you kept looking hard at the sky, a few little stars appeared shining brightly. Distant and solitary, they did not exist unless you could see them. What linked them—he in the belly of the darkness on the west side of the courtyard in their house in Bab al-Shaykh, and this little trembling star on the outer edge of the universe—was solitude, isolation, detachment from the world. This was the nearest to the truth you could get; it was not alienation or separation. It was to be at the center of the world, with nobody behind or in front of you, nothing preceding or succeeding you, to have your own laws which nobody but you could apply. I have nothing to do with the beggars and the unemployed who sell their principles, and sometimes even buy them, for a morsel of bread. The world begins and ends with me; I have to take my own spatial and temporal limits as my starting-point. This is not a sickness, but a healthy egotism. Rational, orderly. The world is mine at any price. Being on your own, being an individual means you go into the world cautiously and absorb it, consume it incessantly, provided that you do not become part of it, as this might stop you achieving your aims. Strong people behave in this way. Strong in the new sense of the word. They are not stupid or vicious, over-curious or easily embarrassed. They lie sincerely and are not shackled by morals or families or deep emotional attachments. There is nothing to stop them enjoying the good things of the world, which others have created with the sweat of their brows.

Everything is mine, and there is no shame involved.

He saw his aunt and grandmother coming out of the room where the television was. They had passed through life, nothing more. They would never be able to say that they had known it. He resumed his walking. Clearly, he wasn't going to end up like them. As soon as he had reached a definite conclusion, he would get going. So his journey that summer would be confined to gathering the information which he needed to realize his very first project.

Being on your own in the world gave you the best chance of a full life. And that meant leaving behind these surroundings which were impoverished in every way. He looked at the high wall of their house, built of small stones and clay, almost indistinguishable from the darkness, despite the stars in the sky. This was his worn out, uneasy, cheap world with its narrow-minded traditions and idiotic morality. A world of secret pleasure and acceptable crime. A world where everything was permitted behind closed doors. A world of cowards. His mother came out. He saw her looking towards his room, then turning to the place where he was standing. A world of blind, lachrymose sentiments. She went into his aunt's room. Individualism precluded anger and irritation. If you were a healthy egoist you didn't get psychological illnesses. You could make judgments with steady nerves and a clear mind, without hatred or resentment, even condemning people to death and destroying their world.

He stood at the balustrade feeling that he had discovered something which could be useful to him. The yard was dark and the sky above it very black, shining with stars. The wooden pillars in the big gallery, which supported the roof, looked spindly and on the point of collapse. Would he ever be able to leave these ruins behind? They were kneaded with his blood. Ruins of stone and humanity. A series of muffled knocks could be heard at the outer door. But they could become a deadly prison if he decided to stay there all his life. Added to which, this sort of attachment to places and people, as well as being intellectually unacceptable, represented an embarrassing obstacle on the path to being alone in the vast, rich world outside. And then there were women, too, those lethal toys.

The knocking persisted. Who would think of visiting them at this time of night? He looked at his watch. Past eleven-thirty. He went to his aunt's room. The women's voices, merging into one another, were incomprehensible. When he opened the door, they looked at him in fear and perplexity. His mother stood up without a word and followed him downstairs. As they reached the end of the passage the knocking grew more rapid and insistent, and he began to feel anxious himself.

His brother Abd al-Karim rushed in as if he had been propelled over the doorstep by an outside force. He didn't speak to either of them and hurried away up the passage. His mother went after him while Midhat fastened the big door and followed them in. His brother didn't seem to be himself, but that didn't do anything to dispel the annoyance he was feeling. These lost children of the night were stupid by nature. And here were he and his mother following their own spoiled nocturnal child without protesting at his lack of concern for their feelings. He heard his mother saying something which he couldn't make out, and didn't reply. He continued to feel annoyed with Abd al-Karim and, although he was worried about him, decided to leave him to his own devices. He went into his room and lay down on the bed. Suddenly he heard his mother shouting his name. He lay rooted to the spot, his heart in his mouth, then jumped up and ran into the next room. There he saw them, his mother and brother clinging together in the glare of the light, screaming at one another. Abd al-Karim had a mad look in his eyes. As he demanded to know what was wrong, he noticed the blood on his brother's trousers. For a moment he was afraid that he had been seriously wounded. Pulling his mother aside, he knelt down beside him, examining him all over. Between her screams his mother managed to articulate a few breathless words: "He's not hurt. It's not him. It's Fuad. His friend Fuad."

Abd al-Karim was waving his arms about involuntarily with a lost expression which upset Midhat suddenly. He took hold of his brother's arms, trying to calm him down, and was talking gently to him when his father burst in on them like a whirlwind.

"What's wrong with my son?" he shouted. He would have fallen on top of Karim if Midhat hadn't caught him. He regained his balance quickly and took Abd al-Karim in his arms and began rocking him to and fro and kissing him. Then Madiha came in wailing, still half asleep. Midhat stood a little apart from the general commotion. He was reassured by the fact that his brother wasn't wounded and watched them in silence. The unholy family experiencing the delirium of shared emotion. They had inherited celebrations of grief, festivals of lamentation. Down the ages, these had been the distinguishing features of their continuing trivial and sterile existence. And with their children—their livers walking the earth, as someone once wrote—these foolish elements would persist forever.

He was lying in bed peacefully. They had all gone to bed a short time before and the crisis appeared to be over, although he could still hear his brother moaning quietly from time to time. He had told them that his friend Fuad had died after being hit by a speeding car. His tone had been curiously disjointed, his face pale. Somehow Midhat had the feeling that it had not been a simple accident, and his brother's relationship with the world had hit rock bottom.

———

Good. Peace. Justice. God. All mere words. It's pointless trying to define them. In real life they don't have any serious meaning. Who am I, or more accurately what am I? What's the real world? What's the soul? What's knowledge? What's thought? Insoluble problems and unanswerable questions, because any attempt to put them in the context of real life is doomed to failure. So who raises these problems in the first place, if they don't come into existence by themselves? It's the intellectuals, or people who call themselves intellectuals, the people who employ their minds for the sake of others, instead of others, most of the time without being directly invited. They're curious in one way or another, and more often than not they're people with no job to distract them from thinking.

In his office that morning, with the raindrops beating hesitantly on the windows, Husayn sat listening to him, his bronze face somber and empty, his cigarette dying between his fingers as he looked at him with surprise and some degree of admiration. Midhat didn't know why he was talking like this, or for whose benefit.

A person has a beginning; this is when he becomes deliberately conscious of life. He does this on his own. His end is death, which is personal in the extreme. Between this uncertain beginning and sudden ending, within this very specific time period, something complex and mysterious comes into being. This is what is sometimes known as the life of the individual. Individual. But even when he repeated this word several times, Husayn didn't respond. He extinguished his cigarette and lit another, and looked uncomfortable, as if he couldn't settle. Nobody had interrupted them, and Midhat didn't know why he himself had also begun to feel uneasy while he was talking.

Husayn had arrived about an hour before. He had developed the habit of coming to his office over the past few weeks. He sat calmly in a corner, once he had asked after Abd al-Karim, and told him that there were brief showers every now and then and it was pleasant outside, then began drinking his tea with assurance and obvious relish. Midhat was temporarily distracted by some papers in front of him, but he wanted to ask Husayn where he got his self-assurance and equanimity. As it turned out, he forgot and began talking about ideas that he considered his personal secrets. First he wanted to tell him briefly about his projects which were the sort of projects anyone had, but the anxiety which appeared on Husayn's face and the exaggerated interest he showed, although it kindled Midhat's enthusiasm, annoyed him at the same time. It seemed forced, although this only made Midhat want to talk more.

The time passed. They chain-smoked, the tips of their cigarettes glowing fiercely, to the accompaniment of sudden short sharp downpours. Husayn fidgeted in his chair as if he was sitting on nails: "Look, Midhat, this is a dangerous premise. Where's it going to lead us, this extreme egotism? I mean, if everyone thought like that it would be a problem. Wouldn't it?"

His hand holding his cigarette remained frozen halfway to his mouth. Midhat answered him in the negative and Husayn's hand moved on, he sucked on the stub, then the smoke burst from his lips like a sigh.

"These ideas aren't for everybody," said Midhat. "What's the point of doing other people's thinking for them? They're for a certain type of person, with clearly defined attributes and abilities. Such ideas exist separately from the world, history, evolution. Those are all circumstances, decor to round off the picture."

Husayn's expression changed. His eyes were red as he coughed and stubbed out his cigarette. "That's impossible, irresponsible," he said. "We live in this society and it provides us with basic services. We should work to preserve it, too. Do you mean we should just think of ourselves? That would be cheating."

Before embarking on the subject of cheating, we should define the society we belong to. Generalizing won't achieve anything. This is Iraq in 1962. An unstable society with no future; a society on the edge of the abyss; a society of indigestion, stupidity, fear, hatred, hypocrisy; where you eat when your stomach's full, don't know what's going on in the world, can't avoid sexual complexes, and are obsessed with poverty. It's a society which has no relationship with its true members and offers you nothing in exchange for the stupid conditions it imposes, because in fact it's not a society but a period of time. That's why talking of cheating in your dealings with it doesn't make sense. There's no cheating involved when you're trying to save yourself.

He found himself shouting angrily: "Look, Husayn, I'm not interested in this rotten society. I don't want to belong to it. I'm attached to it by chance, and I'm not the first or the last."

Husayn was looking at him with trepidation. It occurred to Midhat that Husayn had perhaps reached similar conclusions when he'd given up his home and job and gone off the rails. A vague idea, close to his own, could have formed in the depths of Husayn's mind and pushed him towards this semi-suicidal way of life.

He watched him holding his cigarette in his grubby, trembling fingers and lighting it. Perhaps Husayn had judged the world before him, condemned it and was now working hard to turn his life into a lament for mankind. All things considered, was Husayn not his mad twin? His double who had been formed by the same ideas, but then lacked the will, the determination, the sharpness of vision to put them into practice, and so had abandoned everything and let himself be carried along by the current, a bloated body floating on the surface of the water?

He had an exhausted look, as if the life was draining out of him: prominent cheekbones, dark sunburned complexion, black circles under his eyes and this blank expression in them every now and then, devoid of any reflection of the world around him.

The janitor came in with a pile of papers and files and Husayn asked him for a tea. When they were alone again he turned to Midhat: "These ideas of yours, Midhat. They're very individualistic. They're rebellious or revolutionary up to a point, but they're completely egotistical. They don't have a future. I mean, they don't have a place in the societies of the future. You know, socialism and that kind of thing. What do you want out of life, Midhat? What kind of plans are these? They won't achieve a change for the better. Don't you agree?"

Midhat looked at him in silence. He didn't think the question needed an answer. Then he said that he didn't want to be considered a rebel. What was the point of that? Apart from the fact that it would hinder his plans, it involved confrontation and struggle, and he had a horror of all that. He wanted to achieve his goal by advancing like a snake with deft, silent twists and turns, and in the maximum possible security. He definitely had no illusions about being a rebel. This spurious word did nobody any good and he'd never been able to bear it. The moralities of the time didn't stand in the way of selfishness, exploitation, enjoyment at another person's expense or getting rich by any means but, in reality, none of this appealed to him. He wasn't temperamentally inclined to commit crimes for the sake of having it all. But you only had one life and you shouldn't waste it, so you had to organize it, and as far as possible ensure that it was easy, pleasant and full.

Husayn was sipping his tea and smoking avidly. A beam of white sunlight fell on his face. He didn't appear to be listening to him and Midhat saw a mysterious look of happiness spread over his features as he looked surreptitiously out of the window at the bright sunshine. He put his glass carefully down in front of him and stubbed out his cigarette, his normal prelude to leaving.

"I'd like to talk to you, Midhat," he said. "Come and have a drink one day. We could spend an evening together. I'd like to hear what else you have to say. Will you come?" He had a sudden fit of coughing and turned red in the face. He pulled out his kaffiyeh and began wiping his eyes, nose, and mouth. "Sometimes it helps to talk," he went on, once he'd recovered. "I don't know why. It's soothing." Midhat smiled at him. "Of course most of the time it's just chatting into the small hours. All the same, try to come one evening, Midhat, won't you?"

"Does talking really help you, Husayn?" asked Midhat.

Husayn was about to get to his feet but he checked himself and looked oddly down at the ground for a few moments. Then he leapt up energetically. "Yes, why not?" he said, buttoning his jacket, "I'm someone who benefits from an honest conversation."

"How, Abu Suha?"

As he walked slowly towards the door, he turned round. Uncertainty showed on his face and then for a moment Midhat saw his eyes gleam and his lips curve. "You know. And now, instead of dying on the pavement and annoying people, I'm going home to die in my bed."

His crooked mouth parted in a smile expressing a mixture of confidence and embarrassment. He raised his hand in farewell, opened the door, and vanished.

———

Midhat was sitting with his father on the wooden bench in the corner of the yard, listening to him talk. After lunch they had had a short nap in the small basement room, then woken up around four and were waiting for someone to bring them tea. The sky was pale blue, still bathed in sunlight. His father was talking about his life. He had begun with his childhood and still had plenty of memories left.

"My father, God rest him, loved company. His social evenings were never ending. Friends, drink, women, cards. Life after death didn't interest him, God rest his soul. He was very handsome. Tall, dignified, large eyes, an elegant moustache." He paused and began telling his prayer beads more quickly. "I remember once," he paused again, staring into space, "I was fourteen, perhaps less, and my father hadn't been home for two nights. We were completely dependent on him. I was at home with my mother, God rest her, and your Aunt Safiya and my grandmother. My poor mother was almost out of her mind with worry, but she didn't complain. On the third day my grandmother got hold of me and said, 'You must go and see what's happened to your father. He's in the Naqib's orchard.' I wondered how I would get there. It seemed miles away to me at the time and I was still a young boy, not used to going out of the house after sunset. Anyway, my grandmother hired a carriage belonging to someone she knew and entrusted him with the task of taking me and bringing me back."

Nuriya called from the first floor.

Her husband looked up at her: "What?"

"Tea's ready. Come up and drink it in the alcove. There's nobody to bring it down. I'm staying here in case Karumi wants anything."

He nodded and turned back to Midhat.

"Where were we? Ah, yes. The carriage owner turned out to be an honest chap and delivered me and waited for me, as promised. I was very scared when we got there. It was late afternoon in spring. The sun was low in the sky and the thickly growing trees in the orchard made it hard to see where you were going. I walked for a quarter of an hour like a lost sheep until in the end a black man jumped out of the shadows and shouted, 'What are you doing here?' Dammit, I've never been so scared in my life as I was of that black man. I swallowed hard and said, 'Please, Uncle, I'm Sayyid Ismail's son. My family sent me to look for him.' He towered over me, his eyes like burning coals. 'Stay where you are and don't move,' he said and vanished. I stood shivering like a drenched sparrow, afraid to move my little finger. They didn't keep me waiting long. I heard footsteps and caught a glimpse of my father's shirt among the branches. He emerged in front of me and stopped when he saw me. I was speechless. He was so tall, God rest him. His shirt was undone, his hair fell on to his forehead and his eyes were red, but looked as if they were outlined in kohl. 'Razzaq!' he shouted to me. 'Why are you here?' He leaned against a tree trunk. I was dazzled by the sight of him. 'My grandmother was worried about you, Baba,' I said. 'She says how are you.'

"He began to laugh. The sun's rays were falling on the orange tree above his head, making him look as if he had a halo like an angel. He put his hand in his pocket and before he said anything, I saw the flutter of a red dress between the trees, and a woman appeared at my father's shoulder."

They heard Nuriya calling again. Midhat looked up and saw her looking down at them from behind the wooden balustrade. She gestured that they should come up, but didn't speak.

119

"All right, we're coming," answered Razzaq Abu Midhat, continuing to finger his beads. "You pour the tea and we'll be there."

He lowered his voice. "Fair-skinned she was, amazingly fair-skinned, and plump, with long black hair which was tied back and hung down to her waist. You'd think she was a beauty from the court of Harun al-Rashid. Outstandingly beautiful, glory be to the great Creator! She rested against my father's shoulder and said, 'I want to see your son, Sayyid. Is he as handsome as you?' Her voice—I remember it well—it had a musical note, a sweetness. My father, God rest him, put his arms round her and handed me his wristwatch. 'Go home now, Razzaq,' he said to me. 'Take this watch as a sign to your mother. Tell her I'm fine. Really fine.'"

He said nothing for a few moments. His fingers played with the prayer beads and on his lined face there was a touch of the wonder he must have felt all those years ago.

"It was spring," he whispered. "The woman's name was Rihana. She was a singer. People said she was in love with my father and used to sing some songs about him. She was famous in those days, glory be to the Creator! Come on, let's go and have our tea before it gets cold."

Midhat liked this story and the way his father told it. He was going to ask him how he felt about this woman, and what happened between her and his grandfather afterwards, when the big door facing them squeaked and slowly opened. Munira's face appeared round it, framed by her black *abaya*. Despite signs of tiredness she looked radiant and had a good color in her cheeks. She smiled a greeting at them, and Midhat noticed her mother behind her. His father stopped and turned to welcome them. Nuriya, standing at the balustrade, called to them all to come up to the first floor, obviously glad to see her sister and Munira, who replied enthusiastically to her from the middle of the courtyard. He noticed Munira looking at him once or twice and felt slightly embarrassed that he was in his pajamas. He waited for them to go ahead of him up the stairs. She wasn't wearing make-up, and her and his aunt's clothes had traces of dust on them. Finally they moved towards the stairs and he followed them. Munira must have made an effort to finish up her work at the school in Baquba as quickly as possible. He walked slowly behind them and left them to go and sit in the alcove while he went to his room to change. When he came out, his sister Madiha was passing the door smiling, and he fell in behind her. They were drinking tea and his mother was telling them about Abd al-Karim's illness. He sat down next to his father, facing Munira, and took a glass of tea.

"How's your sister Maliha?" his father asked Munira.

"Fine, Uncle."

Her voice was soft. He looked up at her. She hadn't pushed her *abaya* back off her shoulder, and the only sign of make-up he could see on her face was that thin line of kohl round her eyes.

"I've lost count of how many children she has now," went on his father. "Is it six or seven?"

Her lips parted in a slight smile. "Three boys and three girls, Uncle."

"God bless her. That's right, she was young when she got married." He turned to Nuriya. "Nuriya, how old was Maliha when she married?"

"Maliha? Very young. Fifteen maybe. But God save her, she was a big, strong girl."

Munira's mother nodded her head in agreement: "She was just about fifteen."

He heard Munira asking Madiha in a low voice about her daughters and Husayn. His mother was pouring the tea into the glasses in front of her, whispering with Munira's mother. The shimmering blue of the sky had faded and all that remained on the high wall were the violet reflections of the setting sun. He watched Munira take a glass of tea from his mother and thank her. Her *abaya* had slid gently off her shoulders, revealing her blue dress, her neck, and the swell of her breasts. She looked towards him. The light fell on the right side of her face making her eyes a luminous brownish gold. Her nose, cheeks, chin, and lips were firm and delicately curved. They didn't say a word to each other. The voices around him became indistinct murmurs, then silence descended.

This was broken by his mother, launching into a new conversation about Abd al-Karim and his illness. Munira listened attentively, an anxious look on her face, and asked questions about the nature of the illness, its causes, what the doctor had said. Then she wanted to see him. His mother got up quickly and dragged them along behind her. Munira was tender with Abd al-Karim, kind, soft-spoken. He seemed to revive temporarily, then kept putting a hand to his forehead and wiping the sweat off it. Convinced they were a burden to him, they got up and went out. They were on their way to Aunt Safiya's room when Munira's mother remembered their suitcase. Munira looked perplexed for a moment, then her features relaxed and she hurried towards the stairs.

"Where are you going, Munira?" Midhat asked.

"I won't be a minute," she answered without pausing. "I left the case in the passage."

He followed her. She was two or three meters away from him. Slim. Tall in her heels. She turned round. "You don't need to come with me, Midhat. The case isn't heavy."

"Don't worry. I want to stretch my legs a bit."

They went cautiously down the stairs and out into the yard. In the pale light he could see part of her left cheek and forehead and eye and delicate nose. She pulled her *abaya* round her, and her shoulder and upper back became more clearly visible. He went ahead of her, switched on the light, and opened the wooden door into the passage. The case was propped in a dark corner. When he lifted it up and felt how heavy it was, he laughed. "Come on! Do you call this suitcase light? Were you really going to carry it yourself?"

She was standing holding the door. She laughed briefly and didn't reply, then switched off the light in the passage. Her silence pleased him and he trudged off, aware of her walking beside him, lagging behind a little, her heels gently tapping the paving stones in the yard. He turned to her when he reached the dark stairwell and discovered she had taken off her *abaya* and was carrying it. Thick tresses of hair fell loose on her thin shoulders. She stopped beside him. He couldn't make out her features clearly.

"Is it too heavy?" she asked.

"No. But it's better if you go up the stairs ahead of me."

"Isn't there a light?"

"No."

She went past him and climbed the stairs swiftly. He followed with heavy steps, trying to fight an overwhelming feeling of exhaustion. She waited at the top of the stairs, looking worried. "Leave it here, Midhat. Please."

He put it down by the wall, then they walked along side by side.

"Is that all your things?"

"No. But we thought we'd get settled first."

"So you're going to move to Baghdad, are you?"

She was looking at the ground as she walked. "I hope so. I've written to my brother Mustafa to see if he can organize something with the Ministry of Education. He knows people there."

When they reached the door of his room he stopped, and she kept walking. "Excuse me," she said, and went off towards Aunt Safiya's room, where the noise was coming from.

Beyond the black, dilapidated walls the sky was unruffled and clear. He watched her walk away, her dark blonde hair falling in disarray on her shoulders and back. Her slim hips swayed as she moved. Her legs weren't quite straight, and he fancied that a slight weariness, an invisible spiritual weariness, was affecting her walk.

He went into his room and sat on the edge of the bed. He hadn't seen her for months, since shortly before they went to Baquba. She had been more cheerful then, more open. Perhaps that depressing town had affected her morale. He felt a numbness in his right arm and began rubbing it. The room was fairly hot, and dark apart from the remains of the daylight coming in from outside. He heard the sound of rapid footsteps, then saw his mother going past the door towards the east side of the house where Aunt Safiya's room was. He rubbed the pins and needles in his wrist again. He felt calm and satisfied. However, it occurred to him that Munira staying with them meant he'd have to adopt a certain attitude towards her and, before that, to get to know where they stood in relation to one another. His memories did not provide him with any image of her which he could use as a basis for his future conduct. It was as if she had come into existence shortly before sunset that same day!

He noticed a shadowy figure standing silently on the gallery just to the left of his door. It was his brother Abd al-Karim, and he was looking over in the direction of the noise, leaning against the balustrade, his shoulders bowed. Midhat's heart filled with pity for him. He looked so tired, as if his strength had drained away. What would become of him?

He heard one of his nieces calling Abd al-Karim: "Uncle, Uncle. We're going up on to the terrace. Bibi said we're going up on to the terrace today." Then he saw Suha come running up to him. "Uncle. We're going to sleep up on the terrace today. All of us. You'll come too, Uncle, won't you?"

Abd al-Karim reached out a hand to stroke her hair. "That's nice. Where are you going to sleep?"

She looked up at him. "With Mum and Sana, under the mosquito net. It's going to be lovely, Uncle."

He went on stroking her hair for a few moments without saying anything. Then she turned and ran off round the gallery to the other side of the house, and Abd al-Karim walked slowly back into his room.

Calm prevailed in the house, broken only by the twittering of birds coming from the trees in the little garden. The last of the sunlight had faded from the room, and faint shadows remained. They wouldn't be quiet for long; the noise of dinner being prepared would shortly fill the house. He had no desire to get up; he was aware, in this newcomer, of a mysterious, magical presence, beyond the boundaries of himself.

———

He and his father were having lunch in silence, and his mother was sitting with them in the small, cool basement room. He wanted to tell her that he had seen a girl who looked like Munira when he was coming back from the office at midday. She had been crossing the street and at first he had thought it was Munira's graceful walk and figure. Then after the meal, as he and his father lay down for an afternoon nap, it struck him that this wasn't the first time: a few days before he'd thought Munira was talking to him on the phone, when it had actually been a wrong number.

He tossed and turned on the bed under the ceiling fan and did not fall asleep until the noise had started up in the big adjoining basement room and it was almost four-thirty. He woke with a thick head and sat up in bed. He was alone and it was almost completely dark in the room. He rubbed his eyes irritably. They were all upstairs. He heard his mother calling and his sister answering her, then the two little girls running from one part of the house to another. He got up slowly and went to the basin. The cold water revived him a little and he splashed his face again and rubbed it. It wasn't all that hot although it was the end of July. Perhaps this summer would pass with a minimum of really hot days.

He went rapidly up the stairs and caught a glimpse of her going into Abd al-Karim's room as he reached the big gallery. She was carrying two glasses of tea. His pace slackened. The north walls were still tinged red by the sun's rays, and his father was sitting cross-legged on a sofa in the alcove, peacefully drinking his tea. Midhat went into his room and shut the door behind him. He took off his pajamas and put on a shirt and trousers. He heard her talking to his brother in the room next door. "I don't know why, but it's true you know, tea helps you cool down."

He made some reply and she laughed. It seemed to Midhat that her laughter had a special note in it, a concealed joy. Abd al-Karim spoke again, then there was a brief silence broken by Munira saying, "What do you mean?"

Midhat went out of his room and put his head round his brother's door: "Good evening."

She was smiling radiantly, her eyes shining, as she sat on a low chair next to Abd al-Karim's bed, leaning forward slightly with a glass of tea in her hands. She turned to look at him, and he was dazzled by this image of her, before she said a word: wide hazel eyes, dark blonde hair, and smiling mouth. "Good evening."

The narrow opening of her purple blouse was framed by her high, firm breasts. He asked his brother how he was. He also looked relaxed. Midhat wanted to leave, but that might have been taken to mean he acknowledged their right to be alone together, so he sat on the edge of the bed facing her. She had her knees pressed together, and she straightened up and sat back in her seat.

"Thank you very much for the books," she said to him. "I don't know how . . ." She turned briefly to Abd al-Karim. "You see, I helped myself to them without asking you. Sorry." She talked gently, without gestures, looking straight at Midhat now.

"I bought them with you in mind," said Midhat.

"Thanks," she said quickly.

"So do they help to pass the time?"

"Definitely." She looked back at his brother. "You know, Karim reads some of them. It's not only me." She smiled her broad smile. "I've got plenty of time. But you ought to be studying, Karim. The exams will soon be here."

"That's not true, Munira," replied Abd al-Karim. "I only read novels when I'm having a break. Don't interfere. It's my way of relaxing."

"It's tiring to read all the time, Karim," said Midhat. "And you're not strong enough."

"They're light, entertaining stories. It's not tiring at all. On the contrary." He turned to Munira. "But Munira wants all the books to herself. She doesn't want to share them."

They laughed.

"Did you go to the university, Karim?" asked Midhat.

"Yesterday."

"So you got the timetable?"

"No. They said it'd be out next week." He put his glass on the floor beside him. "The place is in a mess these days. I don't know why. There are all sorts of rumors."

"Such as?"

"They say there isn't going to be a second round of exams this year, or that the students are going on strike during the exams or at the beginning of the academic year. I don't know what the problem is."

"Why would they go on strike?"

"I don't know. They say the strikes are going to be different this time."

"Who says?"

"Lots of people. Apart from the president's supporters, of course."

"Let me tell you, in our current situation, nothing will shift Abd al-Karim Qasim except force. That man's got so much blood on his hands, it's all he understands. It's true he's let things get away from him, but force is the only thing which will work. Strikes, my foot!"

"But look, Midhat," said Munira. "If these strikes spread and there's an agreement . . . I mean, if an anti-Qasim front comes into existence, everything might be possible. You know, the government is very weak outside Baghdad. I mean, in Baquba they curse Qasim openly."

"That reminds me, Munira," said Midhat. "Has anything happened about your transfer to Baghdad?"

The shadows had lengthened in the small, stuffy room, but her face still had a light in it somehow.

"No, not really," she said, looking a little dejected. "My brother Mustafa can't come to Baghdad at the moment. He's thinking of taking some leave at the end of this month. In a couple of weeks, ten days' time."

"What if you don't get your transfer?"

Her face darkened and she was silent, then she began gathering up the tea glasses. "I don't know at all. Let's hope for the best."

Her white skirt fitted closely round her full hips. He followed her with his eyes for a moment as she went out carrying the tea tray, and felt as if the room was empty of light when she'd gone. He stood up, switched on the lamp, watched the ceiling fan revolving, and asked his brother, "How do you feel when you study, Karim? Does it make you light-headed to read a lot?"

"Sometimes."

"That's anemia. You're not eating the right food. Rice and broth every day. That's not enough for someone who's ill. I must talk to Mother and ask her to vary the food a bit."

"Vary it? That's all she knows how to cook. But maybe I should take some kind of tonic, at least during the exams."

"Yes, you should. Your body's healthy and strong. But certain events have affected you psychologically. You should make a note of this and not let it happen again."

"What events? Nothing ever happens in our life."

"You mean nothing major. Don't jump to conclusions. That's not what I meant. Sometimes trivial events can have a violent psychological effect, shake people up, I mean."

Abd al-Karim's face seemed to turn even paler, and the blank look intensified as he wiped the sweat off his forehead and neck.

"Nothing like that happens in our lives. Nothing. Our lives are like dust, without taste or color."

He was irritated by his brother's words. "Look, Abd al-Karim," he said, relaxing his guard. "Your health went downhill after Fuad's death. You must understand that. Understand the reason."

Abd al-Karim didn't appear to be listening to him. He went on wiping his sweat away with slow, deliberate movements. "Is there really something to understand?" he said at last. "Is there any logic to these things? And," he paused, "what's the use of realizing that the death of the person you were closest to has no connection to your life? What's the point? Just to convince yourself that life is a series of mechanical gestures? That there's no difference between the death of a human being and an animal?"

The words came out softly, apathetically from his barely open mouth. It had never occurred to Midhat that Abd al-Karim could express himself like this. In the space of a moment, as he looked at him, he felt shocked by his brother: his illness, his despair, the bitterness of his words. He was gazing through the window at some distant spot.

"What do you mean?" Midhat asked him worriedly. "Do you think the world ought to stop because someone's died?"

Abd al-Karim turned calmly towards him with an innocent expression in his eyes. "Why not?"

"Don't act clever with me, Karim. Nobody's denying these things are hard, but that's life. Who told you life should be comfortable and happy? But you have to understand when it's time to save yourself. That's the important thing. Save yourself."

"Like animals, you mean?"

"What? And why do you despise animals so much anyway? What do we gain from being superior to them?"

"I don't know," he answered in his subdued voice. "I don't want to defend mankind. I don't have anything to say in their defense." A pained look came over his face. "But I feel I'm not equipped for life. Maybe I'm exaggerating, but I don't think I could take the death of someone like Fuad again. I just couldn't bear it."

His hands were quiet still while he spoke, his eyes anxious, lighting up for a moment, then going dead.

"Is there any point in being so gloomy?" Midhat asked him. "Why do you insist on living in the past?"

Karim sighed deeply. "I don't want to live in the past. I don't want to remember it or explain it. I have no desire to understand something that's incomprehensible. You don't need to tell me that." He turned suddenly to face Midhat. "But, you see, Midhat, I feel something pulling me back all the time, back to be with Fuad, even just for five minutes, to say one word to him. It's true it doesn't make sense, I realize, but I can't get over this feeling. I must have done wrong to him, committed a crime against him, but what?"

He wasn't really asking himself the question. On the contrary, Midhat had the impression that his brother had a secret which he wanted to forget about. He watched him cover his eyes with his left hand and press it against his cheekbones. His black hair was carefully combed and shone under the electric light. Midhat couldn't think of anything to say to him. He had the nagging feeling that there was some important aspect of the whole affair which didn't ring true, but also he wanted to be sympathetic, tell him it was all just a passing cloud and that his youth and vitality would ensure that everything would be sorted out in time. He put a hand on his shoulder. "Why do you torment yourself like this, Karim?"

Karim remained with his head bent, saying nothing. Midhat squeezed his shoulder. Karim took his hand away from his face and looked straight in front of him, then his eyes lit up. Munira was leaning against the doorjamb watching them. The fact that she'd come back, and was standing there unabashedly, astonished Midhat. She had the usual thin line of kohl round her eyes, her hair was up, and she was still wearing the purple blouse.

"Sorry. I was going to tell you—my aunt went shopping an hour ago, and hasn't come back yet. I don't know—we're a bit worried about her."

"Where did she go?" He took his hand off his brother's shoulder.

"I don't know. Maybe to buy bread and vegetables." She was looking with concern at Karim.

"How many times have I told her not to make these stupid excursions?" muttered Midhat irritably.

He left the room hurriedly, and as he passed her a sweet smell filled his nostrils. Then when he was walking along the dimly lit big gallery, he saw her going into his brother's room again. He stumbled as he went downstairs. The yard was in shadow, and the murmuring of sparrows in the branches of the olive trees filled it with ghosts. When he was at the end of the long passage, he heard the voices of his mother and Sana and could just see them as they closed the outside door. He called to them and switched on the light in the passage, reproaching them for going out in the first place, and then being so late back. They didn't reply and carried calmly on walking with their bags and packages. He followed them inside, feeling increasingly depressed. Munira was still in his brother's room. He went into his own room without a sound and sat on the bed, soothed by the darkness around him. Suddenly voices could be heard all round the house once more, and lights were switched on. It was time for the dinner ceremony again. The two next door were talking, although he couldn't make out what they were saying. He felt tired all of a sudden and didn't want to listen to them any more. It seemed to affect him personally. He put his head in his hands. He was anxious and had the vague feeling he was in an uncomfortable situation, as if he had been caught unawares in an invisible net. He began walking about in the darkness. They were still talking. He slipped out of his room and made for the television room. The kitchen light shone on the paving stones in the courtyard. The sky was pale, empty of stars. He kept on going, past his aunt's room, and quickly climbed the unsurfaced stairs up to the roof terrace.

The great expanse of the sky opened before him. He noticed a star or two right on the horizon. The air was clear, and there wasn't a soul on the roof apart from him at this melancholy hour. He sat down on one of the beds, glad to be left to himself to ponder. He would never let problems build up around him without at least being aware of them.

That he must guarantee to himself. Adopting a strategy for living had to involve taking account of the difficulties and obstacles which might stand in its way. The vital thing was to understand the nature of these obstacles and their range of influence. He stood up and walked slowly around. The red had disappeared in the far west and left behind it dark ashy purple, and the walls hid their misery in the darkness.

He stopped by a bed in the corner of the terrace. He could call the problem by its name: Munira. There was nothing preventing him. He smiled. This bed was where she slept. But as a problem she was harder to pin down. And what did she represent, apart from sexual and emotional attraction, beyond this world of solitude and loneliness and boredom?

They were shouting at one another down below, and the smell of burnt fat wafted up to him. It was no secret that she attracted him, and he didn't feel himself resisting. It wasn't every day you found a pretty girl, and there was some mutual attraction between you and her! Someone called him from the yard. But what about the way she and Karim were always talking together? The stars had multiplied in a colorless sky, and the white bedcovers looked like tents in the desert. He kept his distance, and perhaps this was the position which suited him best. But she had begun to take shape in front of him, a clearly defined person whom he couldn't do without. For the first time, she had become an individual.

They kept calling him. He didn't feel like answering. Suddenly he had the urge to stay there in the dark and silence away from the world's demands: without people, plans or projects, free from the eternal, anonymous fear.

———

Just before he reached the house, he heard the mosque clock chiming its soft mellow chimes. The alley was deserted, enveloped in shadow. He opened the door as the clock began to chime again and went slowly and cautiously along the narrow passage. He stumbled a little way along, then forgot the final dip in the ground and lost his footing again, bumping against the big wooden door leading into the yard. He stopped right up against it. The light from the yard filtered through its broad cracks. He peered through them but couldn't see anything, so he gave the door a hefty push and went in. The light was on in the big gallery on the first floor, hanging directly over the chair where his brother Abd al-Karim was sitting. Midhat looked at his watch but couldn't make out the position of the hands. He took a few steps forward, then stopped again. The wooden pillars supporting the roof from the gallery cast shadows on the high walls, and the branches of the olive tree had withdrawn into themselves. He was fascinated by these alternating segments of light and shadow surrounding him in the yard and spun round twice like a giant windmill. The giants of Don Quixote. The giants of Bab al-Shaykh.

He heard someone calling him. "Midhat. When did you get back?" His aunt was leaning on the wooden balustrade outside her room.

"What's this, Aunt?" he called back. "Why are you still up?" He spoke slowly and deliberately, slurring his words slightly.

"How can you ask such a thing, Midhat? I haven't slept a wink. The night seems endless."

"Why don't you end, you wicked night?"

"What?"

"I hope you get to sleep soon, Aunt. Can I do anything for you?"

"I pray you never have to do a tyrant's bidding, son. But I'd like a bottle of water from the fridge. I'm on fire, and I haven't eaten a thing."

"God is great! Why didn't you have dinner, Aunt?"

"God only knows. I couldn't eat a thing. Bless you, go and have a look for me. Maybe there's a bit of watermelon I could have with some pastries."

"At your service."

He took a swig from the bottle of ice and water, then carried it and a slice of melon back upstairs. As he crossed the yard he was entranced once again by the palette of light and shade, like the columns of a ruined Roman temple. He noticed his aunt watching him as he spun round in a circle again, and raised the bottle to her.

He hailed his brother from the top of the stairs, then went off along the small gallery towards his aunt's room. She was sitting on her bed with her hands in her lap. The big windows were all open, and the distant light illuminated the edges of the room.

"Are you all alone, Aunt?"

She opened her arms resignedly and didn't answer.

"Where's Bibi?"

"She's gone up on to the roof. She couldn't stand the heat, my dear. Where are the water and melon?"

He stepped inside the room and an invisible blast of heat hit him. He put his burden down on the floor in front of her and waited hesitantly. She filled a glass with water and drank it, then said quickly, "Sit down, Midhat. Why are you standing? What's the time now?"

"I don't know, Aunt. Past midnight probably. So have they all gone up to the terrace?"

"All of them, my dear, all of them. Except your brother, who hasn't taken his eyes off his book for the past four hours. It breaks my heart to see him, but I daren't say anything."

She seized the sliver of melon in her fingertips, broke off a piece, put it in her mouth, and began chewing it with gusto. It pleased him to see her enjoying her food like this.

"Why are you standing, Midhat dear?" she said again, ferreting around in an ancient paper bag. "There's a slight breeze getting up now. That should revive us."

He wanted to exchange a few words of banter with her, then leave, but she started talking again.

"Immediately after you went, we heard Munira had got her transfer to Baghdad. You probably hadn't even reached the end of the street."

"What did you say, Aunt?"

"Didn't I tell you to sit down?" she answered, munching a pastry. "There's a nice cool breeze now. Munira's been transferred to Baghdad. To a school in Haidarkhana, they say."

"Who says? Who brought the news?"

"Adnan. Maliha's son. You'd just left when he knocked at the door, wanting to see Munira. Sana was the one who told me."

He suddenly felt slightly agitated. He drew up a chair and sat down. "Adnan? What's he got to do with it?"

She looked up at him. "Midhat, dear, why does it matter to you? In a few days everyone will be going about their business again."

Her eyes were sharp in spite of the wrinkles round them. It vexed him that he didn't understand the strangely muddled set of circumstances she was referring to.

She repeated slowly, "The message went to Baquba. To the school where she used to work. And he brought it immediately to Baghdad."

She seemed to take pleasure in pronouncing these words softly and gently.

"Then what?" he said abruptly.

She ignored him and concentrated on cutting up the pastry and stuffing it into her mouth. She seemed to have completely forgotten he existed.

He raised his voice. "Yes, and then what?"

"That's all. Her mother said they'd have to look for somewhere to live and move out of here." Her jaws moved continuously. "Why shouldn't she? Her daughter's a teacher with a salary, and she's not married. I didn't have her luck. God have mercy on all those who made me suffer. God have mercy on them. They need it. They left me to sit and stare at the walls. Every time a nice boy approached them they said he wasn't good enough. As if they were the only ones with no flaws and the right background. I pray God has his revenge on them. They don't deserve any mercy."

She plunged her fingers into the remains of the melon and seized hold of a large red morsel which she kept in her hand for a few moments. The faint light fell on her face, leaving the rest of her in darkness. In spite of her wrinkles there was a harmony in her features, lingering traces of beauty.

She sighed. "There's no point thinking about it. What's done is done. But you be careful, son."

"What's wrong with you today, Aunt? You don't seem to be yourself."

"Was I ever myself? Our life's just a mess." She drank a mouthful of water. "Look, Midhat. You're sensible. I don't want you to tell them I told you this. It was Sana, poor little thing, she came to me trembling like a leaf, her face the color of turmeric. She said, 'Auntie, he pulled Munira by the arms, then he started shouting and threw a piece of paper at her.'"

He felt his emotions flaring up again, and his heart beat faster. "Who? What do you mean? Who are you talking about, Aunt?"

"I'm talking about Adnan, my dear. I told you he came after you'd gone out. He was bringing her a message. They said it was about her transfer, I don't know. But why did they fight, Midhat? Why don't they go and fight in their own homes? What's it got to do with us? Poor little Sana was scared stiff. She'd done nothing wrong."

"Why were they fighting? What about? What's his relationship with her?"

"He's her nephew, dear."

He leapt out of his chair. "I know, I know. But what does he want from her?"

"How would I know, son? I've already told you he heard the news and came flying to Baghdad in his father's car. It's all right for some. A car and no work to do. All right for some. What's it to you, anyway? You haven't told me where you come into it."

"What's wrong with you today, Auntie? Who said it was anything to do with me?"

She looked at him in openmouthed disbelief. "What do you mean? What are you so bothered about then?"

"That's not fair. It's all the same to me. Why should I care?"

Her face lit up. "God have mercy on your ancestors and all deceased followers of the Prophet everywhere. You've reassured me tonight, my dear. God bless you!"

He wanted to go, but hesitated. He was tense and felt as if he was being suffocated. "What about Munira? Didn't she say anything?"

She waved her arm in an expansive gesture. "Nothing at all. Silent as the tomb."

"And my father? Did he know about it?"

"What's it to do with him? Who'd tell him?"

"You mean someone like that idiot can walk in here, act outrageously to people, and then leave without anybody teaching him a lesson?"

"Don't talk like that, Midhat. Haven't we just asked for God's mercy on all the pious, dead and alive? Nobody knows about this except Sana, and she came and told me in secret, poor little thing. May God protect our secret. God preserve you. Praise be to God. But now I must tell you . . ."

"Don't worry, Aunt. Your secret's safe with me. But doesn't your conscience trouble you?"

"Of course it does. What do you think? Who wouldn't be troubled by such behavior? But didn't we just say it's got nothing to do with us, son?"

He was uneasy, but felt he had reached a dead end with his aunt. "Okay, Aunt. You're right. God will judge him."

"Yes, but how?"

"God will judge him," said Midhat, on his way out of the room.

As the cool breeze touched his face, he heard her saying, "May God give His people some sense."

Karim wasn't sitting on the gallery any longer, but Midhat heard the pages turning in his room. He took off his clothes, which were damp with sweat, and put on a thin pair of pajamas. His head and stomach felt slightly heavy. He had eaten too many nuts and chick peas that evening. He looked in on Karim and asked him how his studying was going, and Karim muttered something inaudible. Midhat went off to wash his face, hands, and feet. The cold water invigorated him. As he climbed the stairs to the roof, he heard the Bab al-Shaykh clock chiming gently and deliberately. He didn't count the chimes, just heard them, and when he left the darkness of the stairs and his eyes were lost in a sky crowded with pale stars, the clock began to chime melodiously again. He breathed deeply. The cool air worked a strange magic, inflating his chest with life. His eyes took time to adjust to the darkness on the terrace, and the white beds looked like night birds perching there. He walked quietly over to his bed and sat down on it. There were random snores from all around the roof, but this did not mar the silence of the night. He looked over to where her bed was, but couldn't make it out.

His feelings were confused. The story his aunt had told him had made him angry, and he was annoyed by this damned stupid idea of their moving to another house. He lay down on the bed and closed his eyes, and his head spun. Too bad. With the cool air and rest it would pass. There was something strange in what Sana had reported to his aunt, something not right. What was Adnan's reason for coming to have an argument with Munira here? What was there between them? Perhaps there hadn't really been a fight, but he had just happened to insult her in passing. But why? His tension returned. He opened his eyes, and they were filled with the dancing stars. And in their house too, without caring who heard or saw. What if he had jumped out at Adnan from nowhere and punched him, savagely, with deadly calm? He would have been proud to do it, and she would have collapsed into his arms. He sighed contentedly at this image. But things had been very different, if Sana was telling the truth. What was strange about her story was that it had no logical explanation. It should be cut out of the tape, then burnt, and anyone who inquired should be told that the censor had cut it because it went against the truth. But the punch would be left in and replayed many times. His eyelids drooped and the stars were extinguished. The punch would be replayed many times, by popular demand. Many times . . .

He sat up in bed, his mouth dry, his throat burning. He looked around him, then got out of bed and walked unsteadily over to the water pitcher by the railing, rubbing his eyes and adjusting his pajamas. Everyone was asleep at this uncertain hour of the night. He reached the pitcher and picked up the earthenware mug covering it. The moon in the east had a chip out of it, like a damaged plate, and shone in a crystal sky. The first light of dawn rose and spread in a fine red veil, while the silent world around him turned silver blue. He stood immobile, holding the mug. The dark mass of her hair tumbled over the white pillow and part of her bare shoulder was visible over the edge of the bedcover. He was only a couple of paces away from her and the cool breeze ruffled the bedding. His mouth was dry again, and he bent to fill the mug with water then gulped down the cold, magic liquid greedily, so that it ran out of the corners of his mouth. He took a long, deep breath. The silence at this time of night was uncanny; even the sleepers held their breaths. A movement from her startled him, then he saw her suddenly sit up in bed and place her hands on the cover, looking at him. Her hair fell over her shoulders and upper arms, and her nightdress, blue or white or gray, revealed her neck and chest. He wasn't surprised that she was awake, but an incomprehensible sense of wonder took hold of him. As he peered more intently at her, he thought her eyes were shut, but a glimmer of moonlight reflected in them proved him wrong. They went on looking at each other.

"Water?" he whispered.

As soon as he said it, she sighed as if she thought he was a ghost. She covered her face with her hands, leaning forward slightly so that her hair hung down around her. He felt suddenly disturbed: in that position, she looked excessively thin to him. He bent and filled the cup with water, then took a step towards her and whispered again, "Would you like some water, Munira?"

She looked up quickly. Her features were clearly visible in the moonlit dawn. He thought her eyes looked blank, her lips slightly slack. Perhaps she would say something, but everything about her suggested she had neither seen nor heard him. Her skin looked pale, and her thick hair framed her face and fell on her shoulders and chest. He noticed the opening of her nightdress revealed the meeting place of her breasts. He felt anxious about standing so close to her, but stole another quick look at the beautiful swell of her breasts. She was sitting stock-still, with an air of bewilderment. He held out the pottery mug to her, sincerely hoping that she would take it and that would be the end of it. Her eyes looked larger in the shadows, and the bow shape of her lower lip almost round. She raised her arm slowly and took the mug, and their fingers touched gently. A magic touch of infinite tenderness. She raised the mug to her lips. He noticed the fine parting in her hair, partly covered by unruly strands, then she handed the mug back without a word. He paused in front of her for a moment, but she wasn't looking at him; she seemed to be in another world. He retreated and put the mug back in its place on top of the pitcher. She had lain back down again and pulled the cover over herself. He walked wearily over towards his bed and turned to look at her again. She was fast asleep, motionless. He sat on his bed. The dirt floor of the terrace was stained silver, and on the western horizon only a few faint stars remained. He had a sense of well-being, tinged with disquiet. She had seemed like a different person. He noticed the rapid beat of his heart subsiding gradually. Such encounters with her were too much for him, especially in this lost time between night and day, moonlight and dawn, when you couldn't predict what you might do next. Perhaps she had feared the worst, thought he was waking her at dawn to slip into bed with her. Just like that, without an invitation. One man attacking her in the afternoon and another completing the humiliation before the next day had dawned. A weak, defenseless girl whom they could abuse with impunity. He recoiled at the painful images. In the end she might leave them, move out of their house. Who could tell? Then the light footsteps, gentle laughter, whispers, smiles, and glances from those honey-colored, kohl-rimmed eyes would vanish from their daily life. He withdrew further into himself. She had become a part of his life, there was no denying it; although she kept her distance, he felt the invisible effects of her youthful spirit on him.

He lay on his bed. The sky was on fire in the east, extinguishing the brilliance of the moon and stars. The sparrows, far below in the yard, began singing the day's first songs. He heard the muezzin switch on the speaker and then the rasp of his fingers and heavy breathing against it. Midhat was not excessively perturbed and, as his eyelids closed, felt that soon he would be able to do something wonderful.

Chapter Six

Sana broke the white dish with red flowers on it while she was helping her mother wash up after lunch. Her mother yelled at her and clipped her round the head a couple of times. Shocked, Sana put up her hands to protect herself from her mother's blows.

"You stupid little girl," shouted her mother. "Don't put your hands on your hair when they're all greasy. Anyone would think those plates belonged to your father, the way you smash them all the time!" She clouted her across the shoulders and gave her a push, still shouting. Choking with tears, Sana stood back, holding her hands out in front of her to stop her dress getting wet. That was the first plate she'd broken; it had slipped out of her hands without warning. Her mother threw the pieces in the bin. "Clumsy little wretch," she shouted. "You should be more careful."

The sweat ran down Sana's face and the back of her neck. This was the first plate she had ever broken, and she said so to her mother.

"Get out of here, you bad girl," screamed her mother, coming at her to hit her again. "You're just like your father: you think I'm stupid. The first plate indeed! There are hardly any left in the house. Get away from me. Go upstairs. You're not having a siesta in the basement today. I don't care if you die of heat."

The sun burned Sana as she ran across the yard towards the stairs. Her grandmother was heading for the kitchen from the opposite direction. Sana hesitated for a moment. She felt like talking to her, but in the end she kept running, the tears trickling down her face. She hadn't broken anything before today. This was the first plate, and her mother knew that very well. She tripped and fell on the top step and started to sob again, then blew her nose, wiped her eyes on the edge of her dress, and ran along the gallery towards the room she shared with her mother and sister. Her right knee hurt. She heard her name being called and saw Umm Hasan gesturing to her through the open window of her bedroom, but she shook her head without replying and went into her own room. It was in semi-darkness and there was nobody there. They had all gone down to the basement to sleep on the soft mats in the cool breeze of the fan. She picked her doll up off the chair and lay down on the bed, holding her and stroking her bright yellow hair. Her heart was still pounding and her knee hurting, but she didn't feel hot. She sat up in bed and wiped her nose, then sat the doll in front of her and began talking to her. "Don't cry, Fadwa darling. Don't cry. Why are you crying, sweetheart?" She pulled the doll's dress down and wiped her nose. "How many times have I told you not to break things?" She waited in silence, as if expecting the doll to reply. "No, no. It was you. Who else could it have been? You bad girl. Don't cry. Why are you crying, Fadwa darling?"

She picked her up and held her close and began gently rocking her to and fro. "Go to sleep now. Go to sleep. Come along, let's go to sleep now." She lay down on the bed and put the doll beside her. It was very hot now. She could hear her mother and grandmother talking in the kitchen and tried to hear what they were saying, but did not understand a word. She wiped her face and smelt the grease on her hands.

"How many times have I told you to wash your hands?" she whispered. "It's so hot in here, sweetheart. Never mind. Go to sleep now." She fanned her face and the doll's with her hand. "Go to sleep, dear. Never mind about the heat. I'll tell your Auntie Suha to put the fan on. But where is she? Lying in the basement, eating ice cream, where do you think? Doesn't she think of her sister and say, 'Poor Sana. Poor thing up there in the bedroom all by herself in this boiling hot weather'? No she doesn't. Let's be like her! We'll eat ice cream in secret, and biscuits, shall we, dear?"

Her imaginings upset her and she hugged the doll tight, then began playing with her hair and torn clothes. She closed her eyes. "Tomorrow," she whispered, "we'll get ten fils from Uncle or Grandfather and buy ice cream or sweets. Why shouldn't we? We haven't got a father and our mother's always cross and hits us. Go to sleep, you naughty girl. How many plates and glasses have you broken? What can we do, dear? She ended up at the top of her class, but she's a bit cheeky. She's broken lots of plates, and she's scared of the rats that run along the ceiling."

Sana looked fearfully up at the dark wooden ceiling. The house was quiet. Then the clatter of wooden shoes across the courtyard reassured her. She kept her eyes pinned to the ceiling for a few minutes. The sweat was damp on her forehead and cheeks and around her mouth, and she felt dreadfully thirsty. She began patting the doll's back lightly.

"Don't be afraid, dear. There aren't any rats now. This isn't the time they come out. Everyone's asleep or eating ice cream and it's only Sana's head that's full of rats! Don't be frightened. Go to sleep. School starts soon and Dad will come to see us, and you'll be top of the class and we'll get ten fils to buy ice cream and chocolate and manna-from-Heaven sweets. Go to sleep, dear."

She heard her mother talking, but couldn't make out what she was saying. Her eyelids closed gently, and the monotonous thud of her fingers on the doll's back faded away.

———

Sana stood hesitantly in front of the little pond, examining her feet in their red leather clogs. Above her head in the luxuriant tangle of the olive branches, the sparrows feverishly sang their sunset song. She wanted to dip her toes in the water, just for a moment, then pull them out again quickly. The still surface reflected the light sky, crisscrossed by the twisted branches. She hadn't heard or seen her mother for some time now. She must be in the kitchen making supper. Sana looked up and saw her sister Suha standing on the small gallery holding the doll. Suddenly her mother came out of the kitchen, and then Sana heard someone knocking at the outside door.

"I'm going to take the doll on the roof with me," Suha called to Sana.

Sana saw her mother going over to the middle door. "Who's there?" she called down the passage, then turned to Sana. "Why are you standing there like a stone? Go and see who's at the door."

As Sana started to move, she called up to her sister, "She's my doll. Leave her alone. You can't take her on the roof."

She ran off along the dark passage. "Who's there?" she asked, before she opened the door.

The caller was standing to the left of the door with his back to the light. She thought she recognized him. "Yes, Uncle? Who are you looking for?"

He was tall and spoke in a fierce, rough voice. "Munira? Is she here?"

He was wearing a fine white shirt and dark trousers. She couldn't see his face clearly. She hesitated.

"What are you waiting for?" he shouted. "Go and call her. I've got her transfer here." He waved a piece of paper at her.

She backed away, then ran off inside, her heart pounding. She didn't know who he was, and this worried her. Her mother confronted her at the kitchen door: "Who is it?"

"A man looking for Auntie Munira."

"Who?"

"I don't know him, Mum. He says he's brought her transfer."

"Her transfer? What do you mean?"

Sana said nothing. She heard her sister calling, "Auntie Munira, Auntie Munira."

Her mother took a few steps along the passage and shouted, "Who's there?"

Then Munira appeared on the gallery, and Sana's mother looked up at her. "Munira, my dear. I don't know who's come to see you, but Sana says he's got your transfer."

"My transfer? The official document? Thank you, Madiha! That's such good news. It must be the school janitor, Husayn. Poor man, coming all the way from Baquba. Mother! Mother!" Munira turned and went back into her room.

"It's the official transfer, you silly girl. You wouldn't understand," said Sana's mother, and walked slowly back into the kitchen.

Sana stayed where she was, leaning against the wall, suddenly uneasy. This unknown man frightened her for no reason. She heard a movement in the gallery, then saw Munira heading for the stairs with a spring in her step. The sparrows were hopping about on the branches of the olive tree as darkness descended. Sana put her hand to her chest in the place where her heart was. Her grandmother came out of the kitchen.

"Why are you standing there, Sana dear?" she asked. "Come and give your mother some help."

Sana let her arm drop to her side and looked at the floor. She heard her mother from the kitchen: "No, Mum, please. Let me get on with my work in peace."

Her grandmother walked off, and Sana's mother said, "Go away, Sana. Go up and see what your sister's doing."

Munira was crossing the yard. She smiled at Sana and held out her hand. "Come with me, Sana," she whispered.

Sana smiled back and took her hand. "Okay, Auntie Munira."

Together they went down the gloomy passage. Munira's fingers were soft and cool, and Sana felt her anxiety diminishing slightly. When they reached the front door Munira pulled it open slowly, peering round it. "Yes? What is it?" she asked.

Sana wanted to see too, then she heard that rough, harsh voice. "It's me. Don't you recognize me? Were you expecting someone else?"

Munira stepped back so abruptly that she bumped into Sana and pushed her against the wall. Sana could feel that she was shaking, even when their bodies weren't touching. She heard her draw her breath in sharply and whisper a name which Sana couldn't pick up. She and Munira stood leaning against the door in silence.

"Where have you gone? Munira?" he called. "Why are you running away from me? Do you want to make me crazy?" He raised his voice. "Huh? Why? Do you want to get rid of me? Is that it? You move to Baghdad and Adnan can go and jump in the river, is that the idea?"

He pounded on the half-open door and they clung together, terrified. Sana found herself squashed between the door and the wall, her hands and feet ice-cold and her legs trembling, and felt Munira trying to squeeze further into the dark corner beside her. She was seized by a greater terror than she had ever experienced before, and as he began to kick the door repeatedly she was sure she was about to die. His hoarse voice rose disjointedly above the noise of his feet striking the door. "You won't get rid of me. I promise you. I can tear up a dozen documents like this one. It won't help you to escape from me. Nobody . . ."

Sana felt Munira steeling herself during this last speech, then she turned and gave the door a sudden hard shove, so it slammed shut, making a noise like an explosion; she pulled the latch across and leaned against it as the dust rose in the air around them. There was silence. Sana looked up at Munira. She was white, like a wax effigy, and was breathing loud, rasping breaths, her chest rising and falling.

"Open the door," they heard him say in a surprisingly unsure voice.

Sana stood pressed against the wall. She could feel the sweat running down beside her left eye. The long passage was in darkness, its walls black.

"Open it. Please, Munira. Please," came his voice again, low and despondent.

These whispered words scared Sana; she put her hand up cautiously to wipe her eyes and forehead, then looked at Munira. With her closed eyes and waxy face, she appeared unconscious. Sana summoned up her courage and took hold of her wrist. It was so cold, and she could feel her quivering at the touch of her fingers. Finally Munira drew her hand away, opened her eyes, and looked up in the air. The sky was spread out above the high walls of the passageway, a luminous pale blue with not a star in sight. They'd be making the beds on the roof by now! A faint, barely audible knocking started up on the door behind them. She noticed a piece of paper at their feet. White. Folded over several times. Munira had seen it at the same time. They looked at one another. The knocking stopped for a moment then began again, accompanied by indistinct murmurings. Munira signaled to her to pick up the paper. She bent down to get it and put it in Munira's outstretched hand. Munira's fingers closed round it, and she indicated with her eyes that Sana should go on ahead. She slipped reluctantly away from Munira's side, her shoulders slightly hunched, then felt Munira coming along behind her and turned round. Munira waved her on, putting a finger to her lips. The strangely subdued knocking continued. Once they got half way along the passage, Sana walked faster and was about to run ahead to open the middle door when Munira grabbed hold of her. Her eyes were full of affection. She embraced her silently and kissed her on the hair and forehead. She smelt nice, and her clothes and body were soft. A fresh breeze blew on Sana's face when they opened the door into the courtyard. She leaned against the wall and wiped the sweat off her face and neck. Munira walked quickly off towards the stairs. Sana was tired and thirsty. How that madman had scared her! She went dejectedly into the kitchen and found her grandmother sitting on a stool smoking peacefully.

"What's wrong, Sana?" she asked. "Why are you so pale?"

Sana didn't reply. She went on standing uneasily in front of her. Her grandmother blew smoke out of her nose and mouth. "Who was at the door?"

"I don't know, Bibi."

"What d'you mean, you don't know? Who was it, dear?"

Sana's mouth and throat were dry. "I'm thirsty, Bibi. Let me get a drink of water."

"Give me one, too."

She hurried to the fridge. The icy water revived her, and she took a glass to her grandmother who was standing turning over the rice on the hob, her cigarette hanging from her lips. She gave the cigarette to Sana to hold while she drank the water. As Sana took the glass back to the sink, she emptied the last few drops into her hand and moistened her face with them. Without saying anything more to her grandmother, she ran off upstairs. She heard a noise coming from the roof, but couldn't be bothered to go up there, and ran along the gallery to their room. She found it empty and dark; even the television was switched off, and she heard them calling her from Aunt Safiya's room. They were all there. Munira smiled at her, and Aunt Safiya welcomed her exuberantly.

"Sana, when are we going to eat?" asked Umm Hasan. "See if your mother's come down from the terrace, there's a good girl."

Before she could answer, Aunt Safiya shouted, "Let her have a rest, Umm Hasan. Come here, Sana dear. Take this bottle and fill it with cold water. Go on, dear. Are you thirsty, Umm Hasan?"

Munira's mother, cigarette in hand, was listening intently as her daughter whispered in her ear. Aunt Safiya handed Sana an empty bottle and she took it unenthusiastically. As she went out of the room, she heard Munira saying, "We're not going to Baquba any more."

———

Sana hurried along with Munira beside the high cement wall of the

Kilani mosque. The sun shone full on the narrow pavement. She didn't understand why they were in such a hurry. That morning just before breakfast, she'd heard Munira talking to her mother. "Madiha, is it all right if I take Sana with me to see the new school? It's supposed to be in Haidarkhana. Do you need her for anything?"

Then the two of them had hurried to get dressed and leave the house. Sana was over the moon! Suha had to stay and help her mother!

"Auntie Munira, I want to be like you when I grow up," she said as they crossed the street.

Munira looked beautiful and elegant to her: she wore sunglasses with her *abaya* and had a lovely smile. Munira didn't reply, and Sana accelerated to keep up with her.

Where Kilani Street crossed Kifah Street they turned off towards the bus stop. Under the hot, white sun they joined the crowd waiting for the bus. At this time of day Kifah Street was filled with the roar of speeding cars and people. Sana didn't recognize him at first and didn't hear him speaking to them, but then Munira returned his greeting and Sana shouted, "Uncle! Hello!"

The three of them stood together apart from the waiting crowd. Midhat stroked her hair, smiling at Munira. "Where are you off to so early in the morning? Going shopping?"

"No. Shopping indeed! I'm going to look at the school. I don't know where it is."

Munira seemed happy somehow. "I though we'd be there and back in no time," Sana heard her say. "Why's there such a hold-up?"

"It's like this every day. Didn't you know?" He looked into her face as he spoke. "I've been standing here for about a quarter of an hour. Three buses have gone by full."

He turned towards the street then seized Sana's arm suddenly and called to Munira, "Come on! That taxi's empty."

He went ahead of them and signaled to the taxi to stop, then opened the rear door for them. Sana jumped in and sat by the window. Munira followed, then her Uncle Midhat. Two other passengers took the two front seats. A gentle breeze blew, ruffling Sana's hair and letting her breathe. Delightedly she began observing the scenes in the busy street, the cars, and big buses. She hadn't been on an excursion like this for ages. The last time had been before the summer holidays, when she went with her mother and sister to buy new shoes for the Feast.

Midhat gave the driver some money and Munira looked at her. Sana smiled.

"Be careful of the door, Sana," said Munira.

"Yes, Auntie," said Sana, then went back to her determined contemplation of the street. She would tell her mother what she had seen, and Aunt Safiya and her sister Suha. She would describe everything she saw in detail. A big bus passed close to them sending a blast of air into her face, and she sat back in alarm. She had the impression that Midhat was resting his hand on Munira's.

"What's the school called?" she heard him asking.

"What did you say?" asked Munira.

"The school. What's its name?"

"Oh. Petra. Petra School."

He smiled. "As if there'd be a school with a name like that in Haidarkhana!"

"Are you serious?"

His smile broadened and he patted Munira's hand, which was hidden under her *abaya*. "No, no. I'm just joking. But . . ." He laced his hands round his knee. "Do you always have to go first thing in the morning?"

"Yes, of course. Once the term starts, I hope things will work out."

"Auntie Munira," said Sana. "Can I come with you to this school?"

"I don't see why not, dear. Except I'm afraid your mother might not like it. Perhaps she'd rather you went with her to her school."

"Do you like your Aunt Munira very much, Sana?" her uncle asked her.

Sana looked at him in surprise, then nodded hesitantly. "Yes, Uncle."

He half turned to look at Munira. "Everything's fine then. It seems we're both in the same camp."

"Yes, Uncle."

"So shall we draw up an agreement and present our demands?"

He was talking to her as if she wasn't there and looking almost directly at Munira. "What do you say, Sana? Do we have an agreement?"

Munira laughed and covered her face with her *abaya*. Sana was glad to see a big smile on her uncle's face, although he looked round with some embarrassment at the other passengers. The cars, people, shops flashed before her eyes. She had no idea when they would reach their destination and hoped it would be never, but a few minutes later she heard her uncle asking the driver to stop. Still smiling, he explained to Munira that his office was here and told her where they should get out. Then he said a quick goodbye and slammed the door behind him. Munira sat watching the route attentively, all traces of joy gone from her face. The car had not traveled on much further when she said to the driver, "Here. Can we get out here, please."

Sana moved quickly from her place at a nod from Munira, and the two of them stood at the side of the road. They still had to walk a short distance before they reached the school, so they crossed the street and hurried along without a word. After a while they reached Jumhuriya Street and were confronted by some derelict houses. When Munira inquired, a passer-by directed them to the other side of the street.

"Come on, Sana. Be careful," said Munira, taking her hand.

They hesitated before turning into a narrow dirt alley, which curved unexpectedly, then forked off in different directions. For the first time Sana noticed Munira looking perplexed. An old man went past, and Sana asked him shyly where the school was. He pointed out the way with no difficulty and they set off again. Sana was elated when she caught sight of a smile on Munira's lips.

Chapter
Seven

I went back to my room, shut the door behind me and sat on the bed. Then I stood up and switched on the light. I had eaten well and after the meal drunk tea and talked to my parents. I told them about the last exam, which hadn't been bad. Two questions had come up on a subject I had reviewed on the bus on the way to the university. They considered this a blessing from on high, a good omen.

I myself had come to the conclusion in the course of the exam that if I carried on thinking the way I had been, I wouldn't get anywhere. Nobody before me had got anywhere by being obsessed with the idea that life wasn't worth the effort and everything was a sham. I had accustomed myself to thinking that I was only one person among billions, and that even if they were not all better than me, millions of them must at least be intellectually superior, more balanced, more determined. Even though I was not in a position to make an objective evaluation of myself vis-a-vis other people, it wasn't the sort of subject one could just forget about, and it seemed to me that talking about the murky depths of the human mind and spirit could never be a waste of time.

So I sat on my bed in my brightly lit room, wondering why I had restrained myself from telling my father, not to mention my mother, how I had wasted half an hour of the exam trying to free myself of the dispiriting idea that everything was futile. This notion had been tearing me apart, and I had been observing myself being demolished by it for a month or more, like a sparrow watching a snake swallowing it bit by bit. On this occasion it had occurred to me that if I got up and left the exam hall, without anger or heroics, pretending I'd finished the exam, then . . . I had stopped as I did every time, wondering what my master plan would be. That was if I wanted to put off suicide for the time being, simply because I wasn't in a fit state of health to contemplate it.

During those moments of reflection, I could possibly have understood some important things or reached a fruitful conclusion, if the student next to me hadn't dropped his pen and made me jump, interrupting the unusual rapport I had established with myself.

I stood up and opened my bedroom door to let in the cool night air, then returned to my seat on the bed. I could have a break tonight, because the next exam wasn't for two days. I looked at my bookshelves, but didn't have the energy to choose a book to entertain myself with over the next few hours. I was exhausted by the September heat and the effort of the exams. So perhaps I could go to sleep early. I put my head in my hands, not thinking of anything in particular, even though I would have liked to: I had the feeling that if I was involved in some normal enterprise or led a normal life, I might become an ordinary, normal, contented human being. It seemed to me that what stopped me from being at ease in the conventional framework of life was the way I turned my back—emotionally and intellectually—at the first sign of a crack opening up in my personal universe. Although I wasn't made of cast-iron, it would really help if I was more ready to retain an interest in life; it didn't make sense to spend all your time in a complete vacuum, as I was doing now. Even a brief spell of it was enough to shake up your life forever. But I was waiting, wasn't I? I looked up and let my eyes wander round the room and out at the night sky. I was doing something with my life which was similar to work: waiting. My days would not go by in vain because I was counting them and waiting, and it wouldn't matter if appointments were missed. Appointments were irrelevant when you were concentrating on waiting.

I went and stood in the doorway of my room. The weather was pleasant, the air slightly heavy and damp. I'd been among the first to come down from the terrace, with my parents, the old people, and the little girls. Munira had slept up there two days longer than me, and Midhat and Madiha were still there. The heat was strange that year, reluctant to gather up its skirts and depart. The door and windows of Aunt Safiya's room were wide open, and the electric light gave out a reddish glow. My grandmother, Umm Hasan, was curled up in bed, and my aunt watched her in silence. Both of them had had a good supper and now they were relaxing. A noise came from the crowded television room. There was not a trace of daylight left in the dark sky. It must be past ten o'clock, and they had not yet returned. Perhaps the light had been left on downstairs for their benefit.

Before I went into the exam that morning, when I was standing in the sun outside the university buildings, it had occurred to me that if the intelligent people in the world knew the earth was cooling down and the human species was on the road to extinction—that every civilization with its achievements and dreams was going to be swept away—then they must surely also be aware of this gloom which habitually engulfed people and plunged them into the abyss, into nothingness. So how could they live their lives with the enthusiasm of the ignorant? Were these knowledgeable people not impostors who didn't really believe in their own ideas?

But I think I'm mixing up the chronology of my thoughts now, because I remember clearly that I had this idea about the earth cooling down and death while I was coming home after the exam, not before it. The only thing occupying my mind while I was standing in the hot sun beside the university was the image of a person listening to his own death rattle, hearing himself dying; even if it was only for a moment, a second, a tenth of a second, he could hear the sound of his death. Or perhaps he heard a collision inside him, two objects colliding somewhere in his head—bang!—then darkness. Or—a third possibility— maybe he heard an explosion and was about to look round, thinking it was some distance away, when he was swallowed up by the darkness. I was thinking of the huge amount of fear which surrounds human beings and how it exists primarily because of them, and how when you have a good chance of encountering such fear in your life, absurdity becomes meaningless. It's enough to make it your aim in life not to be filled with terror to the point of madness.

They came in laughing and shut the middle door behind them. Munira looked radiantly happy in the distant glow of the light as she listened to Midhat talking to her and Sana about something. I stepped back a little when the door next to mine opened and Suha came out. Holding on to the wooden balustrade she observed them, then rushed back inside shouting that they were here. Aunt Safiya asked who was here, in the tone of one not expecting an answer. I went into my room and sat down on the bed. They started calling to one another from upstairs to downstairs and back: questions, answers, more questions. I could hear my mother, Madiha, and Suha all talking at the same time and Sana answering them, except once Munira spoke to say she wasn't hungry. Her voice sounded soft and melodious. Then there was the clatter of crockery and cutlery and the noise of the fridge being opened and shut, interspersed with cheerful laughter and conversation. I stood up, turned out the light, and lay down. Several shadowy figures passed along the gallery and went downstairs. Aunt Safiya called my mother again, asking who had come, and who was eating at this time of night.

I was seriously trying to collect my thoughts, see what my life meant and work out what I felt about death. But—in the darkness of my room, lying listening to the distant clamor in the kitchen and staring at the black patch of sky visible through my partly open door—I was aware of one thing only: my sense of defeat—again. I had no practical experience of life because I couldn't overcome the particular conditions of the society in which I lived. Nor could I overcome the feeling that I was waiting, in some remote corner, to be allowed to experience life. I remembered standing by the bridge over the river one evening a few months ago. I had recovered from my illness and gone to the university in the afternoon to find out about the exams. The empty building and the janitor's pale face depressed me, and I was put off by the complicated exam timetable. I stood in the street beside the empty café, not far from the bridge, looking at the setting sun. I was in an endless cemetery. A big white car passed with a girl driving. God, how far away it seemed! Like a shooting star on the distant horizon. To have a house, a car, a wife—it was all such a long way off.

———

I told her all that, explained it to the sad hazel eyes. She listened to me, sitting on the edge of the bed. She was still wearing her green dress with short sleeves. She dropped in on me after they had finished eating and those who wanted had gone up on the roof to sleep. I had switched on my lamp and sat down at my desk to try and use the time profitably before I went to bed. So she came in and sat down on the edge of the bed. Her green dress showed her knees, too. Her long blonde hair was arranged with care on her shoulders, and faint traces of make-up were visible on her face. She seemed a little tired.

"Where were you?" I asked. Like her, I was tired and it showed in my voice.

She looked around the room. "At the cinema. How did you get on in the exam today?"

"Which cinema?"

She parted her lips in a half smile and closed her eyes for a moment, then looked at me. "No, really, how was the exam?"

I told her unenthusiastically what I had been thinking before and during the exam, listening to myself, no longer feeling that what I was explaining to her was important. She looked at me in silence for some time. "Why do you think in this way? I mean, are you serious, Karim?"

"Why not?"

"No, I mean, why do you bother about these things? Even with this interruption, you can still finish university and things will work out all right."

"And if I finish—then what?"

A flicker of anxiety showed on her face. "What are you talking about? You'll get a degree, then find a job. After that you can live your own life and settle down, can't you?"

"A degree, a job, stability . . ."

"Why don't you have some respect for these things? You've got no right to despise them; there's nothing else in our lives."

She was more concerned than I had expected, frowning at me as she fiddled with a strand of hair beside her left ear. She spoke again, more softly. "Karim, you've got to do well. Please. Why are you upsetting yourself talking like this? You're young and you've got your whole life in front of you. Why bother with such ideas?"

"You know, Munira," I told her, "What you're saying reminds me of something that happened over a year ago, after Gagarin's space flight. I was having my shoes polished by an Armenian on Kilani Street. His face was twisted to one side and he was goggle-eyed."

She was listening solemnly, this beautiful creature, and crossed one leg over the other as I was talking.

"I was alone in the shop. The moment I sat down he asked me, 'Is it true they've gone up into space?' 'Yes, so they say,' I replied. 'And Christ? What about Christ?' he screamed at me. I was really taken by surprise. He seemed quite agitated. His eyes were blazing, and he was gasping for breath. I mean, it looked as if it were a matter of life and death for him." I smiled. "You see, you've reminded me of this story. I

160

also wanted to say to him at the time, 'What concern is it of yours, you idiot? Why are you thinking these thoughts?'"

She interrupted sharply, her cheeks on fire. "No, no. That's not what I was saying."

"That's roughly what you were thinking though—that I read too much, have an odd philosophy of life, take no interest in the world around me!"

She raised a delicate finger in protest. "No, Karim. Please . . ."

"Just a minute, Munira. First of all, I don't read that much. Hardly at all, in fact. Secondly, these ideas—I myself don't know where they come from. Perhaps it's quite natural to have them. They're not structured or logical. They just come and go. I'm influenced by them a bit more than I ought to be, that's all."

Her eyes clouded over briefly, and a few small wrinkles appeared underneath them. She raised her finger in protest again. "Look, Karim. I don't think you understand me. I really respect your ideas and opinions. But I want you to take more interest in your personal affairs and sort out your studies. I mean your future is important, and this wouldn't be in conflict with—philosophy, would it? And anyhow, philosophers don't care about anybody. They're spongers."

"Spongers? Who do they sponge on?" I was interested by these new ideas of hers.

She smiled. "Us, of course. Why are they concerned about us? Why don't they leave us in peace? As Midhat said, they don't have proper jobs, so they spend their time chattering. People want to get on with their lives, so God lets these philosophers do all the talking."

I smiled back at her, at her animated, flushed face and sparkling eyes; at the sweet life she embodied. I shook my head. "I don't know which philosophers you're talking about, but you know, there are people who don't talk rubbish, who understand life, or at least some parts of it, and write about it. They're not parasites. Perhaps we're the parasites. Sometimes we can't survive without some help. Life wears us down without us realizing it. I know that only too well. We burn up in the air. Believe me, I know. The hot air kills us sometimes."

I hadn't intended to talk like this, or for my words to have this peculiar emotional ring to them, but all of a sudden my thoughts had been filled with an image of Fuad and his life, his love, his efforts to confront his problems, and his death. I was talking to myself more than to her.

"Sorry, Karim," she said. "I wasn't meaning anything specific. I was joking. And you must be tired; you probably want to read and I don't even know what the time is." And to my consternation she made to get up.

"Where are you going, Munira?" I said quickly. "It's not late."

"What time is it?"

"It doesn't matter. Tell me about the film. Which cinema did you go to?"

"You don't want to study. That's what this is all about."

"I'm not trying to avoid working. I had an exam today. It should have been me who went to the cinema, not you. Especially since you don't even seem to know the name of the film."

She looked at me in astonishment. "Of course I know its name. But I didn't have the chance to take it in. On the one hand Sana wanted to know about everything in the film in advance. And Midhat—God bless him . . . I don't know . . . They wouldn't let me follow it. The cinema was new—it was beautiful. The Nasr cinema. But the film—as you say I didn't have a clue what was going on in it."

We both laughed.

The house was silent, as if everyone had gone to bed, and Munira was in front of me, laughing. Sharing a joke with me. Some color had risen to her cheeks. I could see her upper arm, smooth and golden brown where the sleeve of her green dress ended, and her white teeth, and hear her voice. I forgot about death. I had a sense that she possessed some knowledge which was relevant to me and which I had to hear from her lips.

"How was it at school?" I asked.

"Fine. But it's a bit far for me to travel. If we go on living here, I mean."

"What do you mean, if? Where would you go?"

Her hazel eyes clouded over again, and she grimaced slightly. "Look, Karim," she said after a pause, "everything has its cost. It's not right for us to go on staying like this. We're a burden." She raised her hand, anticipating my objections. "I know. I know what you're going to say. But, all the same, I'm going to write to my brother Mustafa and see what he thinks. Of course we don't want to live on our own—my mother and I. Our situation doesn't help. You know, our financial situation—and other things, but . . ."

Very slowly, she bowed her head and was transformed into a different creature. She stretched out her arms and put a hand on each knee, then her hair fell forward around her face, and she seemed to have been transported to another world within moments. All I could see of her was the parting in her hair, her eyebrows and eyelashes, and the tip of her nose, as if I was looking at a slave kneeling at my feet. She was turned in on herself, absorbed in something deep inside her. She reminded me of how she had looked that dawn several months before when she had stood in the pale flood of light in her blue nightclothes, communing with the invisible, and listening with her whole being to the silence. Then, as now, she had left our world, the uninterrupted sequence of life going on around her, and moved into a private world of her own.

I tried to bring her back, speaking slowly: "You know my friend Fuad, Munira?"

Her face didn't change. She said nothing. She hadn't heard me.

"He was a very dear friend to me," I whispered. "He died a few months ago."

She frowned. "Died?" Then she went on quickly. "Yes, yes. I remember. Your mother told me about him. An only child. You were with him when . . ."

"That's not important," I interrupted. "But Munira, why do you . . ."

A vague look of anxiety began to spread over her face, beginning in her eyes, which were a little damp, and reaching her mouth. She tensed her lips.

"Why do you remind me of Fuad?" I concluded.

She went on looking at me. In place of the worried expression there was one of indifference or resignation. "I remind you of your friend—who died?" she asked coldly.

Then she paused and blinked several times. I nodded my head and she looked away and said, "Look, Karim, I don't feel very strong at the moment, I mean psychologically as well as physically. Today at the cinema I had a shock, and now you're . . ."

"Sorry, Munira. I was just thinking, I mean when you love people, even if they're different, you see strange similarities between them. Wouldn't you say so?"

She looked at me again, her eyes clear and sparkling. "You mean you can see death—on my face?"

She was teasing me, but she scared me. "No, no," I said hurriedly. "Why do you twist my words?"

She stood up. It seemed unexpected and I stood up, too.

"What?" I said enquiringly.

She was smoothing down her dress from just below her breasts to the top of her thighs. She repeated the exercise several times, gazing abstractedly at the floor. Then she spoke. "It's late, Karim, and this kind of talk is never-ending. I'm a bit tired today."

"Another day then," I said quickly.

She smiled with affection and understanding. Her lips were parted, her oval face framed by wild clouds of hair, and her hazel eyes shone with love and happiness.

Then she left me, quickly and gracefully, wishing me good night. Her smile lingered in the air: a tremor, an ethereal image, an invisible rainbow. Something that I couldn't pin down made me intoxicated for hours afterwards. I couldn't sleep or read, but lay on the bed in the darkness listening to the night sounds: a bird asleep on a dry branch; a vague tapping in the kitchen; the distant howling of dogs; the sound of light footsteps coming and going with the breezes; the subdued sounds of myself; and the morning which had not yet broken.

My mother insisted on bringing me up a cup of coffee. She stood in the kitchen doorway and called me as I sat in the big gallery by the alcove, concentrating on the book which lay open in front of me. I'd heard her and her mother talking in the kitchen for a while, but not been able to make out what they were saying. The sky was clear, an autumn sky, and the noisy members of the house were all out. The two women's conversation was like the murmur of water simmering on the stove. Then my mother appeared. I said I could easily come down. I wasn't particularly keen on having coffee; I'd slept for a few hours before dawn and felt greatly refreshed. But she insisted. She was smiling broadly, and her plump, pale face conveyed her pleasure. She asked me how I'd slept last night, how my studying was going, how I felt. As if she hadn't seen me at breakfast!

Then she sat down beside me. A long time seemed to pass before she spoke. The olive tree was still, bathed in the sun's golden rays, and the sky was very blue. Her words were not preceded by any unusual sound or gesture. The house was quiet—the things in it and its inhabitants—and so was the world and the whole of existence, even the sky.

"Karim dear," she said, "Midhat wants Munira. He spoke to her at the cinema yesterday. That little devil Sana heard him and told her mother and Madiha told me. As if it was nothing to do with me. I had to find it out from your sister."

I could see a few white hairs in her eyebrows and small folds of skin underneath her eyes. I remained calm, apart from the rapid beating of my heart.

"She didn't give him an answer," continued my mother. "So now her mother's all confused and doesn't know what to say. I don't know. Did Munira mention it to you last night?"

I shook my head. The house was still quiet, an absolute theatre of indifference. I shook my head. So this was it. I told her I knew nothing. But she guessed my unspoken questions, perhaps from some vague aura I was giving off, and answered them.

"He's your older brother, Karumi dear. He's a graduate with a job and some money. And you—what I'm saying is, the world's not going to end, is it? You're all young, my dear, and God willing you'll all live to see your grandchildren."

She seemed to be bearing the guilt for other people's crimes, and I felt somehow that I was a victim, that it was up to me to make sacrifices again. I shut my book and with it all thoughts of the future. I turned to my mother. The sun was reflected on the wall in the distance to my right, its light bisected vertically by the wooden columns supporting the roof. My grandmother appeared in the doorway of her room.

"You know I'm fond of Munira, Mother," I said, "and Midhat, too. But neither of them has told me anything. And I don't know how you can believe . . . I mean why you trust the stories that little girl tells you."

"My dear, she's little but she's a devil. She hears every single thing that goes on in this house. But you're right. Somebody should ask." She stared into the distance. "But ask who? The subjects Midhat is prepared to discuss can be counted on the fingers of one hand. I don't know, but perhaps you, Karumi, my dear . . . What I mean is . . . she might talk to you if you ask her." She paused. "There's your grandmother. What does she want at this time of day? She's had breakfast, and it's not nearly time for lunch yet."

She got up to go and see.

The book was lying closed on the table in front of me with a pen beside it. I picked up the pen and opened the book. I noticed that I hadn't touched my coffee. Had Munira wanted to tell me something yesterday evening? She hadn't looked for a moment like a girl who'd received an offer of marriage a few hours before. And my future and whether I succeeded in my studies—since I was to be deprived of her, why had she bothered asking all those questions about them?

I wanted to write something, a name on the page. Then I changed my mind. I felt somewhat anxious, as if I was in a void. Ill-defined thoughts kept coming to my mind. I hadn't seen her that morning, but the image of her luminous skin, the shadow of her green dress on her upper arm, and the reflection of the color on the delicate fold of flesh came and enveloped me as I sat looking at the open book, holding the pen.

I shut the book again and put the pen down.

Chapter
Eight

Her daughter Sana woke her from the deep sleep that comes around dawn.

"Mum, Mum," she whispered in her ear. "The jinn's in the kitchen washing the dishes. Mum. I'm scared. Please, Mum. The jinn."

Sana's voice came from a bottomless cave. Her mother gathered her bemused senses. "What? What's wrong?" she asked. "What jinn? What dishes? Why are you awake?"

"Mum. He's in the courtyard washing the dishes. Listen!"

She sat up in bed, straining to hear. The milky light of the sky flooded in through the open door, and from down in the courtyard came an inexplicable, irregular knocking sound, as if the hard ground was being hit with a hollow metal pipe. One, two, three knocks, then silence, then three more knocks. She felt Sana gripping her arm.

"Can you hear it, Mum? Can you?"

"Shh. Be quiet."

Two rapid knocks, then another, followed by silence. She was afraid; she felt her scalp tingle. It didn't make sense. Not even jinns talked like this! She swung her legs down from the big bed, stood up, and put her feet into her sandals. For some reason she asked Sana where her sister Suha was, and Sana replied that she was snoring her head off in bed. Madiha went apprehensively towards the door. The pale blue sky and the olive tree appeared in front of her. The morning birds had not yet begun their song. The banging came from below, heavy, irregular. She stood hesitantly in the doorway and stuck her head out. As the cool breeze touched her face, she felt her daughter's trembling fingers clinging to her arm. It was barely light in the courtyard, and she had trouble making out the ground. She wanted to cross the small gallery and look over the balustrade, but was afraid of what she might see. It could be something that a human being like her ought not to know about: the world of jinns or some other creatures who had no desire to be spied on by a wretched mortal.

Her heart beat more powerfully as she continued to stand in the doorway, her reluctance fuelled by all the fairy stories and tales of jinns she had heard in childhood. Sana was clinging desperately on to her from behind. She was about to go back inside, shut the door, and return to bed, when she heard a movement from Aunt Safiya's room to their right. She looked round and saw her aunt leaning on the door post, her hennaed hair disheveled; she was looking vacantly in the direction of the courtyard.

"God keep you, Umm Hasan," she was saying irritably. "Do you think my eyesight is good enough to see dragons and monsters? Strong, healthy people sleep on full stomachs. But I'm starving, so my vision's blurred. God heals all. God bless you, Umm Hasan. You've woken me up and it's not even daylight."

She was talking quietly to herself, as if she wanted no one else to hear. But Madiha was reassured to see her aunt.

"Auntie, what are you doing standing there?"

Her aunt turned towards her, shading her eyes with her left hand. "Good heavens. Is that you, Madiha? Something odd's happening down in the yard. Bang bang all night, from the evening prayer till now. Can't you tell them . . ." she stopped and gesticulated towards the courtyard. "Talk to them nicely. Why are they washing their hair all this time? There's no more water in the pipes. Talk to them, Madiha, please. Nicely. Don't be cross with them."

Madiha breathed easily again as she listened to her aunt's raving interspersed with the strange knocking, which continued unabated. Hesitantly, she approached the balustrade. The sky, the high walls, and the top of the olive tree were bathed in the dawn light. She looked down. There was another thud, then silence, followed by a weak, muffled groaning which she hadn't heard before. The courtyard was like a mirage, the things on the ground indistinguishable from one another. She squinted, trying to see, feeling a prickle down her spine. Nothing. Then she heard Sana whispering to her: "There, Mum. There, beside the pond. What is it?"

The thing was moving, a shadow lost in the shadows, a smudge of black in the blackness. She couldn't make out a specific shape, just a dark, truncated blob turned to the right. There was another of the mysterious bangs, then the blob turned slowly to the left, accompanied by the moaning sound. She was more surprised than frightened by what she saw.

"Please, Madiha," said her aunt in a low voice. "Recite 'God is One' and put the light on beside you. You don't know whether you're going to die of hunger or fright around here. Recite, my dear. Recite the Quran."

Madiha felt a movement behind her as Sana put the light on and its reddish glow flooded the yard, driving the shadows away. She tried to follow the movement beside the pond, but couldn't make out what was happening. There was a short tail and four short legs, but no head.

Sana let out a yell. "It's the tomcat! Its head's stuck in the kettle. The stupid thing. It scared me, Mum."

The cat was swinging its head slowly from side to side, weighed down by its strange helmet, producing the cacophony of sounds which had interrupted their sleep. Madiha continued to observe the scene with some annoyance, feeling her tension draining away.

"What cat? What are you talking about, Sana?" demanded Aunt Safiya. "Why didn't you recite 'God is One' before you put the light on? See how the jinn's turned himself into a cat to make fun of us."

"Auntie dear, it's the white cat that ate your kebab the other day."

"Curse it! See how God's punishing it! It's no more than it deserves."

Madiha moved heavily away along the small gallery towards the stairs. She was thinking about what she would have to do, since she was the one responsible for putting right any such disruption to the domestic order. She passed her sleeping brothers' rooms, and when she was almost halfway along the big gallery, her mother looked out of her room, her round, pale face still bearing traces of sleep.

"Where are you going, Madiha?" she asked. "It's not time for morning tea yet, is it?"

Grumpily, Madiha told her mother what had happened to the cat and said she was going down to free its head. She was tired, moving her legs as little as possible and supporting herself on the wall as she went down the dark staircase. Her mother had not even seemed surprised, which disappointed her and made her uncomfortably aware of her unenviable position in the house. The courtyard was gray and desolate. She heard the cat's copper head banging on the ground again, bringing her back to the task in hand.

"Be careful the cat doesn't scratch you, Madiha," she heard her mother call.

"Shall I come down, Mum?" shouted Sana.

The cat grew calmer when it heard her approaching. If the damn thing would stay like that for a few more minutes, she could deal with it. She took hold of it by the scruff of the neck and it quivered and mewed faintly. She tugged on the copper kettle with her other hand but nothing happened, and she inadvertently joined forces with the cat to make two more metallic thuds. Its legs were splayed out and its skinny tail was trailing on the ground. She gripped the vessel with both hands and lifted it and the cat high in the air. The cat flailed its legs and began mewing piteously. Agitatedly, Madiha shook her burden again and again, then she had the idea of throwing it across the courtyard. The cat and the kettle rolled along in the shadows behind one of the wooden pillars, then she saw the cat bounding nimbly away and heard the empty kettle continuing to roll in the direction of the middle door.

"Bravo, Mum," called Sana, clapping her hands. "How clever you are!"

"Quiet, Sana," interrupted Madiha's mother, "don't disturb your uncles."

Madiha found the kettle upside down by the wall and picked it up and took it into the dark kitchen. She still felt slightly numb as she tipped a bit of Tide into it and began scrubbing it. It was badly dented, and there was a white deposit in the bottom of it. She filled it with water, lit the oil stove and put it to boil. As the asphyxiating smell of oil started to fill the kitchen, she hurried outside and sat on the little bench by the door. She couldn't see anyone on the gallery.

"Sana," she called softly. "Where are you?"

Her daughter appeared up above. "Wake up your sister," said Madiha, "and both of you get dressed and wash your faces."

"There's plenty of time, Mum. I'm sleepy. Suha hasn't even opened her eyes."

"I said wake her up. She shouldn't still be in bed. Don't start annoying me first thing in the morning, when I've got five hours of classes in front of me."

"Take it easy, Madiha," came her mother's voice. "Make the tea, and I'll go and help the girls dress. Leave it to me."

She saw her mother up on the gallery, going towards their room, and shivered slightly, drawing her black cardigan more closely round her and pulling her dress down. The morning light filled the courtyard and woke up the birds in the olive tree; their first calls rose joyously in the air. A packet of cigarettes and a box of matches lay on the ground near the bench; she picked them up and lit herself a cigarette. There wasn't a sound from the floor above: she could still relax for a bit longer, crouching there like a kitten waiting for its masters to wake up. She took a long drag and tasted the acrid smoke, swallowed it, and blew it out through her mouth and nose. She looked all around her. Where had that wretched cat gone?

They were all asleep still. She had been the only one to think it her duty to go down and put an end to the nonsense in the courtyard. She alone was afflicted with this mysterious illness which made her wait on them all, as if it was a condition of her being accepted back in her father's house. Although she hadn't been a lazy adolescent before her marriage, she had never felt driven by this inner compulsion which drove her now. She used to be able to stay in bed, any time she wanted, until nine or ten in the morning and had not felt terrified, as she did these days, if she failed to put the water on to boil before sunrise.

She could hear her mother and daughters moving around and whispering together in their room. They were best friends, and the age difference didn't seem to matter; she hoped the affection would last. The kettle was beginning to sing. She took a last drag on her cigarette and threw it away. Then she leaned forward, hugging her legs. Even her cousin Munira was treated as a visitor; they never expected her to do any housework. Still, she might agree to marry Midhat, then she would become part of the household and nobody could go on thinking of her as an honored guest.

Munira hadn't given a straight answer so far and seemed unaware that everybody knew and was waiting to hear what she said! Yes, Munira was pretty, but she herself had been just as pretty when Husayn approached her family asking to marry her. All the same, they hadn't given her any time to think or express an opinion. As if he was the Aga Khan, when he was only a branch manager of the Rafidayn bank and couldn't even express himself clearly half the time. She hadn't been against the idea of marrying him, but her parents' eagerness to settle the affair quickly had made her feel aware of what a huge burden she represented to her family.

The kettle's familiar song grew louder. She rose to her feet disconsolately and went in to make the tea and prepare breakfast. Their first years together hadn't been that bad. A normal Iraqi family life. Work, food, sex, visits in the neighborhood. She had bled in the train to Basra; the color of the blood on the white sheets had particularly alarmed her. She didn't know how she'd survived when the fool had sex with her a second time before they arrived, and she bled even more violently. She hadn't been fully aware of what was being done to her—she was twenty-two years old and had never seen a man's genitals even in her dreams. So she believed that everything had happened properly and according to the rules, despite the pain and terror and revulsion and embarrassment.

As she put the milk to boil on the stove she heard rapid footsteps behind her, but didn't pay any attention. Then she heard Munira's voice. "Good morning, Madiha."

She turned round with some surprise and saw her in her nightdress. "Good morning. What woke you, Munira? It must have been all that racket."

Munira took a bottle of water from the fridge and helped herself to a drink. "No, really, Madiha. But every day I say to myself I'm going to get up in the morning and come down to help you with the breakfast. I'm sorry."

She was wearing a blue robe over her white embroidered nightdress. Madiha smiled at her. "Why, Munira?"

The robe was wide open at the neck and part of her right breast showed.

"Why be in such a hurry to wear yourself out? Don't you want to break yourself in first?"

"What? Break myself in to what?"

She paused with the glass of water in her hand. Madiha was embar-

175

rassed that Munira didn't pick up what she meant immediately. She had no make-up on her eyes, but the contrast between their light color and the blackness of their lashes gave them a particular beauty. Madiha returned to her task unenthusiastically. "To work, my dear Munira. To work."

"Really?"

"Yes, really. Don't delude yourself. What else have we got to look forward to?"

Madiha didn't see Munira as being of more than average intelligence, but she sensed that she shrank away from their world, obviously preferring her male cousins' company to Madiha's, spending hours talking and laughing with Abd al-Karim, or going out with Midhat and Sana to the bright lights of Bab al-Sharqi, or to the cinema. Anyway, who could blame her if she liked talking to young men?

Madiha could see her out of the corner of her eye, standing contemplating the olive tree.

"Munira, I was wondering," she said, "didn't you get a reply from your brother Mustafa yet?"

Munira glanced rapidly at Madiha and the breakfast table, then turned back to the olive tree. "No, not yet."

Madiha put the teapot down next to the other breakfast things and went towards her. She wasn't meaning to say anything in particular, but she took hold of both of Munira's hands. "Look, Munira, it's not because Midhat's my brother, but I do know him well and I know he's a good person. I mean, I don't know how to convince you, but I swear to you, you'll be very happy with him."

She saw a faint smile on Munira's lips, but a few moments later her eyes seemed to fill with bitterness and anxiety.

"I know, Madiha, I know," she said. Her voice was hoarse, as if she hadn't spoken for several days.

"Then why haven't you given him an answer, my dear? Why leave him to suffer like that? He doesn't know where he stands."

Munira's fingers tightened round her hands, then relaxed again. She gave her another quick look, then turned back to stare at the olive tree.

"Perhaps you're thinking to yourself that I'm the last person to advise people on marriage," went on Madiha. "But . . ." she felt a sudden pang of sorrow, "you see, Munira, nobody knows as well as I do, especially now, the value of marriage and independence. You create your own world and there's nobody looking over your shoulder. Still, if God didn't intend you to be happy, there's nothing you can do," she finished flatly.

Munira turned towards her and gripped her by the arms, her eyes full of affection. Madiha saw her lips trembling slightly.

"Don't blame yourself for what happened to you, Madiha," she said. "Please. You're the victim of circumstances. I know all about it. Don't torture yourself." She lowered her arms suddenly and as she turned away, Madiha noticed the light reflected in her tear-filled eyes. "But please leave me alone now. Let me rest. What have I done? I wish you'd all leave me alone."

She started to walk away, but stopped after a couple of paces and turned back to Madiha. "Madiha, you know, my brother must be going to reply soon. But please help me. Make them be patient."

A mask had descended over her lovely, tearful face. Madiha was shocked by her reaction and didn't know what to say or how to sympathize. She watched her sadly as she walked along by the west wall, thin, listless, her loose hair hiding her pale face. It struck her that, yet again, Munira hadn't helped her make breakfast. Then she caught sight of her mother and her two daughters ambling along the big gallery and remembered that she wasn't dressed yet and it was getting late.

———

Madiha stood beside the lighted stove waiting for her mother to talk. Nuriya was sitting on the little wooden bench in the kitchen doorway, smoking calmly. About an hour before, maybe less, they'd been washing up together and she'd told her mother that the school caretaker, Jasmiya, had come to her that morning in school to say that one of her relatives had heard that Husayn had been ill for ten days and was in a serious condition. Since then, her mother had been sitting on the bench, chain-smoking. She appeared distracted and annoyed.

"What do they mean by serious?" she asked at last, in a low voice. "Has he got a cold? Everyone's got a cold. Just because they call it influenza now, so what? It doesn't make it any more serious."

She looked inquiringly at Madiha, who didn't answer and seemed even more irritated by the news than she was.

"Do what you want," continued her mother. "If you want to go and see him, go. Good luck to you. Take the girls with you. I can't come though—but do you know where his aunt's house is? I've heard it's behind the Café Yas on the other side of Bab al-Shaykh." She inhaled deeply. "If he's going to die of a cold, there's not much we can do."

The sky was black, heavy with clouds, and the air was cold. Madiha had felt more depressed by the hour since the woman caretaker at school had told her about her husband's illness. It wouldn't have bothered her to learn that he'd dropped dead in the street, but the feeling that he was still alive, on the brink of the abyss, reawakened something in the depths of her, a pounding in her heart mixed with a profound pity that ate into her soul. When he used to come home to her, ill after nights of drinking, she treated him like a motherless child. Afterwards she realized that nursing him made her happy. She had never really been worried about him because she knew he was physically strong and she'd enjoyed him being confined to bed, dependent on her. Then the sexual explosion as he recovered always surprised her. It wasn't a painful experience, and yet it resembled a rape. After that the animal escaped from its cage again. She sighed. She no longer wanted to remember all the details of the sex they'd had during their life together. Sometimes it had been extraordinary, but what remained was no more than vague sensations and indistinguishable images, which drugged the body pointlessly.

Her mother roused her from her thoughts. "Take some fruit with you. Go in time to come back before sunset. Do you want—I mean—shall I come with you?"

"No, Mum. Let me go for an hour and come straight back. Just to see what state he's in. Why fruit?"

"No reason, dear. But it's not nice to go empty-handed. A gift from you and the girls."

Madiha didn't reply and went off upstairs.

She told her daughters to get ready to go with her. She had been reluctant to take them at first, but supposed their presence might relieve the pressure of what could be an unbearably embarrassing situation. They washed their faces and combed their unruly hair, a little surprised and full of excitement. She saw her face in the mirror, pale and lined, and her doubts returned. In what capacity was she going to see him?

She sat down on the bed. He hadn't even told her he was going to leave her. He had been away for a few days, then come back, worn out and broke. The fight between them had ended up with him not talking to anybody for a whole week, eating, smoking, sleeping, and never leaving the house. She didn't know what had happened to him exactly, whether he'd lost his job or what, and her pride didn't allow her to ask him for money or try and make up with him. Guessing he had some serious problems that he didn't want to tell her about, she had decided to contact his friends at the bank, but had never got round to it. Perhaps he had invented the quarrel to hide something more worrying from her. One morning he'd gone out and not come back, then she'd received a letter from Kuwait, in which he told her he was working for a company there and was trying to find a suitable place for them to live. He didn't give her an address, and a few months later he wrote her a cold, uncomfortable letter which caused her many misgivings. She realized that she should get used to the idea of his being away from her, and prepare herself and her daughters for a different life without him, so she moved into her father's house.

She noticed Sana standing in front of her, looking at her inquiringly. "Where's Suha?" she asked, then was aware of herself sighing.

"She's ready to go, so she's sitting talking to Uncle Midhat," answered Sana.

"Why isn't he asleep?"

"I don't know. I saw her talking to him. Maybe she went into his room and woke him up. That's what she's like."

"Go and call her."

She stood up to check on her appearance and saw a lot of white hairs, so she hid some of them and pulled some out. She no longer wondered, at moments like these, why she was doing this and for whom. She changed her blouse and shoes, picked up her *abaya* and went out on to the gallery. The sight of the dull gray sky didn't really spoil her mood. The house was empty, which pleased her. She remembered her bag, went back to her room to fetch it, and put a few things in it which she thought she might need, along with some cash. A cool breeze invigorated her as she emerged for the second time. She was surprised to see her daughters standing with Midhat at the end of the small gallery, the three of them looking in her direction. She hesitated briefly, and Sana, holding her uncle's hand, gave her a broad smile.

"Let me take you, Madiha," called Midhat. "I know Husayn's aunt's house. I've been there once before. I knew there must be some reason why he hadn't been around. I told myself he must be ill. It's been two weeks since he came to visit me at the office."

Then he walked calmly ahead with her daughters and she followed behind. Her brother's wish to accompany them gave her a sense of security. She had the vague feeling that there were no solid grounds for her visit; her sole motivation was pity, but the thought of going alone, or even with her children, was painful. Sana hung back as they approached the outside door and began to walk beside her. Madiha ruffled her hair gently, and Sana looked up at her with shining eyes.

Before they walked through the Kilani mosque they bought fruit and other groceries. The sun still had not set, and its red rays were catching the top of the minaret and the high clock tower as they reached Café Yas and made for the dark archway leading to the Kurdish quarter. An unpleasant smell of tobacco diluted by water spilt from the narghiles rose up off the ground. Sana held her nose. They didn't talk much. Madiha wanted to ask Midhat about Munira, to talk about anything remotely connected with her, but he seemed so happy, as he chatted lightheartedly with her two daughters, that she refrained. For no reason that she could put her finger on, she was afraid he wouldn't appreciate her bringing up the subject.

They passed into another world when they went through the dark archway. The narrow alleys were uneven and badly lit, the walls so close together that they more or less denied their inhabitants a view of the sky. There were children everywhere, their voices coming from every nook and cranny, and the whole place was enveloped in a smell of cooking, and in darkness and filth.

She held tightly on to her children and after a few steps turned to Midhat. "Is it far?" she asked.

He shook his head. "We're nearly there."

He indicated a turning to the left. The light there was gray and the walls dingy and dirty, covered in a mass of drawings and graffiti. She felt as if she was creeping along deep in the bowels of the earth and wondered what she could possibly find in this miserable place.

They stopped in front of an old black door covered in dust. The bottom of the door had sunk below the surface of the alley. Midhat hesitated and looked across to the other side of the alley then studied the door again. It was in a dip in the ground and had a high step to prevent water coming into the house. Midhat raised the iron knocker and banged on the door, smiling. Nobody answered. This did not surprise

Madiha, and she hoped her brother hadn't made a mistake. Midhat knocked again, loudly. After a few seconds the door moved slowly, without a sound, and an old man stood in the narrow doorway. She felt her heart beat faster, and her daughters clung to her.

"God bless you, Uncle," said Midhat. "Where's Aunt Atiya? We've come to see Husayn. How is he?"

"What, brother?" came the old man's hoarse voice. "Where are you from?"

"Isn't this Hajji Rahman's house?" asked Midhat sharply.

"What? Yes, it is. That's right, brother."

"Isn't Husayn here? Abu Suha? We heard he was ill."

Madiha could not make out the man's face, and he spoke in an unfamiliar accent. He was silent for a few seconds, then repeated his question in the same mechanical tone as before: "Where are you from, brother?"

"The old man's senile. He doesn't recognize me," whispered Midhat. Then suddenly he turned and shouted at him. "Go and get your wife, quickly. Hurry up. Tell her you've got visitors. Go on."

The old man retreated in confusion into the darkness of the house while they waited in the gray stillness of the alley and cool breezes blew over them from nowhere, bringing with them a vague, incessant murmur of sound.

They heard light, hesitant footsteps, then a small woman swathed in black came into view, indistinguishable at first sight from the old man apart from some anonymous feature of her appearance which proclaimed her gender.

"Yes, sir. Who are you looking for?" she said, the minute she arrived in the doorway.

"Good evening. I'm Midhat, brother of Madiha, Husayn's wife. How are you all?"

"Yes, sir. You're welcome. Please come in."

"How are you all?" asked Midhat again.

She retreated inside slowly, drawing her *abaya* round her. "Welcome, sir. How are we? As you see. Falling apart. Please come in. Excuse us, there's no light in the passage."

"We've come to see Husayn. These are his daughters. This is Madiha, his wife. How is he?"

"Yes, sir. He's here. Husayn. He's better. He slept for ten days. He couldn't move his arms and legs. Like us. Come in, please."

Midhat went ahead down the dark passage and Madiha, having said hello to the old lady, followed him, holding the little girls' hands. The courtyard was quite empty and was lit only by the last traces of the sunset. The old man stood to one side, giving them hostile looks.

"They're Husayn's relatives," his wife told him. "They've come to see him. Excuse us, sir. He didn't recognize you."

The old man muttered in Turkish through his long white beard. "Birum, birum, *afandim*. Welcome, sir."

The woman indicated a staircase. "Please go up. The room's in front of you at the top of the stairs. I can't manage the climb. Give him my best wishes."

Her features were sad, her small face covered in wrinkles.

"Thank you. I know the way," said Midhat, bounding off up the steep staircase.

"Be careful," whispered Madiha to her daughters.

"I'm scared, Mum," said Sana.

"Shut up! We've got here safely, haven't we? Go up slowly."

The three of them made a faint rustling and clattering in their clothes and shoes as they crowded together on to the dark stairs.

"Watch out. You keep treading on my toes," whispered Sana irritably to her sister. "Do you think you're the only one climbing these stairs?"

"Silly idiot," answered Suha.

"Did you hear what she said, Mum?" shouted Sana.

Ahead of them was a landing where it was less dark than the staircase, thanks to a high window through which a distant patch of blue sky was visible. Midhat was standing in front of a closed door to the right, looking at them with some displeasure. He remained there without moving, until they had lined up next to him, then he pushed the door open and went in. Madiha hesitated, but when she saw her daughters following their uncle she too stepped up to the doorway.

She couldn't make out anything as she stood on the threshold. It was almost pitch black in the bare room, and the small window facing her only let in a faint glimmer of light. Then to her right she noticed the outline of a bed, whose colors were distinguishable from the darkness. Midhat reached an arm behind her and the room was suffused in the pale glow of the electric light.

There was the shadow of a smile on her brother's lips as he approached the narrow black metal bedstead. At first Madiha couldn't see anyone under the blanket and dirty raincoat covering the bed, but the way the covers stuck up in the middle gave the impression that a person lay underneath. Although she felt no emotion, she was extremely curious to see him alive, to see his face and try to discern what lay behind it. Dead, he would have meant nothing to her, but alive he might give her some indication of the shape of the future.

"Husayn. Husayn." Midhat drew back the covers cautiously. The thick hair appeared of a man, his eyes closed then opened quickly as he became aware of their presence, looking at them apprehensively. Husayn had a matted beard, full of white hairs. His swollen eyes were surrounded by dark circles. He continued to stare at Midhat without lifting his head, as if he was seeing a ghost. His hair was disheveled and his face the color of copper.

"What is it? What's going on?" he asked in a hoarse voice.

Then he was overtaken by a fit of coughing which forced him to sit up in bed holding his head and mouth and gasping strangely for breath after each cough, like a dog howling in pain. Midhat picked up a glass of water from a little table by the bed and offered it to Husayn, but he pushed it away. As the attack abated he buried his face in his hands, breathing rapidly, his shoulders shaking and twitching convulsively.

His hair was going gray; it was dirty and full of dandruff, the scalp visible in places. Midhat gestured to Madiha to sit on a long couch against the wall by the bed. She hesitated. She had never felt so affected by anything before. Seeing what was left of the young husband who had shared her bed for years, she felt he was saying goodbye to her and that, in a way, he had stayed alive so that she could see for herself how low he had sunk. For a moment she doubted that these dried-up, angular features were really his. But then she recognized a vague line which incorporated his eyebrows and eyes, before descending in a characteristic way towards his nose, which twisted slightly to the left. But the eyes—they had lost their color and sparkle, and the mouth had contracted and withdrawn into itself. He was in outdoor clothes, the small knot on the black tie loosened at his lined brown neck to allow him to breathe.

Suddenly he spoke. "Sorry, Midhat. I can't see properly. I've been ill. Really, really ill, Midhat. Sorry."

He didn't look at her. His dark blue jacket was covered in a layer of dust and dirt, his crumpled shirt collar twisted back over its lapels.

"I'm the one who should be sorry, Husayn. I didn't know you were in this state. I've been busy. How are you now?"

"Now? Fine, fine."

Madiha noticed a trail of snot running out of his nose. As he spoke, he put his hand into his jacket pocket, pulled out a crumpled handkerchief and wiped his nose, eyes, and mouth. He stared over at the three of them for a moment, then wiped his bristly face again, as if he hadn't seen anything that stirred his interest.

"You know, we heard you were ill by chance," said Midhat. "So Madiha and I and the girls have come to see you. It seems you don't recognize them, Husayn?"

Husayn turned mechanically to look at them again. "Recognize them? Yes, of course I do. You know . . ."

185

There was no enthusiasm or emotion in his dull eyes, nothing to suggest he was even attempting to take an interest in them. Madiha spoke for the first time. "The caretaker at school said you were ill. She'd heard you were going to die."

At the sound of her voice, he suddenly became agitated and pulled up the cover. "Me?" he interrupted. "Not at all. I'm fine now. Everything's fine."

These signs of life reassured her.

"Yes," she said, "you seem to be. We came to check. I was afraid you might need to see a doctor, go to hospital."

He interrupted her again. "Hospital? No, there's no need. What for? It's not worth it. It wouldn't do any good." He put his head in his hands. "Nothing would do any good."

Madiha looked at Midhat and found that he was looking at her. She cast her eyes around the room. It was strangely empty, bare, bleak. On the floor, which was thick with dust, she could see traces of dried vomit and cigarette butts everywhere. There were marks on the wall where the rain had come in at the uncurtained window, and they looked as if someone had drawn a graph.

Husayn suddenly spoke in a trembling voice. "Please, Midhat, you must excuse me. I know I don't look too good. Not entirely decent probably." He was talking through his hands. "But this illness—it was grim. I knew very well I mustn't get sick. In my situation, it doesn't help. But . . ."

When he took his hands down from his face, Madiha noticed water collecting in the corners of his eyes, but he didn't look from his expression as if he was crying. He turned his distracted gaze on Midhat.

"I caught cold one night and didn't do anything about it. It was terrible. I had a temperature of over forty degrees and a dreadful headache. Dreadful. And I couldn't stop shaking. My teeth were chattering all night long. And there was no one to help. And in the daytime it was even worse."

He took out his handkerchief, wiped his eyes and nose, and put it back in his pocket, then ran his fingers through his hair. Madiha noticed that his nails were too long and his hands were shaking. He was silent for a moment and breathed deeply, trying to sit up properly. He was becoming aware of the people round him and recovering his senses. He turned slightly towards the three of them. His wet lashes blinked rapidly, and his features seemed to relax.

"How are you, Mad . . . Madiha?"

She didn't answer. She was amazed at how ugly he looked. It was such a tragedy that the only real relationship she and her daughters had in the world was with this broken-down specimen of humanity.

He looked at his daughters. "How are you getting on at school, Suha? And how are you, Sana?"

They answered in sweet, gentle voices. He turned to Midhat.

"What's happening, Midhat? What news of the president?"

"Nothing much. What do you expect in ten days?"

"Ten days! Yes, you're right. But every time I hear a bang, I say to myself, that's it."

"There's nothing going on. What are you talking about?"

"Yeah, it will take time. But every hour of this president's life is numbered now. Every minute maybe. Believe me."

Madiha's gaze was suddenly drawn to an empty, clear glass bottle lying under the bed. Probably the last bottle he drank before he was ill, or even during his illness. And yet he was chatting with Midhat as if he was at an ordinary family gathering. As if he'd never done anything shameful to them, didn't owe them anything, wasn't responsible for them in any way at all. He was behaving for all the world like a respectable person who had fulfilled his obligations to the best of his ability and was now enjoying himself gossiping harmlessly about politics. The idea infuriated her.

"Look, Husayn," she shouted. "Instead of talking about politics, why don't you tell me what you're going to do with yourself? What are your plans? I never imagined I'd see you alive. Never."

He turned his head and upper body away from her involuntarily as if she had hit him, then his lips tightened and he looked down at the bedclothes.

"We don't want anything from you," she went on. "Get that into your head. We don't want a penny from you. We don't need your money . . ." She had been about to say "your filthy money," but as she was speaking to him she had begun to have feelings of regret. "You see, God doesn't abandon His servant. God bless my father and my brothers, they opened their door to me and my daughters. We don't need anybody, but . . ." she hesitated, "but human beings—I mean they're not like animals, so I'm wondering—it's nothing I've done, so why did you do this to us, to yourself? These are your daughters, after all. You can say I don't count, pretend I don't exist, but your daughters?"

Damn, she hadn't meant to talk like this. What was it in him that made her want to appease him or try and get closer to him, even just with words?

These waves of pity and regret and the images of the painful past, but also of her brief periods of happiness with him, had combined with the ugliness and awkwardness of him as he lay ill in bed to make her articulate things she would never have thought of before coming to see him. He was as silent as a black stone. Leaning forward, his hair disheveled, he scratched the back of his hand with a slow, deliberate movement. She looked at Midhat and saw signs of discomfiture on his face. With his eyes he signaled warningly towards the two little girls. She felt compassionate, resigned, ready to accept anything. She was incapable of insisting on the truth of her statements or defending them. She didn't have much proof, despite all the bad treatment he had subjected her to. She decided that it would be best to bring the painful scene to a close.

"I don't really know how to apologize—to you, I mean," he was saying. "But maybe you know—Midhat certainly does . . ." He wasn't looking at anyone. "I mean, I wasn't—you know—the drink and other things. Circumstances. I didn't know where I was. Things were spinning out of control. I was conscious of what I was doing for possibly one or two hours a day, or not at all. But recently, when I was ill, I realized the state I had got myself into. And now I don't know how to apologize. Now I want to do something, to change, so that you all know that I'm really sorry."

"What do you want to do? What do you have in mind?"

Her question drew his wavering eyes towards her.

"What do I have in mind? Why do you ask? Is there a chance I'll get better? Will I ever be on my feet again?"

"Of course," answered Midhat briskly. "Why are you so pessimistic, Husayn? There's nothing wrong with you. It's just flu, soon over and done with. A common cold."

"Thanks, Midhat. You see, I need you to tell me there's nothing wrong with me. I was in another world. Now I don't know if I'm better or not, whether I'm going to live or die. But if you all tell me I'm fine, then I'll be fine. I'm a useless person, Midhat, but I can't leave this world behind!"

He looked distractedly into a corner of the room. "What's all the fuss about? Fear, the day of reckoning, sacred texts—everyone ends up as a heap of bones!" He was talking in a whisper, almost ignoring them. "A heap of bones with no name, no judgment passed on them, not answerable to any holy book. But death's no easy matter, my friend. What dreadful, dark nights I spent with the angel of death above my head and my soul cowering under the bed, while I raved and begged for mercy. But I'm not the same person. I'm not Husayn. I've changed my name. There's no point, night after night, not knowing where you are, so now . . ." He looked up at her, glanced across at Midhat, then looked back at her. "Now I'm as you see me. What do you want? I'm at your disposal, but . . ." He opened his arms helplessly on the cover in front of him. His gesture seemed to suggest that they were the reason for his illness and suffering and his brush with death, because they wanted to come into his empty life, looking for crumbs of hope.

"Husayn," Midhat was saying, "where do you get these gloomy ideas from, for God's sake? You're still young. You've got your whole life ahead of you."

Wasn't he right, in his misery and desolation, to refuse to respond to their calls? He had crossed over to the other side.

"Of course you wouldn't be the first to go to the clinic and be cured," went on Midhat.

He had crossed to the other side, lost his boat, and couldn't find his way back. It was pointless now, pointless and distressing, for them to confront him with all these demands and conditions which he didn't understand.

"That guy Fadil," said Midhat. "Your friend Fadil. Don't you remember him? He wrote long articles for the papers about his experiences in the clinic. I promise you, it's very easy to arrange."

But he was telling them with his eyes, his copper-colored skin, and his crooked mouth that he wasn't going back to them, and that what was left of him was not evidence that he was alive. He had already left them and, at the end of the day, was no more than a memory.

"What do you think, Madiha? Honestly?" continued Midhat.

A wave of dizziness came over her, and she closed her eyes. He was alive, merely to prove the opposite to them.

"What's wrong, Madiha?"

"Nothing, Midhat. I just feel a bit dizzy. It's probably fatigue."

She felt a movement beside her. It was Sana. She touched her soft little hand. She saw an expression of disappointment on her brother's face as he came towards them.

"Things will work out," she said, "but it's late, isn't it?"

Husayn muttered some inaudible words.

"Okay, fine," Midhat said to her. "We'll come back another time."

She stood up.

"We'll come and see you again then," Midhat went on, turning to Husayn. "Okay, Husayn, I hope you feel better. Are you sure you don't need anything now? We'll be back, of course."

"Definitely, Midhat. You must come. All of you."

Madiha said nothing as she made for the door and went out into the darkness, but she heard her husband murmuring, "Before you go, Midhat, have you got a dinar on you by any chance? You see, I . . ."

Her daughters' whispering muffled his words. She couldn't see the top of the stairs properly and realized that she had tears in her eyes. When she raised a hand to wipe them away, she noticed she was still holding the bag of fruit and gave it quickly to Sana.

"Go and leave this by your father's bed."

She dried her eyes. She didn't want to cry here, at the door of his room. Taking Suha's hand, she followed her brother. Sana caught up with them a few moments later. As Madiha went carefully down the stairs and out of the dark house, she felt she was leaving Husayn in his grave.

There was a cold, foul-smelling breeze blowing in the deserted, poorly lit alleys. She hid her tears under her black *abaya* and choked back the sobs. Luckily it wasn't far to her father's house.

Chapter Nine

I was half-sitting, half-lying on my bed in the old people's room, reading a novel. It had seemed interesting at first but I was beginning to think the writer had lost his way when my mother spoke to me. She didn't like seeing me absorbed in something she couldn't understand.

"Munira, my daughter. You should write to your brother, Mustafa. He might talk to his friend about getting you transferred to Baghdad more quickly."

She was smoking a long cigarette and chewing her words like gum, an ugly habit I hadn't managed to break her of. I turned a page of my book in silence, knowing that she wouldn't leave me alone. We were by ourselves in the room, as Aunt Safiya and my grandmother Umm Hasan had both gone to the bathroom or somewhere. The heat was pretty bad, but it hadn't given me a headache as it used to before. Perhaps I was happier in myself here, or God in His grace had cured me at last.

"These people have a thousand things on their minds, my girl. If you don't look out for yourself, no one else is going to do it for you. And you know your brother!"

"Why don't you talk properly, Mum? Keep your tongue still while you're speaking. I've told you before, I'm not writing to Mustafa again, so why do you keep going on about it? I've written to him once, and he understands how things are. I'm not writing to him again."

"People are only interested in their own troubles. I should know."

I put my book aside and looked through the wooden window shutters. I wasn't tired of reading, but it was time for tea and so I had stopped concentrating. My mother's talk, always in the same vein, was not about to provoke a strong reaction from me. Since our arrival I had quickly learned to disregard the hidden meanings in words. I was concerned not to be miserable all the time; it seemed sensible, now that we had found this bolt-hole, not to torment ourselves about the past. The best thing we could do was to lick our wounds and take stock.

They were making tea somewhere in the house, and I felt incapable of talking to my mother, who was squatting silently beside the bed. With a hand to her forehead, which was wrapped in a shiny black bandeau, she was smoking, enveloped in a mass of white, evil-smelling smoke. When she spoke she didn't make the slightest gesture, but just sat there on the floor with her voice coming out of her in a continuous stream of malformed words. "What makes you think people want to help us in our troubles, my daughter? I swear by all the imams that that there's not a living soul who cares whether we live or die. If you don't look after yourself, no one else will."

Then suddenly the stream of words came to a halt, as if she had dozed off or a particularly gloomy thought had stopped her in her tracks. As I lay beside my closed book, I had the urge to tell her that I agreed with her. However, I had recently decided that she was actually more optimistic about life than I was and that my black view of things was of a different order from hers. If I responded now, she would keep repeating the same inanities even more enthusiastically and give me a headache. Besides, as I said before, in my aunt's old-fashioned house with her children and granddaughters, I was helping myself to forget and so I was on my guard, keeping my wound hidden and hoping that life could go back to normal.

"What a wonderful year we spent in Kirkuk," my mother was saying, "like a dream! With your brother Mustafa and his children, Ahmad and Saman, and his wife Bilqis, God bless her! It was like a dream. Eating and sleeping, being with the family. It was lovely!"

"You were the one who wanted to come to Baghdad. You went on and on about it to me and Mustafa."

"So, what's wrong with that? We're from Baghdad, and we wanted to go back to where we belonged. All our relatives are here. But delightful Baquba—or rather dreadful Baquba—how did that come into the picture?" So saying, my mother struck her mouth twice with the flat of her hand.

I had hated this gesture since the first time I'd seen her doing it. It was not only vulgar and crude, but the way she did it repeatedly made it seem dubious and shameful. Eventually it had begun to trigger off vague ominous fears in me.

However, I said nothing this time. Even with her I was no longer open these days. I stifled every impulse to be outgoing and was trying to learn to withdraw from life. All this was against my nature, but it suited my recent habits. So I picked up my book again in silence to continue my search for soothing oblivion—an activity I had not yet mastered. I heard a lot of noise downstairs and an exchange of words between Suha and her mother and sister. Perhaps the tea was coming at last. I wasn't able to read. I looked surreptitiously at the sky, the clear sky of a summer's afternoon. There was more noise from the ground floor and someone calling my name. I put the book down.

"I don't know why they have to shout like that," said my mother.

Suha appeared in the doorway. "Auntie Munira. You're wanted downstairs."

I stood up.

"I hope everything's all right," remarked my mother. "May those who have forgotten their Lord remember Him."

As I walked along the gallery, Madiha called up to me that someone had come with my official transfer papers from Baquba. This seemed odd. My heart started beating, and I ran towards the staircase. Sana was standing by the middle door, so I held out my hand to her and took her along with me. I was always scared of the dark in the long passage. We walked towards the outer door in silence, and it occurred to me as we were about halfway along to go back indoors and let Madiha or my mother see who was at the door. Perhaps there was some mistake, which I wouldn't be able to deal with. But it could be the Baquba school janitor—I had heard them talking about a transfer order or something like that—and Sana was gripping my hand as if she was more afraid of the dark in the passage than I was! So I kept going, now that the effort seemed justified.

The door was ajar, and I stopped behind it. Fear can generate such strange notions. Holding on to the latch, I peered out. The faint light fell on the opposite wall, and I couldn't distinguish the features of the tall figure on the doorstep. I asked him some question, who he was, I think. He was looking away from me, and when I spoke he turned round. If I hadn't spoken, he wouldn't have turned round. I was asking him innocently who he was, not realizing that I was walking along a precipice. He faced me, and in spite of the dark I recognized the eyes, the long black moustache, the square jaw.

The only thing which is important about people is the history of their relationships, and for this reason they carry with them the terror and cruelty of the past. This face had a history, a sharp, cold knife that plunged into my entrails. I pushed the door shut and cowered behind it, but this was an illogical reaction, as I wasn't frightened so much as distressed. My limbs were jelly-like, and I could barely focus on him hammering at the door and shouting indistinctly. I seemed to lack the strength to run back into the house and continued to stare foolishly at a sheet of paper which Sana and I had trodden underfoot. However, I was not in a bad enough state to lose consciousness, although I think Sana thought I had passed out where I stood. He would soon go away. He wouldn't dare force his way in. He wouldn't dare do anything but leave. Noticing the door wasn't properly shut, I summoned my strength, gave it a good bang, and slid the bolt across. Then I leaned against it, my heart thudding. He began knocking more violently. As I held Sana's hot hand, his muffled tones drummed in my ears. Then the door shook violently as he appeared to kick it, repeatedly, and I found my breath suddenly becoming more labored as if a terrible heavy stone had been lowered on to my chest. My heartbeats grew slower and slower, and the rasping voice stopped my breath. I felt my self-control ebbing away rapidly as I stood leaning against the door, looking up at the sky, a chink of it, a luminous pathway far up above the two towering walls. The slow pounding of my heart diminished as I squeezed Sana's hand and felt my reserves collapsing bit by bit.

———

She was with him in the car speeding madly along the winding road which was lined with orange trees in blossom, whose perfume filled her nose and her soul as she moved her head in time to the sentimental song playing gently on the radio. He talked to her, laughing, but she didn't listen, so he began shouting but still she didn't listen. She opened the car window, and the warm spring air rushed in and her hair blew around her face. She was drunk with the smell of life on the blossom-laden breezes, glad to forget the irritations of the morning in her sister Maliha's house—the screaming children, the stupid behavior of their father, the complaints of her own mother. She had not imagined that deliverance would come so easily when she whispered to Adnan that she was bored and asked if they could go to his father's orchard on the banks of the river Diyala. It was a Friday, and as they slipped out of the house, the sun was singing in a diaphanous blue sky. He drove off down the narrow streets at this crazy speed, making people jump out of his way, until they reached the outskirts of Baquba. On the green-fringed country road, the song and the scent of orange blossom in the warm air had combined to intoxicate her; she could no longer hear what he said and answered him with happy laughter.

This was her second spring in Baquba. She had come there several years before, but only stayed a few days, and the vivid memory of the visit was always associated with the smell of orange blossom in her mind. Now she was back again to stay, as she had been transferred to a school there. She had had no idea what to expect before she and her mother arrived at her sister's house one dull evening the previous September. She knew vaguely that there were a lot of difficulties in the family, but didn't bother to go into them, agreeing with her mother and brother that the move to Baquba was the only solution for the coming school year, but hoping that it would be temporary. Her brother promised to talk to someone he knew in Kirkuk who could pull strings to have her transferred to Baghdad.

Adnan switched off the radio. She turned to him, and he switched it on again, laughing. He was a well-developed young man, only just eighteen, tall, with thick black hair and moustache, and fierce dark eyes. Because he was held in awe at home by his mother, brothers, sisters, and, to some extent, even his father, and because he had some ideas, not very clearly thought out, for subverting things, she felt drawn to him and was glad that she was his aunt and could remember his childhood and adolescence and have long, affectionate conversations with him. He grabbed hold of her flying hair and pulled it, and she pinched his hand gently. The trees rushed past on either side like unstoppable columns of mad soldiers. She was not the least bit afraid. She was used to his driving after all their lightning excursions to Baghdad. They would hear of a new film showing in one of the city's cinemas, slip out of the confines of the family circle, jump in the car, and fly like the wind. They came back after dark, not much bothered by anything her sister or brother-in-law might say. Deep down, Adnan's parents were scared of him, and Munira always wondered why. Was it his party affiliations, their concern for his future, or his unrestrained temper? When they complained about the cost of the petrol he used for these trips, they appeared satisfied by his joking reply that it was no more than the cost of one crate of tomatoes from his father's store.

He swerved sharply, and she was flung against the door. She screamed in fright, while he continued to sing. Bouncing in their seats, and leaving a cloud of dust behind them, they turned up a narrow dirt track in the bright sunshine.

She had noticed his rebellious personality when she first arrived. He was completely different from the rest of his family. His mother, her sister, told her that he had left school a year or two before when he was only in second year and had seemed quite capable of continuing with his studies. He had given up a few days after the attempt on the life of Abd al-Karim Qasim, come home, and never thought about school again. He worked with his father in his greengrocery business and began spending his time driving around in the car, sitting in cafés, or attending mysterious meetings. He had a revolver hidden somewhere, he had told his mother, and could get hold of a machine gun if he needed to.

Munira had once talked to him about politics and had been unable to dismiss his ideas as childish. For some reason this had annoyed her, and she had pulled his hair hard in mock aggravation, without knowing why. He had smiled at her with exaggerated kindness, and their friendship was consolidated. He seemed to admire her beauty and enjoy walking with her in the streets of Baquba, or accompanying her to the school, the shops, the cinema, or the railway station, where they used to watch the train leaving for Baghdad at sunset.

At home he was bad-tempered with his brothers and sisters, sometimes hitting them for no reason, looked down on his mother, and refused to acknowledge his father's authority over him. As time passed, he only seemed interested in her, and this pleased her and flattered her pride. She was aware of her power over this violent creature and enjoyed reprimanding him, sometimes intervening when he threatened to hit one of his little sisters. One day his mother had called her to come and help, and she had run down from her room and seized hold of his arm to restrain him. He had stood there, red in the face, like a wild animal about to pounce, looking at her with blazing eyes. His little sister had been in tears in front of him, but he had just stared at the hand on his arm, then walked off without a word. Later on, he had begged her not to come near him when he was in this state. Chewing on his lip, he had told her that he didn't always know what he might be capable of and that she should restrict herself to shouting at him from a distance. She had pulled his carefully groomed hair and for the first time he had responded in a similar vein and twisted her arm. She had felt his strong, rough, warm hand on her and cried out in pain. They had been in the kitchen together, making tea for the family one afternoon two or three months after Munira and her mother's arrival.

He stopped the car by a big gate at the end of the track and jumped out. She followed him, helped him unlock the gate, and they raced off into the orchard. The sun was hot, the damp air refreshing; it was just after eleven o'clock. She ran ahead of him up a dusty path, her body feeling lighter than usual, as if she was about to take off, lightly skimming the treetops which swayed in the breeze, letting her whole being fill up with sun and life.

In those days she didn't feel constrained or ill at ease with him. She was fond of him and unselfconscious in his company. She did not take herself to task regarding her relationship to him and behaved as if she was immune, so she saw no particular significance in the repeated contact between their bodies, their growing mutual affection, or his excessive admiration for her. There were enough prohibitions to do with kinship, tradition, age, and respect to make her feel safe and disregard the signs of veiled desire in his hands, his words, his glances.

She bounded uninhibitedly towards a little copse. She was wearing a light blue blouse and gray skirt which she had picked out for no special reason as far as she could remember. The skirt was tight and short, and her blonde hair was loose on her shoulders. She ran and jumped over the narrow streams, for the pleasure of filling her lungs with the pure, perfumed air, and batted the trees with her hand as she passed.

He followed her in silence, and when she stopped, exhausted, under an orange tree covered in white flowers, he came rapidly towards her. He was red in the face, his black hair flopping on to his forehead, and he carried his jacket over his arm, but she didn't notice anything unusual about him. As she laughed and tried to catch her breath, he threw his jacket playfully over her head. She made to fend it off before it reached her, but it was covering her face as she felt his arms go round her. Hurriedly she pushed it out of the way, and his face was right next to hers, his breath on her, as hot as the sun. Still panting from her exertions, she looked inquiringly at him, then blew in his face to tease him. Her mind was completely blank. He squeezed her tight against him. She shouted at him and blew in his face again. A long time went by. Their bodies were touching; she felt her chest pressing against his, and her rapid breathing pushed her breasts up hard against him. At last she asked him to let her go. She was exhausted, her body and emotions in turmoil. She begged him not to bother her any more and to let her go. He held her tighter and tried to enclose her body within his broad thighs; she couldn't believe what was happening, was reluctant to acknowledge the reality. He tried to kiss her and she moved her mouth away; immediately, in another part of her body, she felt an instinctive movement from him, which told her clearly what he had in mind. She was a little surprised, but not afraid; another word from her would bring him to his senses. She wanted to get free of him and cut this dreadful current passing between them, and she pushed him away. She pushed him gently, somewhat disgusted at the idea which had come to her mind, but her resistance brought their bodies closer and he moved more urgently on the lower part of her stomach. Her limbs were tense, and her weary heart thudded with abnormal force. Her head turned involuntarily for a moment and she was staring straight into his burning eyes and up his broad nostrils, smelling the sweat on his fiery body. She took hold of his shoulders, trying again to break free from him, and felt his body bend towards her violently and his mouth clamp on to hers.

She shuddered, then took in a mouthful of air to avoid suffocating. At that moment she became fully aware of what was happening to her. The events fell rapidly into place in her mind and the sudden horror of the realization made her shake uncontrollably. She shouted something which she couldn't remember afterwards, then collapsed beneath his weight. While he was leaning against her, he had managed to draw one of her legs towards him and keep hold of it. She felt no pain as she hit the ground but as she became aware of her naked thighs she realized the extent of her humiliation. She was being treated like a dirty animal and had this overwhelming desire to cry with sorrow and anger and shame. He was pushing up her skirt, and she clenched her legs together, then she aimed her fist at his head which was buried in her neck. He recoiled slightly and she saw his face, his crazed expression as he fought to hang on to his prey. He slapped her, then punched her in the jaw. Her body went slack momentarily, as she reeled from the impact of the blow. Her legs opened and he pulled off the rest of her clothes. For a split second she had a profound sense of what was happening to her: she was on the edge of the abyss, contemplating her end. Her whole life was concentrated in these few moments when her nakedness, her virginity, and the cruel vertigo within her merged, and she submitted. The fear came belatedly, fear of everything: the distant shadows, the hot earth under her buttocks, the sun, the knife piercing her entrails, the shuddering sighs and the blood which stained the trembling flesh.

She screamed and screamed and screamed, to stay alive, to stop herself from going crazy. He stood in front of her, stupefied, panting for breath, then looked down and tried to cover up his bloody genitals. But she no longer saw him. He had left her world forever. She lay on the ground, which was spattered with her blood, and screamed, dry-eyed, in the spring sunshine among the blossoming orange trees.

———

I sank down and down until I reached the bottom, then came the fluttering of the heart which separates life from death. A tiny pulse, followed by a rush of blood, and I was back in this murky world. The ribbon of sky, shining tenderly above my head, restored my sense of time and place. I breathed hard, to avoid suffocating, and became aware of gentle fingertips touching me. It was Sana, with her round dark eyes and lips tightly closed, begging me for reassurance; the crazy, disjointed whispering and light knocking scared her more than me. Again I saw the crumpled sheet of paper, like a sail, on the dark floor of the passage. Sana rushed and picked it up and brought it to me. We were both equally determined to escape back inside, but when I saw her walking on tiptoe, her head down as if she were avoiding poisoned arrows, I realized that, even though she had nothing to be afraid of, she was more upset than me. In the darkness of the passage, I seized her and held her close.

Later in the hot room I sat on my bed, neither listening to the noise around me nor replying to my mother and Aunt Safiya's questions. I was trying to collect myself, feeling as if I had been picked out at random and crushed between the jaws of a grinder. I was trembling slightly and felt a cold sweat breaking out on my head and chest. Pride, beauty, and insolence no longer served any purpose. The sun had set, and I lay on my bed with the folded paper in my hand. I was not a victim, as tradition required, nor an anonymous corpse lying butchered on the side of the road, nor a feather in the wind, as they say. I was a bit of each of these, lost in the midst of miseries and vile acts which were not meant to be divulged. I didn't complain because I wasn't meant to. I preferred to tell myself that the little I had left could have been destroyed too.

That was how I learned very quickly to think about what was left and care for it. So I erased some of the big headlines from my life and dragged my shattered limbs along to join the tail end of the caravan, where I would remain. Among the spiritually and emotionally damaged, you could live without pride or glory; among them the future and human aspiration had no meaning, and sometimes you found wonderful small happinesses there.

Madiha and her daughters, my Aunt Nuriya and my mother were gathered round me in the shadows, asking me about the folded paper in my hand, the mysterious visitor, the tea which I hadn't yet drunk. I sat up to face them, wiping the sweat off my face, and tried to smile.

———

Before we went to Baquba I used to think of myself as separate from the rest of the world; what concerned other people, determined their destinies, made them live as they did, could not possibly influence the future which I had marked out for myself. It was difficult to know where this feeling came from but, relying on my looks and my salary, I thought I could be confident of finding a comfortably-off, well-educated young man as a husband. We had been told, on dubious authority sometimes, that marriage was everything in a girl's life here, as both a means and an end, and included legitimate sex and children, and other pleasant things besides, and also a man. They did well to keep quiet about the bad side and leave us to enjoy the dreams that always float around these subjects, to hope eternally, since there is no life without hope. A flagrant lie. There are plenty of lives without hope! It may seem impossible to live such a life, but habit and time take care of everything. I for my part was relying on them, and also aiming for a psychological and mental state which could only be disrupted by something totally unexpected.

During my long hours alone before we left Baquba, I began to think what might have happened to me and quickly came to the conclusion that my survival was a matter of pure chance. Also, being able to keep the event a secret had smothered it and transformed it into an obscure incident which meant nothing to anyone else. If it hadn't been for her feminine instinct, and some signs which I couldn't conceal, my mother herself could have been kept completely in the dark. As it was, she had only a confused image in her mind: something had happened to her daughter, some kind of physical or mental crisis, but she couldn't be sure what it was.

Furthermore, I had managed to escape the most obvious outcome of a male-female liaison. I jumped for joy and cried with relief when my period came on time and I saw the first drops of blood. What a violent barometer blood can be, presaging good one moment and evil the next!

This truly drew a line under what had been, and meant I had to make a new start. Without Adnan knowing in advance, I made plans for my mother and me to escape. I begged the school head to accept my exam scripts and marks before the other teachers' and let me leave early to go to Baghdad. So it was that, one afternoon towards the end of May, my mother and I left Baquba behind us. The fresh, damp air was heavy with the scent of the orchards, and I couldn't wait to abandon that unlucky town.

I didn't look behind me as we crossed the bridge and turned our faces to the horizon, and the black, winding road stretching ahead of us. Death, humiliation, and shame were back there, and I didn't think I needed any of them. But to my surprise I wiped away a tear as the lines of green vanished into the distance. I remembered the songs, the faces, the fresh air, and the countryside, and contemplated the tiny thing which my life had been reduced to now.

We reached Baghdad in the late afternoon and made for the old quarter of Bab al-Shaykh, with its ancient houses and kindly relatives. We hadn't visited them for months, but this didn't mean the affection between us was diminished. As we sat drinking tea in the alcove, I felt as if I was immersed in the sun's warmth after the cold of winter. In a way, I felt safe with them. When they told me their son, Abd al-Karim, was unwell I went in with them to see him and exchange friendly words with him. Before I went to sleep, in a room with all its windows open, I cried briefly into my pillow, for different reasons this time: at least I wasn't going to die here. As I came down from the roof at dawn one day some time after our arrival, it struck me that—given that I had no right to anything and ought to be dead now—the damp breeze I smelled as I stood alone in the empty house was in itself a small happiness of the particular kind enjoyed by the stragglers at the back of the caravan, the rejects, those who really notice the sun, flowers, birds, and kind hearts.

There were other small joys. Conversations with that enchanting imp, Sana, every morning as we ate our breakfast together: bread, cheese, and mint tea under the olive tree. Hours reading in the quiet bedroom with nobody watching over me. Family gatherings in the late afternoon in the alcove to drink tea where, whether anybody noticed or not, I felt relaxed and happy to be with them. Endless contemplation of the sky and the stars as I lay in my cool bed on the vast terrace where the breezes played. Listening with apparent indifference to the veiled conversations of the old ladies and even the childish onslaughts of Aunt Safiya, who didn't mean to hurt anybody.

One beautiful morning, a few days after the arrival of my official transfer, my mother, Aunt Safiya, and I were in the room we all shared before the sun had got round to its windows. Aunt Safiya, having had breakfast, had sent my grandmother Umm Hasan on some obscure mission to the kitchen, and I was reading, lying on the bed, when I heard her saying to my mother, "Tell me, Najiya, is Baquba dear? I mean the vegetables, the housing, the cost of living? Is it like Baghdad, I wonder?"

"Why should it be like Baghdad? It's a stinking hole. It's dead. A graveyard. Why would it be expensive? It's not fit for human beings to live in."

"God is great! Why does your daughter live there then?"

"That's life, dear. Didn't you know?"

"Not really. God is the most knowing."

A period of silence. I stopped reading. Then Aunt Safiya's questions started up again. "Wouldn't it have been better for you both to stay in Baquba? What appeals to you about this God-forsaken place? Every day, bang! bang! You never know when all hell's going to break loose. You could have stayed quietly in Baquba without anyone bothering you and telling you things you already knew."

A long silence. I put my book down.

"Yes," said my mother as if she was talking to herself. "He who knows knows, and he who doesn't know is less useful than a handful of lentils."

Aunt Safiya stared sharply at her. "There must be some reason," she muttered.

"Why must there? One of my daughters had some bad luck. Was that our fault? Does it mean we're doomed to go on living the same miserable life forever? To be cheated of our just deserts, I mean? God wouldn't accept it. Everyone has heaven or hell ahead of him."

"God is great. God is great. 'Lord, defend us from . . .' I don't remember how the verse goes. What's going on, Najiya? Is something wrong? What is it? Tell me, my dear."

My head spun for a moment, and I sat up on the bed. They both looked at me in some surprise. Their conversation had ceased to be amusing.

"Aunt," I said, "my transfer to Baghdad has come through and everything is sorted out. Why do you still need to talk like this and ask all these questions? We're not from Baquba, so why should we live there? What's there for us? We're from Baghdad, all our family are here, so we ought to come back here."

"Yes, Munira, dear. You put it so well. But this man, your Aunt Nuriya's husband, he hasn't a thing. You know that. Not a penny. And those cousins of yours—they're grown men. And people don't know how to keep their mouths shut. This area—Bab al-Shaykh—isn't what it used to be. Those who remain don't fear the Lord, can't distinguish truth from lies. What is there here for you? Do you think you can find something in Bab al-Shaykh?"

For no reason, or for many reasons, I wanted to tease her: "Do you mean if we've lost something, Aunt, we'll be able to find it in Bab al-Shaykh?"

She raised her arms in the air and let them fall again. "I pity the person who tries to make a living in Bab al-Shaykh!" she exclaimed. "God help him a thousand times!"

"Why are you talking like this, Safiya?" interrupted my mother with a sudden flash of bad temper. "Aren't we allowed to stay a few days with my sister? Why do you keep on about it? Nobody else cares. What's it got to do with you?"

I stood up to leave. Aunt Safiya was silent as she scrutinized my mother's face, uncertain how to interpret her words. The discussion was turning into an excavation of the past, which I hated. I wasn't scared of Aunt Safiya as a person, but of her instincts. She sprayed us with her bitter truths like polluted rain. Men and the eternal female! I found it strange how much truth there was in her pronouncements. But according to the strict conditions which I had laid down for myself, her words were rubbish and should be disregarded.

When I first saw my two cousins again, I realized that they were mature young men, and it would be pointless to remember the past and try to change them back into silly young boys. We had grown up, and our relationship had inevitably moved on to a different level. I understood this perfectly, and yet I was reluctant to read anything into Midhat's meaningful glances, smiles, private words, or obvious liking for me. I was recovering from a sickness which still came back to haunt me and was happy not to have to analyze things. But as we traveled to work together every morning and lived our daily life in the intimacy of the big house, he moved closer to me, to the point of touching me, deliberately or otherwise. I ought to have done the following two things: been honest with myself about what was going on and taken a decision. I did neither. My pleasure at having him accompany me to school was quickly overshadowed by a gloomy anxiety which snuffed out any other emotion. Somehow I felt helpless and did not want to act. Was I not a typical daughter of this country, suspended eternally between death and prostitution?

Then he bared both our faces and stood me naked in front of the mirror without warning. It began in a taxi which we boarded in a hurry, sitting squashed up next to the driver. He told me he had promised to take Sana to the cinema later in the day. That fine autumn morning, for the first time, he whispered something in my ear. My only answer was an embarrassed smile, or that was what it was meant to be. He rested his arm protectively along the seat behind me. His fingers rested lightly on my right shoulder, his thigh against mine. I smelt the familiar smell of his toothpaste and felt a slight tickle where he'd whispered in my ear. I had no reason to turn towards him, so looking straight ahead with the same embarrassed smile, I asked him what this had to do with me. He told me Sana refused to go without me, and so the decision was up to me. I saw nothing wrong in this indirect invitation to go out with him, and it didn't occur to me to refuse outright. First of all, I wanted to go, to enjoy myself, and secondly, at the time I couldn't think of a polite way to refuse. Similarly, I wasn't particularly conscious of the mysterious relationship between our shoulders touching, our visit to the cinema, and the smiles we got from my aunt and uncle and Madiha when we said we were going. I stifled a premonition that I was hiding from myself things which I understood, or ought to understand, and convinced myself that I was overreacting. However, when he leaned towards me in the dim light of the cinema, asking what I thought about a friend of his who wanted to propose marriage to a girl, but didn't know whether to talk to her parents or approach her directly, I knew I should have refused his invitation. I felt myself turn pale with fear. God, how terrified I was by those few words, whispered so gently! I remained speechless, staring at the moving colors on the distant screen. I had the impression he was looking at me. Perhaps he was waiting for an answer, but what answer? I spoke to Sana, to take my mind off him. She was sitting at the front of our box, completely wrapped up in the film. She answered me quickly and turned back to the film. I felt him moving his seat closer to mine, then he repeated the apparently innocent question. There was no escaping it. I asked him why he thought I was capable of expressing a relevant opinion on such matters.

You're sensible. Balanced. Well-educated. Have a different point of view. Moistening my lips, I told him it would be better for his friend to follow tradition and approach the family to ask for her hand. Then I regretted what I'd said. I could possibly escape from him if I acted on my own, but if my mother or brother were involved, it didn't even bear thinking of. Hurriedly I said that if the girl was broad-minded, modern in her thinking, and knew what was coming, he could approach her in person, wait for her answer, and be understanding. I was speaking in a whisper like him, out of the corner of my mouth, half turned towards him. All the time my heart was beating wildly, and I had a persistent sense of foreboding. I thanked God that all this was happening in a place where the lights were low and intermittent. Then I saw him move vaguely and felt his hand touch my arm, which was resting on the arm of the seat. For a moment I didn't know how to react. I was confused, rather than upset. Should I pretend, like all girls do, that I didn't feel anything, or ask him to explain himself, turn and look at him, move my arm? But he was whispering to me again, asking if I was generally opposed to marriage. I turned towards him, somewhat surprised. He looked handsome: the light was reflected in his eyes and on his hair, and he had an irresistible smile on his lips. It amazed me that this elegant youth was approaching me, talking to me so kindly. His face was flushed, lit up, happy. I couldn't think what to answer, so I turned away from him. He squeezed my arm gently. I murmured that it had nothing to do with me. He asked why.

I had calmed down slightly during this game of words and was in no hurry to answer him, staring straight ahead at the screen, but aware of the pressure of his hand and his eyes on me. Why did he think that I, of all people, was qualified to talk about marriage? But that wasn't the question; the question was are you for marriage or against it? Does it bother you that people marry one another, love one another, have children together?

I had no choice but to say I was for marriage, especially as saying I was against it meant nothing in my view. He said he was with me on this and backed me up wholeheartedly. Suddenly I laughed at the tortuous way he was conducting the encounter, trying to appear as if he had nothing specific in mind. He laughed with me, and Sana turned round and bombarded us with questions. I drew my arm away, he let go and sat back, and we resumed our normal positions.

I took a few deep breaths. Perhaps I had been wrong to laugh, as the victim. Laughter would allow this earnest suitor to think that his prey was looking for a net to throw herself into, and, Lord, it was the first sign of consent.

I withdrew silently, sitting as far away from him as I could. I wasn't sad; by nature I was inclined to be cheerful and happy; but the millstone I had chosen to be tied to was dragging me down, away from warmth and life and sweet folly, and I couldn't abandon it all without regret.

We watched the film to the end without exchanging more than a few words and left with the crowd. He held my arm whenever he got the chance, and I tried to avoid physical contact with him as far as possible. It made me feel uncomfortably tense and apprehensive, and I had never grown used to it, although it had happened repeatedly for over two months. The cool night breeze struck our faces as we emerged into the busy street. He wanted us to take a taxi; I objected, but he insisted. Sana didn't give us the chance to talk on the way home, and he seemed quite happy to listen to her chatter. I was relieved that the film and the perilous conversations which had accompanied it were over. When we reached the dark turning up to the house and got out of the taxi, I heard the mosque clock chiming slowly and melodiously. Sana went ahead of us with her short, rapid steps. The walls of the dimly lit alley seemed to be swaying. Suddenly he said in a calm voice, "Are you going to give me an answer, Munira?"

He was walking unhurriedly, looking at me.

My heart immediately beat faster. "Answer to what?"

"You mean you didn't understand what I was talking about—in the cinema?"

Fear returned, constricting my breathing. "No. Sorry."

"How about now?"

"What do you mean, Midhat?"

"I mean—would you consider—marrying me?"

He stumbled slightly over the last words. My heartbeat was reverberating in my chest, my mouth, at the ends of my toes. I felt a twinge of pain somewhere in my head and pulled the *abaya* more closely round me, covering part of my face. We were just a few meters from the house, and Sana was on the doorstep in the dim light, waiting for us. She looked so far away, a speck on the horizon. If only I hadn't let her go ahead of us, he wouldn't have been able to talk.

I walked on, silent as a mummy, stumbling a couple of times as we approached the door. Sana called out that she was scared of scorpions and didn't want to walk along the long passage alone. As I came up to her, she took my hand firmly.

The three of us entered the house in silence. They were waiting impatiently for us, as if we had been away for years. Midhat smiled as he asked me in front of his mother if I was hungry. I said no. I was trembling all over and just wanted to throw myself down on the bed. My mother asked why we were late, but I didn't reply.

They brought me something light to eat as I lay on my bed in our room. This excessive concern embarrassed me, and I thanked Madiha several times. For no obvious reason, I felt completely numb and had no desire to sleep or change from my outdoor clothes, although I was exhausted. I was told that Abd al-Karim was asking about us. Karim? This person tormented by his fantasies, whom life made ill, who resembled me; would he be able to offer me a word of comfort, a sign, an answer to a question? I got up and went towards his room, my mind blank, just wanting to see him. As if miracles happened on demand!

———

I remembered a woman in a film I had seen several years before. A wretched creature from a village in Italy, deprived of care and affection all her life, and when she found them in a kind, charming clown, her husband killed him in front of her. I didn't remember much about the film—its name or even what the main characters looked like—only the state of the woman after the death of the clown. Something snapped inside her, and she looked as if her life had been abruptly snuffed out. She stopped helping her husband in his work and fell ill, and the whole time she moaned gently, like someone dying or refusing to live. She began when she woke up and continued at intervals throughout the day and the following night. I remembered her when I became conscious that I was sighing repeatedly. It happened, regardless of the time or place: on a crowded bus returning from school; on my bed before the afternoon siesta; at tea time as I turned the spoon round endlessly in the little glass; at night, when I first lay down; at midnight and at dawn. In some way it soothed me to make these wordless sounds, but what did they mean? Was it my soul talking?

I was a ghost, shunning the daylight. I didn't like being alone, but solitude was my last refuge. They were all hounding me. I felt oppressed by their meaningful words, gestures, and looks. They were obsessed by one question alone; it showed on their faces and colored everything they did. Why didn't I say yes, become another bead on the rosary, live on the same plane as the rest of humanity, agree quickly and come and share their lives?

It was worse than those last bitter days in Baquba, when I was escaping the shadows and looking for obscurity in the sunshine, negotiating to stay alive a little while longer. At the time I was certain that the incident in the orchard meant I didn't have long to live, that something would suddenly finish me off. The anarchic atmosphere of the big house in Baquba had changed; it seemed to be entirely directed at gathering together reasons to hate me more. It wasn't clear to me how this son of theirs had managed to convince them that I'd become his mortal enemy overnight, but I took refuge in our miserable, hot room, pretending to be ill. My mother brought my meals up and incarcerated herself with me, forgetting everything but her love for me. When I came back from school to sit hunched up on the edge of the bed in the dark room, running with sweat, and dreading any sound outside, I felt I was losing my mind.

On the fifth or sixth day Adnan confronted me, when my mother had gone out for some reason. I didn't understand exactly what he wanted from me. He opened the door and stood in the doorway, looking at me silently. I hid my head in my arms, wiping away a few tears. I couldn't see his face properly. He walked rapidly up to me as if he was going to throw himself off a cliff or kiss the feet of his dead lover. His dark shape and the bloody memory filled me with terror. I was almost crazy, and I screamed at him before he had a chance to blink or catch his breath. He backed away in horror, gabbling incomprehensibly, and left the room, while I stared blankly in front of me through my tears, then began to emit a series of howls worthy of a ravening wolf. Their dislike of me increased. I cut myself off from them and felt my best bet was to concentrate on staying sane and alive. It helped me if I treated them as enemies, persecuted them as they persecuted me, behaved coldly and resentfully to them.

In Baquba, as time went by, I became focused on saving myself. I didn't sigh day and night as I did now, when I felt I was heading inexorably towards a locked door whose key they had cruelly given to me. Midhat and his mother were the only members of the family who avoided me: they thought they deserved an answer and felt the passing of time put them in an awkward position. But they didn't say anything. Midhat distanced himself from me a little and pursued me less than before, and I was grateful for that. But his mother—my aunt—continued to express her bitter dissatisfaction through her tired eyes. Her greetings, her conversations, her silence, her rare laughter, and her preoccupied air were all accompanied by looks which said one thing: their precious daughter was treating them badly, with no justification.

Then one day I realized that my thoughts weren't going anywhere. They were mixed up with my emotions all the time and went round in circles bringing me no nearer to a resolution. I lived within these very precise psychological and intellectual boundaries that I had set for myself, without profiting from them to help me make a decision. I was indulging my sadness, enjoying going back to lick my wounds, as if I had all the time in the world. It was my mother who made me see this. I was in bed one October night around midnight, not thinking of anything as usual, floating in a sort of invisible sea of gloom and misery. My mother lay quietly on her mattress on the floor beside me in the room we shared with my grandmother and Aunt Safiya.

"Why are you sighing such a lot?" she asked suddenly. I jumped and held my breath, but she went on talking quietly. "You're sensible, Munira dear. I've let you do what you think best. You're all I've got, and you know what makes you happy, what kind of a future you want. But don't torment yourself like this. We have to be able to recognize our own fates. And the two of us alone are nothing, my dear."

All around us was quiet, and her hesitant murmuring touched my heart. She had never talked to me like this before. She was beside me; I leaned against her and she held me, and the warmth of her affection gave me strength. But she couldn't share the crisis with me. She knew

215

that she could no longer give me advice, that I wouldn't listen to her opinions. I saw her forcing herself to hold her tongue, and suffering because I was suffering.

I sighed deeply. She was trying to give me signals, on the strength of her intuition.

"Why are we helpless on our own, Mum?" I asked her, as if I was talking to myself. "What's wrong with the world? I've got my salary, and you've got your pension. Can't we live like that, you and I? Will we really die if I don't get married?"

"No, of course not, dear, God bless you. Why ever would we die? But I'm just saying people are only interested in themselves in this world, and we're on our own. We only have God. We're cut off from the tree."

When she began repeating herself like that, I realized it was pointless to try and discuss anything with her. She only had one idea in her mind, which she repeated again and again, and she still had no effect on me. I felt I would oppose her with all my being if necessary. However, the veiled meaning contained in her pronouncements was reinforced by kind words from an unexpected source. One evening a few days later, they were taken up with entertaining female relatives. I helped Madiha bring them tea and food from the kitchen, then took a glass of tea and a piece of cake to Midhat's father in his room. He was sitting by the open door, playing with his prayer beads, and smiled broadly, showing his yellow teeth under his gray moustache. His unqualified good nature gave him the innocent air of a misunderstood child. He thanked me with an effusiveness which embarrassed me, then, when he saw I was about to go, said affectionately, "Munira, my child, can I have a word with you?"

I stood awkwardly by the door, holding the tray behind my back. His right eyelid trembled for a moment, and his lower lip twitched before he spoke in his broad Baghdadi accent. "A little thing I haven't had the chance to tell you before." He put the beads down and picked up the glass of tea. "I want you to know, to be sure, I mean . . ." He began rotating the spoon in the glass at an extraordinary rate. "This house is your house, and the door is always open to you. Don't say, 'It depends what happens.' Please remember what I'm telling you now. This house will never shut its door in your face."

Then he smiled his innocent child's smile, as if he was apologizing. I went out, muttering some vague words of thanks, and stood on my own in the empty alcove. Then I sat down on a chair in a dark corner and sobbed as I hadn't sobbed for a long time. My tears fell gently through my hands which covered my eyes. I had never felt so miserable, desperate, and alone; it was the painful discovery of my own weakness and insignificance. The road ahead of me was closed, but there was no way back. His words were a continuation of my mother's message. We, who were rootless, severed from the tree, who could only watch while our destinies were acted out, had no room to choose. We could pretend otherwise but the fact remained: we were isolated from society and despised.

The sunset sky, this sad evening, glowed clear and pure, but the courtyard looked as dark as a bottomless pit to me. My heart was empty. The few tears which I'd shed out of the blue had relieved me. I saw Sana coming from downstairs and asked her to bring me a glass of water. The noise of the guests' laughter and conversation continued uninterrupted, making my head ache. I sat the little girl down next to me and drank some of the water, then splashed the rest on my face and smoothed my hair down with my wet hand. Sana watched fascinated, and I threw the last few drops of water over her for fun. I asked where her uncles were, and she said they'd gone out before the guests arrived.

It occurred to me that if I dropped a line to my brother Mustafa, letting him know indirectly about our current situation, he could—what? I didn't have the strength to be scheming and manipulative, even though everybody expected it of me because girls normally were. Anyway, my brother wouldn't tell me anything new, since he didn't know the whole story. Nobody in the world could tell me anything I didn't know already.

I told myself that I shouldn't be looking for any new revelations. My view of things had been shattered, and life appeared full of contradictions. What I needed desperately now was a straightforward perspective on the realities of my life, so that I could accept them and also have confidence in them, for God's sake.

When Sana left me, I had a desire to go up on the empty terrace to enjoy the view of the sky, fling myself into that blue sparkling ocean, and lose myself for a while.

They were coming out of the guest room, still chattering non-stop, five stout women who hadn't shut up for two hours. They passed me standing in my corner and interrupted themselves briefly to say goodbye to me. As I watched them, and myself face to face with them, against the background of the dark courtyard and the clear sky, I had the overwhelming sensation that I had no fundamental connection with this group of people, these compact mounds of flesh, of which I was supposedly one. I stood apart, hovering between life and death, self-delusion and suffering, weaker than a reed and yet responsible for the rising and setting of the sun. I could neither prevent anything happening, nor continue to procrastinate any longer. I was only human. To resolve things, it would be enough to get up one night, instead of lying in bed pretending to sleep, and stand on the gallery screaming into the darkness. Then I would either get peace of mind or go mad. Sometimes I wanted to pray to the Lord to have pity on me. Then I would hesitate: whether our destinies were decided in advance or were in our own hands, any form of hope seemed equally futile.

Then I began to think about him, Abd al-Karim, who was always there, somewhere inside me. I'd been told he'd failed his exams and would have to repeat the year. I knew only too well what such a failure would mean to this creature ruled by his memories and his ghosts. As I considered myself to be close to him, I thought that I should somehow face this setback with him. Besides, he knew about Midhat proposing, and perhaps he understood something which I didn't understand or saw something which I couldn't see. He might be able to do something or give me the strength to wait for a last shred of hope or sign of deliverance. So one autumn afternoon, I climbed the worn, unpaved stairs to the terrace. A short time before I had seen him coming out of his room and walking towards the door leading to the stairs, supporting himself on the wooden balustrade from time to time. There was an invigorating nip in the air, so I picked up a shawl and followed him.

He didn't see me at first. All around me was the immensely clear blue sky, splashed with the red of the setting sun. I stood catching my breath, dazzled by the spread of colors. He was leaning against the wall, his head bathed in the sun's last blazing rays. The empty wooden beds were lined up around the terrace like coffins. Suddenly he noticed me, and I went towards him. He seemed wary of me, buttoning up his jacket uneasily and moistening his lips with the tip of his tongue as he looked at me. This made me uncomfortable. I greeted him quietly and asked him why he hadn't told me about failing his exams. I was shocked by the foolish expression which descended on his face; it was quite unfamiliar to me.

"Sorry. I don't know. It's not important," he said, with his face turned away from me.

He looked thin and bent as he put his hands in the pockets of his wide trousers and wandered aimlessly over to the other wall nearby. He was ill at ease, and I realized I hadn't chosen a good time to talk to him.

"Only relatively important. Anyway, you can pass with flying colors next year," I said.

He didn't answer, making do with a vague grunt and a sarcastic smile, and kicked a small stone without looking at me. Then he raised his eyes to the sunset, where the laughing sun was fading. His nose looked enormous in the middle of his mournful face. I was going to say something more about his passing his exam brilliantly next time but he spoke first. "Don't comfort me, Munira. You of all people. You talked to me a lot before the exam. I remember everything you said. But I thought it was irrelevant because it hadn't crossed my mind that I'd fail." He stood at some distance from me, prodding the ground with the toe of his shoe. "Why do they want to soften the blow? There's no need. What's done's done. If I'd known it didn't matter, I wouldn't have bothered. But now what?"

"What do you mean, now what? What are you planning, Karim?"

"Nothing. What do you expect? I've failed and I have to take the consequences. We're always trying to escape the consequences of our actions. I don't understand why. I want to take the responsibility and be done with it."

"Be done with it how?" He had provoked me and I persisted. "It seems to me you're contradicting yourself, Karim. A few months ago you were saying the exam would be easy. You hardly thought about it. It didn't interest you. Now you're regarding failure as a life sentence. How can you? What's more, accepting the consequences of your actions doesn't mean giving up. Wouldn't that be a contradiction? You accept unfortunate consequences in order to progress beyond them, move on, don't you?"

He continued digging up the earth with his shoe then smoothing it down, again and again. A few of his hairs looked bright red. It was for my own benefit that I was fighting against his weakness, doubt, and confusion.

"I don't know," he said in a low, uncertain voice. "I don't know. It's just that everything has to end. Why don't we acknowledge it?"

"What do you mean, Karim? I don't understand."

He looked up at me suddenly. "Sorry, Munira. I'm not saying anything complicated. But. . . ." his voice was cold and firm and didn't fit with the bitterness on his face. "I'm a failure. I'm no use. I'm weak and incompetent, and I can't tell you that I'm going to improve. On the contrary, I get worse each day. That's about it. I'm done for, useless."

"Why are you talking like this?" My heart was pounding, but I stayed calm. I was fully aware that he was aiming his words at me and knew exactly what he was saying. Ironic, when I'd come to him for comfort. Leaning against a wooden bedstead, he looked at me. I repeated my words slowly. "Why are you talking like this, Karim?"

He clenched his fingers, then relaxed them, and walked over to the far side of the terrace. With his shoulders bowed, he stood staring at the dark wall. My heart was still thudding; I was a little afraid and felt dejected. The vast, brilliantly colored sky above us looked as if it was about to close up forever. It occurred to me that I was listening to the tone of his voice, rather than to what he was saying, and that this was crazy.

Then I noticed he was coming back. He turned round silently and came and sat on the bed in front of me, his hands clasped in his lap as if he was praying, the sunset sky forming a halo around him.

"Sorry, Munira," he said in a deep, muffled voice. "I don't know why you're asking me what I'm talking about. You know very well. All the same, I must tell you, I'm not only a failure with no plans, but I'm also somebody without any hope. I mean I'm a failure not just because I don't have the skills, but because—I don't have any faith, I'm not interested in life." He raised his hand to stop me talking. "No, no, please. Only you, Munira. You're the one unusual thing in my life. You . . ." He dropped his eyes and whispered, "What are you? And what do I want from you? And why should a stupid, useless person like me love you? And if . . ." His voice was lost in the darkness and I listened, trembling like a small leaf blowing in the wind. "Why do I love you so much, Munira? And why are you so far away from me?"

He hid his face in his hands. He was addressing a ghost. I was frightened by the hollow, dream-like ring to his voice. I couldn't lose my hope now in the meanderings of his fantasies. I held out my hand to him. I was trembling too much to speak. First I wanted to touch him, to feel the warmth of life in him, then perhaps I could get inside him, find my image there, but my fingers didn't even reach him. My gesture startled him and he recoiled slightly, staring at my hand in fright, like somebody who had been woken from a deep sleep, then he frowned, and his expression changed. His jaw and lower lip hung slack and something died in his eyes: a light, a mirage, a sun. He sighed and stood up hastily, banging his foot against the end of the bed. I let my hand fall to my side. He walked agitatedly away from me into the shadows, dragging himself along beside the bare earth wall, then stopped and rested his arm on it, looking at the ground as if he'd lost something there: hope or the meaning of life. I was astounded. For a moment I had thought he wanted to take me by the hand, this man who had seemed as if he understood everything and knew the answers to all the riddles. I stood up. A small fragment of the happiness triggered off in me by his confession of love lingered on, and I was confused and hesitant. I was going to go back downstairs, but instead I approached him. My mind was blank, but I didn't want everything to end like this.

He began talking to me before I reached him, not turning round but standing in the same miserable pose, looking at the ground. "I'm sorry, Munira. Don't take any notice of what I said. I didn't mean any of it."

I froze where I was. I had to say something to make sure he knew what he was saying, to convey my inflamed emotions to him.

"Why are you sorry? Karim, do you regret . . . ?"

"Don't delude yourself, Munira. Don't delude yourself. I'm finished. There's no point in me being alive."

"Why? Why, Karim? My dear, why?"

He was as still as a stone for a few moments, then he turned round slowly, still clinging to the wall. His face was wet with tears. "No, Munira. Don't speak to me like that. Please. I've had it. I'm a coward. If I hadn't completely given up hope, I'd never have dared talk about— my love." He put his hand up quickly to wipe his eyes. "I can't be part of your life, Munira. I can't."

As I listened to him I suddenly felt sobs rising in my throat. "Why?" I shouted, interrupting him. "Why can't you? Why can't we . . . ?"

"I can't," he shouted back. "I can't. I tell you, you . . ." He wiped his eyes again and struck the wall with his hand. "You're not mine. You know that perfectly well. They're waiting for your answer. All of them. They want to take you away from me. They know you're not for me. They want to take you away. Marry you off. They've taken her. They've taken her away from me."

Although I'd tried not to, I was crying like him, desperately, sobbing at the sight of him clinging to the wall, talking his foolish, childish words. What could I have hoped to find in this fragile creature, who was even more pathetic than I was?

I sobbed without tears, making unfamiliar sounds, trying to catch my breath and almost choking, then the words rushed out from my trembling lips. "I'm ill, Karim. I can't get married. It wouldn't work. I can't. And my family . . ."

I stopped. I could no longer control myself and buried my face in my hands, then stepped back blindly towards the empty bed. My tears were a culmination of all those painful months; I was crying for the life which was lost to me for no understandable reason; I was crying because in his pale, tearstained face I had seen the last door closing. I fell back on the bed and collected myself, searching through my pockets for a handkerchief. I didn't want to talk any more or hear him talking. I felt that what I had left, which was precious little, had nothing to do with anybody but me. It was an unadorned choice, with no evasion or hypocrisy possible, between life and death.

So when he came back and stood miserably beside me, asking me questions I didn't know the answers to myself, I said nothing. I withdrew into my own world. I didn't despise him, because he was actually right, but somehow I was distant from him now, and from all that had happened between us minutes before. He asked me about my illness, what it was, why I was ill, was I really ill, etc., and I didn't answer, sitting hunched on the bed, absorbed in myself and what had happened to me.

I rose heavily to my feet and was about to go, when he took hold of my arm. His clenched fingers were cold. I looked at him, but didn't ask what he wanted. He appeared almost unreal. In the sunset shadows I watched him talking without understanding the words.

Before fear becomes a habit, it is possible to uproot it from the soul. I discovered that to do this you have to proceed on the assumption that the reasons for the fear don't exist and imagine what you could do on this basis.

I therefore excised several hours of my past and put them in parentheses, then began to think of the life ahead of me. The change was not so great: the circle of despair had now interlocked with the circle of defiance. In any case, during our time on this earth, we should not overlook the need to coexist with the rest of humanity. This is a matter of give and take, and not of assuming attitudes. It is a process of flux and overlap, where walls and frontiers don't exist, only bridges for crossing and recrossing. And I had to think where I stood in all this.

I wrote to my brother Mustafa in Kirkuk, asking for his advice about an offer I had received. I knew in advance what his answer would be and didn't think it would be long coming.

Chapter Ten

H e was listening to a conversation between a couple of customers sitting hunched over the table behind him in the
Murabbaa café. The speakers' accents and the strange nature
of their discussion had attracted his attention. They had northern
accents, and he had guessed as they passed his table that they were
probably restaurant employees or drivers. One of them had red eyes
and looked distraught. They remained silent for some time, stirring
their tea violently, then one of them asked, "What do I do with this bit
of paper?" The voice was hoarse and gravelly. Midhat assumed it
belonged to the one with the red eyes, and after a brief pause the voice
continued. "I think it's forged. What do you think?"

"What do I think? Can't you see the judge's signature at the bottom?
Why do you think it's forged?"

The first voice spoke again, the tone veering between tearful and
pleading. "It's not right. I tell you, it's not right. The Lord's justice has
not been satisfied. Where will I go with the kids? It's impossible. She
runs off and leaves the kids, then sends me this bit of paper saying she
and them have become Muslims, and so she's forbidden to me. So I

225

have to start running after the stupid tart to make her keep her mouth shut about what's happened to me. Me, your friend Boutros, from a family with four priests in it. By the life of Christ, this document's forged. She's just trying to play with my head."

The cannon had only just sounded announcing the end of the day's Ramadan fast, but Rashid Street was already crowded with cars and pedestrians, and the lights had been on in the shops across the road for some time. Midhat had drunk two teas since his arrival a couple of hours before. Although he had not enjoyed sitting in the café the previous day, he had returned today just the same. Shortly before sunset they had drawn back the curtains and removed the tattered awnings from the shop front, and a white sky had revealed itself to him between the high buildings.

"If I go to the judge myself, what shall I say to him? I want to become a Muslim like that tart Mathilde?"

"What are you saying, Boutros? He'll put you in prison if you talk about your wife like that. What's wrong with you?"

It was during this conversation that Midhat saw the man enter rapidly, then stroll casually between the tables and benches, looking left and right. He was short, with red hair and a thin, sickly face. He had been friendly with him for a short time in his student days, several years before, and spent a few evenings with him, and Husayn too, as far as he remembered. He was coming in his direction. Midhat greeted him, and they shook hands warmly.

"Good evening, brother. How are you? How are things? Fine, fine."

He answered his stream of questions and indicated to him to sit down, so the red-haired man sat in the seat facing him. He remembered he was called Said something-or-other and used to work in the Customs Service. His small eyes were framed by bright red eyebrows and eyelashes. Midhat asked him what he was doing these days.

"I was ill, brother," answered Said. "I had to go into the hospital. I'm fine now, but I lost my memory. What am I doing now? I've been pensioned off. I don't have a job. I lost my memory." He opened his eyes wide suddenly, emphasizing his words.

"Why did you lose your memory?"

"I don't know, brother . . . brother . . . forgive me, I can't remember your name. You see? I woke up one morning and couldn't remember a thing. Who I was. Where I'd come from. Where I was going. Who such-and-such a person was. What was going on. I didn't know anything. So they put me in hospital. I'm better now. Sometimes I remember things, sometimes I don't. Now I'll try and think what your name is."

He put a hand up to his forehead and began rubbing it.

"You must go to the judge," Midhat heard Boutros's friend saying, "and make him tell you what's going to happen to you and your children. Do you understand?"

"It's written on this piece of paper. We have to do the same as Mathilde."

"You see what I mean," said Said suddenly. "I can't remember." He closed his eyes. "I'm sure I know your name. It's on the tip of my tongue. But you see, Midhat, how I forget things?" He opened his eyes wide. "Midhat! Midhat!" he shouted. "You're Midhat." He smiled stupidly all over his thin face and repeated, "Midhat. Midhat."

One autumn evening when he had been sitting on the couch with his father near the basement stairs, he had watched her crossing the courtyard in her pale blue dress, her hair hanging down her back, and felt as if she was walking across his heart. He was drawn to the soft curves of her body and her high round breasts as she swung gently along, and he noticed her looking surreptitiously at him with a little smile which told him secretly that she knew.

He heard Boutros's unsteady voice. "I'm going to go mad. If only I knew where she was. They said she's working as a nanny. She called to ask how the children were. She said something then started to cry and put the receiver down. I'm going to go mad."

227

"I don't always remember things as well as that, Midhat," said Said.

"Are you still with Customs?" Midhat asked him.

Said began gesturing violently. "No, no. They pensioned me off. I don't have a job. I wasn't well . . . Midhat."

"So what are you doing with yourself now?"

"Four clergymen and a priest in our family," repeated Boutros. "We're an old Christian family. I'm doomed. Where shall I go? Where shall I take my children? If only God would take her life, or mine."

Said swiveled his eyes round slightly to look behind him, then returned his attention to Midhat.

"I don't have anything to do," he said. "I get up in the morning, have breakfast, then come to the café and sit here like this." He folded his arms on his chest. "Quarter of an hour. Half an hour. Sitting thinking. Then I get up and go home. My wife Umm Hazim's a good woman. I'm happy with her. I sleep by myself so I can relax. Everything's fine. I can't complain. I come to the café every day. Morning and afternoon. Quarter of an hour. Half an hour. Just sitting."

He still had his arms folded, resigned as a red sheep.

"Don't you read or write?" Midhat asked him. "You could write pieces for the paper, your ideas or something."

Said raised his arms and moved them rapidly in a gesture of negation. "No, no. I don't remember anything. What would I write about? Do you think I'm stupid?" He calmed down. "So what are you doing these days, Midhat? Are you still working at the Ministry?"

Midhat nodded vaguely. Said grimaced as if he hadn't had enough information. Midhat felt sorry for his companion's confusion and said patiently, "Yes. I'm still with the Ministry, but I'm on holiday at the moment."

She had left behind her a little movement of her eyelashes, one sunny Friday morning when he had been deliberately waiting near her room and half blocked her path as he asked her a question. She was wearing her *abaya* for some reason, and her flushed face was radiant against the black. She avoided his question and walked on, but as she passed him, stony faced, she lowered her eyelids for a second, and the long black lashes seared into his entrails.

"What's wrong with that?" responded Said. "It's not against the law to take a holiday and relax a bit."

The waiter arrived, carrying a tray crammed with glasses of tea, put one down in front of Said, and looked inquiringly at Midhat, who signaled in the affirmative. The waiter conveyed his approval with a particular gesture of his arm, carefully putting one of the little glasses down in front of Midhat. From behind Midhat came a mixture of noises and conversation, then the sound of someone hawking and spitting and blowing his nose. He didn't look round, but heard Boutros's friend talking kindly: "No, Abu Mikhail, no. It's wrong for men to cry. Everything will work out in the end. You mustn't cry."

Said was looking at the two men, frowning in amazement, obviously finding their behavior hard to comprehend. He raised his glass to his lips and took a mouthful of tea which burnt his throat. He screwed up his face and his eyelashes quivered, then he looked at Midhat, who shrugged his shoulders slightly. Said sat back in his seat and turned away from the two men. For him they represented all the tensions and complexities of the world with which he had lost contact.

Midhat heard them stand up. They walked past beside him, arm in arm, one covering his face with a handkerchief, and moved away unsteadily through the warm smoke-filled café. Midhat sipped his tea. The tortured Boutros had no choice but to lose his memory and forget his wife's treachery and whatever had been her religion or his religion. Said was sitting in silence with his arms folded. He finished his tea and pushed the glass away from him, then Midhat saw his face light up suddenly as he looked to the right and left before subsiding back into his seat again.

"Are you waiting for someone, Said?" he asked.

Said opened his eyes, then shut them, as if he didn't want to reply. "No, no. I'm not waiting."

She had hurt him one evening. He had been about to go out when he had heard an unfamiliar noise coming from his sister's room. Without any definite idea in his head, he had gone to see what was happening and found Munira and her mother talking heatedly together, Munira crying passionately, her red dress open at the neck to reveal her marble-white chest. She had turned to face him, her wet eyes a more brilliant golden color than ever and her lips scarlet, and sobbed in front of him, letting him feel the full force of her emotion, then apologized to him, apologized.

Said was collecting himself and preparing to leave.

"Where are you off to, Said?"

"I'm going."

"What have you got to do? It's still early."

"It doesn't matter. I want my supper."

"So you're not fasting."

He raised his eyebrows in astonishment. "Me? No, no. I'm not fasting. My nerves wouldn't stand it." He smiled weakly and stood up, raising his hand. "Right, my friend. Goodbye. You see, I've forgotten your name."

He was slightly built, short. He walked off between the tables and benches, his head lowered, his mind and spirit empty. Nobody existed inside him, and it didn't matter to him whether he met someone he knew or merged with the crowd. He was happy, like his name, rejecting his memories. He stopped to pay his bill, then suddenly turned back towards Midhat and raised his arm high in farewell, his face brightening. Had he remembered his name again? Then he disappeared out of the door.

Midhat took out a cigarette and put it slowly between his lips. Griping pains in his gut reminded him that he hadn't eaten for eight hours or more. His mouth was bitter as if he was ill. It would get worse if he lit his cigarette. He took it out from between his lips. His fingers wandered over his chin and neck, scraping on the stubble of his unshaven beard. What should he eat today? Syrian kebab in the Mina Restaurant? Something at the Golden Nest?

A wave of bile rose up inside him. Perhaps he should rest for a while. Was Said able to forget his miseries along with his memories? Did losing his memory mean he didn't feel pain or hunger? In other words, if he lost his memory, would it make him forget the night the two of them—he and Munira—came back together and in the darkness of the passageway near the door, through which light seeped and the family's noise and music could be heard, he'd stopped her, held her soft shoulders through the *abaya*, brought his face close to hers, and brushed her velvety, soft, warm, golden lips?

He jumped up as if he'd been stabbed, trembling all over, and looked around him in embarrassment. Some of the other patrons were staring at him. Slowly he sat down again, lit a cigarette, and took a long drag. A faint wave of dizziness came over him, and he put a hand to his forehead and closed his eyes. Four days had passed since it had all happened. Four days. But what was important now was to see it through in an intelligent fashion. He hated nothing more than the clumsy, involuntary behavior which exposed his lack of self-knowledge. To not know yourself to that degree! Even though she was the cause of it for sure, despite all his efforts. But now, before he did anything, he wanted to understand, to understand at this moment what his limits were and put all other considerations aside. The limits imposed by time and space, now, in this place, without hatred, without love.

In the midst of the family's chatter about engagement, marriage, the future, his love for her had taken him by surprise. He'd suddenly noticed her eyes, and his heart had missed a beat. The girl he loved was living amongst them.

Hurriedly he rose from his seat and left the café. Staying in one place didn't help him remain in the present. The opposite was true, and he cursed. The air in the street was cold, heavy with the smell of burning petrol. As he stood outside the café wondering where to go, his legs felt weak. What sort of a wreck was he! He'd sat for an hour or two without moving, and when he stood up his legs were incapable of bearing his weight. The front of the Shaab cinema was dominated by a picture of Abd al-Karim Qasim, insanely huge. He crossed to the other side of the street and went with the crowd down towards Bab al-Sharqi. It was a little after eight. If you thought about it, there was no time or space, or else they existed within fluid boundaries. He, for example, as he walked down Rashid Street a little after eight in the evening, was walking through time and space. Suffering from stomach cramps because he hadn't eaten, he could nevertheless pass with ease from one dimension of human life to another. Here was another example. Near the shops which sold cakes and yogurt, or more precisely in front of Aram's pastry and pastrami shop, right in front of the window, he was standing hungry, weak, and unshaven; for several days now he had stayed away from the house and its people, and those damned bright images and the songs and whispers and beautiful days.

He was afraid for her when he held her to him, and she sighed gently and he felt the pressure of her breasts against his chest. Was this the reality? More importantly, was this the world which slipped through your fingers when you wanted to organize it so carefully? He went into the shop and asked the old assistant for a glass of yogurt and a pastry. For all he knew these constant daydreams might be doing him a favor, stopping him from moving outside the immediate here and now, immersing him in space and time, keeping people away from him, severing his links with them. This daydreamer was not a human being, not begotten, although he might have begat. His hand carrying the pastry to his open mouth stopped in mid-air. He might have fathered a child. He paid the old man and left the shop. The air was cold. Where was he going to go? The street was packed with cars. Was it possible that he had planted his seed inside her, then run away? Songs played on a shop radio. As he hurried along, he bumped into people strolling on the pavement. Would it have changed anything if he hadn't run away?

He stopped on the edge of the pavement opposite the Post Office as if he was about to cross. He didn't see the people around him. He was tired and dejected. The yogurt had left a bitter taste in his mouth. Things were becoming complicated, more than they had been two or three days before. After all the nightmares he had been refreshed by a long sleep in the Rusafa Hotel, but things had begun to change inside him since then. Now he was afraid something awful was about to descend on him unawares, a specific disorder in himself or the world around him, which would destroy his mind or his life.

The blurred shapes of the cars raced past in front of him, making the ground shake. One small jump and he would be under those soft, black wheels, and everything would be over. The shining images, the smiles, the stars, and the tears would vanish with him.

When he embraced her for the first time, she buried her face in his neck and he felt her warm breath as she whispered, "Don't leave me, Midhat. Don't leave me alone, please." She didn't lift her dear face to him until he took hold of her hair and was confronted by the tears trickling out from under her closed eyelids, so he kissed them one after another.

Now, if he made that decisive jump, this image would be nothing but blood and bones and broken flesh. Munira would become a fragment of the remains, when she had once inhabited an anonymous corner of this disintegrated heap of flesh, perhaps been a melody arising from it somehow, which nobody would hear from now on. Even she would never be able to understand that somewhere in that bloody mess echoes of her laughter and glances from her shining eyes used to reverberate. The dark surface of the street reflected dim, distant flickerings of light. Gloomily he turned and walked slowly on, trying to avoid that fatal impulse towards self-pity. What would he gain by remaining in front of the stopped clock on the Post Office building, drowning the world in his bitter tears, which he shed for himself, at the thought of his own suicide? He noticed the Rusafa Hotel entrance on the other side of the street, but didn't feel like going up to his cold, bare room. Such an empty room.

He saw her making his bed shortly before they were married, bending over slightly, and the room, with her in it, appeared full of laughter and movement and light and sunshine.

Suddenly he felt himself lunge forward into the street, in a stupid attempt to cross it, a stupid attempt to cut across his thoughts and the flow of his emotions. A car horn blared in his head and brakes screeched. He didn't look round, but bounded on. He heard swearing and cursing behind him. His heart was beating uncomfortably and, noticing a dark alleyway, he dived into it to escape. He stumbled a few times as he hurried to put distance between him and the noise of the street, and then walked on slowly, panting between the grubby walls. A smell of food and burnt oil assailed his nostrils. A door opened and an old woman emptied a bucket of dirty water out into the narrow alley. A cool breeze touched his face as the alleyway ended and he came out into an empty street. Apartment buildings were under construction on either side of it, and at the far end faint lights were visible. He stopped at the foot of a dark old wall.

He kissed her by the big wooden door in the musty dark passageway, then folded her in his arms so that her *abaya* fell on to her shoulders and her perfumed hair came cascading down.

His heart beat faster all of a sudden, and he leaned against the wall behind him. He was attacked by a fit of weakness, and his legs and stomach trembled slightly. The stones protruding from the wall dug into his bones. He was overcome by a desire to sit down on the ground. His stomach was churning violently. He pressed it and wiped the sweat off his face. His heart was pounding irregularly. What was happening to him? He was a vagrant, an outcast! Then he had terrible cramps in his insides and felt his body refusing to hold up. His legs gave way and his back scraped down the wall, stirring up the dust. His vision blurred and he tried to hold on to the wall, but his hands slid down it with the rest of his body and he thudded like a stone on to the muddy ground. The cramps squeezed and crushed his entrails again and rose in waves towards his chest. He gasped, then took a deep breath. His eyes were closed, his pulse fluttered rapidly, and cold sweat poured down his face. He heard a car roar past. He was dying alone, without any warning. He breathed in and out again loudly. The sound of his breathing annoyed him, and his mouth and throat were dry and constricted. He didn't know what was happening to him but as he crumpled into a heap by a wall at a crossroads in the gloomy quarter of Sinak, he felt that he had finally hit rock bottom. He swallowed and wiped his sticky forehead. It hadn't taken him long on his own to sink to the lowest depths. The stomach cramps abated. He opened his eyes. There was nobody nearby. A breath of sweet, cool air revived him. He saw himself spread-eagled in a dark corner on the dirty pavement.

She trembled in his arms, naked, fragile as crystal, with frightened eyes, moistening her lips constantly, then putting her hands up to cover her full, warm breasts.

He leaned his head back against the wall.

He had embraced her and she didn't tell him, she didn't tell him. He was just an object of derision for her. Instead of having the grace to rouse him gently from his glorious dream, she had slapped him into wakefulness.

He beat his head on the stones behind him.

She had let him subside into bitterness, terror, and impotence. Her thighs were warm, soft, tender. She had wanted him to roll in the mire. Neither the memories, nor his persistent desire for her came to his aid.

He hit his head against the wall again, and his skull reverberated painfully. His pulse and breathing became regular once his guts had stopped heaving. He sat up and brushed the mud off his hands, bent his legs, rested his weight on the ground, and struggled to his feet. Taking out a handkerchief, he did his best to clean himself up. His head was throbbing. He looked around him. His mouth still felt sour and dry. He headed off, making his way slowly back down the alley he had come from. He was weak, his body afflicted by a strange debility. He tripped on a stone, and his feet disappeared into a deep pothole filled with dirty water. In the distance he heard a raucous voice rising and falling, reciting verses from the Quran. He could not distinguish phrases or individual words, but the harsh, unsteady quality of the voice saddened him. He walked shakily along at the side of the alley; he was tired and the back of his head hurt. He would wash in his hotel room and try to rest. Perhaps he would find something to eat.

———

He entered Uwanis's and asked for Husayn then, disregarding the surprise written all over Uwanis's face, walked away and pulled aside the dirty curtain at the back of the shop. They were sitting against the wall on their worn cane chairs with their drinks and snacks on upturned empty barrels in front of them: Husayn, Abu Shakir, and a bedouin enveloped in his *abaya*, whom Midhat didn't know. They turned towards him in the faint red light.

"Al-salam alaykum," he called.

"Alaykum al-salam," they answered with one voice.

Then they peered at his face to see who it was. Husayn jumped to his feet and came over to embrace him, and Midhat smelled his stale body odor mixed with the muskiness of the arak and a whiff of food.

"My dear Midhat," he murmured. "Where have you been?"

This affectionate gesture touched him, and he began looking for a place to sit. He patted Husayn's shoulder without saying anything and pushed him gently away. Abu Shakir stood up, appearing slightly mystified, and the bedouin shifted in his seat, then was still. Husayn pulled up a chair from a corner of the room, put it next to his, and invited Midhat to sit down. "Hello," they chorused the moment he did so.

"Abu Kamal, Abu Kamal," called Husayn.

He turned questioningly towards Midhat, blowing cigarette smoke in his face.

"A quarter of Zahle arak," replied Midhat tersely.

Husayn looked hesitantly at him, then nodded at Uwanis. "A quarter of Zahle, quickly please, Abu Kamal."

"Good evening to you," said the bedouin suddenly in a guttural voice, raising a hand in greeting.

"The same to you, brother," replied Midhat.

"That's a new bird," whispered Husayn as he took out a packet of cigarettes and offered one to Midhat. "Our dear friend Abu Shakir snared him a couple of weeks ago."

Midhat refused the cigarette. The air in the back shop was heavy, dominated by a putrid smell which was hard to pin down.

"What do you want to eat?" Husayn was asking him. "Beans or chick peas? That's all there is today. Or do you want a proper dinner?"

"No, no. I ate before I came. A dish of beans."

"Okay. Abu Kamal, two dishes of beans please." Then he turned back to Midhat. "How are you?" he asked. "I went twice to your office looking for you. They said you were on holiday. And yesterday—no, it could have been the day before—Karumi came to see me at home. That was a mistake!"

"Give me a bit of peace, Husayn. I've got a sore head."

"Okay, fine." He blew out a puff of smoke, turned to look at Abu Shakir for a moment, then glanced surreptitiously back at Midhat again. The people sitting there and the objects surrounding them were a mixture of black and ochre shadows. Midhat was not interested in examining them more closely and wanted to shut himself off from them. The curtain was drawn back violently, and Abu Kamal entered carrying a quarter of arak, a glass, and the beans. With Husayn's help, he put everything down on the empty barrel in front of Midhat.

"Abu Kamal," said Abu Shakir, "you need a few tables in this bar."

Uwanis looked coldly at him. "What bar?"

Abu Shakir made an expansive gesture with his arm. "There's a seating problem here."

"I'm a shopkeeper, and I sell drink. I can't get a license to open a bar. If I had a bar, I'd have had to close it during Ramadan. It's forbidden. This is Ramadan. I'm doing you all a service here."

Abu Shakir went on looking up at Uwanis through his large dark glasses, without speaking.

"What are you making a fuss about, Abu Shakir?" said Husayn, when Uwanis had gone. "He's obviously doing us a favor."

Abu Shakir raised his glass to the bedouin, who raised his in reply, and the two men drank.

"And they wonder why everything's going wrong!" said Abu Shakir.

Midhat was mixing his drink, no longer attempting to join in with them. He'd eaten a few kebabs in a piece of warm bread from a vendor near the hotel, then washed and lain on the bed for a while. He poured the arak into the glass, added ice and water, and watched the liquid turn milky.

"God is great," said the bedouin.

"Our friend has a good story to tell," whispered Husayn. "I'll fill you in later."

"Mr. Midhat," called Abu Shakir, "to your very good health."

"God is great."

They all raised their glasses. Midhat's throat and insides burned for a few moments, then the heat began flowing into the rest of his body. He still needed a bit longer to relax, come out of himself. In the company of somebody he had chosen to be with, because he was confident he would listen to him, he could feel the stirrings of some kind of equanimity.

As they were talking and laughing beside him, the numbness spread slowly into the nooks and crannies of his body, and he felt that he was calmer than he had been for a long time; an invisible envelope separated him from his vociferous companions. Husayn turned to him and brought his face close to his. "If you knew how I've missed you, Midhat. But I've got a bone to pick with you. You'll say that idiot is messing things up as usual. But I swear to you, Midhat, you mean a lot to me and I don't want you to forget me. I know I'm useless. Don't worry about me. I know what I'm like, but to hell with everything. I wouldn't give four piastres for this scabby, precarious world, balanced on a bull's horn, so they tell us. Four is too much. On the other hand, you must realize, nobody can buy me for a few pence. I want my just deserts, brother. But you, Midhat—no. Keep my example in your head as a warning. I've got a bone to pick with you, if you don't mind. Let me get it over with, then I can relax, have some self-respect, tell myself that I'm still joined to the world by a thread."

He raised his glass and drank, then picked up a bean and slipped it into his mouth. The shadows round his head smoothed out the dark lines on his face, so that he looked less exhausted, and his features were almost sharp and handsome. He twisted his head round to watch Abu Shakir and his friend whispering together, then reached for the plate again, so absorbed in what they were saying that he forgot to finish the conversation which he had begun so abruptly with Midhat.

"Now they're bearable," he whispered to Midhat, "but once that bedouin Abu Ab'ub gets drunk, our evening's ruined."

Abu Shakir was talking angrily to the bedouin, who was listening humbly, but with interest.

"How's it going, Abu Shakir?" called Husayn. "Are you getting any-where?"

Abu Shakir's dark face turned briefly in his direction. His glasses covered half of his face, and his long, drooping moustache obscured his mouth.

"My brothers, Abu Suha, Mr. Midhat," he said, "we're discussing an insoluble problem, I and my respected colleague Abu Ab'ub, and we know very well it's insoluble."

"God is great."

Abu Shakir turned half back to the bedouin. "We know, thank God, but I don't remember who said it, we want to grasp the problem in its virgin state or, to be precise, if you'll pardon me, we don't want to let the bitch go."

"Well said, Abu Shakir. Let's drink to that!" shouted Husayn.

The three of them emptied their glasses. Husayn smacked his lips, then whispered to Midhat as he put his glass down, "Don't believe a word he says. But Abu Ab'ub's story is worth hearing. I'll tell you about it. Bitch indeed! They're a bunch of scoundrels."

A feeling of well-being came over Midhat as he listened to all this chatter. The arak had begun to do its work some minutes before and objects, faces, and gestures had taken on unaccustomed hues. He was glad of this mist in front of his eyes and felt almost happy.

"Yes, Midhat, she's the estate manager's daughter. I'm telling you. Her name's Huriya. Couldn't the poor bastard have fallen in love with someone else? And what's he? A shepherd, or maybe an assistant shepherd, son of a bitch!"

Husayn dissolved into laughter, interrupted by a cough that shook his whole body. Abu Shakir and his companion were immersed in conversation and did not look up.

Husayn groaned. "I've still got a cough on my chest. This bloody flu."

"What estate manager's daughter? Who are you talking about?" asked Midhat brusquely.

Husayn signaled to him to lower his voice. "Keep your voice down, Midhat. I've hardly started yet. Abu Ab'ub fell in love with the daughter of Hajj Alwan al-Jalut—no, al-Mahtur. I've forgotten the bastard's name. He was singing her praises to everyone. But he's like a servant, you know. Deputy shepherd, half-time shepherd, according to Abu Shakir. I don't know. That's just what Abu Shakir said. Maybe he is, maybe he isn't. Anyway, lover boy had some really impressive job! But the Lord works in mysterious ways, and there was Huriya, in no time at all, ten months pregnant, fourteen months maybe—I mean about to give birth, a nice girl like her."

He paused and glanced surreptitiously at the two men, seeming suddenly apprehensive for no reason.

"What are they saying, Midhat? Have you been listening to them?"

240

"No. Why are you bothered about them?"

Husayn made a dismissive face. "I'm not. Your health." He picked up his glass and drank avidly from it, his eyes closed, before putting it back in its place. "Those two are half-spy, half-animal. You haven't seen them in their true colors. I don't know what's wrong with me these days. I'm a bit depressed and I feel there's something in the air." He drew a number of agitated circles in front of him. "Every time there's a bang, I jump. I don't know why. But there's something in the air that won't let me rest."

"What about Abu Ab'ub? Did anything happen to him?"

Midhat's question seemed to surprise him. "There he is in front of you. He's still alive. Half a bottle of arak every day, and sometimes a glass extra. Why are you asking about him, Midhat?" He looked at the two men. "I can't hear what those two assholes are talking about."

"And the farm manager's daughter, Huriya, what happened to her?"

"How did you know about her, Midhat? Talk quietly, for God's sake. Don't let Abu Ab'ub hear you. The bastard's got a knife in his belt. Where did you hear about her?"

Midhat did not answer immediately. He took a sip from his glass. "Are you going senile, Husayn? How can you forget so quickly? Haven't you just been telling me about her?"

An expression of doubt appeared on Husayn's face. He looked genuinely mystified. Silently he took a handful of beans and put them in his mouth.

"Yes. Yes, that's right," he whispered. "I did forget. I don't know what's wrong with me these days. Anyway, it's some story. They married him to Huriya. Married Huriya to that scum and were grateful to him. They sent the pair of them to live in Baghdad, all expenses paid. I don't know what they were scared of. What happened? A girl made a mistake. So what? They're all just as bad. Bloody bastards."

Midhat picked up his glass and swallowed its entire contents in one go. His jaw contracted slightly, but the stinging sensation in his mouth didn't last long. The smoke undulated in the air of that gloomy cavern, white and soft, and cigarette ends glowed intermittently. Abu Shakir belched then sighed and coughed.

"Yesterday I had the same dream I told you about two months ago, Abu Suha. I dreamed I was at the head of a demonstration . . ."

"God is great."

"It's true, Abu Ab'ub. I mean, a real demonstration, with yours truly out in front. And we were running along, shouting, 'Very sorry,' and everybody . . ."

She had wanted to say something to him when she let him pull her into his room, one night not long before they were married. She was smiling at first, her hair falling into her eyes as she glanced around the silent house before she went in. Then he took hold of her, embraced her passionately, and planted his mouth on hers. She closed her eyes and gave him her soft, moist lips. He didn't allow her the chance to speak. In those ethereal moments, outside the limits of time and space, he possessed the whole of existence, and his heart was filled with perfect peace. He held her close, afraid, hesitant, wary of his excessive happiness. She withdrew her mouth from his with a heavy sigh. Her chest pressed against his. Then she whispered something, and he put his hand up to her face and passed it over her burning cheek and her throat. Her golden eyes reflected invisible lights. Again she whispered incomprehensible words. His eyes misted over. His body was taut, filled with crazy desire. Perhaps she had been trying to communicate some significant information in those words which he never heard. He put a hand out and took hold of her full breast. She was trembling, and when he saw her moistening her lips, he pressed his mouth to hers again. Nothing else existed but the sweet taste of her mouth and that softness under his fingers, which had gone beyond the confines of the material and pushed their way in, gently at first, in pursuit of the tender flesh. He felt her yielding to him and her constant trembling never penetrated his consciousness. He was touching part of her naked left breast, which was like a small, warm bird. The narrow opening of the dress stopped him putting his hand right round it, so he pushed his hand in more forcefully and heard the tearing of threads and something dropping on to the floor. Suddenly his fingers were encompassing the trembling smoothness of the breast, and he heard her gasp under his mouth. He was startled at what he had done. Then he moved his mouth down towards her throat and chest, covering the side of her neck with kisses and trying to lift up her dress and kiss her down below. But she drew away slightly and sat on the edge of the bed behind her. No, no, no, she sighed, putting her hand gently on his, hidden beneath her dress. Her heart was beating rapidly and irregularly. He felt as though he were holding it as he squeezed her warm breast. In some obscure way she was giving him her life, and at the time it had not occurred to him to question the mystery of it.

"Cheers. Good health, everybody. Let's drink to that."

"God is great."

They were shouting, laughing, raising their glasses high. He picked up his own glass and drank eagerly from it.

"Look, Abu Suha," said Abu Shakir loudly, "it's not a question of whether the demonstration's peaceful or not, it's why I have this dream all the time. Ah, Mr. Midhat, what's the difference between life and dreams? It's all a dream, believe me, Abu Ab'ub . . ."

"You're quite right, Abu Shakir," interrupted Husayn. "But we're interested in your slogan. 'Very sorry.' What's that about? Why are you very sorry? Why bother to mount a demonstration if you're very sorry?" He guffawed loudly.

"All I know is I have this dream," replied Abu Shakir. "And I want to know what it means."

"Who says it means anything?"

Abu Shakir paused in surprise, the glass halfway to his mouth. "Why wouldn't it mean something? The whole of humanity would die if there was no meaning to anything, I'm telling you."

"Where's this taking us?" murmured Husayn. Then he said out loud, "My dear Abu Shakir, I'm not against reality in any way. But our ancestors said dreams were just confused jumbles of images, not me. What have they got to do with reality? Don't you agree, Midhat?"

"Why aren't you saying anything, Abu Ab'ub?" said Abu Shakir, turning to his neighbor.

Abu Ab'ub exhaled the smoke forcefully from his cigarette and did not react.

Abu Shakir repeated his question. "Abu Ab'ub, my brother, why the silence?"

"Bless the Prophet, my friend, and say God is great," said the bedouin suddenly.

They all laughed.

Midhat closed his eyes and his head went round. This relaxed him, and he wished he could sing a sad song or abandon himself to the roaring cascades within him, and let them transport him deeper and deeper inside himself. Perhaps then he would discover secrets about himself which remained hidden under a thousand layers. His flight from himself was like the flight from the sun or death, a pathetic act doomed by its nature to be temporary, circumscribed by time. Maybe it would give him breathing space.

"Karumi's a real gentleman," Husayn was saying to him. "Refined and sensitive and yet tough at the same time."

Midhat remembered that his brother had visited Husayn. "What did Karim want to see you about, Husayn? Why did he visit you?"

Husayn was stuffing his mouth with beans. He stopped and turned to him in surprise. "You've reminded me, my dear Midhat. These days my tongue runs away with me. But you've just reminded me—Karim came to ask about you. Why? Where were you?"

Her radiant, calm face was the same when he came to inquire what her brother's letter had said, when he asked her to fix a day for their wedding, and when, at dawn after the first night of their marriage, he had been about to shut the door of their room behind him and go out of her life, and had found her half sitting up in bed, their bed, her beautiful face calm as she abandoned him to his fate.

"I said to him, My dear Karumi, give me some of the facts. I wasn't feeling too good. I'd drunk a lot the night before. I swear, every time I drink a bit too much, all the problems of the world descend on me the next day. Try solving their awkward questions when your head's all over the place!"

"Your health, brothers," yelled Abu Shakir. "Are you with us, Abu Ab'ub?" .

"Cheers, brother. Cheers."

There was the clatter and thump of glasses being put back on the empty barrels. Abu Shakir clapped his hands. "Abu Kamal. Water and ice, please. Are you having another drink, Abu Ab'ub?"

"Half an arak, thanks."

"Half a Mistaki, Abu Kamal, with some of your famous snacks, please. Are you up for a party tonight, Abu Ab'ub?"

"God is great," said Abu Ab'ub, then he began to sing. "*As if my love . . . Oh, Mother. Where have our loved ones gone? Where are they now?*"

"It goes downhill from now on," whispered Husayn. "Where were we? Ah. So I was under the weather, and Karumi, bless him, only told me half the story. I was completely confused. You mean Midhat's not there? He's moved out? He got married? I said to him, 'My dear Karumi, stop. Give me the facts one by one, or at least in some sort of order.'"

Abu Ab'ub belched, then apologized and started to sing again, while Abu Shakir took the dishes of food and the bottle of arak from Abu Kamal and put them carefully down in front of him.

"So—why did Karim come to see you?" Midhat asked Husayn haltingly, the drink getting the better of him. "I mean—what did he need to talk to you about?"

His voice sounded unclear to him; it gave way at certain points when he didn't mean it to.

"I told you," answered Husayn. "He came to ask about you. He said, 'Is Midhat with you? Have you seen him or not? Do you know what's happened to him?'" He raised his glass to his lips. "My dear Midhat, I said to him, 'Karumi, my brother, why are you asking me? I don't even know where I am, so how would I know where Midhat is? Anyway, did Midhat leave home?'"

They were finally alone together after midnight. She was wearing a simple white dress with a little red artificial flower on her left breast, and had make-up on her face and kohl round her eyes. Her apprehension was plain to see. He had asked his family in no uncertain terms to go to bed and not to expect anything from them. He was tired, worn out by his passion, combined with the trivial rituals which they had both had to undergo. She seemed distant from him somehow, and he put this down to the fact that they had only known each other for a short time before they were married.

"*Where have our loved ones gone? Where are they now?*" sang Abu Ab'ub. Then he said, "He didn't want to tell me that the engagement, dowry, and marriage had all been fixed up without me knowing anything about it. I felt he was embarrassed for me. It touched me. No, I was really very upset."

"Sing it again, Abu Ab'ub! You're a real gem."

The courtyard was silent. She was sitting on the edge of the bed looking at him. Her eyes were golden brown and her lips deep red. She was pressing a handkerchief between her fingers and seemed more worried than their situation merited. He went up to her and kissed her without touching her with his hands, and she continued to look at him. Behind the beautiful features and all these colors on her face, he could sense that something was wrong. He embraced her and touched the soft, cool flesh and smelled her scent. For a few moments he forgot his tiredness and the doubts reverberating within him, and began responding to the demands of his body, which was excited and ready for her. Those few minutes were a brief respite for them both, but did not last long.

He knocked back the contents of his glass, unconcerned at the burning taste of the bitter liquid. He was aroused, but his emotions simmered quietly without provoking any painful physical effects. Husayn's conversation and Abu Ab'ub's mournful singing gently soothed him.

"These symphonies fortify the muscles of their souls," Husayn was saying with some effort, his features dark. "And we . . . our brother here, I mean . . . is crying over his family and his dead ancestors' bloody camels. An under-shepherd bellowing in our ears! What's the world coming to, Midhat?"

"Why have you got it in for Abu Ab'ub?" asked Midhat indistinctly.

He had not meant to slur his words like this and decided it would be better to avoid long sentences.

Husayn whipped round to look at him, gesturing towards the bedouin. "Got it in for him? Not at all, Midhat. I haven't got the strength. I'm not the sort to hate anyone. I don't have the energy."

"I'm just the same. I don't hate anybody."

"Why not, my dear Midhat? You're young, you've got a job and a wife. Your whole future's ahead of you. Why don't you have the strength to hate?"

Things were becoming slightly muddled in Midhat's head. He didn't know if Husayn was joking or not. He passed the palm of his hand over his eyes and face.

"*Oh Mother, Oh Mother,*" sang Abu Ab'ub. "*Where have our loved ones gone? Where are they now?*"

Was this idiot really missing his family and the special smell of his homeland, and refusing the life they had arranged for him with his erring sweetheart?

"Keep it down, please, brother. It's Ramadan and the police will be round here any minute." Abu Kamal was standing impatiently in front of them, speaking in low tones. They fell silent then busied themselves with their drinks as if his words didn't concern them. Abu Kamal went out into the front of the shop. Abu Shakir smacked his lips and Abu Ab'ub belched.

"Beautiful music, a human symphony," said Husayn to himself. "But it doesn't always stick to the rudiments of music. If they had a good conductor, they'd be fine." He laughed noiselessly and turned to Midhat. "This is the next phase of our evening just beginning, and if our luck holds out, you might see some of the wonders of nature, Midhat. You're my guest today, you know, the drinks are on me. Do you understand?"

"What did Karim want?"

Husayn looked at him in astonishment. "What's wrong with you, Midhat? Why are you so obsessed with Karumi? There's nothing wrong with him. I don't remember him saying anything important. Maybe one of the old ladies had some aches and pains, but I don't remember which one."

"Oh Mother. Where have our loved ones gone? Where are they now?"

"No. What did Karim say? Are they all well at home?"

"They're all fine. Why shouldn't they be? It's you . . ." He struck the edge of the chair with the flat of his hand. "It's you, Midhat. What's wrong? Why are you sitting with us in this stable, leaving your lovely wife alone at home? Do you know what you're missing?"

Midhat watched his own arm reaching for his glass of arak and raising it slowly to his lips. He felt the bitter liquid's stinging heat in his entrails.

"Thanks, Abu Suha. I'm quite at ease with you all now. This isn't a stable, by the way. Or a barn. I feel comfortable with you. I mean nobody's sitting here planning to cheat on his brother, are they? There's nothing like that going on. We're both here to have a drink, the same as Abu Shakir and Abu Ba'bu, sorry, I mean Abu Ab'ub. We're all friends here. Nobody's cheating on anybody. Okay, so why do you say this is a stable? Animals, Abu Suha, if you want to talk about animals—I mean, they don't know how to cheat on each other. They don't have the time. Would I have any interest in hatching plots just to amuse myself? What are you talking about? Are these crossword clues? And secondly, I'm not missing anything, because all you've got to lose in this stinking world is your life. My life, in this case . . ."

"I'm sorry, Midhat."

"My life's with you. With the stupid, pure-hearted herd. I'm happy with these good folk. Why? Because they don't trample on other people's rights. Why not? Because they're cretins."

Midhat heard stifled laughter and turned round. Abu Ab'ub was staring gravely at him, while Abu Shakir tittered vaguely. Midhat had the feeling someone was talking to him. Husayn had his mouth full and was chewing with difficulty. Midhat looked back at Abu Ab'ub. "What did you say?" he asked him.

"Have a drink, my dear friend."

"Your health, Abu Ba'bu . . . Ab'ub. I'm very sorry I didn't get to know you before. And by the way, Abu Suha, I'm not missing anything. And the people you're talking about—actually I have nothing to do with them. I don't understand them. That's to say, I don't know what they want from me. I mean, what they wanted."

"Are you far away from your family?" Abu Ab'ub put his glass down, looking at him with eyes dark as a wolf's. It was easy to believe he was a shepherd.

"My family? First of all, what's a family, Abu Ba'bub . . . Ab'ub?"

"Abu Ab'ub, my friend," interrupted Husayn. "Mr. Midhat's a civil servant from an old Baghdad family and what's more he's a relative of mine."

"Sorry. I didn't mean . . ."

"It's all right. I don't have a family. Abu . . . Abu Ab'ub. Husayn's mistaken. Believe me."

"What are you talking about, Midhat?" asked Husayn.

Midhat raised his left arm in the air. "No, no, no. Look, Abu Suha. Abu Ab'ub's question is relevant, as you well know. You, for example. Who are your family? Who have you got in your life now?"

"A drink and a dish of beans," answered Abu Shakir with a loud laugh. He raised his glass and gestured with both hands, urging Abu Ab'ub to do the same. Without appearing to be annoyed, Husayn joined in the laughter. Despite their responses, Midhat wanted to pursue the conversation. Never before had he been possessed by such a desire to open up and express his opinion.

"What you're saying is partly true, Abu Shakir," he said, not seeming to realize that he was raising his voice. "These things don't let you down, in a way. I mean, a glass doesn't suddenly become a pitcher before your eyes, and arak doesn't turn into date jam."

Their laughter rose in the air, and amid the uproar he made out Abu Ab'ub's words. "Or chick peas into goat turds. You're right, my friend. What's the reason?"

In their dingy hideaway, heavy with their breath, they exhaled cigarette smoke and alcohol fumes from their wrecked lungs, and their coughing filled the air. Midhat thumped the barrel in front of him several times, and the plates and glasses jumped.

"Your comparison is . . . apposite, brother Ba'bub. I mean Abu Ab'ub," he continued, shouting above the noise.

"It wasn't deliberate."

The interruption annoyed Midhat. "Let me finish, Mr. Ab'ub. Abu Ab'ub. Let me finish."

They were silent briefly. He forgot what he was going to say for a moment. "I wanted to say one thing which made sense, my friends. For an hour now we've been indulging in pointless chatter. Let's have at least one sensible conversation."

He was breathless, panting slightly as he spoke. This was not how he wanted to finish. He felt the need to go on talking indefinitely.

"I'm joking," said Abu Ab'ub. "I just wanted to cheer you up."

"Come on, Abu Ab'ub," said Abu Shakir. "We were all joking. Don't worry about it."

"Why are you joking now, Abu Ab'ub?" Husayn went on. "When Mr. Midhat's wanting to tell us something?"

The bedouin looked as if he was trying to apologize. "I'm at the end of my tether," he said after a short silence.

"What's the matter with you this time, Abu Ab'ub?"

"Nothing serious. I'm not happy. They're the problem. My family. I miss them. I want to be near them, near the sheep, the songs, the sunrise, the fresh air, the warm bread, the milk, the smells."

He began shaking his head from side to side, as if he was singing or nursing his pain.

"What smells, Abu Ab'ub? Dung and farting donkeys and camels? Surely we're better off here with our handsome brothers, who smell of rosewater!"

Then Abu Shakir raised his glass, and Abu Ab'ub imitated him in silence. They drank together. Husayn was muttering something which Midhat could not make out. His desire to talk had subsided, and he felt tired and deflated. His eyelids drooped and his head began to spin. He lit a cigarette, thinking it would be a good idea to go and splash his face with cold water. He turned to Husayn, who was talking to Abu Shakir, and touched his arm. His head was going round.

"Look, Husayn. I think I feel a bit sick."

Husayn brought his face up close to him. "What do you mean?"

"I said I feel funny. A bit queasy."

"Why, my dear Midhat? The night's only just beginning. The best is yet to come." Then he called. "Abu Kamal. The bill, please."

"It's a bit early, Abu Suha."

"Let them go home if they want."

"Yes, Mr. Husayn?"

"The bill, Abu Kamal. Yes. Just for the two of us. Hurry, please."

She was lying there quietly, not intending to divulge her secret to him, while a fire blazed inside him, engulfing his heart and mind. She reached out and touched his forehead, revealing her rounded breasts, and let him look at them, stroke them, kiss them. She didn't speak. He sucked her lips, taking the pink lower lip into his mouth and biting it, his eyes closed as he abandoned himself to her warmth and smell and softness. He felt her move her tongue and touch his lip with it. She had her eyes half open, and he could see the gold tinged with mysterious hints of green through her black lashes. He felt the first stirring of desire in her and a flicker of love. She seemed to like all this. Perhaps she was less afraid of it than him. He held her close.

"Leave me alone. It's nothing to do with me."

"Don't play games with me, Abu Ab'ub. Get your money out and pay our bill."

"What's wrong with you, Abu Shakir? Are you quarrelling with the air?"

"Come on, Midhat. Let's go."

Midhat stood up to leave with Husayn; he was more unsteady on his feet than he had ever known himself, and his vision was blurred.

"Do you think it's my turn, Abu Ab'ub? Look at me. Do I seem as if I was born yesterday?"

The fresh air revived Midhat briefly and he took in lungfuls of it.

"Driver! Driver! Stop!" shouted Husayn.

Then the world went round and everything turned upside down in front of him. Closing his eyes, he leaned on Husayn's arm.

"Come along, this way. See where the driver's stopped. You're going home, aren't you, Midhat?"

"No, no."

"For heaven's sake. Where are you getting off then? Where do you want to go? What's the problem? Back a bit, driver. What's that? Who's drunk? Neither of us. Keep an eye on your horses. I'm afraid you're the one who's drunk! So where do you want to go, my dear Midhat?"

Midhat did not answer. Husayn put a hand under his arm and helped him up the steps of the carriage, where he collapsed on the seat.

"We come from God and to Him we will return," pronounced Husayn. "Take us to the Kurdish quarter in Bab al-Shaykh, my friend. Behind Café Yas. Do you know the area well? It's your patch? Glad to hear it. So why are we having this long discussion? Let's go."

She was wrapped in his arms, soft and yielding beneath him, breathing rapidly and exhaling that strange fragrance. He moved away from her slightly, raising his chest off her nakedness, relishing the sight of her like that: his Munira, his wife, his lover. Her skin was delicate, her breasts and stomach rounded. Her pelvic bone momentarily attracted his attention and he saw her gently closing her thighs. She was underneath him, tight against him, not talking. Her rosy brown body was telling him something which he didn't pick up. When she pulled him back towards her as if she didn't want him to look too long at the secret parts of her body, he felt her opening her thighs again to take him inside her.

The air was cool and smelt faintly of burned food, the horses' hooves pounded the street monotonously, and songs drifted vaguely to his ear from some unidentified source. Not feeling Husayn next to him, he opened his eyes and saw him sprawled out, like him, with his legs up on the seat opposite. The driver was humming a song to himself and to Kifah Street, which was empty, all its shops closed, apart from a couple of cafés. Midhat let his heavy eyelids droop shut again and abandoned himself to the swaying of the carriage and the gentle breeze. The moment he shut his eyes his head went round, and he was seized by a violent whirlwind which lifted him up and spun him round in spiraling eddies, vertically and horizontally, an unbroken sequence of movements without sense or purpose. He didn't resist them and felt his insides succumb to the gyrations and heave and churn.

"Where did you say you were going?" he heard the coachman say. "Which street?"

Husayn coughed violently and lit a cigarette. "Don't pretend you don't know. Bab al-Shaykh's your patch, remember? Where are we now? Isn't this Fadwa Arab? So we're near Bab al-Shaykh, aren't we? Didn't I say behind Café Yas? Straight ahead, brother, then when you get to the cemetery at Kilani Mosque, go right. Where the police station is, that's the street. What do you mean, which police station? The one in Bab al-Shaykh. You're going too far now. Don't you understand Arabic?"

Listening to Husayn talking helped take his mind off his nausea. There was no escaping it, sooner or later it would come, but for the moment he could fight it.

When it was all over, he went out of the bedroom and walked up and down in the dark. It was past three in the morning, and the night hung heavily over the ghastly world. He was distraught. He wanted to go downstairs, but didn't have the strength and stood in a remote corner of the gallery, leaning on the chilly wooden balustrade. He was trembling, his insides churning. He did not want to see another living soul. He became convinced of this out of the blue and remained convinced. Not a soul. He was revolted, humiliated. He wanted to keep silent forever. At that moment, as he looked over at the faint light from their bedroom, he had an attack of nausea. His body was rocked by two violent spasms, his mouth filled with bitter liquid, and his eyes watered. He was crushed, his thoughts not connecting to the reality of his situation. He retched for a third time and leaned against the railing, panting. He could die quietly there, but he mustn't see anyone. He turned round in a panic when he thought he heard a movement. The dark sky gleamed with stars, and the high black walls encircled him like the sides of a well. He mustn't see anyone. He went quickly back to the bedroom and got dressed. She was dozing, her hair spread over the pillow and covering part of her face. He slipped on his clothes like a thief, afraid of making the slightest noise, but she woke up just as he was about to leave the room and sat up, resting back against the bedhead, her face radiant despite the fatigue which showed on it, and a look of hurt questioning in her sleep-blurred eyes. Just before the door came between them, he noticed the curve of her right breast and the fine creases in the skin around her armpit.

"Midhat. Don't you want to go home? See, we're in Kilani Street and there's still time, if you want . . ."

"No, no," interrupted Midhat in terror. "I said no." Then he called, "Take me to the hotel. Who told you . . . ?" He paused. "Where are we? Where are we, Husayn?"

"Take it easy, Midhat. Take it easy. If that's how things are, leave it to me. Don't worry about it. I know where to take you. It doesn't matter. Straight on, brother. The way we were going before. Keep straight ahead for a bit, then when you get to the street with the police station, turn right. Understand, my friend? Carry on." He patted Midhat on the shoulder. "It doesn't matter, Midhat. You can stay with me for the night. But if you'd told me a bit earlier, it would have been helpful. Just given me an indication. Never mind. I'm ready for anything."

Midhat did not open his eyes. It felt pleasant surrendering to those spirals of dizziness and not immediately dangerous. If he got through the night without throwing up and having to deal with the repercussions, he would be able to say it had been a successful evening. However, the continuing upheaval in his guts and throat and head made this an unlikely hypothesis. So he had to look at things from another angle: how much damage would it do to him? Or, to put it another way, what would be left of him after the impending bout of vomiting? Obviously the answer . . .

"Yes. On your right. What do you mean, where's the police station? Go on a bit further. We're just about there, and he's asking me where the police station is. What's wrong with you? Midhat, have you got some small change on you? I've only got a half dinar. I don't want to give all that to our friend from Bab al-Shaykh."

Midhat reached into his pocket and brought out a handful of coins. Husayn snatched them unceremoniously from him. The carriage lurched violently, and the driver swore at his horse.

"Stop. We're here. What's all that about? Take it easy. Why are you swearing at the horses? They've done nothing wrong. Here's a hundred and fifty fils. Come along, Midhat. What are you saying, my friend?"

"Nothing, sir. I'm just cursing this filthy, stinking world."

"What's that got to do with us? Go and swear at home, not in front of the mosque. Not in front of God's house. Am I right? We're at the beginning of Ramadan, sir. That's a fine way to talk!"

The lights were still burning brightly in Café Yas, and there were a few customers smoking narghiles. Midhat climbed slowly down from the carriage; his limbs drooped and his vision was blurred, but he steadied himself and stood up straight, waiting for Husayn to decide which way they should go. He breathed heavily, feeling as if there was a dead weight inside him. He passed the flat of his hand over his temples and it came away cold and clammy.

"What do you think, Midhat?" Husayn was saying. "Do you want to clear your head with a cup of coffee or a glass of tea? We've still got time."

Midhat signaled his reluctance. He felt no embarrassment or annoyance being here with Husayn. It was a perfectly normal state of affairs. Husayn was talking, and Midhat turned as if he was expecting to see someone else beside him.

"Come on, then," said Husayn. "I'd been thinking of going into that thug's place for something to eat. I'm starving. Watch out, the ground's been sprayed, and it's full of potholes."

They walked along, supporting one another, between two rows of seats. A foul stench of tobacco and dust and water penetrated Midhat's nostrils. He slipped a couple of times. They entered a dark alley, dark as a cave. Husayn left him to walk alone.

"My dear Midhat," he began in a loud voice. "You know how important you are to me, how much I like you, but I don't want to interfere in your life. There's just a small idea that's been hammering in my brain for the past two hours. I don't want to intrude on you, but just think of me as a brother. Don't destroy yourself like I did. It's true, I don't have much advice to give. Anyway, who'd listen to my advice? People aren't stupid." He interrupted himself with a snort of laughter. "But I've just got one small thing to say. Look at me now. Just look at me, Midhat. What am I? I can't solve problems. I put it off, run away, duck and dive." He was waving his arms around like a pair of snakes. "But believe me, over time it's surprising how putting things off becomes an actual solution. It's a fact. You could construct a philosophy on it if you wanted to. I can give you all the data. That, my dear Midhat, is how your brother Husayn's gone on fighting like a hawk, but a hawk hung up by its tail, not knowing whether it's coming or going. Yet all the same I can dance with the wind. Look . . ."

He moved a few steps away and began to leap about and kick his legs out to either side, a crazy black shadow. He burst out laughing. They were in a small dimly lit square where several alleyways met. In the middle of it was a pool of stagnant water. Husayn came to a halt, panting.

"This way, my dear Midhat. You're going to sleep in my bed tonight. You're the guest of honor. Luckily it's not at all cold." He went off to the right, still bounding into the air at intervals. "There's no problem without a solution, my dear Midhat. The fact is, you see, the solutions are lost and if we look we'll find them. But that's not really what I was getting at. To hell with your ancestors, Abu Ab'ub." He snorted with laughter again. "What a man! He wants to go back to his family and eat shit!"

He stopped in front of a faded black door, part of which had sunk below ground level. "Come here, Midhat. Help me look for the key. I don't know where the devil I put it."

Midhat approached him hesitantly; his head was gently going round and he had no idea where to look for the key.

"Just a minute, Midhat."

Midhat felt Husayn take his arm. His voice was clear and quiet, and his fingers gripped him firmly. Midhat wanted to see his face, but it was too dark, so he went on waiting, unconcerned, abandoning himself to the spinning in his head.

"Midhat, please," whispered Husayn. "Take care of her. Don't lose her."

His voice was suddenly muffled, tearful, unsteady. They remained without speaking for a time, mute as the dark walls around them. In the distance Midhat could hear a drumbeat surfacing momentarily above the noise of the street and the café. The fingers gripping his arm irritated him. He disengaged himself and leaned against the wall behind him.

"Have we come here to sleep," he muttered incoherently, "or to listen to a lecture."

Husayn remained stock still beside him, the shadows he cast mingling with the feeble street lights. His ebullience had suddenly deserted him, and he appeared unable to carry on his search for the key. He let his arms drop by his sides, came down off the doorstep, and sat on the ground in the street, sighing, then buried his head in his hands. Midhat looked at him with annoyance. From the start he had lacked any confidence in him. His good nature was no use when there were serious matters to be dealt with. He heard him giving more long sighs, followed by another noise which he couldn't identify to begin with, but he didn't say anything, assuming that the situation would eventually be clarified. He was completely exhausted, weighed down in body and soul, incapable of exchanging opinions or recalling an image or a memory. All he wanted at that moment was somehow to cease to exist. As he stood helplessly in the darkness of the alley beside this drunk, who seemed unable to control his mood or emotions, he felt he couldn't go on any longer.

Then he heard a stifled sobbing coming from nowhere. He looked around him. Darkness hid the turning into the next little alley, and a splinter of red light from behind him fell on the opposite wall. There was nobody in sight. The sobbing rose up louder this time, but more disjointed. Husayn's shoulders were twitching and sagging alternately in time with his sudden strange fit of tears. Midhat continued to stare impotently at the dark heap of disheveled hair and clothes. These were not ordinary tears: long sighs followed by a short sob, then more lengthy exhalations.

She gasped when he entered her for the first time and wrapped her arms around his naked back, then began panting like him. The way she opened to him took him by surprise; he had the impression he was falling into a bottomless pit. His feelings had been in a state of confusion as he prepared to enter her. The smell of her body, her sweat, her perfume, the touch of her soft fingers, her eyes, her lips, her open thighs had made him want to cry out wildly in a way that was quite unfamiliar to him. The incessant heat welling up in him, threatening to suffocate him, was suddenly extinguished by a jet of ice-cold water. In a few seconds his life was turned upside down. At the moment of penetration, his woman, his beloved, turned out to be a mirage. The next moment he withdrew but his desire left no room for his reason or doubts to operate, so he plunged in again and immediately lost his restraint, and his soul overflowed with the water of life which spurted from him like blood, like the heart's blood.

Now Midhat too was sitting in the dark hollow in front of the locked door, listening to Husayn continuing to sigh and snuffle ignominiously. Midhat did not speak to him.

The memory had hit him like a physical blow, his legs had buckled, and he had sat down slowly on the damp ground. Perhaps the end he wished for was not far away now. The end of his confusion, his weariness, and his hopes. He was empty, unable to cry, as he realized when he felt his shoulder come into contact with Husayn's shaking body. Would he never be able to extinguish the fire inside him by this simple human expedient?

The heavy door squeaked and opened slowly, revealing a skinny apparition lit from behind. Husayn abruptly stopped all the noises he was making and raised his head. A small old woman swathed in black was standing before them in the doorway.

"Who's that? Who are you, son?" she said.

"Aunt Atiya, is that you? Good evening. We've been knocking on the door for an hour. Why did you wake up now? It's because of the fast and the meal before dawn, isn't it? Thank God! I'm dying of hunger, Aunt. Some hot soup and a shish kebab will do nicely. Come in, Midhat. Auntie, this is Midhat. Nuriya's son. You know him. I've invited him to eat with us. Come in. How's my uncle? I haven't seen him since this morning."

259

Husayn coughed repeatedly as he got to his feet, blowing his nose and wiping his mouth and eyes. Midhat glimpsed him for a moment in the light from the house. His nose was red and damp, and a strand of hair was stuck to his forehead. He was like a child who had just been woken up.

The old woman went back inside without a word, leaving the door ajar. Husayn pushed it open and went in, holding Midhat's arm. The entry was narrow. Some light filtered into the yard of the house, and it was full of the smell of food.

"All we need now is to find that our brother the Hajji has eaten all the soup," murmured Husayn, still wiping his nose and eyes.

Chapter Eleven

They walked cautiously along next to the tumbledown wall avoiding the middle of the alley, which was full of mud and puddles. Her sister Suha was in front of her, talking loudly.

"Today Miss Suhaila gave Aida ten strokes of the ruler. She began to cry like anything. You wouldn't believe how much she cried and screamed."

"Why does she get hit all the time? Is she cheeky?"

"You're so stupid, Sana. Do you think you only get hit when you're cheeky? She can't do her sums. She's useless at arithmetic. She's really stupid."

"You're the stupid one."

"Shut up. It's none of your business anyway."

"You shut up."

"You."

"I swear if grandfather wasn't ill I'd tell him you hit me, Suha."

"Liar. Idiot."

"You're an idiot."

Suha did not reply but gave a little jump across the alley and continued walking on the other side. The sun shone brightly from a clear blue sky, but there was a cold breeze every now and then.

"Do you know what, Sana?" began Suha again. "I found a sweet in my pocket. From Uncle Midhat's wedding. I was so happy. It was really good!"

Sana stopped and looked at her."Did you eat it all?"

"What do you expect? There was only one. It was hidden in my pocket. It was lovely."

"One?" Sana was sad.

"Yes. I just said, there was only one and I ate it."

How they had danced and played that night! There was singing, lots of food, and people with their children. She hadn't woken up till midday, when her mother had woken her. It was a Friday, but they were all silent and cross, enveloped in an air of mystery and not answering her questions. Her Uncle Midhat was nowhere to be seen, and she hadn't been able to get close to Munira, the beautiful bride. She loved her so!

She saw that her sister was a long way ahead of her, so she summoned all her energy and hurried to catch up. She was always hungry after morning school, but she had a vague feeling that her appetite was not as good as usual and she might not be able to eat anything. Maybe she should fast like her mother and grandmother. Her grandfather had fallen ill after a week of fasting. Her grandmother said that every year it was the same: he fasted for a week then got ill. How Sana hated to see him in bed, huddled up under the covers like a helpless kitten. And he moaned constantly; it had upset her to hear him when she went up with her mother to take him his food and medicine.

"What's wrong with you, Sana?" shouted her sister. "You're treading in the mud, you stupid thing. Look where you're going."

Her sister's voice made her jump. The edge of her white shoe was splashed with dark specks of mud. She moved to one side, stamped her foot hard a few times, then continued on her way without looking up. She had felt for the past few days now as if there was a black cloud hanging over her. She could not even understand most of her lessons any more. Luckily the mid-term exam had gone well, and there were no more exams for the time being.

As she turned into the alley leading to the house, her sister began to run. She watched her dress and hair dancing as she moved. How she had scared her when she shouted! She would tell her mother. No, then her mother would ask her about her dirty shoes. She'd tell her grandmother and Umm Hasan and Aunt Safiya, and also Munira, her beautiful friend. She'd go to her room, where she shut herself in these days, knock gently on the door, as Munira had taught her, and ask permission to tell her how that stupid Suha had scared her by shouting at her all of a sudden.

She went in through the half-open double doors and quickened her pace down the long passage, wondering if she was ill: she didn't feel like eating, couldn't understand the lessons at school, and was too tired to run. She must tell her mother about it. She opened the middle door slowly and saw her grandmother in the yard outside the kitchen.

"Hello, Bibi," she said.

"Come here, Sana, my sweetheart," exclaimed her grandmother. "The Lord must have sent you. Run and buy us ten rounds of bread, quickly. That wretched sister of yours doesn't hear a word anybody says to her. Come along, dear. Here's the money. Hurry up, now. You know the old women are going to start making a fuss shortly. Come along. Let's try and avoid that."

"Yes, Bibi."

She put her books down on the bench outside the kitchen door and took the money from her grandmother but hesitated a little before heading towards the door again. Should she tell her grandmother how tired and lethargic she felt, how she couldn't run? But then who would go and fetch the bread? She would wait and tell her everything when she returned.

She went back down the chilly passageway and out into the alley, and set off for the baker's in Kilani Street. Her grandmother loved her more than Suha. She gave her a lot of sweets and extra food, but she also made her work too hard, just as she made Sana's mother work too hard. It didn't matter. Still, they ought to know how rough Suha was with her, and how she was always yelling at her and frightening her. She was crazy, talking at the top of her voice whenever she wanted to say something. Why didn't she speak kindly and patiently to her like other people did, especially her Aunt Munira? She'd broken a tea glass and saucer on her way into Munira's room the day before yesterday. Munira had jumped out of bed in alarm, but when she saw who it was, she had calmed down and hugged her and kissed her and not said a word. Then together they had hidden the broken pieces away out of sight. She had smelt so nice, and her arms had felt so soft! Then Auntie Munira had told her that from now on she shouldn't come into the room without knocking and waiting for a reply, and Sana had said she was sorry she'd forgotten although the teacher had taught them that a long time ago. She had been going to tell her aunt something important, but it had slipped her mind when the silly glass broke. The alleyway was empty and in deep shadow, and the cars and carriages sped past at the bottom along Kilani Street. All of a sudden her Uncle Abd al-Karim came round the corner. They exchanged smiles.

"Where are you going, Sana?" asked her uncle.

"To buy some bread, Uncle. Bibi gave me money and told me to buy ten rounds."

"Fine. Come on, then."

He took her hand gently and they walked towards the baker's. She was delighted to have his company and looked up at him gratefully, pressing her fingertips into his palm. He looked sad and pale and was walking heavily. He wouldn't give her the bread to carry although she pleaded with him.

"Uncle, are you fasting?" she asked him, darting all around him as they approached the house.

"No."

She pushed the double doors wide open. "Uncle, where's Uncle?"

She closed the doors and followed him. He was walking ahead of her in silence.

"Uncle. Where's Uncle?"

He gave her the discs of bread just before they reached the end of the passage, then pushed open the middle door, and indicated to her to go in. For a moment she looked at him, crestfallen, then went towards the kitchen. She put the bread away. The kitchen was empty and warm, filled with the smell of food. She hadn't wanted to annoy her Uncle Karim, but had thought that he was the only one who might give her an answer at last. His silence had hurt her. She went to fetch her books and found someone had knocked them carelessly on to the ground. She bent to gather them up without a murmur. Why hadn't her uncle told her anything?

She heard her mother calling, "Sana. Sana."

"Yes, Mum."

"Where on earth were you?"

She was looking down at her from the gallery outside their room.

"Buying bread, Mum."

Her grandmother called from somewhere below, "I sent her, Madiha, love. I sent her."

"Warm bread?" came Aunt Safiya's voice. "For God's sake give me a taste. We're dying of hunger here, people."

Her grandmother emerged from a room near the basement carrying dishes and cooking pots and other utensils. She saw her noticing her Uncle Abd al-Karim as he was about to go upstairs and calling him. He stopped, and she hurried over and began talking to him. Sana remained standing in the doorway of the warm kitchen, her hands hanging despondently by her sides, watching the two of them whispering intently together in the sunshine. She knew they were discussing important matters which she wasn't allowed to hear. She was just a little girl with no opinions and nothing to say. She couldn't even ask questions about people she loved.

Her legs felt as if they were about to give way. Buying the bread had tired her out this time.

"Mother, please, serve the dinner," called her own mother from the gallery. "All hell's about to break loose up here."

Then she fell silent when she saw Sana's grandmother and uncle talking and hurried towards the top of the stairs. She was going to join them and share in their conversation. Sana went towards the stairs herself. She walked slowly, carrying her books under her arm, head down, looking at the ground as if she was counting the bricks. Perhaps she would catch a few words. She heard her mother's footsteps on the stairs and hoped she'd reach Uncle Karumi and her grandmother first. As her shadow fell on the two of them her uncle's voice reached her ears. "No," he was saying. Then before she could hear any more, her mother said sharply, "Sana. Have you washed your hands?" Her eyes were blazing. Sana drew back, afraid. "No, Mum. I forgot. I'll go and wash them now."

She ran back over to the washbasin which was next to the kitchen and put her books carefully on the ground against the wall. Her heart was pounding, and she felt as if she was about to burst into tears. The youngest in the house, she was the only one who had all this trouble, and nobody bothered to listen to her. The water was cold but she didn't feel it. She was observing the drops running down between her fingers as she rubbed her hands together. They were dirty, almost black. She heard footsteps in the passageway. She washed her hands with soap again, trying to increase the volume of the brownish lather. Had that pest Suha washed her hands? Nobody had stopped her going upstairs. She had eaten a sweet before lunch, and they hadn't asked her if she'd washed her hands. They'd left her in peace. The middle door, next to the kitchen, was opened abruptly and Munira walked in. Sana was surprised by the brusqueness of her actions. Munira's eyes were sad.

"Hello, Auntie Munira," called Sana.

Munira pushed the *abaya* down off her shoulders, looking sharply over at the group by the stairs. "Hello, Sana. What are you doing?"

"Washing my hands, Auntie. My mother told me to. Me and Suha have just come back from school. I went to buy some bread and came back with Uncle Karumi."

Munira was still looking anxiously towards the stairs. Sana wanted to look too, but her grandmother's voice stopped her. "Hello, Munira, dear. Aren't you back early today?"

"Yes, Aunt. Today's Thursday. Can I help you with the cooking?"

Sana's mother detached herself from the group, went silently into the kitchen, and disappeared in the shadows.

"No, dear, there's nothing to do," answered Sana's grandmother. "We just want to shut the old ladies up."

"Has Karim come back?"

"Yes."

"Does he have any news?"

Sana stopped drying her hands. Her senses were alerted. She wished she was invisible. If only she was hidden somewhere close by. Her grandmother shook her head expansively. "Not a thing. We'll just have to wait. Today he went . . ." Then she looked at Sana. "Off you go, Sana, dear. See if your grandfather wants something to eat now."

Sana looked imploringly at Munira, and Munira reached out a hand and stroked her hair gently.

"Yes, Bibi," she said to her grandmother, and walked away as slowly as she could.

"Today he went to the office," she heard her grandmother continuing. "Nobody. They said he was on holiday. He couldn't . . ."

Sana began going carefully up the poorly lit steps. They would never leave her in peace. Once she had seen her grandfather she would go down again to tell them what he wanted. They would stop talking as she approached them, then ask her to do some other task. They would make her go up and down the stairs again and again, while that sister of hers was sitting in their room playing with the doll or combing her hair. Her grandfather was sitting cross-legged on his bed telling the large yellow beads of his rosary with his spectacles on. She smiled at him. "How are you, Grandpa? Why are you sitting like that?"

"Hello, my pretty little Sana. How are you today?"

She went up to him and climbed on to the bed. "It's me asking how you are. Not you asking me." She took hold of his hand and squeezed it playfully. "What kind of illness have you got? I've never seen an illness like that. Sitting up on the bed with your glasses on. Why aren't you lying down, Grandpa?"

She jiggled his hand gently, still smiling at him. His fingers were bony and wrinkled. He raised her hand to his lips and kissed it.

"What a nice clean hand, and its smells so good too!"

"Thank you. But your beard's tickling me, and Bibi said what would you like to eat? I know you're not fasting. Bibi says you've been ill since the beginning of the week." She hit him lightly on the back of the hand. "Why do you always get ill after the first week of Ramadan and make us worried about you? Tell me."

"No I won't."

"Why not?"

"I said I'm not telling you."

"Why not? Don't you like talking to me, Grandpa? You're like them."

"Like who?"

"All of them. Bibi, Uncle, my mother. Even Auntie Munira."

The joy she normally felt in her grandfather's company began to ebb away. He took her hand and kissed it again. She moved close to him and snuggled up against him in silence.

"What's the matter with Auntie Munira?" he asked.

"I love her, Grandpa. I really love her. But she's sad. Maybe about Uncle Midhat. Where is he, Grandpa? Nobody will tell me."

He squeezed her hand and she clung to him, feeling warmth spread through her. She had a strong desire to cry. He put his arm round her. "Don't upset yourself, little Sana. You're still young, my dear. When you're older you'll understand everything. Do you know why they don't talk to you? So as not to upset you. They say to themselves, she's still young, poor thing, why make her sad?"

"But I won't get sad, Grandpa. It's only Suha who upsets me. She's so naughty and rude and stupid. She never stops. She's worse than anybody else." Then she disengaged herself from his arms and confronted him: "Grandpa. Where's Uncle Midhat?"

His face seemed to crumple slightly and his mouth twitched. He took his eyes off her face. Again she had a secret desire to cry.

"He's gone away, Sana. He'll be back in a couple of days. Didn't you know that?"

His voice was calm and gentle, leaving her no room for doubt. She remained silent, looking into his eyes framed by their spectacles. "Is that true, Grandpa? Swear to God."

He played with her hair, pulling it down over her face. "Why would I lie to you, little Sana?"

She was watching him through the black hair which fell down over her eyes, and he never once smiled as he caressed her. She sighed audibly. "I can't quarrel with you, Grandpa. So what do you want for lunch? Tell me."

His lips were dry and pressed shut. He seemed unable to answer her. The door opened violently, and her grandmother burst in carrying a large tray with difficulty.

"Is this what we can expect from you, Sana? While we're working our fingers to the bone preparing lunch, you're sitting up here tiring your grandfather with your chatter instead of letting him rest. Get up and fetch that table for me."

Sana jumped off the bed and rushed to bring the little table from the side of the room and placed it by her grandfather's bed. Her grandmother put the tray down with a thud.

"You know I'm worn out today, Abu Midhat," she said to her husband. "One day I'll drop down dead into the food in that filthy kitchen."

"God protect you, Bibi."

"Don't stand there like that, Sana. Run down and help your mother in the kitchen. Those people upstairs are going to start screaming for their lunch soon. Hurry up, dear."

"Yes, Bibi," and she hurried out of her grandfather's room without looking at him.

The smell of food filled her nostrils, enticing her downstairs, but she stopped on the gallery by her grandparents' window. She could vaguely hear them talking. She was afraid to go closer to the window in case either of them saw her. It was a beautiful day and she felt less tired now. She heard footsteps coming up and walked on to the top of the stairs. Munira appeared carrying a huge tray, her face flushed and her hair hanging down on her dark blouse; she was obviously having a lot of trouble walking with the tray. Sana went towards her.

"Why are you carrying that tray, Auntie Munira?" she exclaimed.

Munira gestured to her to move out of the way. "Leave me alone, Sana. It's none of your business. Go in front of me, but give me some room. Don't worry about me."

Her face was red; beads of sweat gathered on her forehead and she pressed her lips tightly together. Sana raced ahead of her, feeling a pang at the sight of her. She stumbled at the old ladies' door because of the clumsy way she was walking, only half looking where her feet were going and half back at Munira's face. This wasn't what normally happened. Her mother was the one responsible for taking the food up to the old people. Munira stopped at the corner where the gallery became narrower and balanced the tray on the balustrade. She was breathing rapidly, her lips parted now. "Open the door, Sana," she said, waving a hand in her direction.

Sana threw herself at the door of the old people's room and it flew open, banging against the wall behind it.

"God is most great," shouted Aunt Safiya in alarm.

Sana walked in calling, "Auntie. Supper's ready."

Aunt Safiya was half sitting up in bed, eyes popping and mouth open, fear written on her face. "How can you make make such a commotion, Sana?" she demanded. "Do you have to open the door like that? You'll kill us, God forgive you. Now, is this our lunch or have they finally decided to poison us?"

Munira's mother raised her head unenthusiastically. She was lying on the big iron bed opposite the door.

"Sorry, Aunt Safiya," said Sana. "I was in a bit of a hurry."

Munira entered with difficulty and stood in the middle of the room with her burden. Aunt Safiya looked at her in astonishment.

"Auntie Munira, shall I bring the table so you can put the tray down?" asked Sana.

"No. There's no need." She turned to Aunt Safiya. "Can I put the tray on the floor beside you?"

"Yes, my dear," answered Aunt Safiya at once. "God give you strength, Munira. Bring it here. Put it in front of me, dear. Umm Hasan's been asleep for an hour. Come along, dear."

Munira put the tray down carefully beside Aunt Safiya's bed, as Sana hovered around trying to help.

"What time is it, Munira?" asked Munira's mother. "When did you get back from school?"

"Not long ago. How are you today?"

"I feel a bit dizzy. What time is it?"

"After one."

Then Munira sat down beside her mother, looking at the floor. She seemed tired and began wiping the sweat off her face and neck. Aunt Safiya was inspecting the food, gathering herself up, and moving over to the edge of her bed.

"Shall I wake Bibi Umm Hasan?" Sana asked her.

Aunt Safiya shot her a searching glance. "As you wish, my dear. She's a heavy sleeper. Like one of the seven sleepers of Ephesus. I don't know if you'll be able to or not. It's up to you." Then she reached for a circle of bread.

Sana went over to her great-grandmother. The old lady was fast asleep, breathing deeply and peacefully. Sana squatted down and took hold of her shoulder and called gently, "Bibi, Bibi, wake up. Sit up and have something to eat."

The old lady opened her eyes and turned slowly towards Sana.

"Wake up and eat, Bibi. Lunch is ready," the little girl repeated.

"Lunch? Aren't I fasting?"

"No, Bibi. When do you ever fast? Sit up and have your lunch."

With some effort Umm Hasan sat up in bed. Sana rose to her feet. Munira and her mother still had not moved, and Aunt Safiya, her mouth full, was watching Umm Hasan out of the corner of her eye as she edged towards the tray of food. Sana reached out a hand to help her great-grandmother into a more comfortable sitting position.

"Water, Sana," grumbled Aunt Safiya. "A glass of water, please, dear. I've got something stuck in my gullet. Who's put a curse on this food?"

"All right, Aunt. I'll go and get some water." As she went out she turned towards Munira. "Auntie Munira. I'm going down to get a glass of water for Aunt Safiya. Do you want anything?"

Munira's eyes were solemn. She smiled weakly at Sana and shook her head without saying anything. Sana's hopes were dashed. She wanted Munira to ask her to run some errand for her, which she could feel enthusiastic about, but to go all that way for the sake of a glass of water to shift a bit of food stuck in Aunt Safiya's throat would only make her more tired and hungry.

She saw Suha coming out of the kitchen and stopped and called down to her. "Suha, Suha. Bring up a glass of water for Aunt Safiya. Quickly."

"Who do you think I am? I'm still eating my lunch."

"She's going to choke, you stupid thing."

"It's nothing to do with me."

"You're so stupid." She hurried crossly along the small gallery and down the dark staircase and met her mother coming out of the kitchen.

"Come and eat, Sana," said her mother.

"Aunt Safiya wants a glass of water. A piece of food went down the wrong way."

"All right. You'd better eat with them."

"They won't let me, Mum."

"Come and take some food from here then and go and eat upstairs. Bring the tray down when you've finished. Come along. I'll dish some out for you. I want to wash up and have a bit of a rest before the end of the fast."

"Yes, Mum. But let me take some water up to Aunt Safiya. She's going to choke. That stupid Suha wouldn't get it."

"Fine. I know that little madam can be a bit naughty sometimes."

"Yes, Mum. She's really mean. And stupid."

"Take your food and go upstairs then. Don't keep your aunt waiting."

Carrying a glass of water and her plate of rice mixed with broth, Sana walked carefully back upstairs and along the gallery to the old ladies' room. Munira's place was empty, and her mother was lying with her back to the door. Aunt Safiya seized the glass eagerly and gulped down some water.

"Where were you?" she exclaimed. "I was dead and now you see me come back to life. I couldn't stop eating." She jerked her head towards Umm Hasan. "The food would have been finished and I would still have been hungry. But I couldn't eat with the food stuck halfway down my gullet, God help me. God bless you, Sana. You've saved me from the fires of hell."

Umm Hasan looked up from the tray with her mouth full. "Why did you say hell? Does one talk about hell when people are eating? What kind of manners do you call that?"

"My dear Umm Hasan, let me eat and fill my stomach if you don't want me to think about the people who are going to hell for their unjust behavior."

"Why don't you fear the Lord, Safiya?"

Sana sat cross-legged on the rug between the two windows with her plate on her lap and began to eat, taking small helpings of the rice and broth between her fingers and listening to the two of them arguing. She leaned back against the wall. The room was hot with the noon sun, and she could hear the faint sounds of her mother washing the dishes. She didn't enjoy the food; it seemed to lack the particular taste which she liked. Umm Hasan produced a strange noise out of her mouth. Aunt Safiya stopped eating. "What's that, Umm Hasan?" she demanded. "It's neither a hiccup nor a belch. What's wrong with you?"

Sana laughed to herself. Umm Hasan didn't reply. Aunt Safiya turned to Sana. "Sana, my dear. Where's your uncle?"

"He's been gone a week now. Since his wedding night," pronounced Umm Hasan. "As if an angel came down and spirited him away."

"I'm asking about her Uncle Karumi," interrupted Aunt Safiya vehemently. "You're like a broken record. I'm talking about Karumi, not Midhat."

"I don't know, Aunt," replied Sana. "He might be reading in his room." Then she added, "But where is my Uncle Midhat anyway?"

"You see?" said Umm Hasan at once. "She's asking about him. Are you deaf? She's asking about her Uncle Midhat." She turned to Sana. Her small, lined face, framed by the black headscarf, was devoid of emotion. "An angel took him and flew off with him, dear. Came down on his wedding night and took him away. What's wrong with that? He's not the first. Is he, Safiya?"

Aunt Safiya swallowed her mouthful hastily. "What are you talking about? We all know you're senile, but why are you talking such rubbish in front of the child? An angel indeed! You could say it was luck. How many times did I say to him, and these four walls are my witnesses, 'My dear Midhat, this isn't for you. Everyone must go his own way.'?"

"That's exactly what I said to him."

"You? You'd be better off keeping your mouth shut. You sleep day and night and don't know whether it's sunrise or sunset."

Her great-aunt's words upset Sana in some mysterious way, and she didn't understand what the two of them were talking about. "So when's Uncle Midhat coming back, Aunt?" she asked suddenly.

There was a note of pleading in her voice and she hoped one of them would answer. Neither of them really liked Munira, so for this reason perhaps they would tell her the truth. But they remained silent. Aunt Safiya licked her lips then had a drink of water. Umm Hasan was wiping her mouth with a piece of bread. Sana waited anxiously, while the sound of dishes being washed in the kitchen continued unabated.

"God knows. God knows, my dear," said Aunt Safiya indifferently, putting her glass down.

Umm Hasan returned to bed. Once more Sana felt let down. As the two women prepared for a nap Sana remembered that she had to take the tray and the empty plates down to her mother in the kitchen. She was tired.

———

She saw the red sun's rays brush the high rooftop as she fanned the coals under the kebabs. She and her mother were working quickly to finish the last few and her grandmother had already heated the lentil soup and taken it up a few minutes before to the alcove where they were going to break the fast. Suha had also run off with the bread and condiments and a dish of pickles, pretending that she was weighed down by her load. The sun was receding from the treetops in the little garden and falling on the tall brick walls. Everyone was hurrying, and the voice of the man reciting the Quran came from several places at once; it was hoarse and trembling and touched Sana's heart. Some beads of sweat gathered on her mother's forehead as she concentrated on turning the kebab skewers.

"My dear!"

Sana lifted her head. Aunt Safiya was standing by the wooden balustrade looking down at them. "Madiha, dear, God give you strength.

The smoke's killing us and there's been a smell of kebabs on and off for an hour now, but nobody's got their hands on one yet."

"Be patient, Aunt," interrupted Sana's mother. "Patience is a virtue. You ate two hours ago. Everything will soon be ready. Don't be in such a rush. There are people who've been fasting, you know." Then she lowered her voice and muttered, "Will God not take back what belongs to Him? Why remain a burden on this earth? But you do as you wish, Lord."

"Madiha, dear," came Aunt Safiya's voice again. "Take your time. But I'm starving. The people fasting will get their reward in heaven. If they fast ten minutes extra, their reward will be all the greater. Please, Madiha, just a small kebab and a few pickles and vegetables rolled in a piece of bread, God bless you."

Sana's mother shook her head. "There's no power or strength save in God," she murmured.

"Madiha. Madiha," called Sana's grandmother from the alcove. "Hurry, girl. The muezzin's about to announce the end of the fast."

"All right, all right," she answered wearily. "Don't make me crazy, all shouting at me at once. Be a bit patient."

"What does 'Patience is a virtue' mean, Mum?" asked Sana.

Her mother looked at her resentfully. "Don't talk rubbish. I'll dig the grave of anyone who tells me patience is a virtue. Keep fanning and shut up."

Sana moved her arm faster, her eyes downcast. The red coals glowed under the kebabs, drops of fat fell on them, and a white spiral of delicious-smelling smoke rose in the air. The yard had filled up with shadows round about Sana and her mother, and the clatter of dishes from the alcove mingled with the whispering of the water put to boil on the stove a while before. The tea wasn't made yet; her mother would make it when the kebabs were done, then leave the embers to rest. Her grandmother and grandfather, her mother, Munira's mother, Auntie Munira herself, and Uncle Karim would drink the tea when they'd eaten the kebabs.

A puff of smoke took her by surprise. She jerked her head back and felt her eyes stinging and began rubbing them with her free hand.

"Go on, keep fanning. We're nearly finished. Hurry up. I've still got a thousand things to do."

"The smoke went in my eye, Mum."

Her mother began gathering up some of the skewers and emptying their contents on to a large dish, then covering them with herbs and discs of white bread. "Get up," she ordered Sana. "That's enough for now. Take this upstairs. I'll make the tea."

Munira appeared from the shadows and hurried towards them. "Sorry, Madiha. I got held up. You go and eat with Sana. I can finish here."

"No. There's nothing left to do, and the cannon for the end of the fast hasn't gone off yet. I'll make the tea and then I'll be up. I'm really tired today."

"I know you are, Madiha. You're tired all the time. Let me help you."

Aunt Safiya was calling above their heads. "Don't forget us, Madiha, dear. We're at your mercy. Collapsing with hunger."

Picking up the big dish of kebabs without even raising her eyes to look at Aunt Safiya, Munira asked Sana to bring bread, clean plates, and water and walked off towards the dark staircase. Sana stood watching her, her heart overflowing with a fierce emotion. She was never bored being with her, listening to her talk. Earlier in the afternoon she had gone into that magical blue room of hers. Munira was lying on the big blue bed fully clothed, with an abstracted look in her eyes. Sana had come to tell her that they were about to begin making the kebabs. Munira sat up and listened, shoulders hunched. Sana kept talking unnecessarily, just to be with her in her room, touching her and hearing her reply.

She heard her mother coming and got up from in front of the brazier.

"Why are you still here? Take the bread and water and go up before me. Let me finish what I've got to do. Don't forget the plates."

Sana ran into the kitchen, got out the bread, filled the water jug and put it on the table, slipped the bread under her arm, then picked up a pile of plates in one hand and the jug in the other and went out slowly, avoiding looking at her mother. She climbed the stairs without incident, although she could hardly see where she was treading, and proceeded towards the alcove. They greeted her with smiling faces and relieved her of her burdens, and she was glad to sit down next to Munira's mother on the sofa. The big tray was on the table, loaded with all sorts of plates and dishes, and in the middle of it sat a huge bowl with a lid; she guessed this must be the soup. Shortly after she sat down, Suha came in with Uncle Abd al-Karim.

"Where have you been, Suha?" asked her grandmother. "You left your little sister to do all the work. That won't do, my dear. You're the older one."

Sana was delighted at these words and waited eagerly for Suha's reply, but Suha sat down next to her without a word. "Where were you then?" said Sana angrily. Suha didn't reply. Munira slipped into the room and sat down with them on the sofa.

"Have you given Aunt Safiya and Umm Hasan their kebab sandwiches, Munira?" asked Sana's grandmother.

"Yes, Aunt."

She was actually sitting with Munira on the sofa. She was at one end, with her sister Suha sitting next to her, then Munira's mother and Munira. Facing them was her Uncle Abd al-Karim, morose-looking and silent, staring into space. Her grandmother was sitting cross-legged on a cushion on the floor near the tray. Sana leaned forward to look at Munira. She had more make-up on than usual. She was always pretty and nicely made-up. She noticed she was looking over in Abd al-Karim's direction. The light was dim in the alcove, most of which was in shadow.

"Madiha. Madiha," called her grandmother. "Come along now. Leave the tea to brew and come up. The cannon's about to go off."

"Yes. I'll be there in a minute," her mother's voice came from below.

"How's my father today?" asked Abd al-Karim suddenly. "Isn't he going to eat with us?"

"No. Let him rest now," replied his mother. "He drank some tea with milk this afternoon. He hasn't got a temperature, but he's still tired. He's getting better, God willing."

A loud bang from the radio made her jump; it was followed by the voice of the muezzin.

"See, that really scared you, Sana," whispered Suha.

Their grandmother lifted the lid off the soup tureen, and a white cloud of vapor rose in the air accompanied by a pungent smell of fat. Munira's mother went and sat beside the tray, and Sana and Suha jumped up in unison and sat near her on the floor.

"Madiha," called their grandmother again. "Come on, for heaven's sake. We're breaking the fast, not having dinner!" She turned to Munira. "Come along, Munira dear. Shall I give you a little soup, Karim?"

Munira rose wearily. "Give me a plate. I'll serve it," she said.

"No. Thank you," said Karim. "I'll do it." He stood up, taking the cushion from behind him, putting it on the floor and sitting on it next to her and Suha and his mother, opposite Munira and her mother. Sana pictured that when her mother finally came she would sit on the sofa between her grandmother and Munira's mother. Her grandmother was ladling the soup into bowls and distributing it to those sitting there. All Sana could see was the steam rising from the soup tureen and the ends of the herbs and bread on the dish of kebabs, because the tray was too high up.

She sat waiting in silence, her hands in her lap. She was hungry and hoped the food would reach her as soon as possible. She could hear some of them eating, and the clatter of spoons against china, then she noticed Munira sitting there quietly, her face in the shadows, its features indistinct.

"Here you are, Suha," said her grandmother.

Her sister took the plate and immediately began drinking the soup. Her Uncle Abd al-Karim had been eating for a while; she and Munira were the only ones still waiting and this pained her a little, although she did not want to complain.

"Bibi. Auntie Munira hasn't got anything to eat."

They all paused momentarily, spoons in mid-air.

"Don't worry, Sana," said Munira quickly. "I'll have something in a minute. You eat."

"Why aren't you breaking the fast?" interrupted Abd al-Karim. "You shouldn't put it off. You ought to eat now, shouldn't she, Mother?"

"That's right, Karumi. It's not good to wait once the cannon's gone off. I'm just serving her soup. And Sana's. I forgot yours, dear."

"Thank you, Aunt," said Munira in a faint voice, and Sana felt her looking reproachfully at her and hung her head. As she waited for her bowl of soup and kebab sandwich to reach her she heard her mother's footsteps rapidly crossing the yard then fading away. Her grandmother handed her down a bowl of soup, and Sana balanced it on her lap and brought the spoon gingerly up to her mouth. Again she heard her mother's footsteps coming along the gallery, then she appeared in front of the alcove carrying the brazier. She put it down next to the balustrade.

"What's all this, Madiha?" exclaimed Sana's grandmother. "Why put yourself to so much trouble? We would have come down for our tea. You didn't have to bring the brazier up here when you're so worn out. Come along, dear. It's not good to go without eating once the cannon's gone off. The soup's getting cold."

"I'm coming, Mother. I'm washing my hands. Are the girls with you?"

"Yes, Mum, we're here."

The soup had a nice taste, but it was cold. When no one was looking, Sana licked up the last few drops then put the spoon back on the plate and returned it to the tray. Munira was eating slowly and looking in her direction. Had she noticed her licking the soup bowl after all? But she had kept her head well down below the level of the tray. Her mother came and sat between Munira and Karim. "Where's your bowl, Sana?" she asked.

"I've finished my soup, Mum. I'm waiting for the kebab."

"What about you, Suha? Have you finished? Mum, please make everybody a kebab sandwich while I have my soup."

"Yes, dear. At once."

"Are there any human beings there, anyone born of a mother's womb? Where are you all, people of the house?" Aunt Safiya was standing in the doorway of her room calling interminably. "Has the ground opened and swallowed you all up? Madiha, my dear, what's become of you, my darling? And my little Sana? What? Are you mad, Umm Hasan? Who would they go and visit? This is no time for social visits. They're sitting eating in the dark there. That's it! Lucky people! And I'm left with you, you miserable old crow. We're stuck in here, two hungry old women about to die of hunger. Perhaps we deserve it." Then she called again, "My dears! People of the house! Mothers' sons!"

Sana laughed and Suha copied her.

"Didn't you make them kebab sandwiches, Madiha?" asked their grandmother.

"Half a round of bread, a kebab, pickles, and some salad each. But they've never had enough."

"My dears. My brothers and sisters . . ."

"Take it easy, Safiya," interrupted their grandmother. "We're here."

"Where were you, dear? I've been calling you for two hours."

"All right. We'll bring you something to eat. Just wait a minute."

"Hurry, please. We can't last much longer. We're hanging by a thread."

Sana took the piece of bread wrapped expertly around the kebab by her grandmother and bit into it eagerly. The taste of the meat mixed with pickles and salad was delicious. She chewed it slowly, observing the shadowy faces around her. The light had faded in the alcove, and she could no longer make out their features. However, this did not concern her much. Eating when she was so hungry and tired made her pleasantly drowsy and gave her a sense of great satisfaction with the world around her. Later she would have tea with them and help herself to an extra spoon of sugar. The tea would have a very special taste after the kebab and pickles, as long as she drank it before rinsing her mouth out. This would give it more flavor.

She pushed the last piece of bread into her already full mouth, then looked up to see what was happening round about her, chewing unhurriedly. They were all still in their places, eating in silence, enveloped by the darkness.

"Have you finished, Sana?" asked her mother.

"No, Mum."

"What about you, Suha?"

"Yes, I've finished."

"Then take this plate to Grandmother Umm Hasan and Aunt Safiya."

"Why me? Sana can do it."

"Off you go, you little wretch, or it'll be the worse for you. Come on, up you get, or I'll give you a slap. I've had just about enough of you."

Her sister stood up laboriously, giving Sana a nudge with her foot as she did so, not hard enough to bother her, then she took the plate and went off towards the old women's room. Sana's heart was full of joy as she continued to chew her last mouthful of food and watched her sister trail miserably away. She would get her tea before Suha. If Suha had been sitting next to her mother, her mother would certainly have slapped her hard round the head to make her hurry.

"Can I have a glass of water, Mother?" Uncle Abd al-Karim asked.

"Yes, of course. Sana dear, pour your uncle a glass of water."

"Yes, Bibi."

She stood up quickly, filled the glass and brought it back to her uncle. He caressed her affectionately and thanked her as he took it. She sat down on the sofa.

"Mum, shall I put the light on?" she asked after a moment.

"Yes, dear. I can't see where I'm going," answered her grandmother.

Sana jumped up from her place and switched on the light. Her uncle was going over to sit on the long wooden seat away from the rest of them, and Munira was putting her plate on the tray. Her mother and grandmother and Munira's mother remained in their places.

"Shall I pour the tea?" said Munira.

"In a minute. It might not have brewed yet."

Munira went off to wash.

"Can I go and see Grandpa, Mum?" asked Sana.

"Why? He's not there for your entertainment."

"Let her go, Madiha," said her grandmother. "I'm afraid he might want some water and not have the energy to call us."

"All right. Off you go, Sana."

He was sitting up in bed, telling his prayer beads. "Ah, little Sana. Have you broken the fast?"

She sat down on the edge of the bed. "I'm not fasting! But you should have tasted the kebabs, Grandpa. They were out of this world!"

"You had a good meal then?"

"Yes, thank you, Grandpa. Can I get you something?"

Her grandfather reached out to stroke her hair. "A bit later, Sana. I'd like soup with some lemon squeezed into it."

"It was such good soup today! It was out of this world! Shall I bring you some now?"

"No. Later on. Let Bibi bring it and tell her to squeeze some lemon juice on it. Do you understand?"

"Yes, Grandpa. But not now, later on?"

He nodded.

They were in the alcove, preparing tea. Her sister Suha was sitting next to Uncle Abd al-Karim. Sana looked for Munira but she wasn't there, nor was her own mother. She repeated her grandfather's request to her grandmother who acknowledged it in silence with a slight dip of her head. She was busy arranging the tea glasses on a small tray on the floor. Munira's mother sat next to her, stolidly smoking a cigarette.

The silence was complete, unexpected, and Sana suddenly felt confused, not knowing where to sit although there was plenty of space in the alcove. She thought of going to their room to watch television and saw her mother approaching slowly from the east side of the house, her dark dress merging with the surroundings so that her pale face stood out. Her feet made no sound. Munira's mother muttered something to her grandmother, too quiet for her to hear although she was so close to them. Everything—the air, the house, the light, the walls—was wrapped in a fragile, indefinable veil of silence. She leaned against the edge of the wooden couch and looked at the sky for a moment, then back at her mother making her way towards them. All at once there were strange muffled bangings on the outside door. Astonished, she turned to look at her grandmother, then at her mother and her uncle. Her mother stopped by the brazier, peering vaguely into the dark courtyard.

"I pray it's not bad news," said her grandmother.

"I'll go and see who it is," said her uncle abruptly.

As he passed her, she glimpsed his face for a moment, filled with anxiety.

"Wait a minute, Karim," said her mother. "I'm coming with you."

He didn't answer and the two of them disappeared down the stairs, then Munira emerged from her room. "Is that someone at the door?"

"Yes, Auntie Munira," Sana answered. "Uncle and Mum have gone down to see who it is."

"I hope everything's all right."

The knocking continued: a double knock, followed by a single knock, then another, and another. Light flooded the courtyard. Sana ran to stand at the balustrade. Her mother and uncle were hurrying to the middle door. She noticed Munira heading for the stairs.

"Where are you going, Munira?" called her grandmother. "Stay with us, dear."

"Yes, Aunt. I just want to see who it is."

She kept walking on slowly, looking at the courtyard, at the big far door which separated the outside passage from the house. Sana followed her in silence, moving very cautiously so that no one would notice her, then she heard her grandfather calling her grandmother.

"Bibi, Bibi," she shouted. "Grandpa's calling you. I don't know what he wants." She was anxious that her grandmother wouldn't notice her closing in on Munira, who had disappeared down the stairs.

"What's wrong now, for God's sake?" said her grandmother, rising wearily to her feet. "All right, dear, I'll go and see what he wants."

Resting a hand on the wall beside her, she walked off without looking at Sana. Then Sana noticed Suha in the light from the alcove, sitting in her place watching her. Munira's mother was smoking and seemed to be in a world of her own. That pest Suha was the only one who might tell on her. Her grandmother disappeared into her room. Nobody could stop her going downstairs now. She started to run.

"Hey, you idiot, where are you going?" shouted Suha, "I swear I'm going to . . ."

Sana didn't wait to hear the rest of the sentence. She hesitated at the top of the dark stairs then, supporting herself on the wall, began descending in a series of little jumps. She saw Munira standing by the middle door, holding it open slightly, and watching what was going on at the end of the passage.

"Sana?" she said, turning round, then put a hand gently on Sana's shoulder. Sana was breathing rapidly and felt the soft touch of Munira's arm as she stood close to her.

"I'm going to see who's at the door, then I'll be back, Auntie Munira," she said, but received no reply.

The passage seemed darker and longer than usual as she tried to see where to put her feet by the light from the sky. They were standing at the end by the outside door. As she stumbled on the step leading down to the door she began to be able to hear their conversation and thought she knew all the voices. Her mother was holding the big door open and leaning against the doorpost, and her uncle and a third person were standing out in the road.

"Why don't you come in and talk to them?" said her mother, her voice raised. "What's wrong? Are you embarrassed?"

"No. Why?" said the third person. "I mean, there's nothing stopping me, but is there any point? It's nothing important."

The long drawn out way of speaking, the indolent, hesitant tone, were not unfamiliar to her; they were part of her life.

"Look, Husayn," said her uncle. "Have you got something to tell us or not? Do you need anything? Or do you want the two of us to talk alone?"

He was dressed in black or dark blue. Only his crooked nose was visible. "No. There's nothing to discuss. Nothing important. Why would you and I need to talk? No, no. It's just the question of Midhat."

"Midhat? What's wrong with him?" interrupted her uncle and her mother with one voice.

Her father looked from one to the other for a second. "Didn't I just say I'd come about him?"

"Why don't you tell us then?" shouted her mother. "Have you got some news of him? What's wrong with you? Can't you talk? Have you usually had a drink by now?"

Husayn backed away.

"Take it easy, Madiha. Calm down," said Uncle Karim.

"What do you mean, a drink? You've got a right to be angry, I suppose. Anyway, the point is . . ." He straightened up and it seemed to add inches to his height. "Yes. You've got some news. I mean, I've got news of Midhat, of course. And for your information—I haven't had a drink today. That's the problem."

Uncle Karim took his arm and led him indoors. Her mother stood back for them, and Sana jumped to one side.

"Come on in, Husayn," said her uncle. "You must see my mother and father and Munira. Come along. We should all see you."

Her father tripped.

"Whatever are you doing here?" said her mother, noticing her as she was shutting the door. "Get inside quickly."

Her mother followed her father and uncle down the passage, and Sana fell into step beside her.

"Why don't you get an electric light in this damn corridor, or a candle at least? Sorry," she heard her father saying.

He tripped again just before the passage opened out and muttered irritably as he gripped her uncle's arm. They pushed open the middle door and entered the yard. The light was on above the kitchen door, casting its red glow over part of the garden.

"Where are we going, Karim?" said her father. "I don't have much to say. We don't need to sit down. I'm quite happy to stand."

"My father's not well, Husayn. You ought to see him. Don't you want to say hello to him? Have a cup of tea at least."

They crossed the yard uncertainly, her uncle and father still ahead and her mother in the rear. It was then that she noticed Munira standing in a corner near the door, and she took hold of her mother's hand and squeezed it urgently. At once her mother went over to Munira and whispered something in her ear. Her father and uncle had almost reached the stairs. Sana stood waiting anxiously beside the dark water of the little pond. Munira and her mother caught up with her and she felt a hand gently take her arm, then the three of them followed the men upstairs, in a somewhat awkward silence.

Her mother and Munira hurried ahead of her into her grandfather's room. She slipped in with them and sneaked behind a pile of cushions and bedding on the far side of her grandfather's bed, breathing rapidly as she peered out at them from her hiding place. She saw Munira close the door behind her and sit down on a chair next to her mother just inside the room.

Nobody spoke for some time. Her grandmother was sitting on the bed beside her grandfather, and her father and uncle occupied two chairs standing a short distance apart from one another at the foot of the bed. Still no one was speaking; the atmosphere in the faint reddish light of the room was unusually mysterious, like dreams or frightening scenes on television. Sana could hear her grandfather's prayer beads clicking against one another. Her father, in a dark suit, his face drained of color, was sitting with his feet neatly together and his hands in his lap.

"Well, Mr. Husayn, how are you?" said her grandfather finally, in a soft voice. "We don't see much of you these days."

Her father raised a hand, touched his nose and his mouth, then let it fall back on his lap. "Fine, thank you. You're right. I owe you a visit. I've been a bit busy. How are you, sir?"

"Thanks be to God. Thanks be to God. This will pass, God willing. It will pass. You're well, are you, Mr. Husayn?"

"Yes. I'm fine, Uncle. Can't complain."

He raised his hand again and pushed his hair back, then wiped his nose. Sana could see the left side of Munira's face, watching Husayn attentively.

"What's going on, Mr. Husayn? Where's this idiot taking us?"

"Which idiot's that, sir?"

"What? No, you're right. There are a lot of them around these days, and our fate is in their hands. Who else but Abd al-Karim Qasim?"

Husayn lifted his hands from his lap and intertwined them in front of him, then let them hang by his sides. "I really don't know. I mean . . ." He gave a short laugh which he checked abruptly. "I really don't know what's going to become of us."

He twisted his neck as if he was clicking a bone back into place. Sana's mother suddenly spoke. "Husayn, why are you acting as if you don't understand? Do you have any news of Midhat? Tell us quickly. We're desperate to know."

Husayn sat back in his chair, frightened by the unexpected burst of words. Sana saw his eyelids blink rapidly. He looked at Munira, appearing to notice her for the first time, and examined her intently. She neither spoke, nor lowered her gaze.

"Er—Munira, isn't it?" he said, then turned inquiringly to Karim, who nodded his head. Her father seemed to be coming back to life. "Very pleased to meet you."

Munira inclined her head slightly but said nothing and continued to stare sharply at him.

"You know, I don't have anything to say," he almost shouted. "Nothing important. But I wanted to tell you, I mean Midhat's like a brother to me, and his problems are my problems."

"What's going on between you and Midhat?" asked Sana's mother loudly. "For the love of God, tell me!"

Husayn stared at her in amazement, then stole a glance at Munira, before looking bewilderedly back at Sana's mother. "Nothing, really. I mean, I don't think there's anything going on between us. You know—where does he stand, where do I stand? But the thing is that he's been—for the past two or three days—he's been living in my room with me, if that's of any interest to you."

"What? Where?" shouted her grandmother, mother, and aunt in unison.

Munira leaned forward eagerly, her eyes fixed on Sana's father.

"How long has he been with you?" asked her grandfather.

"A couple of days, sir. Maybe three."

"I came to ask you about him five days ago," said Karim. "He must have only arrived after that."

"Yes, that's right," said Husayn. "But please . . ."

They looked upset. Sana stretched out her leg and it knocked against something. She breathed in sharply and withdrew into her corner. Her father spread his arms wide, raising his voice. "Please, I beg you, I came without him knowing. I left him and came to see you. I said to him, 'It's Thursday today and I've got things to do'. He thinks I've gone drinking. Please, I swear to God I haven't touched a drop today.

But he doesn't know. I didn't tell him where I was going, I mean. So please . . ."

"How is he?" asked Uncle Karim. "Is he well? I have to see him. I'll go back with you."

"So will I," exclaimed her mother. She turned to Munira. "We'll both go."

Her father raised his arms high above his head for several moments. "No, no, no. Please, no. For God's sake. You don't understand. Slow down a bit."

He brought his hands down and covered his eyes as if he was in pain. Sana heard her mother whispering to Munira, "He needs a drink. I know the signs." Munira reached out and patted her gently on the arm, nodding her head. Husayn returned his hands to his lap. "Sorry, everyone. You don't understand. And I'm a bit—a bit tired. But it's Midhat's life we're talking about. No. Please. Give me a minute, just a minute, so that I can concentrate and finish what I'm trying to say. The problem is—how can I put it, damn it—the problem is, he hasn't eaten or drunk anything for two days, maybe more. No, no, he's not ill. No, my dear Karumi, I can tell whether someone's ill or not. But he doesn't want to eat or drink."

"Why?" shouted Grandmother Nuriya in anguish. "He should have stayed here. God knows what the food's like there."

"Take it easy, Mother," said Uncle Karim.

"Honestly, Auntie, you know . . ." began Husayn.

"Leave it, Husayn," said Karim.

"Yes, but there is food at my place," finished Husayn.

"Listen, Husayn," persisted Karim. "I want you to tell me a couple more things. First of all, and this is the main thing, is Midhat ill? Does he need medical help?"

Sana's father opened his arms randomly and crossed one leg over the other. "No, I've already told you. He's not ill." He looked around him, and Sana had the impression his eyes came to rest on Munira again.

"But I mean, he's got things on his mind. You know Midhat. But I'm a hundred per cent sure he's not ill. That's definite. Yes, he's not eating or drinking, and doesn't seem to be sleeping that well, but he's not ill."

"Where's he sleeping? Why didn't he stay with me?" said Grandmother Nuriya.

"At my place. In my room, Auntie."

"The sultan's palace!" whispered Sana's mother sarcastically.

Husayn turned to her and laughed suddenly, interrupting himself with a series of coughs. "Yes, but, to make up for it, I'm sleeping on the sofa."

Uncle Karim interrupted him. "Please spare us your comments, Madiha. Listen, Husayn. There's something else I want to ask you. When can I see him? Can I come with you now at least, even if nobody else does?"

"No, no. Give me some time, Karumi. Please. Two or three days. Let me discuss things with him. You know, it's a bit complicated, everybody. But let's hope it's nothing. I came purely to reassure you."

"God bless you, dear," said Grandmother Nuriya.

"Thank you, Auntie. I'm only doing my duty."

A sudden silence descended. It was broken by Sana's grandfather. "Look, Mr. Husayn," he said in a quavering voice. "I know you well. You've got a good heart, and you're decent and godfearing." Sana's father looked at him with surprise as he continued: "But sometimes circumstances intervene in people's lives and change them against their wishes. Despite the twists of fate, Almighty God allows compassion and love to remain in their hearts because they are fundamentally noble and good. Husayn, Almighty God has put my son Midhat in your safe keeping and nobody can resist God's will. Neither you nor I nor anyone else. He's entrusted him to you, Husayn. Do you understand? You are responsible for his safety."

Her father looked around him in some astonishment. "Yes, yes, sir."

"We don't oppose the judgment of the Almighty. My son Midhat, who didn't consult me before he left, when he knows that I . . ." He paused and began on a different tack. "I'm a believer, and I have faith in God and His Prophet, and now I'm on my sickbed and everything is in the Lord's hands. I want you to take him one message, Mr. Husayn, one message from his father, blessed words I want you to deliver to him which I've borrowed from the Holy Quran." He lowered his voice and began to murmur, "In the name of God the Compassionate the Merciful. 'Have you seen the man who has turned his back and has given little? Does he possess knowledge of the Unknown, so that he is able to see it? Has he not . . .'" he paused, forgetting the words, then resumed, "'been informed of what is in the books of Moses, and of Abraham . . .'" he raised his voice in the silence which had descended, "'and of Abraham who was faithful? That a burdened soul shall not bear the burden of another. That Man shall only have that which he has striven for. That his strivings shall be seen, and thereafter he will be fully rewarded. That with your Lord is the end of all things. That it is He who causes people to laugh and to cry.'"

Sana heard a stifled sob.

"'That it is He who causes people to laugh and to cry. That it is He who causes people to live and to die.' Let us trust in the word of the Almighty."

Grandmother Nuriya was sobbing with her hand over her eyes. Sana noticed a sudden movement from Munira and saw her stand up and leave the room rapidly without a sound. Sana's mother looked questioningly at Munira as she left, but when there was no response, she transferred her sad, surprised gaze back to Grandmother Nuriya. Sana's father sat frozen in his seat. So did her uncle. They hadn't even noticed dear Auntie Munira leave. Sana felt a heavy weight descend on her heart and began to be afraid. She didn't understand much of what was going on.

"Let us trust in the word of the Almighty," pronounced her father, then coughed several times and resumed his immobile stance.

"Why are you crying?" Grandfather asked Grandmother. "Is there a reason? Do you despair of the Lord's mercy?"

Her grandmother stopped crying at once and wiped her eyes with her hand. "I'm not crying. Why would I be crying? I wish I had tears to cry. But every time I hear the Quran I feel a sob rising in my chest."

"Glory be to God."

"Go and make the man a glass of tea, Madiha."

At the sound of the word tea her father started and jumped to his feet. "No, thanks. I'm fine. It's not tea time. Excuse me. I have to go now." He paused. "I hope you don't think badly of me. Don't worry. In two or three days everything will be fine. Be a bit patient with me."

"Let's hope so, son. Don't forget to give Midhat my message. Tell him his father wants him to hear God's word and understand it and be guided by it. Tell him his father's on his sick bed and this is his bequest to him. Do you understand?"

"God willing, not a bequest . . . Yes, yes . . . I'll tell him everything you've said. Excuse me now. I hope you get better soon. Good night, everybody."

He raised his hand in farewell and walked towards the door. Sana's mother and uncle stood up. Her mother stood to one side, and he passed without looking at her. Uncle Karim followed him out.

"He never once asked about the girls," said her mother to Grandmother Nuriya.

Grandmother clapped her hands in a dismissive gesture, and Sana's mother said as she left the room, "God help Midhat if he's got people like that looking after him."

Sana got up quietly and edged along the wall without looking at her grandparents. She could hear the regular click of the prayer beads dropping on to one another. Her grandmother sighed. Sana reached the door and slipped out.

The gallery and alcove were empty. She hurried over to the balustrade and saw her uncle and father disappearing through the middle door and her mother walking slowly across the dimly lit yard. The water gleamed for a moment in the little pond. She wanted to call her mother but stopped herself. She was bursting with a mixture of incom-

293

prehensible feelings. She was tired by everything that had happened that day, and nobody had taken any notice of her. She gave a small yawn, resting her hands on the wooden balustrade. A slight shudder passed through her body. She yawned again. Her mother stopped at the middle door to watch her father and uncle disappear. "Little Sana," she heard someone calling softly.

She turned round. The voice was gentle and musical. She saw Munira beckoning to her from the door of her room. Sana didn't need to be asked again and ran towards her. Munira drew her into the room and closed the door behind her.

"Listen Sana," she said, talking rapidly. "I want you to do something for me. This note," she held up a folded sheet of paper, "I want you to get it to your father. Run after him and give it to him and tell him to give it to—Midhat. To Uncle Midhat."

Her hazel eyes were clouded over, and the kohl had rubbed off them. Sana continued to look at her. Munira took hold of her arm. "Sana, do you understand?" She gave her arm a squeeze.

"Yes, Auntie Munira," answered Sana.

"Do you love me, Sana?"

Sana gulped and tried to answer, but Munira began talking urgently again. "I want you to run after them now. Don't let anyone see you. Give this note to your father and tell him this is from Auntie Munira for Uncle—Midhat. See? Go on, Sana darling. Hurry."

She gave her the note and opened the door for her. Her heart pounding, Sana ran off along the gallery and down the stairs, then stopped at the bottom. Her mother had moved away from the door and gone into the kitchen. The kitchen light was on, and there were sounds of dishes being picked up and put down. Sana ran along close to the wall furthest from the kitchen until she reached the middle door, which stood ajar. She slipped through it and confronted the long passage. The two of them, her uncle and her father, were standing out in the street by the open front door, talking. She stood silently catching her breath in the darkness, clutching the note in the palm of her hand. Her mother wouldn't remember her for a while. She was busy washing the dishes and thinking what she needed for the dawn meal before the fast began again. If she was asked when she returned, she would say she had been with Uncle Karim. She inched forward silently, went up the step, then stopped again. She didn't understand what they were muttering to each other. She could see the red glow of the cigarette in her father's hand. He raised it to his mouth every now and then, coughed, and blew out smoke. It was pitch dark around her, and she could only make them out with difficulty by the light from the road outside. She started walking forward cautiously again and saw them shaking hands.

"Yes, yes, of course. Good night," she heard her father saying. Her uncle responded and her father disappeared. She was seized with anxiety. Her uncle went on standing there, looking after her father. She kept walking, with no specific plan in mind, until she was close to her uncle.

"Uncle," she called, and he turned abruptly, seeming startled by her voice. "Who's there? Sana? What are you doing in the dark?"

"I've got some business with my father," she replied at once.

"What sort of business?"

"I have to tell him something. I've got a message for him."

He was looking at her, but she couldn't make out his face properly in the dark. Would he ask her who had sent her? What would she say? Munira had told her not to let anyone see her. Perhaps her uncle would force her to show him the note, would open it, and read what was in it. She was torn by doubts and, without waiting to find out what her uncle might decide, she climbed the step leading to the street. "I'll be back soon, Uncle," she said, and ran off in the direction she had seen her father take.

"Careful," her uncle called after her. "Don't run like that. Have you gone mad or something?"

The alley, which she knew so well, was illuminated by the faint light from a distant street lamp. The important thing was for her to catch up with her father before he was lost among the crowds in the main street. She saw him suddenly beside the house of Mr. Mustafa, the joiner, the house with the huge jujube tree, swaying from side to side in front of her. He held himself erect but as he walked he rocked in a strange way to the right and to the left. He veered abruptly over to the other side of the road, then straightened up again and continued swaying in a regular rhythm.

"Dad. Dad," she called.

He didn't look as if he had heard. She called him again when she was two meters or less from him. The she tugged gently on his jacket. He didn't turn round. He kept on walking, unaware of her presence. She smiled in amazement. They were a few steps past Mr. Mustafa's house when she realized that she had no time to lose, so she pulled hard on his jacket and shouted, "Dad."

He jumped in alarm. "Huh? What?"

"Sorry, Dad. I've been shouting at you and you didn't hear."

He was staring at her face. "Where have you come from? What do you want?"

"Dad, I'm Sana."

"Who? Yes, yes, Sana my dear. How are you? Where are you going? Do you want something?"

"No, Dad, but . . ." she gripped the little sheet of paper. "Auntie Munira says, she says . . ." She held out her hand. "Give this note to Uncle Midhat."

He remained stock-still, looking at her, with his arms hanging at his sides. She didn't know what to do. She jiggled the piece of paper in her hand. "Dad. Here's the note. Take it and give it to Uncle Midhat. Tell him it's from Auntie Munira."

"Yes, dear. All right. But," he took the paper cautiously, "I'm afraid I may not see Midhat tonight. Tomorrow will do, won't it?"

"I don't know, Dad. Auntie Munira told me to deliver it quickly."

"Okay, okay. That's fine."

He put it away in the inside pocket of his jacket, then leaned down towards her suddenly. "Tell her not to worry about it." He kissed her twice on both cheeks. He stank unbearably. His voice shook as he straightened up. "Give her my very best wishes, Sana dear. Tell her the letter's arrived and she shouldn't worry about it for a moment. Go on, dear. Go home now."

"Yes, Dad."

Sana ran off home along the dark potholed alley. She saw her uncle in the distance, waiting where she had left him, and felt glad. As they made their way along the passage into the house, he told her off and kept asking her why she had gone after her father. Her refusal to give him a straight answer annoyed him, and he began to scold her again. They bolted the door behind them and followed Sana's mother upstairs. Sana noticed that Munira's room was in darkness. Her uncle went in to see her grandparents and she ran off lightheartedly, feeling she had an important secret which made it easy to bear reprimands, fatigue, and other inconveniences. She found them sitting in front of the television: her mother and sister, Munira's mother, and Great-grandmother Umm Hasan, but not Munira. She sat down quickly to one side, afraid that her mother would see her and ask where she had been, and even more afraid that she would be unable to lie to her. Her sister turned to look at her once or twice, but didn't say anything. Gradually her heart stopped pounding.

"Here, Suha. Is there a film on today?" her mother asked her sister.

"Yes, Mum. An Arab film."

"You'd better not be lying."

"I swear, Mum. Either a film or a play."

"It'll be a miracle if you ever learn to tell the truth."

"Honestly, Mum."

"Shut up, you stupid little girl."

Munira's mother was smoking in silence, eyes glued to the small screen. Sana heard footsteps on the gallery, which she recognized as

Munira's. The door opened and in she came. "Madiha," she asked, "can I talk to you for a minute?"

Sana looked at Munira and tried to signal to her surreptitiously.

"Is something wrong?" Sana's mother asked Munira.

Munira shook her head vaguely. Sana's mother rose to her feet with some effort, and Munira didn't look in Sana's direction as she took her arm and went out with her. Sana had to tell Munira that the letter would reach Uncle Midhat tomorrow, as her father had said, and that she shouldn't worry. But they never left her alone with Munira. In a while she would try and see her in her pretty bedroom with its soft blue light and describe to her how she had handed over the letter to her father. But Auntie Munira seemed busier than usual, as if she'd forgotten that she had entrusted her with a very special mission, which she had carried out faithfully and at some cost to herself. They always grew suddenly preoccupied like this when somebody brought them a piece of news. It occurred to her that her father's visit might have some connection with their present air of distraction. Another thought pleased her, which was that her Uncle Midhat was at her father's and could come back to them any day. So he hadn't gone away and nothing awful had happened to him, as she had vaguely felt it might have. Perhaps he would soon be back.

"Are you still here, Najiya my dear?" she heard great-grandmother Umm Hasan ask.

"Yes, Mum. What is it?" answered Munira's mother.

"Nothing. I was just asking, dear."

Sana was sitting in an old chair with a red blanket thrown over it. Her eyelids grew heavy and her head spun. She closed her eyes for a moment and was almost sucked down into a whirlpool of languor. She wasn't going to be able to talk to Auntie Munira on her own tonight. She got up out of the chair and went to lie down on her bed. Euphoria spread through her body as her limbs relaxed, and she delighted in the cool touch of the cover on her arm. She would see her tomorrow and tell her what had happened. Tomorrow, for sure. And she would laugh as she told her how she had pulled her father's tail. The tail of his jacket. Auntie Munira would laugh, too, and Sana would be so happy to see her laughing. So happy.

Chapter
Twelve *(1)*

Brief Shining and Survival

His own scream woke him. He opened his eyes in the gray darkness, jaws trembling and heart thudding. As he sat up in bed, a cold tear ran down from one eye. He was breathing hard and fast. He wiped his damp face and neck. From the start he had known that he was dreaming and told himself that he would soon wake up. And yet, despite this, he had seen her in front of him. He had seen her when he was dreaming, aware that he was dreaming, and had pointed a knife at her. She was submissive and docile, accepting the mad thrusts of the knife which tore at her flesh and caressing his other arm very gently. So he had screamed and covered his face with his hands, emerging defeated from hell. Then he wept. His chest exploded with sobs like the waves of the sea, his tears running out between his fingers and the sobbing rising from deep inside him. He wanted to take his hands away from his face and force himself to calm down but, in the darkness of the bare room, he seemed to have lost all resolve and willpower, and his tears continued to flow. He had stabbed at her chest and stomach and head. He recalled that he had begun to cry as he committed his illusory crime. The only thing which had really frightened him was seeing her caress him. She had not stopped him doing what he was doing, but had caressed him with understanding and affection. He screamed, suffocated by a great anguish which had taken hold of him by the throat and pressed down on his chest. Or perhaps he hadn't screamed, but had been on the point of exploding or dying of asphyxiation.

He took his hands away from his face, searched in his pocket for a handkerchief, and wiped his face and neck and eyes, noticing an intermittent snoring and muttering beside him. The darkness in the room was shot through with light; on the wall near the window the moon cast silver rays. Husayn must have returned without him realizing. He could see him asleep on the sofa, a dark mound standing out from its surroundings. Midhat's mouth and throat were dry. He pushed back the worn cover and lowered his feet on to the floor, feeling for his shoes. He couldn't find them and tried again without success. He stood up. His thigh muscles hurt him. The floor was cold. He tiptoed towards the door, wiping his nose, and as he went by the sofa he heard Husayn breathing noisily and mumbling alien words. He opened the door and it squealed like a cat. He turned on the light and looked at his watch. It was a few minutes past four. He stood in front of the basin, and the cloudy mirror reflected his unshaven face and red eyes. He washed his hands and face in cold water and passed his fingers through his unruly hair, feeling how dirty it was. He washed his hands again and reached for the towel. As he was bringing it up to his face, he was overcome by the stench of rottenness it gave off and put it back in its place. He felt the coldness of the floor eating into the soles of his feet as he took out his handkerchief to dry his face. He looked in the mirror again. His features were expressionless; nobody examining his face would ever take him for a man who had been unjustifiably persecuted, although perhaps there was a sort of appeal in his eyes, which he had seen somewhere before. There was certainly nothing in his face to suggest that he could be a killer. On the contrary, the lines on either side of his nose and mouth, the faint twist of his lips, along with the

unfathomable look in his eyes, were the signs of a person who was himself heading for destruction.

A faint quiver ran down his back. Were people's fates written on
their faces? A brief image of the eyes of the run-over dog flashed into
his mind. The eyes like glowing coals, distress signals flaring for the last
time, receiving no response. He felt annoyed, turned the tap on again,
drank some cold water, washed his eyes, dried them on his handkerchief, and went off towards the lavatory. He was seized by a slight fit of
vertigo. Coming back, he switched off the light and paused at the bedroom door. The room was hot, the air heavy with the smells of shoes,
dirty socks, breath laden with onion and arak. He hesitated before
going in, then took a deep breath of the relatively pure air outside the
room and went in and shut the door. The smells disappeared after a few
paces. His bed was further from the door than Husayn's sofa, and he
began feeling his way towards it. Husayn seemed to be breathing quietly now. He reached his bed and stood beside it. The silver moonlight
had retreated into the little window recess. Husayn gave a sudden snore
and sighed several times. Midhat raised his leg, about to climb into bed,
when he was overcome by an uncontrollable flood of emotion. Her soft
gentle hand was back responding to him again, acquiescing to the horror which he had brought upon her. In the faint shadows, it took hold
of him like a dreadful reproach, leading him back into his dream, into
the crazed state he had been in when he was stabbing her. His whole
body trembled, and a brief sob burst from him. He clamped his mouth
shut, then tried to stand up straight, but his legs refused to obey him
and he fell like a log on to the floor beside the bed.

He did not feel great pain and had let his arms go loose at his side
as he fell, surrendering to this unexpected collapse of his body. The cold
floor stung his back and he sat up and began rubbing his forehead and
shoulders until a muscle in his upper arm went into spasm. His head
was ringing and he understood the nature of the physical weakness he
was suffering from now. He had not actively desired it, but had neglect-

ed, or forgotten, all the things he needed to do to preserve his energy. Neglect and oblivion were easy where he was currently living. In any case he had hoped that if he were physically weak he would be more relaxed, but now he doubted if this were true: he would still be left with his mind operating on all levels, conscious and unconscious, balanced and unbalanced. He would have had the same dream even on his deathbed. It—this dream and what lay behind it—was what connected him to the depravity and pretensions of his forefathers, their complexes, and their crazy love of honor and killing. It was, after all, the illusory acting out of their will, the deed they demanded from him, and he had done it; what did it matter if it was a dream or reality, since everything would pass, taking him with it?

He was sitting cross-legged on the floor by the bed in the dark, unable to see and not wanting to. What did they want from women? What was it they had wanted all down the ages?

If only she had told him. He struck the floor with his right palm. Precious woman. Beloved female. Wife of his heart. If only she had told him. He raised his hand to hit the floor again, then paused, aware of the tears rising in his chest and threatening to spill out. This terrified him. He put his hand over his mouth, forcing it shut, as if he wanted to strangle his own cries. His heart was pounding, and he felt something pressing on his skull from the inside, pushing his eyeballs out of their sockets. Moments passed; he sat with his hand clasped to his mouth as his breathing regularized gradually and calm returned to him.

If only she had told him. His body was shaking, from the tips of his toes to the hair on his head, like a leaf blown about by the wind at the top of a tree. But despite the shaking he maintained a fraction of equilibrium, just enough will power to ensure that he wouldn't take leave of his senses again. He relaxed his hand. This was what was new: he would never kill somebody without being aware of what he was doing. This was what was really new. What would have happened if she had told him? Now these words would never frighten him again. He could repeat them to himself in the same form, or a different one, and it wouldn't matter. What if she had told him everything? Why hadn't she confessed her secret to him? Why? Why? He was muttering aloud, making a noise as if he had difficulty breathing. He could hear her talking and began to tremble violently again, his heart racing. But it had not happened; she had said nothing. If she had told him, he would have left her. He would still leave her. He felt calmer. He would have saved his own skin. Perhaps she had realized this and had chosen to destroy him slowly, to kill him in several installments.

The first morning in this rathole of Husayn's he had woken up late, full of images of her in a long, uncensored dream of sex. To begin with, he had been amazed to find himself there, then, coming to his senses, he had reconstructed the chain of events. Then he had vomited, retched, vomited again, on the floor, in the basin, and in the toilet, until he had almost heaved his guts up, not knowing why he was doing it, unless it was to remove all traces of the erotic dream.

It was like a slow death, but she hadn't wanted him to die. What language was she talking for him not to understand her? He was even beginning to doubt if he had heard her right. Had she betrayed him, or shown him a particular kind of trust? Or been insanely provocative? Kill me and cleanse your souls in my blood.

He hauled himself up, resting his weight on the bed, flung himself on to it and pulled the cover over him. A dull light came in at the window, and Husayn's breathing was unusually regular.

Kill me without committing murder; this was obviously how she had thought of the equation. It was acceptable verbally, but unrealizable and inherently ridiculous. People did not die, then come back to life, and it made no difference if the person was a beautiful, beloved woman like her. Even supposing she had been allowed to rise from the dead, would she have come back pure as the morning dew?

He was sitting up in bed looking towards the small window. He had been here a little while now. He was not thinking about himself.

He was no longer able to. Even his food and drink were decided for him by Husayn or those imbeciles who owned the house. He used to think they were a gentle, kindly old couple but they had wanted him out the second day, taking advantage of the absence of Husayn, who probably cheated them and controlled them in ways Midhat knew nothing of. They tried to drag him along by the ear like a wet dog and put him out in the alley. He remained silent and withdrawn, thinking about the attacks of sickness which had beset him all the previous day, and the man and his wife didn't pose any real threat to him. Munira was with him, too, throbbing like a wound that wouldn't heal; he was busy going through the reasons why he had run away, deter-mined not to see anyone, and when the old man grabbed hold of him by the edge of his crumpled jacket he looked at him and saw, behind the small dirty eyes with no lashes, the caved-in mouth, the henna-stained beard and moustache and the deformed language, profound impotence, thinly veiled by a childish ferocity and hardness. He remembered he had brought some cash with him; he didn't know if he still had it and reached for his wallet. The old couple were standing behind him, talking angrily about the chaos and filth and drunken-ness, and the amount of food consumed, when he found his money. Without answering any of their accusations he took out a five dinar note and offered it to them.

Husayn turned over on the ancient sofa where he was sleeping. He had furnished it with a pillow and a few blankets, boasting that he never knew when he was going to go to bed or wake up. But he didn't enjoy sleeping there, cursing the old couple when he woke up late in the morning, and complaining that his bones were broken. Midhat was not offering to swap the bed for the sofa as long as he had any money. What he would do when his cash ran out was another question. It was a prob-lem of crucial importance in his life, which he had no desire to con-front. But did he have a choice? For a while now he had dug deep down inside himself like a mole, but not for his own personal pleasure.

Nobody could believe that he enjoyed these internal conflicts, as if he gratified himself secretly by banging his head against walls.

The wall? She was standing by a mud brick wall. No. His breathing came faster. He had dragged her there, had taken hold of her as he was looking into her face, noticing the hint of determination on her full lips. It was not obvious at that moment what he was planning to do. They had walked around for a while, until they reached a mud wall, and he brandished his knife at her. He didn't see her face from then on, not even the fine eyebrows which he hacked at with the knife. Her eyes were what he loved most in the world, even deep inside his warped unconscious mind. How she smiled when he was kissing her in the corner of her left eye, dark with kohl, and immediately afterwards he began cutting up her chest and stomach, at the foot of that dirty mud wall.

Nobody had applauded him, nobody at all; and if she hadn't touched his arm so tenderly everything would have ended peacefully. He wouldn't have shouted or wept, as he was doing now. His tears would have fallen gently, like little streams, as they ought to have done. In complete calm.

He was sitting on the bed in the bare room with another day breaking outside, wearing the clothes he had been in for over a week now and crying like a child at the images and dreams coming and going in his mind. What did it all mean, anyway? What did anything mean, whether you looked at the parts or the whole? Tears, for example, salt water stored somewhere behind the temples which, when pressure was applied for one reason or another, flowed from channel to channel before finally spurting out of the eyes. How could anybody conclude that this salty liquid, coming from such an unlikely place, was a sign of weakness, defeat, lethargy, loss of willpower, resignation, frustration? What was the salt related to? Heaven and hell? Adam and Eve? Our fathers and grandfathers and what they said or would have said if they'd had time? Did every human act really have an explanation or a meaning, an antecedent, a consequence? Was that why mankind transmitted its fear of certain acts and their significance from one generation to another? Did human beings have any significance, other than that they existed? Did his own life have any meaning? What could shame him? Could he be shamed? Yes, for doing nothing, so they said. What about her, on the other hand? She who had forced him into contact with failure and impotence, what significance did she have? Now that she had lost something, she had acquired a significance which she was lacking before. Was that torn membrane what gave her a meaning? Was it even the key to whether she lived or died?

He buried his damp face in his hands. Her meaning was in him. He was the one who had imparted those negative traits to her, the sediment of past generations deposited deep inside him, when he held her like a warm bird next to his heart. He had not respected that delicacy and transparency; he had gone ahead at full speed, soiling it, then walked away brushing the dirt off his hands, saving his own skin, emerging from the skirmish with his honor intact. But how had she allowed . . . Ah, where would it lead him if he tried to fathom out the sources of her pain? Was he really the person to get to the heart of it, acting with discretion and motivated by love?

He had not said a word to her as he closed the door on her and left her on her own. He was allowed to save himself, wasn't he? He had slipped out silently, like a thief in the night. Never at any time had he degenerated into screaming and shouting at her, despite all the dirt deposited in him by previous generations. He had just been surprised that she wanted this for him. His head had reeled from the shock. In her clouded hazel eyes he had not detected a single cry for help. Had she despaired of him, even when she was holding him close and he felt her slim arms around him, pressing on his back, or when she covered her throbbing breast in embarrassment? When she was whispering in his ear, his heart? When she smiled at him with all her being, shining on him like the sun, like life?

He took his hands away from his face. So were they doomed, two hopeless creatures without a future?

It was growing brighter outside the little window, as the darkness in the room gave way to the murky light of early dawn. She had taken hold of him, with all her womanly affection, and led him towards the abyss. It had been her choice. She had known what was wrong with her and not told him, because she hadn't wanted to be left alone, wasn't strong enough to face the world by herself. Or perhaps she had trusted him and loved him, really loved him, and wanted him to understand the plight she was in. Then he would be at the root of this whole thing. Could she have really loved him? It was a crazy idea. She hadn't told him. Perhaps she had seen him as a hero. If they loved each other like that, it meant they shared the shame, were bound by hidden ties for the rest of their lives. Had she, too, played with similar notions and married him after making certain calculations? But they had both been damned from the start because they had not broken free of their roots. If they had cut themselves off from these roots they would have been sure of finding a way out. However, she knew nothing of all this, and the person she had taken a chance with was the one who subsequently stuck a knife in her. What difference did it make that it happened in a dream? There was a situation, whether it was in a fantasy world, heaven, or a remote corner of the universe, in which he was able to stab her and carry on until she touched him and said, "Enough. Enough death. Enough purging the shame. Enough of wanting to cleanse the air with your blood and erase the stars with your fingers."

As he clenched his hands together under the cover, the room grew lighter and the wall facing him became visible in the daylight coming through the little window in the right hand corner. The dark crack which split it from top to bottom looked deeper than ever now, surrounded by a network of smaller cracks and fissures and patches of damp. It reminded him of barren steppes devastated by an earthquake, like a crazy giant running amok with his scythe, slicing off children's heads, destroying all traces of life. He thought of the line from the Quran: "And when the baby girl who has been buried alive shall be asked for what crime she was put to death . . ." They buried her before she had tasted her mother's milk. That really was extermination. And who was going to stop it?

Husayn snored and turned over again, and he and the sofa emitted a medley of sounds. His face was a coppery brown with dark circles under the closed eyes, and he had covered himself with something that looked like an overcoat or a thick army blanket. He was curled up tightly and reminded Midhat of a silkworm in a cocoon; only his face and tousled hair were visible. Midhat wondered when he had come in. He hadn't had the price of a drink and had been anxious because it was Thursday, the day he was obliged to go drinking with his friends. Not that this made much difference, since he went drinking every evening, but somehow the night between Thursday and Friday had a special quality for him. Still, he hadn't asked Midhat for money and had left shortly after the Ramadan sunset meal, although he had hung about and seemed preoccupied. Midhat had not wanted to give him money that he might need later, so he had reluctantly stopped himself looking up, pretending to be deep in thought. He would have liked to help Husayn somehow, especially as Husayn had opened up to him over these past few days, telling him strange details about his life: his laundry and eating arrangements, his relationships with others. This time he had not tried to deceive him with grandiose statements about literature and philosophy, or the self and others, declaring he knew precious little about anything. Midhat found him better natured than he had expected and had the impression Husayn's present way of life was the only one which would suit him. He wasn't rebelling against life in general, but rejecting society's ties and obligations and paying a hefty price for it in terms of self-respect, going dirty and hungry. Yet he was enviably content and satisfied, but also firmly convinced that he would be dead before long. Fear sometimes seized Husayn out of the blue, a blind terror which defied logic, and he would hurry to seek reassurance from the bottle, where he usually found it.

He snorted again as if he was dying. In his own particular way of looking at things, he was teetering on the brink of destruction, but would expend his utmost efforts to keep his balance for as long as possible.

His face, with its high cheekbones, looked as if the life had already gone out of it. It upset Midhat to look at Husayn when he was asleep. He was no longer a person, but an image of death, a dream, an illusion, an ethereal being. If he had seen himself looking like this, he would have been terrified, but Husayn dealt with the future, or the end of anything, by choosing to believe in the worst possible scenario, then he could relax. What kind of self-deception was that!

He shifted his gaze away from Husayn on to the cracked wall, illuminated by the early morning light. Somebody had drawn on it in pencil—a heart stuck through with an arrow and some letters—and there were marks left by rusty nails and a large stain of black ink, as if an inkwell had been hurled at it. He closed his eyes and felt shooting pains in his chest and stomach. He pressed on his stomach and massaged his chest, breathing deeply. These little actions might eventually help. He was drained and tired, his body limp. Almost the only thing disturbing him now was that he was sexually aroused. Damned lust, still there, inflamed by his thoughts. He squeezed his legs together but the fire kept burning. The way she moved as she opened her rosy legs, the divine feeling of being deep inside a beautiful woman, the woman you loved. The way she covered her trembling breast with her painted fingernails, but when his lips fastened on to it she held his head and caressed it gently.

Wide awake now, eyes open, he stared at the murky void in front of him, suffused by a feeling of secret delight, which stirred restlessly deep inside him and rose up to his neck. A mysterious delight in life with no reason or justification other than itself. The delight which was the justification for life.

It was like an almost physical pleasure spreading timidly from an obscure spot in his insides, and its anaesthetic effect made him forget his troubles for a moment. He closed his eyes. How ridiculous everything seemed sometimes, impossible to take seriously. People even engaged in dialogues with death, made fun of it, skillfully neutralized it, and rejected it, not involuntarily but out of conviction, making up their minds to do so. In the distance he heard a bird cheeping. Surprised, he opened his eyes. It was almost sunrise. Husayn was sound asleep. Midhat turned on to his left side. There was no sign of Husayn's shoes under the sofa. Perhaps he hadn't got round to taking them off. What did it matter? He smiled. He was tired. His eyelids drooped.

When he opened them again, Husayn was sitting on the sofa looking at him. Their eyes met in the silence of the sun-filled room. Some time went by and neither of them spoke, although they continued to exchange glances. The atmosphere in the room was strange and vaguely disturbing, then he suddenly heard a muffled explosion in the distance. He sat up in bed.

"Did you hear?" said Husayn. "That's the fourth one."

"What is it?"

"Either the Hajji ate a lot of onions," said Husayn scratching his head, "or, my dear Midhat, this is the revolution we've all been waiting for. I think today's going to be critical for our friend Karim Qasim." He stretched and yawned, opening his mouth as wide as it would go.

Midhat felt faintly anxious listening to Husayn. It was a beautiful morning, more appropriate for a stroll with someone close to you than another new revolution. Still, if those in power thought like him, the revolutionaries had chosen their time well. His train of thought was interrupted by another explosion, followed by a volley of shots.

"No, it's certainly not the Hajji," said Husayn, putting his feet to the floor. He laughed and stood up, stretching again.

He was in his crumpled blue suit; the collar of his light colored shirt was undone with the black tie still tied. Midhat's anxiety returned as he sat, his feet dangling over the side of the bed, listening to Husayn talking and yawning. "Can I use the bathroom before you, Midhat? I'm in a bit of a hurry."

"Of course. Go ahead."

Husayn scratched his right leg and hobbled off towards the door. Midhat found his shoes under the bed, with his socks stuffed into them, and put them on disgustedly, then stood up. He felt somewhat dejected, realizing that he had not reached any concrete conclusions in his thinking. He had retreated from the world, from all of his family, because he felt humiliated, ashamed of everything. He had not taken any action and, up until a few hours ago, considered that a heroic achievement. But now, as the explosions grew louder in the distance, it seemed he was no longer in control of his world, and time was running short. He felt afraid, too, because the significance of human beings and their actions was breaking free from his logic and expectations.

The door burst open and Husayn came in, drying his hair and smoothing it down. "Sorry. I'm running late. Did you hear anything?"

"No. Like what?"

Then Midhat hurried out himself. In the landing the air was warm. He stood in front of the basin. His eyes were red and slightly swollen, his hair disheveled. He washed his face in cold water and soap, making his eyes sting, and thought he heard an explosion or two. Anxiety jagged at him from time to time like a pin in his side. He was drying his face when he saw Husayn coming out of their room.

"I'm off, Midhat. To see what's going on. Do you want to come with me?"

"Me?" said Midhat hesitantly. "No, no. You go, Husayn. If there's anything to report, you'll come back, won't you?"

"Of course. I don't have anywhere else to go." And he stumbled off towards the stairs.

Midhat put the towel back and looked at his distorted reflection in the mirror, feeling his heavy black stubble. The explosions reverberated in the distance. He went back to the room, but stopped in the doorway. What a stinking hole it was, the sunlight shining into it only making it appear more miserable. He retreated and went down to look for something to eat. There was no one in the gloomy kitchen. He lit the stove and put a pot of water to boil. He called out to the old woman, Atiya, and her husband, the Hajji, but nobody answered. He felt dizzy and his head throbbed. His thoughts had abandoned him and he could remember nothing of them. The water boiled and he made himself a glass of tea and took it upstairs with a piece of stale bread he had found. He sat on the bed, then stood up and opened the window. The warm spring air drifted in, together with the noise of more explosions and general racket. He dipped the bread in the blood-red tea and took a mouthful, which he found tasted surprisingly good. He looked at his watch. Just after half past ten. What had happened to him last night? He sat back on the bed. His and Husayn's feet had left prints in the layer of dust on the floor. Down by his feet now he also noticed the impression left by his body when he had fallen. He took a sip of tea. That terrible dream. Killing her, then screaming, then weeping for her. All these anonymous forces struggling together inside him, and he was powerless to intervene.

His hands were trembling slightly. He took another mouthful of bread and felt some bile rise into his throat. The sound of shots being fired reached him at intervals, sometimes followed by very distant explosions. What had really happened last night? Had he personally been important in the dream, or had he simply served as an arena for certain primitive tendencies to fight it out? Who was he?

Midhat Abd al-Razzaq al-Hajj Ismail. Iraqi. Baghdadi, from an old established family in the Bab al-Shaykh quarter. Law graduate. Civil servant for the past five years. No money, no home, no particular future mapped out. He had a brother and a sister and had been married—for a week. That's what they could write on his tombstone, and they might add certain other details. But none of it was really him, the person sitting in a bare room in the Kurdish quarter, drinking black tea in clothes he had not taken off for about a week, eating stale bread and not caring if there was a revolution going on or a despot was being toppled. What was the vital factor, the thing that made him what he was?

The purple liquid in the glass quivered gently, reflecting the sun shining in through the window. He noticed some dark oily stains on his trousers. He would enter the house as if he had never been away. Nobody would receive him formally. He would go to the bathroom to wash, then sit down to a good meal, relax a little, and go up to their room. He would see her. She would see him. They would exchange glances. He would stab her once in the heart, then go down to tell them what he had done. She would see him. He would see her, with her bright eyes and her blonde hair falling on her shoulders. His woman. He would wrap his arms round her, hold her close.

The sunbeams danced in the glass of tea. His hand was shaking. Yesterday phantoms had torn him apart, spears made of wind. Today, awake and in broad daylight, he was shaken by memories of her. So was this guilty, sinful girl the umbilical cord attaching him to life? Was it his love for her that was doing these strange things to him, as he circled round it like a bull around its fate? He would have to be crazy to believe that. If it were true, then he would have gone back before now to fall at her feet and ease his mind, or he would never have been able to run away from her in the first place. But had he really escaped from her?

He rose heavily to put his tea glass and the remains of the bread on the window sill. The sky was a brilliant blue, and the morning sun felt pleasantly warm on his face. He heard a dull roar in the distance, the drone of an aircraft and muffled shots. Out there they were fighting passionately, using all the material and spiritual weapons at their disposal, and here he was within these four bare, dirty walls, having a discussion with himself about what had happened to him.

He wasn't living in the same world as them. She had flung him out of its orbit. Because he loved her and she had turned out to be flawed, she had made him break the rules, be an exception. He was no longer trapped in the dark caves of his forefathers' moods and desires, no longer floating with the herd on the filthy tide of dross left by those who had secretly carved out his unconscious. He had been freed from this black mud and cast up on a shore of light, and he could choose how he lived and died. But what could one person do? Be an example? Surely the route which began by rejecting extinction should end in some kind of happiness, since this was acknowledged as the legitimate goal.

He walked slowly back to the bed and sat down. His body felt tired and the burst of sexual energy, which had taken him unawares in the night, had subsided. He withdrew into himself, aware of his heart beating unevenly. Anxiety was still gnawing at him, not focused on any particular object, like a mirage, inaccessible but always there. But the horizon no longer stretched ahead of him to infinity. Momentous events which he had not foreseen blocked him in on all sides. Was he afraid that something awful was going to happen to him, or was his anxiety directed at the fate of his family? Did he ultimately want to be with them, whatever the circumstances?

Through the open window he heard the roar still faraway, but continuous now and frightening: a crazy mythical creature which spoke an incomprehensible yet terrifying language. There was another hollow explosion, then light footsteps outside, a hail of shots, and the dull roar always in the background. Somebody was pushing the door open. It was the old woman, Atiya. "Good morning, Mr. Midhat."

He was shocked how pinched and pale she looked against the black headscarf.

"Good morning, Aunt."

"Sorry, Mr. Midhat, I don't want to bother you." Her face was thin and lined, its features indistinct. "But the Hajji, God bless him, isn't in a good mood this morning, and your aunt doesn't have any bread for the soup and you're precious to us. I'm afraid you'll be wanting your lunch and there won't be any bread, and things are in a mess out there today. I don't know if I can hear something, or if I'm going senile."

"Do you want me to buy some bread, Aunt?"

"Yes, Mr. Midhat."

"Where's the baker's?"

"In the square. Behind the café."

In the square behind the café people stood around in groups talking enthusiastically and examining the sky, then hurrying away or into the café or to join another group. The radio was blaring, broadcasting a mixture of political statements, music, and patriotic songs which rattled the café windows. Shortly after he left the house he noticed three people passing him at a run, and in front of the lofty, ornamented gate leading into Bab al-Shaykh was an excited group, gesticulating towards the horizon. Instinctively he looked in the direction where they were pointing, but could see nothing. Nevertheless, he grew increasingly anxious. In this open area the explosions sounded deafeningly loud; the beautiful weather and clear blue sky evoked an innocent joy, which seemed to have no place here. He asked where the baker's was and a boy of about eight directed him to it. All round him he picked up conversations about pro-government demonstrations, failed plots, the destruction of the Ministry of Defense. Standing in the middle of the square with the radio communiqués, frenzied conversations, and explosions all assaulting his senses, he realized what a calm world he had been living in. The clock chimed. It was around noon. He went into the baker's; there were only two loaves left and the long stare the shop assistant gave him made him uneasy. He walked away slowly; his body was limp and weak and he took small steps. When he entered the alley the deep shade rested his eyes. Several groups of people passed him at a run and disappeared into the labyrinth of alleyways, including four or five armed youths panting, their eyes almost spouting blood. None of it made any sense to him.

He found the old woman waiting for him in the kitchen, sitting on a wooden chair. He asked where Husayn was, but she didn't answer so he assumed he wasn't back yet. He watched her light the stove and begin preparing the soup, then tried again. "What's going on in your neighborhood, Aunt Atiya? There's a lot of activity. What are all these people doing here?"

"You can find anything you want here," she said, putting the soup on, "and lose it all, too. God alone knows how to untangle the skein."

She gave him a quick look, in which he sensed some spirit of accusation. It occurred to him that perhaps she found him a troublesome guest in these circumstances or wanted more money from him. He asked how her husband was and was told he was still asleep. Suddenly it annoyed him to be here with this old woman, who had no desire to converse with him. He excused himself and went upstairs. He did not enjoy his contact with these people. He lay down on the bed, his arms under his head, looking up at the ceiling, seeing only an expanse of patchy white. He wasn't hungry or tired now. He was haunted by a feeling, a presentiment, a general impression that an idea was gestating in him, and that something important might be about to happen to him. It was not comparable to the sexual feelings he had experienced the previous night. His insides churned with expectation, as if he was having labor pains.

She was looking at him through half-closed eyes, which gleamed a troubled gold between her black lashes, and a strand of her hair had fallen on to her damp forehead. He breathed faster. Munira. His wife. These words had a strange ring to them. This girl whom he had loved, had sex with, who had revealed herself to him and broken his world apart—she was enclosed, like him, in a frighteningly dense framework of relationships and symbols and signs. Depending on how you looked at them, these could be taken as meaningless words, or could be invested with the power to kill a person, just like squashing a mosquito. It was pointless to ask, when you knew there was nobody to answer, pointless to wonder, in this situation, about the baby girl who was buried alive, and the reasons why she was killed and cast to the wind. Useless to ask questions about extermination and its causes.

He heard the old woman calling him from the floor below. The sun was lower in the sky. The distant explosions continued to reverberate. He sat on the bed wondering why he should feel something big was going to happen to him. Was he finally going to reach a point where he would be able to see clearly and make a decision? He got up wearily. There were no clear boundaries in this world. It was up to the individual to make a choice and put certain things in parentheses before he could act. That was how strong men began. They did not give in to presentiments and fantasies; they eliminated trivialities from their lives, then decided what they wanted and set out to get it.

She had put a bowl of soup on the small table by the kitchen door. He heard her and her husband talking together in their room. He took out a spoon and stood by the table. Steam was rising from the mixture of broth and bread. A loud explosion shook the house. He jumped and spilt the contents of the spoon. The old woman hurried out, and her husband peered round the door of their room.

"God is great, Mr. Midhat," she said.

He looked at the couple as if apologizing for the noise.

"Good morning, *afandim*," said the Hajji.

Midhat nodded at him. The crackle of gunfire came from somewhere nearby, followed by a faint explosion. He happened to notice the time on his watch. It was around two-thirty. They were all looking at each other expectantly.

"*Afandim*, do you have a radio by any chance?" said the Hajji politely.

He shook his head. He was annoyed that he felt scared, his guts knotted. The Hajji disappeared back into his room, and his wife was about to follow him when there was a knock at the door. She looked nervously at Midhat.

"I'll go and see who it is," he said.

The Hajji stuck his head out again. Midhat opened the door and in flew Husayn like a whirlwind. "God help you, Midhat. How are you, Aunt Atiya? Please tell me you've made the lunch. I'm starving to death." He saw the bowl of soup on the table. "Hello, my rosy-cheeked beauty. Whose soup is that? Full of tomatoes! It looks so inviting, damn it."

He reached out and scooped some up in his fingers, stuffed his mouth and carried on talking as he ate. "The news is dreadful, Midhat, dreadful. Huge demonstrations for nothing. Just a show of strength, probably. Now they're saying our friend Karim Qasim has blockaded himself inside the Ministry of Defense."

Midhat stood listening to him, then picked up the spoon again and began to share the soup. Husayn breathed heavily as he chewed his food and licked his fingers at intervals. "But there are going to be a lot of casualties. For nothing. On all sides." The red broth had stained his mouth and moustache and part of his cheek.

"Why?" asked Midhat.

Husayn stopped his spoon in mid-air before it reached his mouth. "What do you mean, why? It's a volcano, my friend. A huge eruption. I've been round almost all of Baghdad. By chance I met Abu Jalal. He had his car, so we toured around everywhere. It was quite dangerous. It's not just a coup, my dear Midhat. The whole place is erupting. Everybody's joining in. There are going to be a lot of victims, and all for nothing. That's my view."

He opened his mouth and swallowed the spoonful. His cheeks were purplish bronze, and under his faded eyes there were dark circles. "Aunt Atiya, a glass of water please," he demanded.

She stood up and went slowly into the kitchen.

"And a little more soup, if there is any," he added. "I'm really tired. It's hot today." He looked at Midhat. "I've got something to tell you, Midhat. I forgot this morning. Let me rest for a bit. I didn't sleep well last night. I'm going to have a quick siesta after my lunch." He took the glass of water. "Don't go out now, Midhat. It's not worth it. Wait until things calm down."

Midhat nodded. He was still eating, enjoying the food and the sense of well-being it gave him. Perhaps Husayn, this surprisingly perceptive drunk, was intending to talk to him about returning home, going back to her. But it wasn't the moment now. He couldn't go back to them like a frightened child. It would achieve nothing. Husayn was talking to the Hajji.

"What? It's nothing to do with you, believe me, Hajji. Nothing at all. You're well out of it."

"I agree, Abu Suha," said the old woman. "God bless you."

"Yes, *afandim*," acquiesced the Hajji. "But don't forget the story of the fox that shed its hide, *afandim*."

Husayn choked on his mouthful and, coughing and spluttering, retreated into the kitchen to hawk and spit and blow his nose at the sink. "Oh! Oh God! Where do you get these stories from?" He gave a resounding laugh, interrupted by a violent fit of coughing, and came back in wiping his face on a towel. "Don't worry. God willing, everything will turn out all right." He threw the towel on to the table. "I'm going up to have a nap." A loud explosion rang out in the distance, followed by another smaller one. Husayn looked up. "If they let me." He strode towards the stairs.

Midhat raised the last mouthful to his lips and swallowed it down, then took the empty bowl into the kitchen.

"Don't worry, Mr. Midhat. I'll wash the dishes," said the old woman.

"Thanks, Aunt Atiya."

Midhat went slowly upstairs and washed his hands and face several times, disconcerted by the greasy smell clinging to the unshaven stubble round his mouth. When he went into the bedroom he saw Husayn lying fully clothed on the sofa, without a cover. The sun was confined to a corner by the window.

"Midhat," he said. "I've got something important to tell you, but I can't remember what it is at the minute. Let me have half an hour's sleep and then I'll be able to remember it in detail."

Midhat didn't reply. He sat on the bed for a moment then lay back with the pillow behind him. A delicious languor spread over him after his lunch. He no longer particularly noticed the sounds of shelling. Perhaps he could have a nap like Husayn. The night before he had only had a few hours of disturbed sleep, less refreshing than insomnia. His energy would come back to him if he could sleep.

He took off his shoes, pulled the cover up to his chest and closed his eyes. He wondered what Husayn had been going to tell him. Had he really forgotten?

"Husayn, have you been to see the family?" he asked.

There was no reply. Midhat opened his eyes to look at him. He had his arms crossed on his chest, as if resigned to the unknown, and was breathing out loudly through his open mouth. His face looked wan and thin. Midhat turned away from him again and closed his eyes. Husayn must have met someone from the family, but it was stupid to imagine that it was of any significance to him. Even if he had seen Munira it wouldn't have meant anything, because Husayn didn't know about her. Even he, her husband, knew no more than anyone else what she was really like, and so ultimately he was fumbling in the dark, unsure what he was looking for. He felt himself grow tense and again had an inkling that he was about to make some amazing discovery. His heart was beating violently, as it usually did after a meal, but this time it was for a different reason.

For example, she had certainly been a virgin, like any other girl. Weren't they all virgins once? But their lovers always wanted them to remain intact, their virginity to be renewed after each encounter. Impossible, unfortunately! But if only she'd preserved it, the dear, reckless girl. If only she hadn't . . . He felt oppressed by his desire for her. She was warm and soft. He rested against her and she put her arms round him and held him tight. She wanted him and pressed him to her.

He wiped his forehead; he was breathing fast again, but felt he could put these images out of his mind. Then, while he was in this dream world of his, an iron fist seized hold of him and hurled him brutally into space.

He was clenching his hands together, his whole body tense and ready to spring as if he was about to defend himself against a wild animal. He opened his eyes and sat up in bed. The room, in the gloom of early dusk, appeared to have no walls, and the low roar came uninterrupted through the open window. Perhaps he was up against an unidentifiable beast whose power lay in its obscure origins and unknown intentions, but if you dared to look it unwaveringly in the eye, it would appear ridiculous and as flimsy as cardboard.

Husayn's arms lay limply by his sides, his face was leaden, and he seemed absent from the world. Suddenly Midhat felt alone and extremely tired. He rested back against the pillow again and closed his eyes. He was exhausted and afraid. He had to expose the face of the beast and confront it. This was the last call to him to look again at his life and the reasons for what had happened to him. It was an invitation to topple the foundations. But how could he do that when the facts were as solid as night and day? How could he fundamentally change his view of the fact that his wife Munira had not been a virgin when she married him? She had had a relationship with someone before him. Perhaps she had loved this person. The tears threatened to come but he held them back easily. When she agreed to marry him she had known she wasn't a virgin and knew this would hurt him, maybe destroy him. That was no longer important, but what could be constructed out of this reality?

She was not a virgin; therefore she had lost her honor and must be punished by him or any other member of the family who volunteered. Everyone knew this equation. Honor resided in the woman's hymen, and she was entrusted with preserving it until the appointed time. Why? This was a question which nobody investigated, but it lay at the heart of the matter. Was it out of concern for the purity of the stock, the family, the tribe, the nation, and the whole of humanity? How ridiculous that was! Why did the word purity come to his mind?

She was as soft and clear and radiant as light, the most far removed of all creatures from ugliness and filth. All the same she had been deflowered and soiled and she knew that; she had known it when she married him, and said nothing to him. There he was coming back to his old obsession: she had said nothing to him. But if she had told him, would it really have altered the essential problem? From a perspective deeply ingrained in him she was deemed to have lost her meaning as a woman and a wife and mother in the society, and she had done so illegitimately. That was the truth of the matter. She had lost this damned sensitive piece of human flesh in an illicit, forbidden fashion.

The point was, she could lose it, but in a legitimate manner. This was another essential problem. The loss of it was not important in itself, because it would happen sooner or later anyway, since in this perverted world a woman was not allowed to be a virgin more than once. But the means by which she lost her virginity was a subject mired in human evasiveness, sentimentality, hypocrisy, weakness, spite, irresponsibility, and fear, over which you could cry a river of tears and they would be insufficient.

His eyelids began to grow heavy. A distant explosion reverberated oddly. He was tired for no reason, wishing wholeheartedly that he could find a time, however short, for rest and oblivion. The tangled complications of life, trying to explain the inexplicable, engendered feelings of anxiety and depression.

His thoughts were not pleasant. He realized he was thinking for her, ordering the facts in her favor, defending this girl he loved in spite of everything—her bright laughing face, her smiling eyes, her gestures, her movements, her expressions, her body, her delicacy, and that halo of light surrounding her!

Was it because he loved her that he was denying the facts, distorting them, trying to cover them up? Where would it all lead him? He would never reach a decision or understand the truth. No, that wasn't right. She had not only given herself to him, he knew that. She had entrusted him with her shame, mixing it with his love, their two lives, his memories and dreams, and slept in his arms, resigned to his judgment, whatever it might be. What an unbelievable picture! Her rosy face, slightly damp with sweat, beautiful, radiant, bearing the mark of her surrender to him.

She had given herself to him willingly, with a woman's love, not fawning or trying to deceive him. He recalled the moment when he had seen her warm brown stomach under him, rising and falling in time with her rapid breathing, the soft flesh coming up to meet him, and how it had occurred to him then that she desperately wanted him to possess her.

He turned over agitatedly in bed, feeling his blood tingle, and adjusted the position of his neck and head on the pillow. There were not so many explosions, but the noise remained like a storm on the horizon.

Did she have the right to make him pass judgment on her, on both of them?

He was dozing, the ideas floating in and out of his mind, his head going round as he felt himself disappearing into the chasm of sleep which rose up to meet him, then slowly engulfed him.

Chapter
Thirteen

It was barely six when the visit ended, but after we left the dreary hospital building we wasted a quarter of an hour waiting for a taxi that didn't come. A gentle breeze blew in the empty street, and the last of the sunlight gave the place a tinge of mystery and unreality. The two little girls and Madiha, swathed in her *abaya*, stood next to me in silence. It must have been the dust storm and the rain which had made the weather so pleasant. We weren't used to having spring in the middle of April; in fact, we weren't used to having spring at all. The winter cold gnawed at your bones, then all of a sudden they were disintegrating in the dreadful summer heat. So at sunset we had given up on the taxi and stood near the river looking right and left for a horse-drawn carriage to take us back home. The visit had lasted no more than an hour.

When we opened the door of his room he had welcomed us with delight. He was lying on the bed in a long white robe and bounced up like a spring to embrace his two daughters. He looked as if he would have embraced Madiha as well, but he got shy and flushed slightly, then gave a little grimace, wiped his nose, and clasped his two daughters to him again. We sat around him and put the bags containing our gifts for him down on the floor by the bed. Sana and Suha sat on the bed next to him. His face was pale, and he had more lines on his neck and round his mouth. When he talked, he hesitated constantly, seemed unsure of himself, and waved his hands about haphazardly. The moment we sat down, he told us that he hadn't slept for two days, that his old manager had come to visit him, and that he was desperate for a cigarette and didn't know why they wouldn't allow him to smoke.

"The dove sounded beautiful this morning," he said, as if he was talking to himself. "I wonder where she is now."

Madiha looked at me with a bewildered, anxious expression. "Husayn," she said. "The main thing is, how do you feel in yourself?"

He raised his arms slightly, then his shoulders. "Me?" he said, without turning round. "I'm fine. Why wouldn't I be?"

Silence descended on us for a few moments. The two little girls were perched on the edge of the bed like two birds, looking from me to their mother with shining eyes. I had been uncomfortable about the visit from the start, but in these dark days I was used to withdrawing into my shell and distancing myself from the world around me. I was not particularly cowardly or desperate, but I had convinced myself that I was going to die in my own way. During the last few weeks I had come to think that this ought to be put in writing. In this crazy, shattered world, death had suddenly lost the special quality which philosophers and poets had always pontificated about. You also had to pay for it now and, in addition to being offered wholesale, it had become bestial.

Husayn came away from the window and stood facing us. "There's nothing wrong with me, Madiha," he said. "I mean here, inside me." He struck himself on the chest a few times, producing a hollow sound. "Inwardly, I mean to say. Spiritually, there's nothing wrong with me. On the contrary, believe me, Karim knows, I'm fine mentally, spiritually."

His shoulders were thin, one higher than the other, and the soft material of his robe hung down over his rib cage and concave stomach.

"I told my old boss how I'd chosen to admit myself to the clinic. I said to him nobody could have made me if I hadn't wanted to. I became— I mean—suddenly I had faith. Life's changing. No bastard can tell me . . ." He glanced hurriedly at his daughters. "You can go back and pick up the pieces, can't you?"

I looked at him, wanting to believe him. He had described to me, the first time I visited him a week after he had entered the clinic, how this fear of death had taken him unawares. He had been walking near Bab al-Shaykh Square one morning and had been gripped by a feeling of terror, an overwhelming conviction that he was going to die soon. It wasn't just a fanciful notion but a dread, as if someone was actually standing there aiming a gun at him. Disturbed, he found he couldn't walk properly, and he went into a nearby café and threw himself down on a seat. He had not drunk anything the night before and so was panting like a wet, hungry dog which had been given a sound kicking. In that wretched condition, near to collapse, terrified and disoriented, he had the idea of escaping from the closed circle of his life, changing it. "I told the boss I had faith," he was saying. "Great hopes for the world. The revolution would come and a new horizon, maybe new horizons, would open up. There would be reform, and this encouraged me. But these bastards are making things hard for me. Why do they forbid smoking?"

He hurried over to the window, but turned round just short of it and came back and sat on the bed next to his daughters.

"Did Abu Sarmad want anything?" asked Madiha.

He looked blearily at her. "Who?"

"Abu Sarmad."

"Who's he?"

"God please don't let him lose his mind. Abu Sarmad. The man who used to be your boss."

"Abu Sarmad? He didn't want anything. He came to visit me. I told him I was going to write an article about my experience—it could be useful to someone. He said that would be excellent."

"You mean he didn't say anything about your job? Nothing at all?"

"Yes, of course he did." He began tugging at the bristles under his chin, wincing each time he pulled one out.

"What do you mean, of course?"

He paused for a moment. "Just be patient, Madiha dear. Give me time to write the article and publish it, then we'll see."

"What article, for goodness' sake? We want you to get better and go back to work."

"Never mind. Don't worry. Be patient please. Everything will be fine. If you could just have a word with the doctors about smoking." He began stroking Suha's hair. She smiled shyly and looked at her mother. "The thing is, Madiha," he went on, "there's been a change in me. I know now that I've been ill and have to get better. I mean, that's an enormous step. Before I didn't know what kind of a state I was in. Now—I do." Then he withdrew into himself again, folding his hands in his lap. "Now I know. The Almighty allowed me to know. After Midhat's death, God rest his soul, I went for ten days without touching a drop. Not a drop. Ten days! I was like a sleepwalker. I had no time to drink or think about drinking. How did it happen? I don't know. But God be praised!"

He talked sincerely, truthfully, a drunk who'd come to his senses. His haggard face and wild eyes had taken on an inspired look which didn't suit him. In my view, the Almighty had only intervened to put immense fear in his heart. These days fear was in the air, in the tiniest particles of the air at any time. Not his fear or mine, not a personal fear. I had seen it, come right up against it in faces, gestures, voices, and we were weighed down by it. When Husayn came to us, pale and stinking of arak, one Saturday morning when nobody in the house had slept, and told us his story, he was oozing fear. He described how he'd spent the night roaming around the streets and alleyways of Baghdad with some friends and had been unable to get back to where he was staying because the quarter was blockaded. All he could tell us was that Midhat hadn't been with him and that perhaps he was caught inside the besieged zone. We were clustered round him in the yard by the kitchen door, myself, my mother, Madiha and her mother. Then my father joined us. We had no alternative but to extract whatever information we could from this broken-down creature.

It was no time to reproach or criticize him, but I was afraid that everything he said was a lie. As soon as he'd washed his face and had a bite to eat, I made him go out with me. She insisted on accompanying us; she wore her *abaya* and half her face was covered, leaving her tear-filled, hazel eyes visible. We walked without talking. Husayn hobbled along reluctantly, as if he wanted to let us go ahead of him. When Munira asked him if Midhat had answered her note, he nodded but didn't look at her, and I noticed his mouth twitch and his eyelids quiver.

There was a tremendous uproar in the street and repeated explosions competing with radios turned up loud in the cafés. It was a beautiful day, with a few clouds and brilliant sunshine. We went into the mosque, crossed the courtyard, and stopped by the far door. The blockade was real: we had come face to face with it. We stood for a long time in the same place. I saw her looking unblinkingly past the Café Yas at the entrance to the besieged Kurdish quarter. The people passing, some of them armed, some hurrying, frightened, did not enter her field of vision. For her the world consisted of one person, and there was no sign of him. Eventually the waiting and hunger, and the din and chaos round about, wore us down, and she and I went home without exchanging a word. We had stopped talking to each other weeks before. This idiot Husayn had remained behind, hoping to be able to sneak back into the quarter, and had promised to come and see us later. We would have been stupid to believe him.

"The doctors here say this is a step in the right direction," Husayn was telling us now. "They say you have to want to help yourself. If you want to be cured, you will be. They say, we can help you, but you . . ."

"So how long will you be here?" asked Madiha impatiently.

"How do I know? The doctors are the ones who decide when I get out. This isn't an ordinary hospital, Madiha. I mean, the doctors look at this as an experiment. They say it's a pioneering venture—in Iraq, I mean. They treat addicts, then let them out to confront the world again. I don't know if it's true or not, but I'm confident . . ." He broke off and went to stand at the window again.

I didn't want to talk to him. I wanted to remain a bystander. It seemed to me that he was talking to himself in an attempt to repair the damage he had done in the past. I was neither sorry for him, nor enthusiastic about his plans to change his life. Perhaps I didn't see the difference between his past life and the one he was trying to create now. I didn't understand his optimism, since he was surrounded by the ruins of an innocent world. How could someone find life beautiful when death was closing in on the horizon?

That afternoon, as the rain fell after the announcement of Abd al-Karim Qasim's execution, I had been aware of a strange taste in my mouth and told myself that I would soon be dead. I was sheltering under the olive tree, staring at the main door. Since they had stopped being able to put a brave face on things, my parents stayed in their room. No doubt they were weeping together, hidden away from the rest of us. They must have realized, like Munira and me, that by a deadly coincidence Midhat's fate was now bound up with the commotion outside, and whether he lived or died depended on matters we had no part in. The rain was pouring down and the leaves whispered cheerfully together.

First I saw my grandmother Umm Hasan coming out of the old ladies' room alone, then stopping to look up at the sky. She went on looking up for some unknown reason, as if she could see a sign in the dense clouds or was talking to someone up there. After a while she went back into a different room. She was muffled in black, her face white and devoid of emotion. Then, amidst the beating of the rain on the olive tree, I heard a door slam somewhere upstairs and noticed another dark shape out of the corner of my eye. Munira was carrying her *abaya* and hurrying towards the stairs. She paused briefly in front of my door, then walked on. I felt slightly uneasy, guessing where she was going and staying where I was. She hesitated at the foot of the stairs. She was wearing a dark blue dress and her face was pale. As she opened out her *abaya* and was about to drape it over her head, she noticed me. For a moment she stopped what she was doing and looked at me, then she continued wrapping her *abaya* round her determinedly. There was about ten meters between us, which she covered in short, rapid steps.

"I'm going out again, just in case," she whispered as she passed.

She walked straight on, her almond-shaped eyes shining above her delicate nose. I followed her. Raindrops fell on my face and hair. I asked her if anyone knew she was going out, and she replied that they were all asleep. We made our way carefully over the muddy ground in silence. Then, without looking at me, she asked if all this would stop now that Abd al-Karim Qasim was dead. Although I meant to tell her that I honestly didn't know, I said nothing. We stopped at the corner of an alleyway near where we had been before, facing the besieged quarter, and were told that the area was about to be shelled at any moment. Gunfire reverberated constantly from all sides, but she was completely focused on the dark mouth of the entrance to the quarter. She stood against the wall, only her face visible, beautiful despite the tension and fear there. I wished I could inspire such anxiety in a woman like her! Unaware that I was observing her, she sighed and wiped some drops of rain off her forehead. We remained there for some time. I was apprehensive, fearing the worst; around us people were running, jostling one another, cursing, and laughing, and the shots were louder and more frequent. I heard the mosque clock striking, but lost count of the number of chimes. I was standing a short distance from her when I noticed someone walking closer to her than was proper. Slowly I moved forward and she turned to look at me. I went up to her and looked into her eyes. The suffering that I saw there seemed too

333

much for the world to contain; she was misery personified. I leaned against the wall beside her in silence.

Then within minutes the atmosphere grew tenser. Groups ran from the direction of Kifah Street and armed individuals moved back towards it. There was an uncommonly loud rumble of machine gun fire and all the bystanders, including us, moved back. Before we had the chance to talk, there was a huge explosion not far away. Someone shouted that the bombardment had begun and they were going to destroy all the houses in the quarter. She looked so horrorstruck, her features pinched, her gaze moving rapidly over the people and objects surrounding her, that I took her arm through her *abaya* but she pulled it away sharply. Insistently I took hold of it again. I was the one clinging to her, to the symbol which she continued to be for me. She looked at me. Her face was pale, her lips trembling, and I caught a glimpse of her silvery-white neck under some loose strands of hair. Her eyes blazed with anger, demanding to know what I was thinking of, and in the space of a moment, a speck of time, in that wave of noise and death and destruction and infinite fear, as we were pushed to and fro by hands and bodies, the phantom of that other symbol in my life, Fuad, seemed to radiate from her. His once familiar features merged with the soft lines of her lovely face, and before my eyes she was transformed into a creature with a double life. The vision vanished with the sound of shouting and panting and running feet across the square behind us. We were separated in the panic. But I found her again and shared her sense of defeat as we walked disconsolately home. She turned back in horror as another huge explosion reverberated in the distance, as if the shells had struck her in the heart and soul. As she walked along the pavement in the sunset, between day and night, looking thin and fragile with her head bowed, she brought back memories of past anguish. I wondered not why these two had become so closely identified in my mind, but what the effect of this would be on me. Fuad had been snatched away from me before I could get through to him; and here she was, enveloped in mystery, about to slip out of my grasp. Something had been missing since the evening we talked together; I felt unable to be close to her once she was married, given my feelings and hers. But I had not lost the right to suffer beside her, to taste my wounded darling's blood. However, I had been absolutely deprived, with all the intransigence and stupidity of the absolute, of the right to address a word to her. But she remained deep in my heart and I wanted to believe, with all these rules and regulations weighing me down, that I had also made a personal sacrifice that evening on the roof and that both of us might be able to be happy. I was out of her life, and she regarded that as a permanent state of affairs. As I said, we hadn't exchanged any meaningful conversation all those months, and I hadn't objected, because she might have been enjoying her life, and I might eventually have recovered, or shriveled up and died like a plant in the desert.

Then, for no apparent reason and out of the blue, everything went off the rails. Life ceased to have a structure and an order. Bewildered as we were, we would not have been surprised if the sun had fallen on us in the course of the day. We were confused because, with the exception of her, we had become a single person, a small child overcome by a desire to burst into tears because the riddle of life was insoluble. When I set out to look for my brother, like a character in a folktale, it was not for anybody else, but so that I could go on living. I failed to find him, but she did not come near me. Even when she lost her color and her eyes clouded over, she remained further away from me than anybody. She would sit listening to me talking to them and the sight of her face would light me up inside, but she never addressed a word to me. Then events unfolded at such a pace that I hardly had time to consider my own fate. But as I walked home behind her with a heavy heart that dark February evening I decided that I didn't want to survive her.

We climbed aboard the old-fashioned carriage without complaint, tired of waiting fruitlessly in the deserted street. I sat beside Madiha, and Suha and Sana squashed up in the little seat in front, smiling and whispering together. All that remained of the sun was a patch of dark red in the far west. The carriage lumbered along and a cool breeze blew in on us. We had left Husayn when he no longer had anything to say to us and the silence had begun to weigh heavily on us all.

Suha laughed. "Mum, do you know what Sana said about Dad?"

"Karim," said Madiha, ignoring her, "what's the point of it? All this fuss, doctors coming and going, and yet I don't see any change in him so far, any progress. What do you think, Karim?"

"At least he's better than he was before. I'm sure of that."

How could you measure a person's progress and development when you knew that, in the long term, there were no fixed values or opinions? I wanted to say to Madiha that I wasn't interested in her husband, not at all interested. The whole thing was a mirage. But as long as he was alive she couldn't live without a mirage of this sort.

"Mum, Mum," repeated Suha.

"What do you want, for heaven's sake?"

The carriage danced in a stately fashion over the potholed road.

"Mum, do you know what Sana said about Dad? She said he's like a scarecrow. Really, Mum. She did."

The air was refreshing, and stimulated the imagination for some strange reason.

"Aren't you ashamed of yourself?" scolded Madiha. "When you were ill the other day, you couldn't speak a word of sense. It's your father you're talking about."

Sana looked at her in silence, then said, "Mum. Why's Dad ill? He doesn't look as if there's anything wrong with him to me."

Sana had become ill when they were all taken up with Midhat's death, but nobody had paid her any attention until in a dreadful fit of delirium she had woken us up in the middle of the night with her piercing cries. I had run to their room and there she was on their big bed, clutching on to her mother, her short hair on end, her eyes and cheeks as red as blood, shrieking, "No, no. No, Mum, no."

Her mother held her close, reciting Quranic verses and charms, then my mother and aunt came in and tried to help Madiha calm her down.

"It's her teeth, dear," said my aunt. "Don't worry about it."

The little girl had broken away from her mother and begun giving the bedcover terrified looks. Her mother tried to take her in her arms again, but Sana resisted instinctively, muttering and grinding her teeth together. At this point Madiha had begun crying and shrieking too, and my mother had rushed over, pushed her aside, and taken the little girl forcibly in her arms.

I had been too miserable to help them calm Sana down, hovering at the edge of the room, my nerves on edge, watching them trying lovingly to restore her to her senses, bring her back to our rational world. My aunt settled down on the bed, repeating her pronouncements about the reasons for Sana's hysterics, and I heard the child say, "No, no. Come and help me, quickly, Uncle." Then she gave a loud cry and lost consciousness.

Now here she was in front of me, and all that was left of her first confrontation with the harshness of life was this unmistakable tinge of sorrow on her face. She didn't keep herself apart from us like Munira and was as enthusiastic as ever about everything that went on in the house, but she had lost a note of joyfulness and spontaneity in her relations with other people. She was more or less the only one to keep Munira company, sit with her, talk to her, even daring to laugh with her sometimes. I had seen her kiss Munira's hand quickly as we left one gloomy Tuesday—myself, Munira, Husayn, and Sana—to go to the Kurdish quarter in a final attempt to discover what had happened to Midhat. Despite her childish insistence, it wasn't logical for her to come with us. We knew that we might be seeing some unpleasant sights and that our mission was serious and difficult enough without the added complication of having a child around. But Sana complained so much to Munira, begged her, hugged her with tears in her eyes, that Munira managed to overcome her mother's objections, and that was when I saw Sana kissing Munira's hand as we went up the street, away from the big door.

Days after the events the quarter was still like a paper house which had been trodden underfoot. The alleyways were not as dark as I had pictured them, and I thought we were hurrying more than we needed to. An urgent pulse went driving through me, convincing me that we would find my brother or at least see where he was staying. So I was hugely disappointed when this white-faced old woman opened the door to us and showed us into a dim courtyard, then asked Husayn if he had any news of Midhat. How we were going to find any clues to his whereabouts there if they were asking us about him? The old man, the Hajji, whose mind was obviously confused, saw us and began repeating names and strange stories in Turkish. Then Munira talked with the old woman, who seemed to realize intuitively that she had something to do with Midhat. She took her by the hand, sat her down beside her on the wooden seat, and began talking to her about the last few days. I was upset and sad, and felt that I was crumbling to pieces inside. Munira listened with an expression of desperate curiosity as the old woman told her how Midhat had gone out a few days before, Saturday evening as far as she could remember, when it was raining heavily, and not come back. He had left them on their own with nothing to eat. She said that she had known that he wouldn't come back and had tried to make him stay indoors, but they had both known in their hearts that his mind was taken up with other matters. She had said goodbye to him and told him to take care, and perhaps after all he was safe and sound somewhere out there. Then she instinctively reached out a hand to Munira and squeezed her arm, telling her not to worry because he was a good man whom nobody would wish to harm.

As I listened to the old woman's halting words, I couldn't shake off the feeling that I was listening to Midhat's funeral oration. The Hajji's demented chanting came from the small room off the courtyard, a soft, uninterrupted burbling, and I had the urge to free myself of this hateful feeling by any means possible. I asked her where Midhat had slept and spent his days while he was staying with them, my voice breaking several times in the course of this short sentence. She and Munira turned to look at me, Munira's expression fierce, despite the tears glistening in her eyes. As the old woman pointed upwards, Husayn said, "Upstairs. He slept in my bed."

Munira stood up suddenly to go upstairs, as if it was settled that this would be her next move. Sana managed to stay close to her one way or another, disappearing among the folds of her black *abaya*, squeezing in next to her, or hurrying along beside her. We found nothing of interest in the bare room and stood looking blankly around it. Munira went over to the grubby-looking bed and hesitantly turned the pillow over and looked underneath it, then retreated. The floor was covered with dust and dirt. We weren't looking for anything in particular, except that we had a vague feeling, perhaps to do with Midhat having been in the place previously, that we would come upon a sign of some sort. It was then that, out of the darkness and silence hanging over the room, Munira asked, "Did you give my note to Midhat, Abu Suha?"

Husayn was already embarrassed at having to accompany us to his room and kept apologizing, but when she asked him this question he really looked as if he wanted to run away from us. He lit a cigarette, and a strong smell of sweat came off him. "Of course I did."

"I mean, you didn't forget, did you?"

"Of course not. What do you think I am? How could I forget?"

"Sorry. Thanks," she said. Then she suggested we go downstairs again.

After that we wandered aimlessly along the dark winding alleys, not knowing what we should be looking for or where to begin. There were a lot of people about, houses with their doors standing open and others in ruins; the cafés were closed and the effects of the uproar and the horror were imprinted on people's faces. I was bitterly sad, my strength depleted, but I tried not to show it. It was easy to be sad then, and we needed somebody cheerful to be a token of optimism in our lives.

We went back home shortly before midnight, Sana stumbling along beside Munira. Husayn slipped away from us shortly before we came out of the mosque. We were drained not so much by sorrow or exhaustion or terror of various sorts, as anxiety, a sharp, nagging fear that anything could happen to Midhat and we were powerless to prevent it. My parents were huddled on the wooden bench by the door to the basement waiting for us, with the light on in the distance. Munira and Sana hurried on upstairs without a word, and I sat down next to them. They were wearier than I was, and my father seemed to be on the verge of tears. With a dark wool scarf wrapped round his head, he gripped the edges of his *abaya*. They interrogated me relentlessly, as if I was privy to my brother's fate and was keeping it from them. I would have liked to tell them my impressions of our search and say that I felt in some vague way we would soon know what the future held for us, but the mass of wrinkles on my mother's face, deeper in the pale lamplight, her mouth twisted in pain, and the look of eternal supplication in her eyes, made me hold back.

The gently swaying carriage rocked Sana and Suha's heads to right and left, and the streetlights accentuated the tiredness on their faces. I was enjoying the cool breezes, not wanting to arrive anywhere. Goals were no longer something I could deal with. All the same, there were secret decisions which deep down I was certain would have to be made. Because the end often lay between two extremes: the infinite on one hand and the fluctuations of the heart on the other. That evening towards the end of Ramadan, when Adnan and Husayn had finally appeared, looking like messengers of doom, I felt in a way that I was confronting the end.

They arrived without advance warning, making an exaggerated amount of noise. On the brink of despair, we were ready to grasp at the most trivial signs relating to Midhat. They wanted to see Munira. She came out of her room on the first floor, not knowing who was asking for her. They were sitting on the wooden bench outside the smaller basement room, exhaling cigarette smoke ferociously. I hurried ahead of her. Madiha and my mother were already with them. I noticed straightaway that Adnan was wearing khaki and appearing somehow inflated with pride. He looked intently at me, then shook my hand indifferently. My mother was talking to them in her inexplicably humble, imploring tone of voice. I didn't know what they wanted exactly, but guessed their presence had something to do with my brother. They were silent, not answering my mother's incessant questions. As far as I remember I asked Husayn whether there was any news, and he gestured towards Adnan with a jerk of his head. I turned to look at him, then heard the sound of Munira's feet at the bottom of the stairs. Adnan stood up suddenly. He was tall and broad-chested. He crushed his cigarette nervously underfoot. She approached us wearing a loose blue dress, with an inquiring look in her eyes, but when she recognized Adnan she stopped a few paces away and said nothing, her face pale, her right arm frozen in front of her. None of us spoke for what seemed like a lifetime. Then Adnan addressed her. "How are you, Aunt?"

The tremble in his voice, it seemed to me, betrayed some fear. Her large eyes shone and she blinked rapidly, but didn't answer him.

"I'm sorry," he said, feeling around in his pockets. "I haven't come at a good time. But I wanted to help under the circumstances. Husayn came to see me the day before yesterday and we went, I went with him," he took a little card out of his pocket, which he kept in his hand, "I went with him to—the important thing is we don't forget our relatives." He hesitated. "I'm sorry, Aunt Munira, but I think Midhat . . ." he hesitated again. "This is his ID card. I got it from some friends of mine. They found it in his pocket. I'm sorry. My condolences."

My heart beat violently. Madiha's wails, followed shortly by my mother's, did not stop me observing Munira as she leaned against the wall and put her hand up to cover her eyes. From that moment—when I was surrounded by them all, but alone with her in a world where only she existed, as they exchanged expressions of condolence and she collapsed on to a nearby chair and they clung to Adnan, asking him for details of the killing, the body, the burial, and my father came down and the children were shouting—from that moment, all I could see was the end, as clearly as could be. There were two different routes to it: one began that evening with Fuad's face in the sunset, when I was swept away with him into the dark abyss and he remained in my soul, his death imprinted on my life forever; the other began with the red dusk when she filled the sky around me. But I hadn't allowed myself to be swept away with her, because of my cowardice and stupidity. I had escaped with the loss of some limbs and reached this second death still carrying the first within me. And so I became aware of the fact that endings always repeated themselves, and that was true hell.

The carriage with its tired old horses dragged itself along the street with us silent inside it, and I marveled how everything came to an end and people saw that and did nothing to stop it and still went on living. We buried my brother Midhat with our imaginations and didn't let our sorrow inconvenience anyone. Until the end we remained embarrassed and bewildered, unaffected by myths of martyrs or heroes. Relatives and a few friends came shyly to offer their sympathy. Husayn sat with my father in the alcove, and I sensed he was happy with this new feeling of belonging, his untidy beard, and all the little duties he rushed to perform. Adnan also visited two or three times with his parents, and on each occasion he wanted to see his Aunt Munira, but such conduct did not fit well with the traditions, and his wish was not granted. At night when they were all asleep I felt that she wanted to bring my life to yet another ending. I was unable to talk to her, and her pale face aroused unparalleled emotion in me. Even enveloped in black she shone out, and each time I tried to look at the world around her I failed and my eyes remained locked on to the hair falling around her thin shoulders and the resolutely closed mouth.

As the carriage turned the corner we were all thrown to one side. The two little girls laughed and Madiha scolded them. The lights in

Kilani Street were a faint red and the noise there was at its height. The driver stopped a short distance from the entrance to our alley, and we got down and walked. I lagged behind them and they soon became no more than shapes moving ahead of me. The desire never to arrive was still strong in me.

We pushed open the big door, which stood ajar, and went along the dark passage. The yard was silent except for some intermittent twittering of birds. Madiha and the girls went upstairs while I sat on the bench by the little basement. I was tired, but not only because of this sad, upside down way of life, or the dearth of openings ahead of me, or the poor flawed creatures I lived with; I was weary of my own impotence and confusion, of the way things slipped through my hands. She was my only concern. This had been the way it was since Midhat's death; she had begun to take up more of my attention with each passing day, and everything that concerned me and her tired me out, everything.

I heard someone calling my name. I thought it was my mother and was amazed to discover that it was my father, his voice soft and broken.

"Karumi, why are you sitting down there? Come up and be with us for a bit."

"Yes, all right," I answered, getting to my feet unenthusiastically.

I found my mother lying on the couch in the alcove, swathed in black, with a ragged piece of black cloth tied around her forehead, and Munira's mother smoking quietly beside her. I inquired how they were and they answered noncommittally. I sat at my mother's feet, taking hold of them and squeezing them gently through the cover.

"How's Husayn, Karumi?" she asked. "Why didn't Madiha tell us anything? She disappeared into her room with the girls."

"He's fine. Very well. He said Abu Sarmad came to see him. His old boss."

"Why? Is he going to give him back his job?"

"If he gets better, why not?"

"Praise God," commented Munira's mother.

343

"Are you saying he doesn't drink any more?" persisted my mother.

"God knows. Maybe not."

"Praise the Lord."

"May God hear you. Perhaps he'll go back to his family and sort his ideas out."

"About time!"

My father came out of his room. "Why are you sitting in the dark?" he said, switching on the lamp, then sat down with us.

I heard the sound of light footsteps. It was Sana in her short black dress, looking like a bird whose feathers had been dyed.

"Sana dear," said Munira's mother. "Where's Munira?"

"She might be in her room. Shall I go and see?"

"Not now dear. In a bit. I want the bottle of sleeping tablets. She took them the day before yesterday and hasn't given them back yet."

"Where's your mother, Sana?" my mother asked.

"She's asleep, Bibi."

"What do you mean, asleep? Why?"

"She feels a bit sick from the carriage, Bibi."

"There is no power or strength but with God!"

"How do you mean sick, dear?" my father asked Sana.

"I don't know, Grandpa. She said she felt sick and her head was going round."

"Maybe she's tired," said my mother, attempting to get to her feet. "Let me go and see to dinner for you all."

"How's Husayn, Karim?" my father asked me.

"Fine, Dad. He's getting better."

"Let's hope so. He deserves it. He's a good lad."

"If he was such a good person, God wouldn't have abandoned him," retorted my mother, looking for her sandals.

"Where are you going, Bibi?" asked Sana.

"To the kitchen."

"Can I come, too?"

"No, you go and see your mother, Sana."

I was anxious, weighed down by random disturbing thoughts. I needed to see her; she was avoiding me just as I was avoiding her, but something had to happen between us.

"I'll go and see how Madiha is," I said, getting up.

"Relax," my father commanded my mother. "There's still plenty of time before dinner. Madiha's probably recovered by now. Let her make the dinner."

The sky was clear as I passed Munira's door and caught sight of her through the window, sitting in a corner. I found Madiha sitting with her head bowed and her hair disheveled, but when I asked her what was wrong she looked at me hollow-eyed, gave me some vague reply, then got up calmly and went out.

I stayed on my own in the gray, bare room. The world was falling apart around me but I felt disconnected from it, the chaos inside me making me indifferent. I threw myself down in a chair to relieve my agitation. As usual they were making a racket outside. They would never change their eating and drinking habits until the end of time.

I heard a door open and close. She had been in the next room and had just come out of it to share our life with us again. I say again, because she had systematically withdrawn from the daily routine. She had begun to cut down the amount of time she spent with other people. She didn't talk to anybody, and nobody talked to her, either out of fear or respect for her sorrow. In my case it was because I was terrified of breaking down in front of her. She no longer helped with the housework; she went to school two or three days a week and stayed at home the rest of the week, sometimes claiming to be unwell. What was she planning to do? What was there left for me if she vanished? I was overcome by my fears, incapable of understanding anything.

The darkness enveloped me, making me feel relaxed and secure, far away from everything, as if I had realized my wish never to arrive anywhere. I stretched my legs out in front of me and closed my eyes for a moment. There was a sequence of structures, which I did not understand, but which shaped my life in some way. A sequence composed of my past and the characters in it, what I had done or not done, my regrets and my hopes. If I thought of it—this sequence—as an abstract concept, it would destroy me for sure. But I simply felt it. I neither understood it nor denied its existence. Like this sense of foreboding which had been gnawing at me for some time, an insane fear lurking in a corner which I could neither take hold of nor banish. Lord, what was the reason for it? Was it a warning to me that I was going to die soon? And did the fact that I was continually haunted by this idea mean that it would come true?

I had a hand up to my cheek and was staring into the semi-darkness, not really convinced by any of the thoughts passing through my head. I was letting my apprehensions and obsessions run away with me, but in order to avoid this, I should at least know the reason for the damned things. I was always thinking, but I never formed a definite idea. The mind's eternally flowing spring took me here and there, on excursions both happy and sad, but I never worked out where I stood. In the course of these intellectual-spiritual sallies, I was prone to being misled by an idea which would push me into a destructive act. I was a weak person, unable to make a decision because I was driven by inclinations which I didn't understand. Was everybody this twisted?

Someone called me suddenly. I jumped to my feet but couldn't work out who had called me because they were scattered all over the house. They were all busy with something, rushing to and fro. All except her. My father was sitting cross-legged on the couch in the alcove. Perhaps it was he who had called me; he was strangely afraid of being alone. I went towards him, passing her door, which was shut as usual, then paused at my door, changed my mind, and went into my room. Again I heard my father calling me but I didn't answer. I wanted to be by myself for a few more minutes. I lay down on my bed and reached out to touch the wall. This was what was separating me from her. This stupid agglomeration of matter was keeping us apart. Except that it wasn't like that, as I very well knew. It was impossible to separate two people if they wanted to be together. The opposite must also be true; and if no power in the world could join two people's hands, what was to be done?

Of course I was sad as I lay there, letting my thoughts run on and affect my mood. This year, if I failed in my classes I would be thrown out of the university and give the family something more to be sorry about. But they wouldn't blame me; on the contrary they would find every possible reason and excuse to justify my failing again. So I would be saved, but would the torture be over?

The door of my room opened slowly, and my father's form appeared tentatively in the doorway. "Karumi, son. Are you asleep?"

I answered him, got up off the bed, and went out.

———

What was death? To lose someone dear to you, lose their physical presence and not be able to see them again, what did that mean?

Nothingness was inexplicable. Like infinity, it was impossible to accept. This was why religions developed, possibly. But why was death so painful to the living? Was it because it brought home to them the eternal contradiction between the present and the absent? Because their loved ones lived on inside them when they were physically no longer there.

Take Fuad. I knew that he had gone forever, but he would die a second time when I died. And again when his father died. Then the pain in our lives would be at an end, the contradiction over.

I was walking in the darkness near the stairs on the far side of the first floor. The sky was clear as crystal, lit by the invisible moon. They had gone quiet for the past hour or two, since supper, and I had spent the time wandering alone in the gloom. Then the lights went out one after the other, except for a very faint light in her room. I was examining my life, trying to shake off the anxiety which had dogged me for so long. Some mysteries had suddenly presented themselves to me. Why did I feel an obscure sense of guilt about my brother's death? How had I contributed to Fuad's death? Was I some warped creature who fluctuated between evil incarnate and the innocence of a new-born babe?

That night when we were together, Fuad and I, I had been at the peak of my arrogance, confident not in my own strength but in his weakness, and reveling in this confidence. He was unable to get close to her, to possess her, for the simple reason that he knew it would destroy him. In the smoky hall where we sat surrounded by the continuous comings and goings of the clients, whores, and pimps, I watched him intently, mentally totting up the signs of weakness, hesitation, and fear in him. That dear friend! I was almost happy at the thought that I could do what he was afraid of doing, because he knew that his life would never be the same again if he possessed her in this way. I was euphoric because my soulmate was suffering. How despicable can a person be!

As I stood wearily in the shadows by the uppermost branches of the olive tree, these thoughts terrified me. In this moment of truth I was afraid of discovering other things which might be the death of me. The light was faint in her room, and she was far away from me. She had formed a relationship with him, agreed to it because I had said nothing to her. Then they had met with this calamity because I had said nothing. Could this really be how things had happened? Was it possible that I had been involved? It was true that she hadn't talked to me since that evening on the roof. I didn't know why I was thinking of all this now. What about Midhat? What possible reason could he have had for choosing to distance himself from her of all people? Was there really any connection between our conversation and Midhat's action?

I was scared as I struggled to remember everything she had said that evening on the roof at sunset. I hadn't been listening to the individual words, only to the sound of her voice, whose music set my heart on fire.

I had wanted to fly above the sky with her, leaving all these different worlds of mine behind me. The thing was, she had said nothing to me. And I had understood nothing and continued to understand nothing.

I looked across the courtyard towards her room, feeling desolate. She seemed like the last beacon of hope in my life. After her there was only darkness and futility. I thought I glimpsed a shadow crossing briefly in front of the dim light in her room, just for a moment, the blink of an eye. Was she still awake then, like me?

I was afraid of everything, of her, the world, the very fact of being alive, and yet she was my only refuge. I advanced very slowly, holding on to the wooden balustrade. She had acquired the keys to my soul, to my destruction and also, possibly, to my salvation. Total silence enveloped me as I crept hesitantly towards her. She wouldn't slam the door in my face, because I wasn't demanding anything of her. I would stand on the margin of her world purely to ask questions. I stumbled as I went past my room, but held tightly to the balustrade and paused, mustering my strength for the last step or two. Her door was ajar, open and closed at the same time, not giving the impression that there was somebody inside. I moved laboriously towards it, and a pale column of light fell across my face. I saw her notice me. She was sitting on the long couch in the corner facing the door still in her black dress, her arms folded, looking at me. Once I had pushed the door open, I remained frozen on the threshold. Standing before her, I saw nothing clearly but felt violent emotions welling up within me. She stared at me, her eyes bright yellow through her long black lashes.

"Sorry," I whispered. "Are the sleeping pills here?"

She shook her head and went on looking at me. Saying these words to her had tired me out. I stood there waiting for her to speak. Her mouth was shut and strands of her blonde hair played around it.

"The sleeping tablets? Where are they?" I asked.

"I don't know." Her voice was as cold as the blade of a knife.

"Why are you keeping them here?"

She seemed to straighten up slightly. "I told you, I don't have any sleeping tablets. Go and look in the medicine cupboard downstairs. Why come to me?"

I hesitated, then said, "You've got them. You took them from your mother. She said so. You took the whole bottle."

She closed her eyes for a few moments then let her hands drop crossly into her lap and tilted her head to the right. "What are you talking about? What are you trying to say?"

She was no longer looking at me. I noticed that my voice trembled all the time I was speaking; there was a catch in it, no firmness. I was silent like the world around us. I felt that I had reached the dividing line between us by talking to her like this. I was anxious, as I had been for ages, but now I understood why; only now and because I was standing in front of her like a beggar asking her wordlessly to give me some meaning in my life, to give me her life. She knew very well that my words had other implications, and I couldn't deny this.

Suddenly she looked up at me with her large, captivating eyes, bright but troubled. "No. I don't have such thoughts." Her voice was sad, her expression, her whole demeanor. "I'm not ready to die, if that's what you mean." She looked away from me and was silent for a time, then continued, "You have a strange image of me, Karim. You always have had. I don't know why. Maybe you're influenced by my physical appearance. Maybe you have feelings you yourself aren't aware of. I don't know." She shrugged her shoulders almost imperceptibly to give these last words the painful emphasis she intended. "But I'm one of those girls who don't have any luck, whom God is displeased with. I must have committed some sins without knowing it. But God has to have mercy on me in the end and let me forget."

"Forget?"

"Why not?" Her tone was sharp and full of anger. "I'm the same as other people. Perhaps I don't have . . ." She paused. "Perhaps I don't have any hope of a future, but . . ."

For some reason I interrupted her. "Munira." Her name was a song in my mouth, a glad shout from my heart. I couldn't stop myself saying it.

She sat back slightly and turned her face away from me. My eyes fell on her chest, on the two mounds rising and falling a little faster than usual.

"There's obviously no point in talking plainly," she said. Then, after a moment, "Please, Karim, I'm tired. This can't come as a surprise to you. We're all tired. But everything has its limits. There are people who can put up with . . ." She stopped with a perplexed air, rested her chin on her hand as if she was waiting, and looked sideways. She appeared to have lost her train of thought all of a sudden, and to have no desire to retrieve it.

"Munira." This time I was calling her, trying to make her listen to me. "Munira."

She looked up at me and I saw her radiant face, the face of my beloved, far away from me.

"Don't leave me alone. Don't go, Munira."

The movement of her eyebrows betrayed faint signs of astonishment. She bowed her head and her hair hung in heavy clumps round her face. "Where would I go if I left? Don't you know I've become the family's property now? Registered in your name?"

"Don't talk like that. You know perfectly well what I mean."

"Please, please. I don't know anything."

"No. You know. You know how I feel about you, Munira."

"You can keep your feelings to yourself. Do you understand?" Her eyes blazed. Between one sentence and the next she had become an angry lioness. She raised her hand decisively, putting up a barrier between us. "Keep them to yourself. Don't bring me into your personal affairs. You've got no connection to me. Do you understand?"

Her voice, despite its fierce tone, was not loud, but it tore at my entrails.

"I've had enough of feelings," she went on, "and I don't want you bringing me into your life. Get away from me. Leave me in peace. I'm tired. Tired of all of you. I don't want anything. Just leave me alone."

Although her hands were trembling and she was breathing somewhat unevenly, her voice was steady. I felt confused by what she said, but had been expecting it. She didn't understand that I wanted nothing from her.

"Munira, I just thought I might be able to help you. I'm sorry. I just thought . . ." I sounded more desperate than I expected to and stopped. She remained quite still as if she hadn't heard, her face turned away from me. For some reason I imagined she was on the point of collapsing or shouting uncontrollably.

"Munira, please," I said. "Don't be hard on me. You're the most important person in my life. But I'm weak and indecisive. I don't know what to do. Believe me, Munira. You're all I've got now. Don't let me lose hope."

"You're not weak. You're like me and everybody else here. Warped and sick." Her eyes were cold, her face pinched. "I knew this. I knew it only too well and I wanted to stay on my own, on the margins, but none of you would let me. He wouldn't let me. He was sicker than me. He was weaker and more warped than either me or you, and he was a coward." Hatred overflowed from her face, from the sockets of her eyes, as she spat her words out in a controlled frenzy. "You're afraid of him. But I'm not afraid of anyone. You're all cowards. You don't know who needs help, who's sincere, who's having bad luck, whose world's falling down around their ears. You're cowards and fools. He didn't want to understand, didn't want to know who was guilty and who was innocent. And now you! Coming to tell me that you're weak! As if I didn't know!"

I clutched on to the edge of the bed beside me and leaned against it. I was trembling. Every atom in my body was trembling. I couldn't bear the hatred of the woman I lived for. "Don't talk like that, Munira. Please don't talk like that."

"Why are you here then? What do you want? If you don't want me to talk, what do you want me to do? What do you want from me? Tell me. Do you want me to die? No. I'm not going to kill myself. The time's past for that. And you're the last person who has the right to ask me for anything."

"I don't want anything from you, Munira. I don't want anything. But give me a chance. Give me a chance to live. Don't ruin our life for no reason."

"What life! Whose life am I ruining? Are you mad?" She looked angrily at me.

I wanted to move close to her, but something in her face stopped me. A slight reddening of her eyes, that tremble in her lower lip, an indefinable change in her appearance: a sort of urgency and uncharacteristic hardness on her face. I went on watching her, feeling that I was slowly being torn to pieces, but was unable to escape.

"Don't make me have to repeat myself," she said. "I've told you I'm really tired." She paused, then went on, "You have to understand, there's nothing between us. And there never will be. I don't want any more like him. Leave me in peace. I can't take any more of this kind of life. They're always asking questions, talking. They all think I'm keeping a secret from them. They criticize me and blame me when they're so cowardly and stupid themselves."

"Please, Munira."

She took out a white handkerchief and wiped her mouth with it. "None of them understands that there might be other people who are unhappy or have bad luck. They're only interested in their own rights. They're crazy! Who gets their rights in this world?"

Without realizing what I was doing, I knelt down at her feet. The tears were flowing from her intensely yellow eyes, but she ignored them, fixing first on one point, then another, and letting her eyes travel over my face as I knelt before her.

"He didn't want to understand," she went on. "He died without understanding. He wouldn't deign to listen to a single word, and I thought . . ." She gestured, the handkerchief still in her hand. "I said maybe he's different. Maybe if he knows my situation he'll be sympathetic."

She pursed her lips in a gesture of scorn and despair, then I saw her take in the fact that I was kneeling inanely in front of her. "You're all cowards, Karim, because none of you is capable of pity. Even when you know that wrong's been done, you're not interested in who's innocent and who's been wronged." She hid her tear-stained face in her hands, sighed vehemently and whispered, "I'm going to go crazy. He told me he loved me, then died without a word, or a sign. Why was he so hard on me?"

Like her, I was crying, as I contemplated her mass of hair at close quarters and her delicate white fingers. Both of us were confronting a closed door. I realized that now, after listening to her, as if I hadn't known it all before.

I stood up, put my hand out, and gently touched her damp forehead. She did not react, but continued to sob, her body shaking and rocking convulsively. I stepped back slowly and slipped out of the room, closing the door behind me.

The night was quiet. Leaning against the wooden balustrade, I looked around me in the darkness. I had nothing more to lose. To be aware of the beginning of the end was an odd feeling, one which not everybody had the chance to experience. My mind was calm, as if I was anaesthetized. I could see nothing ahead of me and felt that, with her help, I could perhaps understand the sense of this end.

Chapter
Twelve *(2)*

Brief Shining and Survival

They realized in a vague way, he and the old woman Atiya and the Hajji, that something was over. The rain fell drearily, the clock showed just after three-thirty, and the explosions continued uninterrupted, with varying degrees of intensity. Earlier they had eaten dry bread dipped in watery gravy, then they took refuge in the little room overlooking the courtyard, making desultory conversation, united by fear and a suspicion that they were approaching the end. Midhat didn't want to tell them what was going on in his mind and what he was trying to decide, allowing them to feel that he was with them in their time of trouble. They were sitting drinking their bitter-tasting tea in the damp room that dull Saturday afternoon, when a strange silence descended on them. The radio orchestra, with its distinctive beat, had suddenly withdrawn, leaving the arena clear for the insane dialogue of war. The roar of the instruments of death became clearer and louder. The Hajji sat on his bed wrapped in a thick green blanket. He had taken it upon himself to recount to nobody in particular the story of his long life, which he had begun suddenly the night before and not yet finished. Midhat had woken up shortly after noon the previous day and found that Husayn was not in his usual place. He had obviously left the house while Midhat was asleep and not returned. Midhat had sat up in bed, listening to the constant reverberation of the machine-gun fire, then got up, washed his face, and joined the old couple downstairs. He found them there like two rats in a trap. Nobody spoke. They made do with exchanging looks in silence, and after a short time he began to feel restless in the gloomy little room and had the idea of going for a walk around the neighborhood. This soon evolved into an urgent desire to escape his tortured thoughts. Having told them he would be back in half an hour, he wandered aimlessly through the streets and alleyways, his mind empty, then gradually became overwhelmed by the situation around him. The people in the street were at war, busy preparing for a long blockade. When they prevented him from going anywhere near the exit points his one idea was to gauge his chances of escaping. The ways through were all blocked. Bullets grazed the walls, spraying chunks of stone about and leaving deep holes behind. People sheltered in corners and doorways. Some houses were empty. It did not occur to him as he moved amongst these people, who were behaving in an apparently organized way, to think of himself as one of them, even though for some obscure reason he was sharing their unknown fate. He was afraid, but anxious that this fear should not be his sole motivation for trying to survive.

He returned after less than an hour, walking wearily beneath the wooden overhangs of the windows. The air was springlike, full of the fresh smell of greenness; it reminded him of burying his face in damp green grass warmed by the hot sun. He saw her among the people hurrying past him, wrapped in her *abaya*, the right side of her face partly showing and some strands of her hair falling on to her forehead. For a moment he was terrified and his heart pounded. She was walking agitatedly, apparently undecided which way to go. He wanted to retreat or hide from her, but she turned round suddenly and the beautiful image in his head was lost in the mass of imperfections in this girl's face. The nose, eyes, chin all pointed to a completely different person. How could he have been so mistaken?

He was still upset when he went back into the house. They received him as if he was the bearer of all the world's secrets, sitting in a fog of cigarette smoke, huddled round the brazier's dying embers drinking one glass of tea after another. He reported what he had seen as he drank his tea, feeling depression replace the emotion he had felt when he mistook another girl for her. The old woman asked him whether Husayn was going to be late coming back. The sound of shots filled the air and almost prevented them from hearing what each other was saying some of the time. He didn't answer her.

"A real celebration, *janim*," said the Hajji.

This mixture of Turkish and Arabic had made him laugh bitterly. He still remembered it now as he watched the rain falling dismally. It had been the very beginning of the Hajji's story, which he had then kept up for many hours the previous evening.

"In the town of Al-Kut, *janim*. At the siege of Al-Kut. Your humble servant was there. We'd come from Qasr Shirin to Sibiliyat. An English general, Townsend, the bastard, was under siege with fife . . . fifteen thousand people. Fifteen *luk, janim*." His face worked violently as he talked, and every now and then his small eyes shone through his dense thatch of white hair. "Half dead. We arrived half-dead. I rested on my arms and slept, *janim*, on the ground like a donkey, on the public highway. I nearly got trampled on by horses. But thank God. The artillery blazed away for two hours. We were in the trench. For two hours the artillery blazed away. Attack. Hand-to-hand fighting. We shouted, 'Allahu akbar. Allahu akbar,' and struck. We bayoneted the English in their stomachs. An Indian queer pulled his trousers down and said, 'I'm a Muslim. I'm circumcised.' Poof! Did he think we were born yesterday? We stabbed him in the stomach and plenty more like him."

He gestured with his arm, demonstrating how you bayoneted someone, his features peculiarly savage.

357

Midhat had wanted to go up to his room, but had decided to stay with them in the end, just as he was doing now, watching the sad rain falling on this gloomy Saturday at twilight. The Hajji chattered on endlessly for hours through the rumble of gunfire. As he listened he was surprised by the impression that came to him unbidden, influenced by the Hajji's stories, that some obscure nameless force—Life, God, call it what you like—was playing arbitrarily with vast crowds of human beings, driving them along for thousands of miles from all directions, bringing them together to fight each other, letting some of them be killed and leaving the others to suffer, go hungry, wander aimlessly over the earth. In the course of these violent and capricious mass migrations, the individual understood nothing and floated like a straw on the surface of a river in flood; if he was spared all the dangers, he was left wondering why he should have been chosen as a player in this game which pleased no one.

"*Naraye kid yursk turk ughli karman shahimi? Naraye kid yursk turk ughli karman shahimi?*" sang the Hajji, his face lighting up with childish joy. "We walked, *janim*, we walked. Oh yes. Sarbul, Karant, Malhadasht. Oh, yes. And Kermanshah. *Naraye kid yursk ughli karman shahimi?* A big, big city. People on donkeys saying, 'Dustur. Dustur.' That means, 'Make way. Make way.' And the bread—a yard long, *janim*. A yard long. And there's great poverty there, *janim*. Beggars kiss your hands. A *sanari* there—that's a hundred thousand dinars—means, *janim*, a fils, one thousandth of a dinar." He gave an abrupt laugh, like a gun going off.

The rain came down harder. Midhat thought he heard a knock at the door, loud enough to be audible over the explosions. He exchanged looks with the Hajji and his wife. The Hajji stopped stroking his beard and put his empty tea glass down beside him.

"O God, most merciful of the merciful," he said.

The knocking was repeated. Midhat stood up, slightly apprehensive. The heavy door squeaked on its hinges. It was two young bearded men with guns. Seriously, without wasting words, they asked him if there was a television or radio in the house. As he answered in the negative, they listened intently, their eyes fixed on his face. The silence in the courtyard behind him confirmed his answer.

"Thanks, comrade." And off they went.

Midhat hurried back across the yard in the rain, which had slackened off, and told the old couple what the youths had wanted. They began talking to one another in Turkish, a picture of fear. Midhat grew increasingly bored.

"Aunt Atiya," he said to the old woman, "if there's something you want to discuss, don't mind me."

She looked blankly at him, not appearing to understand what he meant.

"I'm going upstairs so you can be free to talk."

"We don't have anything to talk about, son. This senile old fool says everything's finished and they're going to kill us."

"Why?"

"I don't know, son. Sometimes the angels talk to him. I don't know if it's rubbish all the same, or what. God is the most merciful of the merciful."

The Hajji spoke without looking at them: "Peace be upon you." A torrent of Turkish words poured from him, without a muscle moving in his face, reminding Midhat of the similar fit of garrulousness which had seized him the previous evening. Midhat had left them after eleven on that occasion and gone up to face his solitude, thinking that they must want to sleep and that he could get some rest, too.

The room had been cold and smelly, and not completely dark. He had been unable to see anything when he first went in, then objects had slowly detached themselves from the gloom. His bed appeared to him, and he walked slowly towards it. The window was the source of the pale silvery light bestowing this comfortable dusky glow on the room. He pushed the cover aside and sat on the bed, then felt a twinge in his back and stretched out, flexing his muscles. The explosions continued unabated. No wonder the Hajji was remembering his wartime past. The way they had been led like sheep to the slaughter was terrifying, of course, but in the minutes preceding the attack when the artillery was already blazing away, as the Hajji had said, would that not have been the appropriate time for them to realize that they were embarking on a lethal game, and were about to be involved in a savage operation of mass slaughter, of which they would not be the only victims? Some of them must have been aware of this, but it would have been too late by then to choose peace, like the Muslim Indian who had shown them his genitals to prove that he was one of them and was refusing to fight his brothers in religion. But what an unconvincing sign to give! Sitting on his bed in the sea of half-light where partially visible objects floated, it seemed to Midhat that the silence squeezed in between the explosions was deeper than normal. The roar of gunfire battered his senses, then halted abruptly and was replaced by this strangely profound silence, like a well, or death, then the thunder of the shelling started up again. This was typical of this era when death and destruction masqueraded as something else, ducking and diving and setting snares. Or was he mistaken in this definition as well? These days death did not bother with masks; it approached with its horrors on show. But still you didn't believe that you were its target until you came face to face with it.

The room was without walls or boundaries, and with these terrifying echoes of death all around him, a particular kind of fear mushroomed inside him: fear with a sharp taste, as if he was looking at his own corpse, examining his remains. He closed his eyes briefly, his whole body shuddering in time with his heartbeats. You couldn't cease to exist. It was impossible to experience your own end. It went against reason, therefore it couldn't happen. His lower jaw relaxed slightly. This was just playing with words. It wouldn't help anyone. She had once said to him, smiling and cheerful, "Everything comes to an end. Everything." When he had asked her what these things were which were going to end, she had blushed and said with some embarrassment, "Everything."

He had told her that this was playing with words and served no purpose.

Why were these simple things she had said coming back to him now? Phrases whose meaning you couldn't grasp, probably because they were meaningless. Perhaps she had wanted to say something specific and hadn't had the nerve. The thought brought him up short. She, with him, saying something specific to him. She was with him, and he was with her. They were together in the same place and time. She was talking and he was listening. And if he wanted, if he had the urge to touch her, he would feel the warmth of her soft hand. A series of explosions nearby startled him. They seemed to come from the next door house. He jumped up and went over to the window. He felt like going up on to the roof. The sky was clear and light. A burst of gunfire sounded in the distance and was answered by another a few moments later. Such a destructive dialogue! He turned away from the moonlit window and stood motionless, confronted by the vague outlines and dark smudges of the objects in the room. Suddenly he felt his nerves tingle, his scalp prickle. She was beside him. He felt her resting against his left shoulder, on the point of saying something as she gently touched him. He felt the weight of her invisible arm on him. If he moved his head slightly her hair would brush against his cheek. He turned around. The stars were shining brightly in a clear, dark blue sky. His childish excitement was marred by feelings of humiliation and dejection. He recalled fading thoughts and memories, but it came to him in an instant how distraught he had been and how lost, and how he had insisted on remaining lost, on running away; he remembered his hollow pride, his wasted emotion, his masochism, his defeated, tarnished love. He leaned against the wall by the window, feeling completely bewildered and shattered. From the struggle to deny to himself that she was still part of him emerged the single, overdue question: what should he do?

There wasn't much left that he could do; the number of options open to him had narrowed considerably. He felt his legs go weak and was afraid that he was about to faint or throw up. He went out of the room and downstairs and noticed the clock's shining hands pointing to one in the morning. He stood hesitantly in the yard. Perhaps they weren't asleep yet. He heard what could have been murmured conversation, went up to the door, and gently pushed it open. In the light of the small oil lamp he saw the Hajji sitting on his bed in a tattered black headcloth, telling his prayer beads and talking to the old woman Atiya, who was lying in her own bed. When he saw Midhat he halted his discourse and the old woman sat up.

"God be with you," said Midhat. "I couldn't sleep. What are you doing?"

The Hajji chanted something in Turkish, swaying his head slowly from side to side in time with the words, which were like a song. He looked from Midhat to the old woman, as the lamp cast waves of red light over his lined face.

"Come in, Mr. Midhat," said the old woman. "We're not doing anything. This is your home. Your uncle here is just remembering the men in his regiment. God rest them, they died fifty years ago, but see, when it pleases God, he remembers all their names."

"Mariush Abd al-Hasan Jafil," the Hajji began.

Midhat went in and sat on a chair facing the old woman's bed. Once he had shut the door the explosions sounded fainter, and their importance was further diminished by the Hajji's strange roll call of his comrades' names.

"Shall I make you some tea, Mr. Midhat?"

The Hajji had his eyes closed and was swaying in time with the words as if he was singing, his features immobile in his old man's face. Midhat shook his head.

"Peace be upon you . Glass Abu Battush, Minshin Gagula."

The old woman laughed unconcernedly.

"Sahan Maya, Hamid Hannun."

The sight of the Hajji shocked him. What was this decrepit old man doing? Why, now of all times, was he evoking these reminders of death?

Was it because he thought there was no escaping it, and it was prudent to train yourself to accept it? Why should anyone accept death, nothingness?

"Rahi Isned, Tahban Mir'id."

Was not man's response to extinction always as clear as the sun: a categorical refusal? Even when things were bad, when a man fell, chose to fall, turned his back on life, was he happy to become nothing? How could he be? It was against nature, against a man's fundamental makeup. Extinction was something that happened to you, not something you willed. It attacked you out of the blue, this terrible thing, and defeated you when you were off guard. You needed to examine the concept closely and understand the nature of your enemy.

"Shall I make you some tea, Mr. Midhat?"

"Goter Madhush, Rekaan Shidhr."

The old woman was sitting up in bed, clothed in black, looking at him, the light from the lamp playing on her wizened face. In her tone of voice and intent gaze he detected a fear which she wanted to hide and was ashamed to reveal to him.

"Thank you, Aunt, thank you. There's no need for you to make tea at the moment."

There was a loud, muffled explosion as if the earth was shaking and grumbling beneath them.

"Oh God, most merciful of the merciful."

However, the absolute abiding principle was survival, not a brief shining, then extinction. You had to survive, however high the price. There was no substitute for life. It was the priority.

"Maadi Nadwan, Durdush Wawi."

"Do you know how it will all end, Mr. Midhat? Is the Almighty going to spare us?"

The Hajji's chanting slowed down, and he stopped moving his head from side to side as if he was waiting for Midhat's answer. Midhat looked at the old woman, wanting to communicate to her the idea which had become clear in his mind, about life and survival. He felt it may have imparted new strength to him, strength which he had been lacking for some time.

"Don't be afraid, Aunt Atiya," he said. "Don't be afraid. It's nothing."

"Shabbut Smari, Kharayyis Mishkil."

"There's nothing we can do, son. There's nothing for us in this world. All the same—praise God—life is beautiful!" She pursed her lips. "Oh God, let us live the time remaining to us as well as possible, for You are the most merciful of the merciful."

Midhat did not know how to talk to her, what words to use to reassure her.

"God willing, Aunt. God willing," he said, then was silent.

They continued to exchange glances, and he felt they had reached an understanding on some basic issues, without knowing why. The sound of shelling filled the darkness around them, shrieking, growling, thundering, howling. She understood that they were in a crazy situation whose outcome was impossible to predict, and that life was too precious to waste on matters you couldn't always comprehend. He was about to say something to her, tell her about his idea and ask her what she thought of it, when the sound of the Hajji's snoring drowned out the shells. He had dozed off as he sat on the bed, his head bent forward on his chest. The old woman quietly got up, made his bed, then laid him down and pulled the cover over him, having taken his prayer beads from him and put them under his pillow.

"Excuse me, Aunt," whispered Midhat, rising from his seat. "You go to sleep, too. Have a rest. Everything will turn out all right, God willing. I'm going up to bed. If you want something you only have to call me. Good night."

Her features were full of resigned misery, the misery of accepting the inevitable. She flung her arms wide. "God willing, son. God willing. Sleep if you can. If you want anything to eat or drink, come down here, son. I'm not going to sleep. Don't worry about us. Good night."

Her tone and manner of speaking saddened him. The air was cold in the courtyard, and gunfire reverberated continuously. He was afraid of sad, despairing people because they robbed him of the strength he needed for his idea, the idea which he had to live by.

He went slowly upstairs. Sometimes the logic of events was such that you were not given the chance to test something you believed to be of central importance in your life. Everything ran smoothly, easily, with no complications, as it always had done for him, until . . . The room still smelt repulsive, the darkness and light mingling and canceling each other out. Again he did not switch the electric light on, but went over to the moonlit window and stood by it . . . as it had done for him until Munira came into his life. The sky was smooth and glittering, glittering. He felt disturbed and his heartbeat quickened slightly. Was he having another crisis like the one a day or two earlier, when it had become clear to him that he was standing at a crossroads and had nothing to show him which way to go?

His guts were in turmoil. He spread his arms and gripped the window frame. Why was he making Munira this cut-off point in his life? Why had he made her the deciding factor in his future, in a crucial choice he was not ready to make? Was she really this fragile creature, with no strength or value or significance?

He rested his throbbing forehead on the cool wall and closed his eyes. That felt better. What confused him, and made him have a circumscribed view of things, was that he mixed up thoughts and feelings, but this was inevitable. There were some basic truths which escaped him. He was acutely aware of them, then suddenly they slipped away. If he was able to grasp the fine thread which presumably connected these truths together, this would be a good start.

Supposing he took his current situation as a starting point—where did he stand? Besieged, driven out of home, at the end of his resources. That would get him nowhere. He felt annoyed by the presence of vague trains of thought which he couldn't avoid: for a start, he was running away from her; that was the basic fact. Running away from the slim body wrapped softly round him, from her warmth, from his love for her. Fleeing from his beloved, his wife. From the kisses and smiles and affectionate glances. From his happiness. But he shouldn't be doing it. It was for appearances' sake only, and at the end of the day it was meaningless. But it was also . . . was there something else behind these superficial tokens? The other sense of Munira, always there behind her radiant image, those aspects of her which scared him to death, mysterious, complex things in her which seemed to have grown into an independent entity and absorbed her, then been bent on destroying him. This was the true nature of the death now surrounding him. It had first appeared to him in his beloved's face and was announcing its presence through the savage sounds of war. But this was not all. His limbs were trembling; he was unable to stand steadily by the window and confront the uproar of the night. Munira, who had bestowed upon him her shame and tragedy, had not chosen to be dishonored. His Munira, soft and serene as the sky, had not wanted her shame. It had happened to her. She was pure as the morning star, and she had chosen him and nobody else, because she wanted to be his. This was what gave her her true significance. The other concerns had nothing to do with her soul. They were the false masks of death, which he had finally been able to tear off.

He clung to the bed beside him. He fancied that the sound of gunfire had receded into the distance and that the night had gone quiet for his sake. He was in a state of high emotion, not knowing what was going to happen to him. She was survival then, his beloved, she was the essence of life.

Joy overwhelmed him and he shouted out loud, rocking the bed violently, unaware of what he was saying. Calling her name perhaps, declaiming his love for her. He burst into tears as he laid his weary body down on the bed.

He wept at length, the feeling of overpowering joy never leaving him, certain that in the darkness of this small, smelly room of his, dawn would break, the dawn of his new life. Then he was submerged in a sudden rush of sleep and slept as he had not done for years, the deep, untroubled sleep of childhood.

The thunder of guns did not waken him until around eleven on that sad Saturday morning.

He had said nothing to them when he joined them shortly before noon. He found the old woman in the kitchen preparing lunch for them and the Hajji sitting on his bed wrapped in the green blanket, sending hostile looks into space and refusing to speak anything but Turkish. They ate the dry, moldy bread soaked in gravy in gloomy silence.

Then the dismal rain had begun to fall, shortly after noon. He drank his tea without a word, having made up his mind to leave them at nightfall. He felt no obligation to let them know this. What commitment did they have to one another, leaving aside the intimacy of those last few hours? The two of them belonged to this place in one way or another and might manage to survive here. Also, he felt that from now on he had something which separated him from them. The world and its little details had become secondary to him. Even fear itself, within his new conceptual framework, was no longer any more than an obstacle of a specific nature that he had to overcome. The one person in the world whose presence with him now might mean something wasn't there. His regrets in this sphere only made him feel more desperately drawn to this absent person—to Munira.

So the two bearded youths went away, and Midhat told the old couple what they had wanted and the Hajji returned to his disjointed ravings in Turkish. The old woman told Midhat that her husband believed they were all going to die this time. Midhat continued to play with his empty tea-glass.

"Mr. Midhat," went on the old woman, "is Abu Suha coming back to us tonight?"

The Hajji paused and looked at him as if he, too, wanted to know the answer. But Midhat had forgotten all about Husayn, much to his own astonishment.

"God willing," he said. "Have you got a cigarette, Aunt?"

"No, son. We've had no cigarettes since this morning."

The Hajji let out a brief stream of invective in Turkish, to which she replied, then went back to his noisy ramblings, his eyes not focusing on them.

Midhat was not much concerned with their reaction and had not interrogated himself over his determination to leave them. He would have left them even if they had been his parents. He was facing the biggest test of his life, which he had chosen to undergo out of conviction. The joy and peace of mind of the day before had not come to him arbitrarily. He had discovered, once and for all, her secret and his own, and the significance of their relationship. In spite of his excitement, he wanted to talk quietly to the old couple and reassure them before his departure, discuss essentials with them, to make the waiting easier for them. The hands on his wristwatch were showing a few minutes before five when the first explosion rang out. The house shook in a terrifying manner, and his tea glass fell on to the floor and smashed immediately.

"God, most merciful of the merciful," shouted the old woman.

Midhat leapt up and went out of the room. In the dim light the yard looked as if it was in ruins. There were people shouting not far away. He went towards the outer door. The old woman called to him. She was standing, her back stooped, resting one hand on the doorframe. "Midhat, son. Mr. Midhat."

Their eyes met. She was crying without tears, her wrinkled face that of someone suffering unbearable pain. He stood there in silence, his heart beating.

"Are you going?" she said.

He did not reply.

"God go with you, son. God go with you. But don't forget us."

"Don't worry, Aunt. I have to go back. Don't worry."

He opened the outside door as he was talking to her and had the impression she did not hear his last words. The lane was in uproar: there was the sound of gunfire, people screaming and calling out and people running terrified, drawn to a particular spot. He ran with them. The house was about a hundred meters away. It had no roof and its walls had collapsed. It was surrounded by armed men and smoke rose from it. Someone told him, without him asking, that a bomb had dropped on it. Some women were wailing and increasing the level of emotion. He learned that the house had been empty and that Abd al-Karim Qasim had been executed shortly after noon. He felt the rain drenching his hair, face, and clothes, although it was much lighter now. Quickly he withdrew from the crowd. Thinking that in this situation he would have to wait until darkness fell, he decided to make a tour of the quarter. After half an hour of wandering the wet, dirty alleyways, he realized that they all led into one another in a never-ending sequence. When by chance he stumbled on an opening from which the main street was visible in the distance, he had to move away quickly to escape the bullets and the warning cries raining down on him from an invisible source.

About six in the evening, when it was already dark, a second bomb exploded somewhere in the quarter. He sat down on a wooden seat outside an empty café to rest and try to organize his thoughts. The café was in some forgotten corner, and as he approached it he had noticed an old man handing over his weapon to another man, shaking his hand, and walking away. This strange encounter had puzzled him. The face of the occasional passers-by reflected an unashamed fear, and he felt slightly uneasy. Getting back home was not as straightforward as he had expected. He wiped the rain from his face and hair and for the first time was aware of the coarse stubble of his beard. What would she say when she saw it? He longed for a hot glass of tea. Would the two of them be able to talk? He would hold her, touch her, feel the softness of her hands and arms and hair, take pleasure in looking at her, run his fingertips over her face, over the almond-shaped eyes, the mouth and lips, feeling his woman, his beloved. He would apologize to her, whisper all his excuses and tell her what she meant to him, and how she had given his life a new shape and direction. He was desperate for a hot tea. He looked around and caught sight of a young lad standing in a corner inside the empty café. He tried to catch his eye but the boy took no notice. God, how he'd love a cigarette, followed by a glass of tea!

He would wait a while until he felt calmer, but he would have to slip out of the besieged area before the moon came up. He gestured to the boy again, who came slowly towards him. A group of women hurried past, dragging their children with them. The boy had a handsome face and wore a large skullcap which came down over his eyes. Midhat asked him if there was anyone serving in the café. The boy shook his head and said nothing. He had delicate features and seemed hesitant and afraid. Midhat spoke to him again gently, but the roar of gunfire nearby drowned out his voice. The boy looked round in terror. Midhat repeated his request, aware of the imploring note in his voice. The child remained silent. He was about twelve years old and looked slightly effeminate. Midhat asked him where he could buy cigarettes, and before he could answer, someone called from inside, "Juwana, Juwana. Come here. Hurry."

A youth stood near the door inside the café gesturing to the girl, as indeed she was, who ran off at once, with a strangely sympathetic glance at Midhat. The youth approached him. He was bearded and hostile-looking.

"Yes, brother?"

"Sorry. A tea, please."

"There's no tea, brother," he said in an unequivocal tone of voice, which took Midhat by surprise.

"Fine. Have you got a cigarette, please?"

"I don't smoke."

The young man eyed him sharply, clearly trying to work out where he was from, what his affiliations were.

"Oh, sorry. Can I rest here for a while?"

"There's nothing to stop you. But this isn't a café, brother. It's a Husayniya, a place where we meet to mourn our dead." Then he hurried off as if he had completed an awkward task.

A few moments later, a feeble electric light went on at the back of the room somewhere. This made him feel better. It was a friendly sign of some sort, and he was badly in need of one. He had become sensitive to every sign, especially those which did not announce themselves and left it to him to plumb their depths, searching for a meaning. It wouldn't have been sensible for her to have discussed the matter with him before their marriage. It would have smacked of cowardice, made it seem like a cheap servile contract, a distastefully cagey arrangement. The fact that she had given her life to him without conditions, because genuine human relationships could not countenance conditions, meant she was sincere and courageous. She hadn't wanted to put him to the test, as she had experienced his love at close quarters and perhaps felt that she could trust him to understand her.

As he sat on his own on the wooden bench in the semi-darkness, he felt an overpowering surge of longing for Munira. He longed to see her, talk to her, feel her near him. His whole chest pounded and he clasped his hands tightly together. He needed to perform some violent act to get close to her, something out of the ordinary and significant, to express to her and to himself that he had a hold on life and survival. He had embraced his misery/death and defeated it, because he had become greater than it, once he understood its nature. She was his supreme choice for this blazing passion which absorbed and subsumed all forms of extinction.

He felt a slight movement beside him. It was the girl Juwana, standing holding a cigarette and matches, her face lit up imperceptibly by a shy smile. He took them from her, thanking her warmly, noticing the few little gold curls showing under her cap and the slight swelling of her chest. He smiled at her and asked her what her name was. When she answered her voice was soft and gentle. If she had talked at the start he would never have mistaken her for a boy.

He lit the cigarette and took a long drag. His head spun exquisitely. He exhaled, his eyes closed. There was nothing to beat life's simple pleasures. He noticed Juwana was still standing beside him, observing him curiously but not unkindly. He asked if it would not be possible to make him a glass of tea.

"No, there isn't any," she answered smiling.

She had big blue eyes which spoke when she was silent. How stupid he had been to think she was a boy! He asked her the way to the main street. An expression of concern appeared on her face, and she looked at the door and then back at him. She pointed hesitantly to the left: "That way."

She was indicating the alley he had walked along already, leading to an open space and a way down to Kifah Street. It was the most dangerous route he knew, guarded on all sides.

"Thanks, but that's no use to me."

"Where do you want to go?"

He swept his arm from right to left, indicating the far horizon. "There. Out. I want to get out of here."

"Why? To find some tea to drink?" she said with another little smile.

At that moment there was a terrifying burst of gunfire. The girl turned in alarm and he noticed her shoulders trembling slightly.

"Don't be frightened, my dear. Go inside now."

She looked at him in silence, a mixture of fear and discontent on her face, then pointed to the box of matches. "Give me the matches," she said.

He returned them to her apologetically, then searched through his pockets and found a tattered half dinar, which he presented to her. "This is for you, dear."

She shook her head, but then put her hand out and took the note.

"Listen, Juwana, my dear. Please, isn't there a back alley somewhere which would take me to the main street? Not that one. Another one. I want to go home to my family."

She was silent and looked as if she was thinking hard about something. She folded the half dinar, pursing her lips together, then looked up, glanced briefly at the door, and whispered, "Through the ruins." Warily she pointed to the right. "That way. The first turning on the right. Go down to the end and there's an alleyway on the left where there are ruins. From there you can . . ."

She broke off and stepped back a little. He turned round, but there was nobody else there. Her eyes were sad. He smiled at her and thanked her, then took a long drag on his cigarette. She walked slowly away towards the entrance and he heard the door bang behind her. He didn't believe she had any reason to trick him. The sound of gunfire still resonated in the air. He would finish his cigarette and go. If you took a decision out of conviction, that meant all doubts and questions should evaporate; but if they continued to gnaw at you, you should regard them as things of secondary importance, or feelings affecting somebody who was not exactly you, although he had some connection with you. At that point it was up to you to become or not to become, to be or not to be, as they say. To put it another way you could choose to be swallowed up or to survive.

He took a final drag on his cigarette, felt the hot smoke in his mouth, and threw the end away. After he had sat in silence for a few moments he stood up, buttoned his jacket and headed off to the right. The air was refreshing after the rain and smelled of damp earth, and the lane was straight, its surface uneven, the single street lamp giving it a tinge of mystery. He moved cautiously, listening out for explosions, aware of footsteps approaching at speed, then fading before he had seen anybody. He made out the entrance of the alley he was looking for on his right after about twenty meters. It, too, was lit by the reddish glow of a street lamp and was no more than two meters wide. He turned into it and moved forward, keeping close to the wall. There was nobody else there. Walking in the cool, damp air restored him. He passed beneath the light, and his long, undulating shadow fell on the dark ground then vanished suddenly. He only saw two doors facing on to the alley and they were both shut. A few drops of rain fell on his head as he walked, and once he slipped and held on to the wall before moving on again. He peered into the darkness, trying to make out where the next alleyway was, breathing deeply and feeling some stirrings of anxiety. What would he do if he didn't find the ruins?

It was almost pitch dark when the alley came out at a little inter-section. To the right it meandered on, but to the left it seemed to be a dead end. Obviously a path like this, no more than a meter and a half wide, could not lead to an exit. He took a few steps along it, then stopped. The faint light from the distant street lamp only illuminated the beginning of the path. He saw a big black door with nails protrud-ing from it on his right, and on the left rose a wall with a rounded top. In front of him was darkness. He felt his way forward cautiously. The ground was soft and slippery. He held on to the wall. The darkness was almost impenetrable, but when he looked up the open horizon was vis-ible, and he thought he could make out the remains of a ruined building by the light of the twinkling stars. He walked firmly on again, trying to see where he was putting his feet. He was neither particularly confident, nor particularly afraid. Many of his misgivings had subsided, but he still felt doubtful and tried to make himself believe that this was natural. A few steps further on, in the faint starlight, he could vaguely distinguish the jumbled outlines of the ruined walls. He stopped, overwhelmed, realizing for the first time that in his heart of hearts he had not believed the little girl Juwana and had given up even before he started. Tentatively he approached the ruined house. It had a low wall round it, connecting to a pillar about two meters high on either side of the bro-ken-down door. He mounted the high front step and stopped in the doorway. The firmament opened out before him in all its pomp and lus-ter. The moon had not yet risen, but it would not be long before it did.

As his eyes grew accustomed to the darkness round about, he began to examine the area close to him and it became clear that the ruin was a small house which, for some reason or other, had never been completed. He had to make his way across to the other side of the house, which looked down on to the main avenue. He jumped at a sharp burst of gunfire, which seemed more alarming than usual. It struck him that it would be possible to keep to the wall and reach the opposite side without running the risk of falling into a hole in the ground or bumping into something. Holding on to the wall adjoining one of the pillars, he set off. He felt his jacket rubbing against the stone and moved out from the wall slightly. As he peered in front of him, his eyes sometimes refused to focus, became blind, then once again managed to distinguish some shapes and dark colors. He tripped against a solid black mass of an indefinable nature and abandoned the wall to circumnavigate it. His foot slipped and he lost his balance and almost fell, but put a hand on the ground to steady himself and stood upright again, his fingers covered in mud. He looked around him. The explosions were more violent now and came one after another without respite. Some reverberated dully in the distance, others sounded very close, as if they came from the street opposite. He could see the wall nearby and stepped up to it, wary of falling, and clung to it. His arms hurt and the sharp stone scratched the palms of his hands. He walked on, brushing the mud off him and breathing hard, annoyed that this simple effort had such an effect on him physically.

The wall turned and he found himself looking down on the main street. The ruin was about fifty or sixty meters from it, and roughly two meters above it, according to his calculations. The street looked frighteningly empty and was in darkness apart from a few anonymous lights reflected on its black surface. The waste ground separating the ruin from the street was surrounded by houses. Looking from behind the wall, he could see the doors of buildings and other smaller streets leading out of the main thoroughfare, but there was no sign of life. He was still breathing hard and his heart was pounding. A cool, refreshing breeze blew. He looked up at the sky. Last summer, on the roof just before dawn, he had stood by her bed as she sat dreaming, completely unaware of his presence, as if she was in another world. The dawn was tinged silver by the moonlight. He had been able to say her name out loud then so that she could hear it. How far away it all seemed, as distant as the stars or eternity. How their world had changed since then. They had committed no crime, but had surrendered to the events which had enveloped them in their perverse, destructive logic. They had become victims of others. Those treacherous others.

He was sad as he stood there behind the stone barrier, fiddling with his fingers, cleaning the mud off them, tantalized by ideas and memories which were meaningless now. There was a high-pitched roar and a car approached from the right and shot along the street in front of him like a demented arrow, the water flying around it and its wheels squealing like a wounded animal. Then it disappeared. The sight of it alarmed him and he wondered what to expect if he tried to cross; however, salvation and survival could only really be measured against the attendant dangers and obstacles. All the same, it was the end rather than the means which counted, and the art of survival would always breed a particular kind of hero.

A powerful light flashed on and off on the other side, then vanished. This reminded him that his time was limited and he had to act. The wall came up to the base of his chest. He felt the top of it and found it was wet and slippery, and decided to go all the way along to the point where the house wall formed an acute angle with the street. This was where the street was at its narrowest. He hoisted himself up and examined the ground on the other side of the wall. In the poor light that transformed everything into a mirage he thought he saw piles of little stones below him. Gathering his energy, he hitched up one of his legs, then with small economical movements edged across and let himself down gradually on the other side. When his feet touched what he thought was the ground, he hesitated, then let go of the wall, but was unable to keep his balance and slipped over on to his back. His fall took him by surprise. He righted himself uneasily and sat on the ground facing the street. He felt a pain in his back and side. He looked to right and left. Nothing was moving, no lights, no people. He felt for the spots on his body where it hurt, and rubbed them. There was a stink of urine, excrement, and rotten food. He stood up, his back painfully bent, and turned right, walking alongside the ruin. He tripped several times and stopped to regain his breath and spirits. The roar of gunfire grew fiercer every now and then. These unimportant sounds were now in conflict with him and worked against his idea. Perhaps he would be safe if he hid in the ruin until things were over. But the significance would be different by then, the significance of him and what he was doing. He clung to the wall which faced on to the broad street, as if he wanted to disappear among the narrow cracks between the stones. He would not be saving himself if he waited helplessly until someone came to rescue him. That would not be surviving at all. The street was long, without bends, its surface smooth and shining. The dirt pavement which lay between him and the street was three meters wide or slightly more; he calculated that the tarred road must be about ten meters wide, and the dirt pavement on the other side was presumably three meters wide as well. Beyond that lay the routes out to safety. So he had sixteen meters to cover, say twenty. How much time would he need to do it at a run?

Trained athletes ran a hundred meters in about twelve seconds, so say he could do a hundred meters in about fifteen seconds, how long would twenty meters take him? The ratio was constant, so fifteen multiplied by twenty divided by a hundred. Answer three. Three seconds! Say five to be on the safe side. Five seconds and it would all be over. Or just beginning.

Warily he stuck his head out. In the distance the street was dark, then closer to where he was it was lit at intervals by the street lamps with their red glow. There was nobody about and that could well be the case for five more seconds.

He drew back again. Perhaps he would knock on the door. His heart was beating violently. Perhaps they would not recognize him at first. Then he would see her. He would call her as soon as he was inside and see her, see that face that he loved so much. He would take her aside to hold her in his arms and apologize to her. No, he wouldn't apologize to her. He moved suddenly, not knowing why he chose that particular moment. He bounded forward enthusiastically and felt the cool night air on his face. He crossed the pavement in a flash, his feet not disappointing him. Of course he would not apologize to her, to that precious creature. He would simply tell her that he had come back for her, his wife, because he had conquered all thoughts of death in himself. He was running confidently across the wet, tarred surface of the street, looking at the horizon and the sky opening out above him, when he felt the shot burn along his right thigh. He hadn't heard any shooting. He dropped heavily to his knees, full of amazement. So these five seconds of his life had not passed safely after all. He held the place where the terrible pain was on his thigh and a warm stream of liquid ran over his fingers. He looked around bewilderedly, but saw no one. He wanted to call out for help, to tell them that they had to let him live, that his death was no business of theirs. When he saw a faint gleam of light in a dark corner on the other side of the street, he understood what it meant. He went on waiting for what was no more than a hundredth of a second, but for him it lasted forever; then he knew, before the dreadful pain tore into his chest and shoulders, that he had not survived. His body, spattered with mud and blood, writhed and shuddered alarmingly on the asphalt of the empty street.

Paris, 9 February 1966—Baghdad, 5 September 1977

This mass of pages does not contain what people believe it does. No sighs, no talk, no groans or smiles. No sublimity, suffering, fear, or desire. No eyes, lips, blood, or tears. If they are thrown away they will not protest. They are dumb pages which are neither harmful nor beneficial, and it is better for them and for everyone if they are left in peace and forgotten.

Modern Arabic Writing
from The American University in Cairo Press

Ibrahim Abdel Meguid *The Other Place* • *No One Sleeps in Alexandria*

Yahya Taher Abdullah *The Mountain of Green Tea*

Leila Abouzeid *The Last Chapter*

Salwa Bakr *The Wiles of Men*

Mohamed El-Bisatie *Houses Behind the Trees* • *A Last Glass of Tea*

Fathy Ghanem *The Man Who Lost His Shadow*

Mourid Barghouti *I Saw Ramallah*

Tawfiq al-Hakim *The Prison of Life*

Taha Hussein *A Man of Letters* • *The Sufferers o The Days*

Sonallah Ibrahim *Cairo: From Edge to Edge* • *Zaat*

Yusuf Idris *City of Love and Ashes*

Denys Johnson-Davies *The Naked Sky: Short Stories from the Arab World*

Said al-Kafrawi *The Hill of Gypsies*

Naguib Mahfouz *Adrift on the Nile*

Akhenaten, Dweller in Truth • *Arabian Nights and Days*

Autumn Quail • *The Beggar*

The Beginning and the End • *The Cairo Trilogy:*

Palace Walk o Palace of Desire • *Sugar Street*

The Day the Leader Was Killed o Echoes of an Autobiography

The Harafish • *The Journey of Ibn Fattouma*

Midaq Alley • *Miramar o Respected Sir*

The Search • *The Thief and the Dogs*

The Time and the Place • *Wedding Song*

Ahlam Mosteghanemi *Memory in the Flesh*

Abd al-Hakim Qasim *Rites of Assent*

Lenin El-Ramly *In Plain Arabic*

Rafik Schami *Damascus Nights*

Miral al-Tahawy *The Tent*

Fuad al-Takarli *The Long Way Back*

Latifa al-Zayyat *The Open Door*